THE CHRISTMAS MARY HAD TWINS

THE CHRISTMAS MARY HAD TWINS

A Novel

RICHARD SHAW

STEIN AND DAY/*Publishers*/New York

First Stein and Day edition 1983
An earlier and different edition was published
     under the title *Elegy of Innocence*
Copyright © 1979, 1983 by Richard Shaw
All rights reserved, Stein and Day, Incorporated
Designed by Louis A. Ditizio
Printed in the United States of America
STEIN AND DAY/*Publishers*
Scarborough House
Briarcliff Manor, N.Y. 10510

Library of Congress Cataloging in Publication Data

Shaw, Richard, 1941 Oct. 9–
   The Christmas Mary had twins.

   Rev. ed. of: Elegy of innocence. c1979.
   I. Shaw, Richard, 1941 Oct. 9– , Elegy of
innocence.   II. Title.
PS3569.H3844C5   1983   813'.54   83-40064
ISBN 0-8128-2940-9

To
Father Bill Hayden
who died September 5, 1972
and
Father Harry Doty
who died July 21, 1972,
for having taught me about
the priesthood

THE CHRISTMAS MARY HAD TWINS

1

ON the night of August 27, 1969, confused and exhausted, I sat at the head table at a Knights of Columbus officers' installation banquet, the youngest man in the hall by at least a decade and a half. I did not want to be there. My presence was not appreciated; but I was a priest, and a priest was felt to be a necessity at such occasions. So, by default and to nobody's pleasure, the lot of saying the opening prayer was mine.

I had come to the K. of C. hall directly from the county jail where I was a chaplain. Sharing the lives of people behind bars—most of whom were poor—meant sharing their constant pain and frustration caused by the stark inequities of the criminal justice system. It tore me apart to leave them in the situation they were in that day to cater to middle-class parishioners, so many of whom voiced smug prejudices about what "the criminal element" deserved. There had been a food riot at the jail several hours earlier, and the two hundred inmates were now being punished by a continuous twenty-four lockup. The whole of my day had been spent going from cell to cell attempting to calm still-smoldering anger; but deep inside I agreed with the men and knew I would have rioted too.

The jail officials had denied that there had been maggots in the soup, and the newspapers had given sanction to their denial; but I had been there when the riot broke out. There had been maggots.

Impulsively, I had wanted to call the newspapers to object, but to do so wouldn't have done the inmates any good. People who mattered in the area had learned not to put too much stock in what I said.

The dinner had begun; the waitresses were rushing around the hall with trays, shelling out the inevitable banquet fare of pressed chicken, peas, and potatoes. I estimated, pushing my chair back a little and settling down into it, that it would be at least two hours before I could bow out of the place politely.

A number of the men in front of me were local politicians, and some were officials at the jail. I began daydreaming about how they would react if, as they dug into their food now, they would discover maggots such as those they denied existed in the prisoners' dinner.

In my imagination I pictured them gagging and pushing back from the tables, screaming at the waitresses, and calling for heads to roll. I began smiling to myself at the idea, almost managing to block out the heavy voice of Mr. O'Brien, the two-hundred-and-fifty-pound chairman who sat next to me, sweating profusely in spite of the hall's cold, damp, air conditioning.

Mr. O'Brien did not like me and had once put his name to a petition asking my removal from his parish. He talked at me now in a steady monologue, stopping only to puff on his cigar. He was listing, as he always did when he encountered me, all the things that he felt were destroying the Church: nuns discarding their habits; priests—like myself—not dressing properly; the new Mass; guitar music in church; the clergy getting mixed up in politics—acting like hippies at war protests; and his grand-slam resentment, that Bishop Maguire had given one hundred thousand dollars of diocesan money "to the niggers" for a slum-area community center.

"Last time I give to the bishop's fund," he concluded. Then, noticing I hadn't touched my glass, he added, "You don't like beer, do you, Father?"

"Uh, that's okay," I said, snapping to at the sound of a question. I purposely hadn't touched my drink. As soon as I could get away from the K. of C. banquet I had to baby-sit our high school hangout center for the evening. Since we were adamant about our rule prohibiting kids who had been drinking from entering the center, we made sure that we ourselves never drank before opening up.

"What do you like, Father? Scotch?"

"Yeah, I like Scotch," I answered, only half paying attention and oblivious of what he was leading up to. A minute or so after this, the bartender came in and placed a glass filled with ice and a bottle of J & B in front of me.

"There you go, Father," said Mr. O'Brien with a patronizing half smile.

I felt myself turn red. I had misunderstood and been taken. Scotch. The priests' drink. Beer is good enough for everyone but Father. I reached over, pushed the bottle to one side, and kept looking ahead. An anger, born of resentment, began to rise inside me. What irked me more than the Scotch was the way Mr. O'Brien emphasized the word "Father," as though it was a suit four sizes too large for me. When he talked about me—one of his teenage kids told me—he didn't call me Father. My surname, Hogan, was enough as far as he was concerned. It was either that or one of the nicknames middle-aged parishioners had given me, usually "Little Red" or "the Sundance Kid"—these to couple me with or distinguish me from the other young priest at St. Mary's who, though older and taller than myself, was almost my twin in looks.

Mike and I were first cousins, and though it was unusual for relatives to be stationed in the same parish, most of our parishioners simply racked it up to coincidence. There weren't that many sets of cousins in the priesthood for any pattern to have been set, and few might have guessed that there had been a purpose in Bishop Maguire's putting us together. In any event it was easy enough for our parishioners to couple us into one mold. We both had copper-red hair, blue eyes, and a ruddy complexion. I was two inches shorter than Mike's six feet, and thus the dubbing, "Little Red"—though the way it was used seemed to refer more to politics than hair. Then when the film *Butch Cassidy and the Sundance Kid* had become popular, a parish wit had noticed what he thought was an obvious parallel. These names were so commonly applied to us we might as well have hung them on our confessionals.

There was a good amount of general dislike aimed at us by what could be called standard Catholics. It was a dislike that seemed to be directed to most priests of our age group. It had been bewildering. We were, so we were told, "the new breed," a term I had quickly come to dislike. Our elders acted as if we were the authors and executors of "the changes" that had torn their Church apart, leaving them with a "new" religion they neither understood nor wanted

11

to understand. They seemed to attribute a premeditated malevolence to us, as though we had carefully planned on careers to do evil, to be the new Huns wiping out civilizations in our paths.

"You know, Father," Mr. O'Brien went on, "this affair was much better when it was a communion breakfast in spring. That way at least everyone got to make their Easter duty. But, then again, you people would never go along with that idea, would you?"

You people. That was where it all became senseless. I could take batting my head against the ills of society, all of the forces of evil outside the Church. But what was the sense of attempting to be something for people who were supposed to be on the same side as you, when for them you were the enemy? My classmates and I were a unique age group in the history of the Church. It was just as I was going into the seminary that Rome had set the Church on a massive cultural overhauling—changing, in what seemed an eyeblink, what had slowly built up over centuries. What we were taught during our four years of theology had been what Rome dictated.

When I was ordained in 1967 and went out (no genius or any kind of theologian, to teach what my superiors had taught me), I and my classmates found ourselves a beachhead group, arriving with a message that our elders rejected upon hearing. From saying that Rome was infallible, they turned and said, in effect, that the Holy Spirit had gone to lunch in 1962 and hadn't come back yet. Rome, they declared, was wrong. They refused to obey, and we who were the bearers of these ill tidings of change became their targets. The volley of fire at first confused, then wounded, then destroyed many of us. I had always been a happy person. I had enjoyed life and still did. But now I enjoyed life only when I could escape or sidestep Catholics.

Any reserve of humor I felt about teaching or convincing or fighting them had long since dried up. These people taking pot shots at me didn't give a damn that I'd dedicated my life to serving them. In the two years since ordination, ten of my twenty-eight classmates had already left the madness that ministry in the priesthood had become. They were living normal lives, off the firing range. Why couldn't I?

Mr. O'Brien tapped on his glass and announced that "Father" would say grace. This was the moment for which my collar, even with me inside it, was wanted. Everyone harrumphed and stopped talking, and I stood. I stared at their scowling faces, trembling a little, because the impulse inside me was growing stronger. My throat felt dry. And yet, I was beginning to feel heady, too, almost as if I had drunk some of Mr. O'Brien's Scotch after all. These people didn't own me. I could be free of them. All that I had to do was make the decision to be free.

I fought momentarily with the love I felt for the Mass and used to feel for the priesthood itself. I tried to connect it with these people in front of me; with the daily tension and pain of being torn apart by them. But I couldn't. The heady feeling grew. It was as if I were at the edge of a high dive trying to get up the nerve to make a leap.

Mr. O'Brien cleared his throat again. The men at the tables, growing restless, looked at me puzzled, as if I were a schoolboy in a play who had forgotten his lines. Mike had told me once that being an actor was essential to being a priest. I didn't want to be an actor anymore. I hesitated at the edge of the board. All I had to do to back off it was say their grace.

"Almighty God . . ." I began. But the words stuck there.

"Almighty God . . ." I started again. And stopped.

They were getting restless, wanting to get it over with so they could eat. My heart was pounding. I wasn't sure I was ready to jump, not this suddenly. No, I *could* do it. I could be free of them. I leaped—and felt the exhilaration one feels just after springing from a board, suspended in air, before diving into the water.

"I'm sorry, but I can't stay to say grace for you," I said. I was in a hurry to be an ordinary human being again. "I have to leave now."

I walked off the dais toward the exit, silence pounding against my back. Only as the door swung behind me did the place well up into startled comments.

For the moment, only I knew that I'd left more than the room. That, as impulsively as I had decided to become a priest, I was walking out on the whole thing. A free man.

2

I don't think my immediate family had much to do with my deciding to become a priest.

My dad and mom parented three daughters and six sons, which was enough to mark them, in the 1950s, as standard bearers of the Catholic faith. But such wasn't the case. They simply liked children, were well-off enough, and had decided upon a large family—a decision for which I, being the youngest of the clan, have always been appreciative.

The strongest orientation toward religion in our home involved weekly attendance at Mass, an exercise usually surrounded by fights about who was making everyone late on the way to and fights about who got what sections of the Sunday paper on the way home from church.

The earliest reaction that I can recall having to that weekly ritual was that it would break me up to hear my older brother Jerry mimic the priest at High Mass. When the celebrant would turn, spread his hands, and sing a greeting to the choir, Jerry would occasionally slip into a monotone and hum along with him, muttering for my benefit, "I can play dominoes better than you can," earning from my mother a hissed, "Jerry, shut up."

For a long time it was the only part of attending Mass that did anything for me one way or another.

It was Monsignor Maguire, a powerfully built, white-haired man who had been born in Scotland, who was the earliest priestly influence on my life. I never knew him as less than a monsignor. He and my dad fished and played golf together; but their close friendship was based, I think, more on their both being professional men in our community than having anything to do with religion.

My dad took care of legal matters for our parish and Maguire was often around the house while we were growing up. Sometimes it was business, more often it was to just sit for an evening and read to "get away from that madhouse for awhile." Because Maguire was at the helm of our parish grammar and high school complex, many an evening's conversation centered on school matters. I can also recall scores of discussions about parish business and political arguments. But I can never recall once hearing any talk about religion. This might sound like an indictment against him or my parents, but it isn't. There was little or no controversy within the realm of the Church in that age. Everyone knew where everyone else stood regarding what they believed in, so what would have been the point in discussing it?

In our parish it was mandatory for every boy to start serving on the altar upon entering the fifth grade. This meant that we spent every other Tuesday after school, crowded into choir stalls, learning the rubrics of the Mass under Maguire's tutelage. Dressed in a Roman cassock with a red sash belt, he spent each teaching session, his hands clasped behind his back, strolling the length of the altar's top step, drilling us with the force of a Marine sergeant. We were more than a little afraid of him and with good enough cause. He was a disciplinarian above all else, and to risk his displeasure was to risk getting one's head put into a wall.

The worst beating I ever got in grade school was from Maguire. It was one of the first warm spring days of my sixth-grade year, the kind of day that awakened hopes for a coming summer of freedom. While afternoon sun and the disappearing yells of friends filtered in through the stained-glass windows, we who were assigned to that Sunday's High Mass settled in misery to hear Maguire harangue away about pageantry for which we had little interest. His authoritative voice echoed off the rafters of the empty church: "All right now. Listen once and get it straight. The choir will begin the Kyrie Eleison . . ."

Bored with the proceedings, wanting only to get outside, I poked my cousin Eddie in the back and whispered, "Hey, Kyrie, you laid my son," totally mindless of the perfect acoustics of a marble sanctuary.

Maguire stopped, and for a moment of deadly silence allowed it to sink into us that someone had sullied the atmosphere befitting the house of God. Then he turned, calmly walked over, and struck me across the side of my head so hard that, caught off-balance, I fell to the floor. He picked me up, hit me again, and went back to the altar. He never even stopped to help pick me up from the floor, and as two of the older boys half carried me, my nose bleeding, into the sacristy, I heard him say, "Now, where were we?"

I was never too good an altar boy. I had a mental block against memorizing the meaningless Latin and couldn't retain more than the first three words of any prayer to be recited. To cover this up I developed, very early in my career, a delivery style in which I would all but shout the first few syllables of each response and then drop to a garbled mumble for the remainder of what I said.

Every now and then after a particularly bad performance, Maguire would stop in the sacristy, lean up against the cabinet table without even stopping to take off his biretta, comment that he hadn't heard a single syllable either altar boy had said, and add, invariably nodding toward me, "Dennis, let me hear that Suscipiat again."

My knees would go weak. I would stumble through half the prayer under his icy questioning stare and finally admit, "I think I forgot it, Monsignor."

I would then be suspended from the roster for two weeks and told to write every response of the Mass twenty times over. It never occurred to me that I might have refused, gotten myself thrown off the altar altogether, and lived a life minus the grief of all that pressure. Instead, petrified that he would tell my parents of my suspension, I would work on the punishment, spending hours copying and memorizing words that had no sense in preparation for the exam which Maguire would exact.

I had little better luck with the rubrics of the Mass, which in that age were as complicated as any battle plan. There were all sorts of half hidden signals the altar boy was supposed to heed as cues for action; but somehow they flew unnoticed beyond me. I invariably rang the bells at the wrong times. There were times when the water and wine cruets were to be handed to the celebrant, and other times when the altar boy was to do the pouring. I once got so wrapped up trying to decide which time we were at that I ended up washing his hands with wine.

I generally missed the hand signal the priest gave when the huge missal was to be moved from one side of the altar to the other. Some priests would impatiently grab the book and move it themselves. Maguire finally got so accustomed to my missing the signal he never bothered with it. He would turn his head at the proper time and order, "Move the book"—a practice he kept up even after I was in high school and he was bishop.

During the first wedding I ever served, Maguire stopped at the beginning of the ring blessing and, noting a lack, said to me, "Go in and get the holy water."

I went into the sacristy, puzzled, wondering what exactly he wanted me to bring, never once thinking of the ornate little bucket used for such purposes. I looked throughout the dark wood cupboards, becoming increasingly panicky and frantic at the delay I was causing, seeing nothing of what he had asked for. Then I noticed in the room's corner a large blue and gray ceramic barrel on an old typewriter table, upon which was labeled in distinct script letters HOLY WATER. I reasoned it had to be what he wanted even though a small voice of common sense tried to cry out that a barrel that size couldn't be used on the altar. But seconds were flying by and Maguire was waiting with the bride and groom.

Quashing further thought I grabbed the front legs of the table and gave a pull. The wheels screeched a rusty protest and I stopped. I was sweating—knowing that somehow I was going to break the thing or worse. I grabbed the legs again, yanked, and it rumbled along the sacristy rug after me, passing several drops of dried bloodstains in the rug where several months before I had stood, recovering from Maguire's beating.

The biggest problem lay in the single step which separated the sacristy from the narrow fifteen-foot passageway leading to the altar. I stopped and quickly figured that my best bet for not breaking the barrel was to get a fast start and get the table off the step, all four wheels in one level drop. I backed into a dragging run, worked up good speed and got us all off at once—the table, barrel and myself—landing intact with a smashing crash against the opposite wall. The worst part was then over, I thought.

I squeezed out from where the barrel had me pinned, pushed the thing down the cobblestoned passageway, the floor causing the ceramic top to dance in a loud clattering jig, rounded the altar entrance and pushed the entire business over to where the bridal party and Maguire waited for me. When the wheels squealed to a stop I turned, out of breath, my face redder than my hair, only to catch a long and penetrating glare from Maguire. He finally found words.

"You damned fool," he said, loudly enough for the bride's mother to drop her jaw in shock. It was the first time I had heard a priest use the word "damn."

I spent the rest of the wedding Mass seeing myself being ripped limb from limb all around the sacristy—wishing I was anywhere else, wishing I wasn't a Catholic, wishing I was dead. I saw myself going home with another bloody nose, to get as I had the time before, another beating at home. When Mass was finished, I put out the candles, took off my cassock, and timidly went through the priest's sacristy waiting for all hell to break loose. I had just made it to the outside door, ready to escape, when Maguire, still facing the vestment case, called out, "Dennie, come here a minute."

I fought a strong urge to bolt out of the place regardless of consequences, but I turned and faced him, although I felt that I was going to throw up. I didn't notice that it was the first time I had ever seen him ill at ease, almost unsure of himself. He smiled and cleared his throat, then said, "Bobby knows a lot about cars, doesn't he?"

It took me a moment to digest that he was talking about my brother. "Uh, yeah . . . I guess he does," I blurted out, momentarily disbelieving he hadn't taken a swing at me. "He's always taking engines apart."

I was lost as to what he was getting at. He put his hand on my back and started walking with me to the door. "I'm going out to look at used cars this afternoon," he confided. "Ask Bobby if he'd come with me, will you? I don't want to get stuck with a lemon. It won't take long. I think I know the car I want."

"Sure, he won't mind," I said, so relieved I was near tears. "He won't mind at all."

"Tell him to call me. You come along too. We'll let you make the final decision."

I couldn't believe it. Later I figured it was because he felt bad about swearing on the altar; but it was still a heady feeling to have been given the final say in choosing Maguire's car. I almost felt that day as if I had lost a drill instructor and gained a friend.

Two weeks after that he threw me off the altar again for not knowing my Latin.

3

WHEN I look now at photographs of my cousin Mike, I am surprised at how baby-faced he was. Even after he had developed a football player's muscular body, his face remained that of both boy and man at the same time. Under light sun-catching red hair, his blue eyes seemed always aggressively seeking action. His face was bright with an eagerness that was almost a kind of jesting laughter, as if, oblivious of anything ugly in life, he saw in his surroundings only matter for enjoyment. Even in a fight he seemed to be doing something that was a sport to him rather than something born of any real anger.

When Mike was barely seven years old, his dad died. He grew up in a house situated in a cemetery where his mother, my Aunt Gert, was caretaker. Mike was the man of the house, having a real authority over his younger sister, Laurie, and his brother, Eddie, who was my own age and best friend. Perhaps it was because of that authority that I always thought of him as an adult. Eddie and I had a healthy fear of him. He had a habit of labeling us "chickenshit" when he got angry. During any family fight, all he had to do was jab a finger at me, say, "Listen, you chickenshit," and I would wait for the roof to fall in.

My dad and Aunt Gert owned a house at the seashore that they had inherited from my dad's parents, and for every summer of my childhood it was our home. It was in August of 1952 when Eddie and I were ten, Mike was sixteen and my brother Jerry fourteen, that Mike almost caused the four of us to be drowned. The first of the season's coastal hurricanes had brushed through the day before, and weather all along the northeast was wind whipped. Waves were high; small craft warnings had been issued, and our family sailboats remained, without even needing parental orders to that effect, lashed to our dock. We had been sitting, huddled in sweaters, by the boats when Mike, impatient with nothing to do, decided that weather conditions had calmed down enough for us to go sailing. I wasn't so sure, but his daring was infectious, and in a matter of minutes we had the boat untied and were headed out.

For an hour we battled winds and water without any problems. When Mike and Jerry finally decided to head in, it was I who got things snarled with the sail, and we caught a wave broadside. The boat turned over, and the four of us were left in the heavily rolling water clinging to the upended hull. There was no chance of getting it righted; we could only hang on, hoping to get pushed toward shore with the tide. Eddie and I were both frightened, but each time we voiced this the angrier our two older brothers became.

It was Eddie who finally dared speak for both of us, "Mike, I can't hold on any longer, my arms are too tired."

"The hell they are," he yelled back. "Hanging on is nothing. We're not even that far from shore. If you two chickenshits weren't with us and we didn't care about the boat we could swim in easy. So shut up and hang on."

In another hour, during which the weather had calmed down considerably, we were picked up by a patrol boat, Mike saying as they pulled alongside of us, "I do the talking, understand?"

He then lightly related to our rescuers that we had turned over only minutes before, thus reducing the time we had been out in the boat to when we might have done so with permission after the wind had died down. He lied so smoothly, laughing and talking with the men on board, he almost had me convinced—but for the fact that I ached all over and felt nauseous from exhaustion—that what he was saying was the truth. All that I knew was that I had been scared of drowning only a little less than I had been of his anger.

I don't know what religion meant to Mike as he was growing up. As I have said, it wasn't a subject that Catholics, or at least my

21

family, discussed. But I would judge that Mike relegated religion to that area in his life wherein he placed matters for which he had scant concern. By the time Mike reached high school he was almost the size of a full-grown man and had taken over many things in Aunt Gert's occupation that better suited a man. He had also gotten into the habit of referring to his mother as "the Boss." He was both proud and protective of her, and when disagreements arose with workmen, the general public, or even the parish priests, Mike would be quick to move in, unwilling to see her argued with. Standing with a scowl darkening his Celtic features and with red eyebrows knotted, he'd pronounce, "That's what the Boss said, and that's the way it's going to be."

Once when a demanding young curate had dared to question Aunt Gert's veracity over a minor misunderstanding concerning a burial plot, Mike turned on him, threatened to punch his face in, and called him a jerk. When his mother, embarrassed and horrified at his disrespect, demanded he remember to whom he was talking, Mike corrected himself by saying, "Okay, Father Jerk."

The incident almost cost Aunt Gert her job and was resolved only after reluctant apologies were exacted from both young men. One was an apology that Mike made to the curate; the other was an apology that Mike insisted the curate make to his mother.

But my earlier impressions that Mike cared little for religion came, I think, from an occurrence that happened at about the same time as the boat incident. Aunt Gert had received a body to bury, that of an old man with no relatives. It had been shipped in from out of town and, with no ceremonies, was to be placed in the ground. It was a hot, sunny afternoon. Mike, my brothers, and a number of their friends were hanging around where the coffin lay, unburied, while the crew was off eating lunch. One of the boys, amazed that the man had been so crudely carted to the graveyard and dumped in, asked, "Doesn't anybody do anything religious for him?"

"Sure," Mike assured him. "That's my job. I give them the old Navajo happy hunting ground dance."

He grabbed a handful of dirt and pebbles, hopped about yelling what were supposed to be Indianlike sounds and then hurled the stones so that they clattered on top of the coffin. Standing nearby, I felt the hair rise on the back of my neck. I had a strongly felt horror of the dead, and his making fun of the corpse seemed to me to cry out to whatever powers might exist to be revenged upon us who had witnessed this mockery. For weeks afterward I had recurring nightmares in which an old Indian—which the man had not been—came back to haunt me for having been a part of that scene, and that incident has always remained with me as a vivid memory.

If Mike was always an adult in my mind, he was very much a child to my dad, who was his dead father's brother. He worried about Mike as if he were his own son, and because school was an incidental factor in his nephew's life, each marking period with its flunking grades brought about an angry session behind closed doors in my dad's study, with all the threats and attempts at reason that my father, as uncle and godfather, could force upon him. But in the final analysis he had no real authoritative hold over his nephew, and Mike remained himself—free, undisciplined, and very much his own man. But the problem with this extended far beyond grades in school, for Mike, as he was growing up, lived life more and more as if no rules had ever been made that applied to him.

Aunt Gert had always supplemented her income by renting out rooms in her large house to college boarders, and though they were generally a good crew and responded well to her friendliness, it very much affected the way Mike grew up. Once in high school and as tall as the older boys in his house, he began to reject having anything to do with companions his own age. By the time he was sixteen he had developed an extraordinary talent as a gambler and began to clear, in all-night card sessions, as much as other youngsters could earn with a weekly part-time job.

This worried Aunt Gert for Mike's sake and worried my parents for the sake of my brother Bob as well—for he and Mike were the same age and had done everything together. It was disheartening for them to think that within the confines of the family one member was a bad influence on another. This meant ugly home scenes after every untoward escapade the two of them got involved with; and such escapades seemed to occur with increasing regularity in their teenage years.

In their senior year, a crisis occurred that had major repercussions in Mike's life. The year was going well for both my brother and my cousin. Powerful athletes, they were co-captains of the football team and, being good-looking and friendly, they were on top of the heap socially in school as well. But in mid-November of that year Mike took a classmate for the whole of his grocery-store paycheck during a lunch-period poker game. The boy's mother, angry and upset, complained to Maguire. When told to return the money, Mike was adamant in his refusal.

On the Sunday afternoon after this incident, I sat unnoticed on the sofa in our living room and watched tensely while an angry scene was played out around my mother's dining room table, with Aunt Gert, my dad, and Maguire trying to keep the matter from blowing up into a major issue. But the card game was only a part of it, for with half of the wash on the line, it all hung out, and Mike admitted to running a regular football pool and even making book on horses—altogether a steadily lucrative profession. But most immediate was the concern for the twenty-three dollars taken in that game.

"I'm not giving Miller back anything just because he cried to his momma," Mike declared. "I'll lay any odds if he had won he wouldn't be rushing to return his winnings to me."

"The money is immaterial to me," Maguire countered, presiding at the head of my mom's dining-room table. "What I care about is that you were using school as a setting for making a dishonest fortune off the other students."

"What's dishonest about it?" Mike asked. "I don't see anything wrong with it at all."

"Making book on games? It's against the law," Maguire said, slamming his fist on the table.

Mike shrugged. "You run bingo every week in the church hall. What's the difference?"

Maguire stopped, dumbfounded at Mike's arrogance. Then he turned an angry red. "The purpose of bingo," he began icily, "is to make money to run the school. And even if it is a modified form of gambling, at least it gives a lot of elderly ladies a social outlet. We're not cheating anybody."

"Who am I cheating?" Mike asked. "Maybe the kids gamble because it's a social outlet too. Anybody who gambles knows what he's doing. Gambling is only dishonest if it's fixed. I play clean. If you agree to stop bingo, I'll stop handing out football cards."

"How big is this whole operation?" my dad broke in, as Maguire started to rise over the table toward Mike.

24

Mike thought for a moment, then said, "I don't know. I take more from the guys in the college." He shook his head and laughed a little. "It's not like I keep records or anything. I just make money playing cards. I'm good at it."

"How much have you made?" my dad asked.

"I've got about two thousand in the bank."

There was a stunned silence. Aunt Gert finally spoke up, almost timidly, as if she were embarrassed in knowing nothing of this side of her son's character, "Why didn't you ever tell me this, Mike?"

He turned red, conscious that he had hurt her and that it had happened in front of an outsider. "I wanted to surprise you," he said quietly. "I didn't want you to worry about Laurie getting money for college. I was just going to say, 'There it is,' when the time came."

My dad broke in, "You never would have wanted for anything, Mike. You know I would have taken care of you, don't you?"

"Uncle Joe, that's not the point," he said, not looking at him. "I don't want charity. I want my freedom."

"Charity . . . ?" My dad was hurt. "Since when is taking care of your own, charity?"

Mike didn't answer.

Maguire broke the silence saying, "Well, this is the end of it. You are to return the money to the Miller boy, and I'm putting you on suspension for a week. And if I ever catch you gambling in school I will expel you without any question. Is that understood?"

He started pushing his chair back as if the affair had been settled, but when he paused for the answer he got none. He looked squarely at Mike.

Finally, Mike answered, "No."

"What do you mean, 'No'?"

"It's not fair, that's all. There's nothing I'm doing that's wrong, and it would be wrong to give that money back. I'm not going to do it."

"Mike, honey," pleaded Aunt Gert who was almost on the verge of tears.

"Look," my dad said, "I'll give you the money to give to him."

"It's not the money," Mike answered, reacting to Aunt Gert's tears by filling up with tears himself. "Please, Mom . . . you're asking something I can't do. I don't want to hurt you. But I can't do it. That's all."

25

It was an impasse. Maguire was bound in duty not to back down and nothing could make Mike change his mind. After twelve and a half years and almost to his high school graduation, Mike was forced to leave the parochial-school system. It was a public embarrassment for everyone. He had been getting a good deal of newspaper coverage because of football, so he was not a person who could be expelled quietly. But it wasn't really an expulsion, a fact that all authorities involved tried to keep attention focused upon. He could have remained in school if he had bent his stubborn will. But he wouldn't. He left to finish his senior year in the public high school. My brother Bob wanted to quit with him—wanted to at least quit the football team before the last games; but, overpowered by our dad's force of will, he backed down.

It was a potentially embittering experience. Indeed, Bobby was deeply bitter about it and refused to wear his class ring after that. But if it had bothered Mike there was no way of judging so by anything he said or did. At first Maguire seemed embarrassed when they met at church or, worse, at the cemetery or at our house. But once he got over the first hurdle of asking how things were at school the two of them moved pretty much back to their former relationship.

If anything, the hurt seemed more on Maguire's part, for after observing Mike's lack of concern and the fact that Mike immediately signed up for track in his new school, I heard Maguire asking my dad, "Could a dozen years in a Catholic school have meant that little to him?"

In June of 1953, when Eddie and I moved on from the sixth grade, Mike joined the navy as soon as school was over, refusing to listen to all pleas that he should go to college. Dad, to say nothing of Aunt Gert, was brokenhearted, and everyone seemed to react as if it were the last we would ever see of him, as if he would become that "black sheep" sort of family member who had "gone to sea," never to be heard of again.

But it didn't turn out that way. "The Boss" got regular mail from all over the world and gift money orders sizable enough to indicate that Mike's gambling talents hadn't diminished. When he returned home in 1955, he surprised everyone by entering college. Now he was only four years ahead of Eddie and me in school, but I never felt

26

any closer to him in age. If anything, his being a world traveler only added to the sense that he was much older than we were. He lived at home and attended the same community college that furnished Aunt Gert with her boarders. Yet, now, if he spent whole nights playing poker he was at least doing it with his peers and was a worry to his family only when he lost.

The only perceivable difference in him was that he was a good student in school and even made the dean's list his first semester in college. Maguire was enormously proud of him, perhaps because he felt so bad about the way he had turned him out of school. After Mike came home, the two of them seemed to develop a closer relationship than they had ever had before. Oftentimes Maguire would ask Mike to join him when he was driving some distance and wanted company. It was surprising to me to see that Mike always seemed so ready to join him.

In the summer of 1957, the year I was starting my junior year in high school, Mike announced to the family that he was going to become a priest. It was as sudden and as simple as that. Instead of going back for his junior year at college, he was leaving for a seminary to begin his studies for the priesthood. It was a total surprise, so total that I have no way of recounting a buildup to the announcement or to say whatever process of thought had brought Mike to his decision. He had never said anything about it. It was so total a change of role I had no way of digesting the fact except to take it and say, "Okay, that's what he's going to do," even though there was no understanding involved.

I don't know if I expected him to turn into a model of holiness or something, but for days after he told us I was as shy of him as if I were Moses hanging around the burning bush. The one time I worked up enough resolve to pry into what he felt, asking him while we were out alone in a sailboat, he shrugged in an annoyed way, as if I'd asked him about his sex life.

In mock seriousness he said, "Well, you know, Dennie, you spend a couple of years of your life staring at water and it makes you think about what you want to do with your life. I started thinking to myself—'Well ... three squares a day, no heavy lifting.... Why not?' Hell, Dennie, I wouldn't work for a living for anything in the world."

While I nodded agreement he looked into what must have been a puzzled uncomprehending expression on my face, burst into a

27

laugh, yanked my hat over my face, and said, "You dumb chicken-shit. You really are dumb, do you know that?"

And then he laughed again, leaving me as ignorant as ever about his vocation.

4

IN July of 1958, I was arrested for public intoxication and for exposing myself while I was working as a junior counselor at the diocesan summer camp. I had gotten the job there along with Eddie and several of our friends because Mike was the head counselor. It was an idyllic job, more play than work. At night, while there was technically a curfew we had to observe, the seminarians were good about looking the other way as long as the violation wasn't blatantly abused.

The lake's one town was a summertime mecca for teenagers. Each weekend the local police waged a losing battle to limit the area's attractiveness to the herds of youngsters who wandered up and down the main street looking for excitement. It was on one such hot, humid night, with the law already hypersensitive about overturned trash barrels, tossed beer cans, and yelling, that Eddie had arranged—since we were underage—for a friend to drive from the city with a trunkful of beer for the seven of us who were off that evening from the camp.

If I haven't said much about Eddie, that's because to say anything about him would be to repeat what I have said of myself. We were enough alike to have been twins. Like myself, Eddie was insecure about relating to others and covered this insecurity with an aggressive bravado. He was a better athlete than I, yet both of us were overshadowed by older brothers' reputations we could never have matched. If we had not grown up comfortably with one constant group of friends from kindergarten onward we, no doubt, would have been shy, quiet people.

It was nearly midnight as we walked around that evening, looking for something to do, and we were fairly well inebriated from the beer we had consumed when Eddie noticed Julie Telaski with some of her friends as they climbed into her parked convertible on a side street. Julie was our classmate, and was known as "Buffalo Oink" since she looked like a buffalo but generally acted like a pig.

Seeing her, Eddie, who was weaving and could barely see at all, was struck with an inspiration. "Let's throw 'em a moon!" he yelled out, grabbing onto me for support. "Wanna? Hey, great! We get 'em with a red eye when they come 'round the corner."

We all balked, but Eddie was laughing gleefully and insisted it had to be done. My own mind was a fog, and with his urging the comic possibilities outweighed my hesitation. We waited around the corner, and, when the girls drove into view, the seven of us lined up, backs facing them, bent over, dropped our drawers, and shot them a greeting that said it all to those of our own age group. The girls screamed, laughed, and Julie, who had a knack for recognizing people even when she couldn't see their faces, honked and hooted a hello.

The police car that rounded the corner after them jerked to a stop, and two cops jumped out, one of them ordering, "Okay, boys, that's it. Nobody move."

My first thought was to run like hell. But as unsteady as I was and with my pants down around my knees it was out of the question. In another second an officer was pulling me up by the hair. The next thing I knew we were under arrest, then shoved into the police station to stand before the massive tribunal-like desk of a heavy-set captain who looked incapable of anything like human understanding.

Sobered and scared witless, I could barely give the information that we were from St. John Bosco Camp, information that only made the Irish Catholic captain all the angrier. When the charges against us were listed as lewd conduct, indecent exposure, and public intoxication, I felt faint from fear and shock. Horrible images of the next morning's headlines loomed into my head, and without even thinking I started to object, "We're not guilty of . . ."

The captain broke in, saying, "You'll say 'Sir' when you address me, and you'll address me only when I speak to you. Do you understand?"

"We're not guilty of all that, sir," I said as respectfully as I could manage. I was holding onto Eddie, who was very drunk, and when I spoke he joined in. "Not guilty," he started to mumble and then threw up, splattering the front of the desk with foaming, upchucked beer.

"Gawd almighty," the captain bellowed in exasperation, throwing a clipboard in Eddie's direction. "Get these kids outta here!"

For about one tenth of a second I thought he meant we could go free. Then we were shoved through a side door and tossed in a tank cell where a couple of old drunks sat looking suspiciously at us. The next hour or so we leaned miserably against the cell bars, having no idea what was going to happen, and listening to Eddie who kept retching in dry heaves. One of the old drunks shuffled over, sat next to me, and grunted a hello that smelled like mildewed rags.

"What'd you fellers do?" he asked, clapping my knee in camaraderie.

Frightened of him, I pulled my leg away and muttered, "Uh . . . lewd conduct, I guess."

"Huh?" he asked, and then *he* looked a little frightened.

"We sort of exposed ourselves."

He stared at me a moment, coughed up more foul air, then got up and walked to the other end of the cell where he avoided us for the rest of our stay.

One by one we were called out to the desk so that we could call our parents and tell them to get us at nine o'clock in the morning. I wasn't above begging. I pleaded, truthfully, that my father was away on a business trip, and told about my mother being sick with worry for my brother with the Marines in Lebanon, practically at war, and how this would probably kill her. When this failed I lied about my phone number, giving the captain the number of a family who I knew would be away for the summer. When there was no answer the captain dialed the camp's number and laconically handed me the receiver.

31

Mike answered the phone. He was already angry. "Where are you guys?" he demanded. "It's almost two o'clock."

"Well..." I told him, "we got in some trouble." I couldn't force the rest of the story out. After a moment the captain grabbed the phone out of my hand.

"This is Captain Turner... Police... Right... In the village. To whom am I speaking?... Well, some of your boys are down here... Right... Right... Well, it seems they like to run around without any pants on... Right... Oh, just lewd conduct, indecent exposure, public intoxication: little things like that. One of them threw up on my desk... Right... You're damned right it's not good for the camp ... You a priest?... Oh... Good enough, Reverend... Fine... In the morning when their parents come... We got hold of them... All but this one and his brother... The other one's having himself a good sleep. Passed right out... You are?... But I want their father... Oh, sorry to hear that... All right... Good... Fine... Good enough, Father ... er... Reverend."

He handed me the phone and his face downgeared from the polite smile he had assumed when he learned Mike was of the cloth. "The reverend wants to talk to you," he announced, sternly.

"Hey, Mike," I said hesitantly.

"You stupid, lamebrained bastard," he rasped, obviously through gritted teeth. "I'm going to nail your ass to a wall when I get hold of you."

"Right," I answered resignedly and handed the phone to the captain.

It was a long, uncomfortable night, and yet as uncomfortable as things might have been, all of us would have readily settled for a life in prison rather than face what the morning was to bring. Shortly after nine the next day an officer came in, unlocked our cell, and brought us out to the front part of the station where everyone's fathers except mine stood along with Mike, and to our shock, Monsignor Maguire.

"I'm responsible for this one," Maguire said, pointing to Eddie. Then nodding in my direction, he added, "This one, too."

Besides the suspended sentence we received, Maguire immediately fired us all from the camp and, worse, expelled us from his high school because we were, he informed us, morally depraved. Each guy was placed in the custody of his father. Eddie and I, luck having totally run out, were ordered by Maguire to get into his car. The ride to the city was interminable.

"The idea of it," he raved. "Catholic young men—Catholic school men—exposing themselves!" The car would lurch forward or slow down according to his inflections. He ranted on and on about the disgrace we had brought upon our family, the parish, the school, the camp—we had managed to do in about everybody.

After he had gotten a lot out of his system and his face had faded from a cardinal red to a more normal color, I tried, feebly, to explain. "Monsignor, please, you've got to understand. Everyone does it. It's not exposing yourself. It's . . . it's . . . like saying hello . . . or something."

"Showing your rear end to somebody is saying hello? And that's nothing? It's mortally sinful! That's what it is!"

Then Eddie tried. "It's not done to be dirty, Monsignor. It's just . . . throwing a moon . . . that's all. Like Dennie says, everybody does it."

Maguire had stopped at a light. Taking advantage of this he turned and angrily asked what he always did when giving sermons about language or purity, "Would you do it in front of the Blessed Mother?" And then he angrily jolted off.

We rode in silence. What happened next is hard to explain because it makes it sound as if we weren't taking this matter seriously. In truth I had never been so depressed in my life; things couldn't have been more down. But as we drove along I began to feel Eddie next to me starting to laugh. He was shaking and breathing in noiseless spasms, but I knew he was laughing to himself. And I knew why. Maguire's suggestion about tossing a moon at the Blessed Mother had hit my imagination with the same blasphemous and graphically clear image. The more I tried to stop laughing the worse it got. I bit into the sides of my mouth, pinched myself, and tried to think of anything but what he had said. But it was impossible. Eddie started to hiss like a pressure cooker, then burst into a cough that was a guffaw. The two of us collapsed into a fit of laughter beyond any control.

Maguire stopped the car, unable to believe our perversity. He waited until we managed, after no small space of time, to quiet down and settle into a sense of shame. He never said another word, but drove to the next bus stop, then stonily ordered us with a pointed finger to get out.

Our expulsion was different from Mike's. Though Eddie and I were registered in the public school, we couldn't carry it off as he had. When it came down to the wire, we wanted so desperately not to be separated from our school we sat in Maguire's office, shedding tears like second-graders, pleading for another chance. There were long meetings with our parents, talks about Catholic honor and public morality, promises demanded about future conduct that only an archangel could have fulfilled, and finally we were allowed to return for our senior year.

The point is that despite the almost incredible family resemblance, which caused people to judge us alike, neither Eddie nor I had much in common with Mike. We were not the stuff of which heroes were made.

5

_A_S if compelled to match the reputation of my brothers, and even of Eddie who ranked several social notches higher than me by playing football, I quit cross-country that fall and went out for the football team. It was a mistake. Track was my first love, and I was a good runner, especially in distance. Nonetheless, football meant high school glory, exactly the opposite of what I had earned after the arrest. Though a night in jail might have won a certain prestige for me in a senior-year peer group, too many people knew how I had crawled and cried my way back into school. Football was how I was going to show the world that I could take knocks.

I was on something like the seventeenth string defensive team and never got off the bench all season until mid-November in the last two minutes of a game that was already won. I scored a ninety-yard touchdown. In what must have appeared to be an interception, the ball, passed to a player behind me, bounced off my shoulder, danced for a moment in the air and plopped unwanted in my arms.

I was shocked, stunned—so stunned I almost handed the ball off to the kid for whom it was intended. Then after what seemed a frozen eternity of standing still, an alarm system within me, or possibly the coach at the edge of the field, screamed, "Run, you idiot."

I darted out along the sideline, easily passing the players of both teams, and ran toward the other end zone. I didn't know if anyone was behind me and never looked. I just ran—my legs and the blood in my head pounding full throttle. The crowd screamed louder with every step I ran, and as each five-yard line passed under me a sense of panic increased: Were they yelling because someone was gaining on me? Or were they yelling because I was running the wrong way?

"Oh, Jeez," I thought irrationally. "I *am* running the wrong way and that's why nobody's caught me. Both teams are probably just standing and watching. I'll never live this down."

The markings of the end zone were under me. I put the brakes on and turned. The nearest man on the other team running after me was fifteen yards behind. I stared back holding the ball. Everyone was cheering, and the band struck up the school song. I had really scored a touchdown. Then everything went blank. I fainted.

I came to in the ambulance, and immediately began protesting that nothing was wrong with me. Nevertheless an overly protective father, along with the emergency room staff at the hospital, agreed that the occurrence was unnatural, and they kept me for twenty-four hours.

That was all that was needed for the incident to become the joke of the year. A bouquet of flowers arrived with a get-well card signed by everyone in my class. These were followed by a visit from Maguire. "Well... missed the big game," he announced cheerily, as he boomed into the room. "I had to give a weekend retreat at a convent. Heard you got hurt."

"I didn't get hurt," I muttered.

"What happened?" he asked, a puzzled note entering his voice as he scanned my body looking for some sign of disability. He obviously didn't know.

"I ran a touchdown and passed out," I told him. "Nobody even touched me."

He looked at me for a moment, broke into a quick laugh, then just as quickly stifled it when it became apparent he was going to laugh alone. "Well, then," he said with a cough, "you'll be ready to be up and at 'em in no time at all."

"I was ready to be up and at 'em when I came to," I said. I was not good at forgiving others when they had hurt me, and at the moment I very much resented Maguire. If he had not made me act like a baby at the beginning of the school year, I felt, then I would not have looked like a fool trying to prove I was a hero.

Two weeks later, when Mike was home for Thanksgiving, clouds of resentment still hung heavily about me. He had barely spoken to me from the time of the arrest until he went back to the seminary. Now I returned the favor, not particularly caring if he was a part of my life or not. Even the day before he went back, when he tried to pull me into conversation on Aunt Gert's front porch, I let him run a monologue, much as I had done with Maguire.

At length, he too gave up and spent a few minutes shuffling through the Sunday papers. Then, abruptly, he demanded: "You're really letting that fainting business eat at you, aren't you?"

"Am not," I said. "That was two games ago."

"Well," he offered, "if it was, I was just going to say that if you'd just forget about blacking out, that was one hell of a decent run you pulled. Nobody could touch you."

"They were caught off guard," I responded.

He accepted the put-down. Then after a moment he agreed, "I could have caught you."

Resentment fired into anger. "How do you know? You weren't even there."

"I'm faster than you," he shrugged. He pointed up the dirt and gravel cemetery road, casually saying, "That turn is about a hundred yards. I'll leave you in my dust."

Suddenly, I wanted to beat him more than I ever wanted anything; I wanted to get back at him, not just for August, but for all the times he had ever played the bully over me. "You're on," I said.

We went out, lined up side by side on the road, and blasted off. We ran neck and neck for fifty yards. Then he began to pull ahead—smoothly, almost effortlessly. I reached for every ounce of physical strength and pent-up fury inside me, feeling I would burst with the effort. I couldn't. I just couldn't catch up with that arrogant, broad back in front of me. He hit the end of the straightaway two full strides ahead of me.

I hated him. When he turned, gasping for air, I wanted to use what little energy I had left to pound him in the face.

"Hey, that felt good," he exulted, almost in a yell. He obviously didn't care so much about beating me as just running the race.

But I cared. Even before we recovered I punched him in the shoulder in a gesture of good nature too hard to be good natured, gasping, "I could beat you doing a perimeter of the cemetery."

"Now?" he panted.

"Right now," I challenged, fighting for each breath of air, "right around to here."

He looked directly at me, then half smiled a maddeningly knowing smile. "Give me five minutes to recoup," he said. "I'll take you."

I had never measured it, but it was well over a mile, and I used it regularly for working out. We started off, easier this time, both of us conserving energy for the end of the race. We ran together, silently. After half a mile he was breathing hard. I knew I had him. He was bigger than I and built for strength. I was lighter but trained for endurance. With a quarter of a mile left I could feel that he was reaching for reserves he didn't have. I pulled away, moved gradually into a sprint, and finished a good twenty seconds before him. I turned and watched him stagger in. I was jubilant—feeling almost as satisfied as if I had punched him after the sprint. Red-faced, he stopped next to me and bent over, kneading a cramp in his side with his hand.

Then he stood up and hung onto my shoulder for support. "Hey, Dennie," he laughed, "you are a good distance runner, you know that? Wait till indoor track starts. That'll be your season."

The flattery melted my anger to a level where I felt shame for it. Then I laughed too, a little awkwardly, nodded and agreed, "Yeah."

We started back to the house, and for the first time since he had come home we started talking. It occurred to me later that I should have told him that he had lost the race, because he didn't seem to notice that. He had gotten kind of taken up in the fact that I had won.

Halfway through my last year in high school, Maguire was named bishop of our diocese. He chose to finish out the school year before fully assuming his new duties. It was a proud moment for the parish and the school, and, though hardly deserved, it was a moment of reflected glory for me as well. Because I was a senior altar boy and in spite of—perhaps because of—all the trouble I had been to him, Maguire kept asking me to serve for him at any special liturgical function. As well, he often assigned me to serve his private morning Mass when he had no public assignment. We shared this transition time in his life.

His new job brought a maze of variations in the liturgy and every now and then I would catch him looking at me as if for directions when I was looking to him for the same. For example, just before the consecration at a bishop's Mass, his beanie is supposed to come off. Once when I reached over at the right moment and whopped it off his head, he jumped and looked around, startled. I held up the beanie, and he turned red, then continued on with the Mass. At times such as that I would get a small urge to poke him with my elbow and share a laugh. It was that intimate a working situation.

There were a few more times during that senior year when I hit rough spots in school, and on some mornings in the sacristy he wouldn't even say, "See you in school," or "Go to hell," or anything. But somehow we had gone beyond the point where we needed that. Once you have been bailed out of jail by someone, there is no need to fall back on small talk.

In that June of 1959 he and I both left the parish world where I had grown and known him, presumably to head down separate paths. I don't think that Maguire was the major impetus in pushing me toward the priesthood; but he was right up there.

6

IN the fall of 1959, I entered Siena College, a Franciscan school, and for the next four contented years never had a single serious thought that I can remember, never opened a book but for all-nighters before exams, and never planned anything about my life farther away than each coming weekend. It was a grand time, one that I wouldn't have traded for anything short of heaven.

Authoritarianism in college was still alive and well then. Students were told how to dress for class—so that even if torn dungarees were worn, a suit jacket and tie had to top the outfit. Dormitory students had enforced study hours and had to sign out at such times even to go to the library. When visiting lecturers gave talks at night, attendance was mandatory under pain of flunking courses, and this was checked by turned-in identification cards. In imposing these penalties the college was only reacting well enough to what we were.

One might think that as a political-science major I would have jumped at the chance to hear an assistant to Robert Kennedy when he spoke at our campus after the federal government had taken a strong stand during a racial dispute at the University of Mississippi. Instead, I opted to watch *The Bugs Bunny Show*—a sacred and untouchable half hour in my life.

In that twilight age of nonrelevance I was by no means alone in the television pit watching Warner Brothers cartoons. Half of my dorm was with me, and the kid who took my card—the sort of guy whose friendship was cultivated in college, who went to classes, studied like it was a hobby, kept a copyable notebook, and who always reasoned out what would be on exams—staggered over to the lecture hall under the weight of some fifty I.D. cards. He didn't mind. We each owed him a beer for the favor; he enjoyed the talk, made out over the coming weekend, and we enjoyed not enjoying the talk. It worked out even.

It wasn't that we were lazy. Most of us worked hard in nipple-headed ways. My summers were spent working with Mike at camp or digging for the power company, and during the school year I delivered for a liquor store four nights a week. But that was to support a life-style. It took money to keep up a car, to pub crawl on weekends, and to mollify one's girl with something occasionally better than a pizza and beer before parking to watch the submarine races at the state park. It was just that thinking had nothing to do with any of it.

It was pretty much the same with religion. For all that the Catholic education system has been branded as having been a brainwashing program, it was not. Measured by our day-to-day lives, my peers and I were, in most respects, a group of happy pagans.

I have one striking memory of a religious experience in college, which, I realized only years later, nudged me further onto a still cloud-covered pathway that led to the priesthood. Chapel on Sunday, much like the guest lectures, was a required function. Most of the dorm students would show up for the noon, hangover Mass and groggily slouch in sit-kneel positions in the chapel's back pews, to be dragged into awareness only by occasional screams from the pulpit or air-stifling emissions of recycled beer vapors from their fellow students.

It was always a pain-filled, interminable experience. But it would never have occurred to us to rebel against going. It was simply the way things were set up. For myself, the dictates of authority didn't bother me, nor was boredom with the sermon or an aching head ever a consideration. Born, perhaps, with a peasant's thick-skulled sense of faith, I accepted without question that Jesus was actually pres-

41

ent, and even if this acceptance was only dim or, at times, totally unconscious within me, it remained a solid basis for my showing up, even if I didn't do anything while there.

One icy February morning, with most of the guys at Mass hating the faculty priests for rousting us out of warm beds and into the sub-zero cold, a superhero from my dorm broke into a sneered whisper, when the priest held up the host after the consecration, saying loudly enough for the whole back area to hear, "Okay, you got it that high; let's see you make it fly."

He got enough of a hushed laugh to satisfy his ego, but his remark startled and awoke me from whatever daydream I was wrapped in and into a slowly growing anger. It was as if he had joked about my mother. I tried to put down my reaction. What was I getting so angry about? It was the kid's own business if he wanted to mock out the Mass. But then again, was it? For perhaps the first time I began really to think about the Eucharist. It either was or wasn't Jesus. If it wasn't, then I was a damned fool for kneeling. But if it was, then how could I remain passive while someone reduced him to a joke? Intent on my thoughts, I knelt up straight. I did believe. If I had grown up with a peasantlike, thick-skulled unconscious faith, I now consciously confirmed that faith to my own mind. Then Maguire's fist-pounding insistence on respect for the presence of God welled up in me. I made the first commitment of my life to any kind of action for Christ. "I'm going to kill that bastard," I vowed to myself, "as soon as Mass is over."

But I didn't. Once outside, this ennobled intent was fast frozen by wintry, drift-blowing winds. I would have felt like an idiot defending Jesus, as if I were some kind of undercover fanatic. Rather, I sat on my feelings, feeding my resentment for almost a month. Finally in a bar I went out of my way to goad the guy into a meaningless hey-watch-who-you're pushing argument, then pushed until, more in confusion than in anger, he was forced into a fight outside, where I did my damnedest to beat his face in. After I had done so, anger bled out of my system, I felt a sense of shame over what I had done, and the next day sheepishly apologized, explaining to him that I had been drunk out of my mind and didn't know what I was doing. I was in no way ready to be an acknowledged defender of the faith.

It was only in our senior year of college, with graduation and the enforced end of childhood in sight, that we began to panic about facing reality. All of us wanted to remain where we were for the rest of our lives. The memoir writers seem to agree that Catholicism was a closed-minded ghetto in that age. Indeed, it was. But it was a great ghetto.

The whole world was a closed-minded ghetto back then: a cold war, plastic, no-think ghetto—all wrapped beautifully and sold in *Life* magazine. But we fitted this world perfectly while adolescents, and not one of my crowd, least of all myself, wanted to grow into the adult end of our society.

For no other reason than that most of my friends had done so, I had spent four years in the Reserve Officers' Training Corps and had gone to a summer basic training camp at Fort Sill, Oklahoma. Although I had almost been dropped due to "lack of leadership qualities" for having nonregulation underwear and for having lost my rifle, I ended my college career receiving a commission as a second lieutenant in the United States Army. It says much, not only of myself but of my whole age group, that, as a future officer, I was not in any way aware, in the spring of 1963, that my country was already involved in a growing war in Vietnam. Neither were my closest friends and fellow officers. We had talked, of course, a good deal about where we might be assigned.

The big hope was to go to Europe since that would be a launching pad for travel. I reasoned that the Far East would be boring. I didn't want to park myself in Korea to watch rice paddies grow, and a place like Laos sounded like you might get shot at. Vietnam, if it ever was mentioned, was passed over in the same light—as a less than good place to have to waste time. But to tell the absolute truth, I don't even remember it being mentioned. My only thought in accepting my commission as an officer in the army was that it would be an interruption in my life and something to be gotten over with. Its only value was in that it was better than getting drafted after starting into a career.

The army was not to come right away though. I had suddenly decided to go to law school first, because on top of everything else that went along with being suddenly grown-up, I had gotten engaged to a girl I had gone steady with from the night we first met at a high school record hop.

43

I had hung about at such events, safely shielded within a group of my friends in a corner of the semidarkened gym, even after Eddie, then on the junior varsity football team, had graduated into sociability and started dating a junior cheerleader named Ann. Then one evening, during routine forays to the lavatory, I kept bumping into one girl with green-gray eyes, soft curly brown hair pulled back into a pony tail, and a flashing, self-confident grin. She seemed to be everywhere I went. At one point, when I walked past her, she suddenly said, "Hi, Dennie."

I knew that her name was Gaelin and that she was a cheerleader along with Eddie's girl, Ann. What startled me was that she knew my name. She was beautiful. She was a social leader among the girls of her class. She was dressed in a soft, white pullover sweater with two small puffballs dangling necktie-like at the collar, a wide pink skirt, white socks, and saddle shoes. Surely she was too cool a girl to notice me. Stupified, I looked at her for a moment, slackjawed, then nodded dumbly and kept walking.

Later I encountered her again in the outside foyer. She was at the soda machine directly in my path, wrestling with the coin return button.

"Do you know the secret of this thing?" she laughed, turning to me, "It stole my dime."

I pulled the button up and down a couple of times for her. Nothing happened.

"Sometimes if you punch it . . ." I ventured, pulling back and slamming against the coin slot with the palm of my hand. There was no doubt about it; her dime was gone.

"I'll buy you a soda," I offered gallantly.

"Oh, you're sweet," she enthused, adding after a pause, "You run cross-country, don't you?"

"Yeah," I answered in a preoccupied half cough. I was preoccupied because I was rummaging through my pockets with both hands and had realized that I had no money with which to make good my offer.

"How far do you run each day?" she pressed enthusiastically.

"About six miles," I answered. I was scanning the speckled marble floor to see if anyone might have dropped a face-saving dime in the vicinity of the machine.

"You must really be light on your feet. I mean like with dancing and things," she offered.

Suddenly Eddie appeared along with Ann. The two girls acted as if they were being reunited after a ten-year separation. Sharing some great mystery through telepathy, they held hands, squealed with giggles, and jumped up and down. I took advantage of whatever they were doing to hiss desperately to Eddie:

"I need a dime."

Ann broke in before he could respond.

"Oh!" she yelled, "They're playing 'Earth Angel.' Let's *all* go in and dance."

Before I knew what was happening, Gaelin and I were hand in hand, and she was leading me into the darkened gym in the wake of Ann and Eddie.

"I'm not really all that great a dancer," I pleaded to her as we passed the sanctuary of my herd of friends. A low chorus of catcalls floated forth from the group.

"Hey, get this. Fred Astaire is gonna dance," announced one.

Someone else pronounced in a tone of finality, "You're outta the club, Hogan."

"Earth Angel" was done, and for a moment I felt reprieved. The disc jockey slapped on "The Great Pretender." It had the same beat; there was no escape. Clumsily I wrapped my arms around Gaelin, placing both my hands gingerly against the small of her back. She cuddled close and through her soft angora sweater I could feel her breasts against the lower end of my rib cage. It was the first moment of real physical contact I had ever had with a girl. I was filled with an electric sense of confusion. My heart pounded wildly, and I almost pulled back, fearing that she would notice this. The Platters kept singing on about the great pretender and Gaelin snuggled in, waiting for me to do something. I didn't know what to do. I was worse than the great pretender. I felt like the greatest fake in the whole world, and I was scared. Finally I blurted, "I never danced before in my whole life."

She laughed reassuringly and squeezed her arms tightly against my back. "It's easy," she whispered. "Just start moving with the music."

By the end of the evening I was in love, and for the next seven years Eddie and Ann and Gaelin and I became an inseparable quartet.

Unthinkingly I just presumed things would go on that way for awhile; but with all the showdown matters about growing up happening, Eddie screwed me up royally when, in January of 1963, he got engaged to Ann. Now all of a sudden Gae and I were odd couple out, and we began to hit long occasional silences when we were together. It wasn't that I didn't love her. I did, and I wanted her to be my girl. But I wanted her to keep on being my girl for awhile. Marriage was petrifying: a house and mortgage, kids, getting ahead in the world . . . It was nightmarish. I kept off the subject and did so with almost total success until the end of March. But with Ann arranging her wedding, Gae was miserable, and finally one night while we were at the state park, right in the middle of some serious necking and not having anything in the world to do with what we were doing, she said, "Dennie, what's going to happen next year?"

"Huh? Oh, I don't know," I said, not wanting to start a conversation. "The army, I guess—unless maybe I get into law school."

"I don't mean that. I mean us."

That put a complete damper on any thoughts about making out. From her tone of voice it was easy to see that she had been working up to a rehearsed argument. I sat up, turned on the ignition, and took the wheel like we should go, but she reached over and turned the key, insisting, "We've got to talk about this, Dennie. We just can't go on hanging."

She was upset and started crying, so I kissed her and said I loved her and that I always would and all that, but she wanted to pin everything down. "We can't go on going steady for another seven years," she said.

I couldn't believe my own voice. "Well . . . we're going to get married. Like we've always said."

"That was childish talk. What about now?"

"Well, damn it, we're not grown-up yet."

"Dennis, we are both twenty-one years old. How much more grown-up can you get?"

"Look, Gae, I want to go to law school. The only reason Eddie can swing marriage is because of the army. And if I go in the army first I know I'll never go back to school."

"You will. We can manage."

We sat for a long time. "You don't really love me at all," she finally said, her voice muffled in tissues.

"I do love you," I replied. And I really did. It was just that I didn't want to grow up all the way yet. She kept on crying, quietly. I didn't know how to handle it, so I started crying too.

We sat silently for another long time. Then, slowly, and dully, I said, "Maybe if I can get a year of school done and save up money I can finish in two years and it will be easy once I'm in the army. I do love you. I do want us to get married."

"Oh, Dennie," she said, and threw her arms around my neck. We were officially engaged. Our families were happy; Ann and Eddie were happy; she was happy, and I was just sick.

I began pushing my dad to get me into law school because if I didn't get in I would be married once and forever before the summer was out, and I simply wasn't ready for it. But luckily, being a member of an over-achiever family was a help. I had done poorly in law boards, and my college average was shy of a B, but the head of the law school where I had applied was a friend of my dad's and I got accepted. I was free to stay just short of adulthood for another year.

And that's where I stood in June of 1963: engaged, graduated, commissioned, headed for great things, and all screwed up.

7

I impulsively announced that I was going to Europe for the
summer to hitch around with a sleeping bag. Gae didn't take
to this too well. Here I was, taking money I had banked for us to live
on in another year and blowing it on myself. She threw a tantrum,
and I took my sleeping bag and left.

Arriving in France, I wandered about aimlessly, poking into cas-
tles and ruins, avoiding cities in order to avoid people, just trying to
figure myself out. I spent a couple of days at the cathedral of
Chartres. It was beautiful and quiet, and there was something
about walking around that cathedral that filled me, I guess, with a
deep sense of history and of Church.

It was a sunny morning when I had decided to leave to move on
southward, and I was sitting in a small park in the center of town
folding my gear and squeezing it into my backpack. I had noticed a
very old priest walking with a cane some distance from me, but I
was busy cramming my stuff together and didn't see that he had
come my way until I saw the bottom edge of his soutane in front of
me.

He smiled, pointed to the ragged sweatshirt I was wearing and
said, "Merton."

I looked at him blankly.

"Thomas Merton. St. Bonaventure's. He wrote there, did he not?"

I looked down and realized he was speaking of the school insignia on my chest. "Oh, yeah, I guess he did," I said, adding apologetically, "I didn't go there. My brother did. This is his shirt."

"Ah, yes. I have read a good deal of Merton. May I join you?"

"Huh . . . oh, sure, Father," I answered, straightening up. Then it struck me that we were speaking English. I added, "Uh, should I call you Père or something?"

He smiled as he sat down and said that it did not make any difference. He was very ancient; he looked to me to be about ninety, and he rested a moment before we talked again. His name was Father Guernier, and he was the chaplain at a nearby hospital.

"I've been to St. Bonaventure's," I told him. "We went to visit my brother. There's a mountain behind the college. They call it Merton's heart. I guess Merton used to walk around on it a lot. It's really beautiful. Nothing like here, of course."

He kept nodding and smiling. He asked if I had ever read anything by Merton. I said, "Oh, yeah," although I had only read about ten pages of one of his books once and had given up. So to be truthful I added, "He's a little hard to get into."

I was suddenly filled with how strange it was that I was talking to an old Frenchman about a small college my brother had gone to in the back hills of New York State. And yet he knew of it right away because of the Church. At home, mentioning a Catholic college's name generally meant having to explain what and where it was as well.

"I must apologize for my English," the priest said. "For many years I taught it in the schools, but I have not spoken it at all since the war, and I must stop and search in my memory for the words."

"You're doing great," I said, and when he smiled I realized that I hadn't said the right thing.

"During the war," he went on, "after the Allied landings and the liberation of my country, they asked me if I would help to hear confessions for the English-speaking armies. I did so as long as the Americans were here, and I made a great many friends."

He paused a moment, then said, "Those were terrible times. Terrible for humanity."

We talked for almost an hour, and when he got up to go he took a small change purse from his pocket, saying, "Do you have money?"

"Oh, yes, I'm all set. Really I am."

"Students never have enough money. Here. Think kindly of an old priest when you buy your supper. And say a prayer for me."

He took out ten francs and put them into my hand, shutting my fingers around the coins. Then he patted my shoulder. It was like he was from my own parish and I was his altar boy or something. We parted. I hadn't planned to, but I went back to the cathedral one more time. I sat on the stone floor for a long while, watched the sunlight play through the bright blue windows, and felt a part of the place in a way I hadn't earlier. This old priest, who was a part of this place, and myself both belonged to the same family. It was a good feeling.

I headed south, going wherever I could get rides. I stayed at Carcassonne for three days. There was nothing to do there, but it was an old walled city out in the country, and in total quiet and solitude each night, I could go to sleep outside the walls, looking up at the stars from under a turret. I kept thinking of the old priest and of the Church and what his being a priest meant.

Somehow it all blended into a sense of mystery. Where I lay falling into sleep I could feel that all time had stopped or that a thousand years of history had all tumbled into a timelessness. I could pick any time for centuries back, and the walls above me would have been witness to all the great and small people who had come and gone; and most all of them, like the old priest and myself, were children of the Church.

It wasn't that I was totally enamored of the Church. So much of what I saw turned me off. All of Europe was marked with memories of man using the Church as a tool for tyranny and worse. Here in the present there were things, as well, that the Church allowed, which were downright superstition. At places like Florence and Siena I looked at all those so-called preserved saints, gold-dusted skeletons, saints' fingers in candleholders, Jesus' footsteps—all of that nonsense. At Assisi I viewed, in fascinated horror, a body stretched out like a slab of overcooked bacon, its seven-hundred-year-old face rotted into a hideous grin. The nun who body-sat with it from behind a grill asked if I had any questions, delicately placing a holy card in front of an "Offering" slot for me as she did so.

"Yeah," I said, pushing a coin toward her and, not wanting to be

50

disrespectful but unable to resist the impulse, asked, "Why haven't they buried it?"

By the time I had traveled through Italy, I was more than turned off by the whole sideshow and gladly would have contributed to blowing it all up. In fact, in Rome it was good to meet American students again—normal people like my own friends. It was like waking up again to be able to sit and laugh with the people who gathered at the Spanish Stairs or who washed their feet in Trevi Fountain, not caring about anything other than what they were going to do for the night. I had had my fill of playing the philosopher. There were hordes of young people in the city, and almost everyone I met, even though a stranger, became an immediate comrade in arms, a part of the world I belonged in.

I felt like I had come back into my own century, and when President Kennedy arrived in the city on some good-will tour, I went to the City Hall to hear him give a speech. It was a routine hello speech—nonsense about how more Italians lived in New York City than in Rome and light matters of that sort. But I was really impressed with him. Catholic and Irish, he was of my own kind, and he was doing a lot for the world. "Why not politics?" I thought. I could do everything that he was doing, someday. I felt good about it. Why not? Dennis Hogan, President of the United States, and Gaelin, First Lady. I'd have taken that. It was suddenly as if a great weight had been lifted from me. I couldn't wait to get home and get started on my life.

Kennedy finished talking, stepped down, and walked along the edge of the crowd, smiling and saying hello. When I shook hands with him I wanted to stop him and tell him how I had just made up my mind and how he had helped me do it. It wouldn't have meant anything to him, of course, but somehow I felt as if he had convinced me of something and we were shaking hands on a decision made.

The next day I went to St. Peter's. I was fairly sick of churches by this time, so I just walked around, not being too impressed. The inside of the place couldn't really be seen anyway. It was filled with wooden bleachers from one end to the other in order to seat the bishops who were participating in the Second Vatican Council. Just as I had no realization that the United States was slipping into an Asian war, I had no idea as to what a Church council meant. I knew that it had been going on throughout the year, but I had reasoned that it was only another one of the fancy-dress shows that the Church was always putting on. The only immediate meaning the council had for me was that if I ever wanted to see what St. Peter's looked like without a track-meet atmosphere, I would have to come back another time.

I wandered around looking at statues and altars as if getting done with a homework assignment. When I came to a knot of kneeling people, I almost moved along past them and then realized that I was at the tomb of Pope John XXIII. He had died only a few weeks before, and flowers banked the walls around his resting place as if he were still being waked. It didn't seem right that John should be encased in such marble surroundings. Everything about the place seemed so medieval. Until a month before, fat laughing John had been as much a vital part of the world as John Kennedy. He was never meant to be part of a museum.

I was surprised to find a small bar hidden not far from the main altar. Grateful to see it I went in, got coffee and sat down. Almost immediately a priest came in, a thin, grizzled American about forty years old. He looked around for a table and, not seeing an empty one, he came over and sat with me. He introduced himself and excitedly told me that he had just said a Mass on St. Peter's tomb, adding that he had almost missed his chance to do so. Priests could sign up, he said, for an allotted time and he had done so. But when he arrived he found he had lost his place in line.

"But thank God," he went on, "the man in front of me finished, and I just had time to whip in and whip out."

He was so happy he was drumming on our small table with the heel of his hand while talking. I didn't know what to say. I managed something polite like "That's good," but I found what he was saying so incidental I wanted to say to him, "Who the hell cares where you say Mass? Why don't you realize what you had in your stupid hands?" And I said to myself that if I were a priest and I had a chance to say Mass on Peter's or Jesus' tomb or any place because it was a place, I wouldn't do so. What did it matter where you were if you had the power to call Christ's presence into your own hands?

And then it hit me full force. It hit me what I was saying to myself and how much I was held captive in my heart to the Mass. I couldn't contain myself with it. I had to go somewhere to see clearly. Without even realizing how rude I was, I got up numbly while the priest was still talking and walked back into the basilica.

I stumbled about trying to piece things together. I thought about men like Maguire and my own cousin. I thought of the old priest at Chartres. I wished I could have made them all somehow present, to make them all tell me what it was that made a man do it. And yet anything they might have said would have been nothing in the face of what I was realizing about the power of the Mass itself. It wasn't even that I was making up my mind. I had made up my mind long before and I was only now admitting it to myself. Nothing else mattered. Every other consideration dwindled, even Gaelin.

For all the shortness of human life, if I could become a priest only to say one Mass, it was something I had to do.

8

I said yes to this without hesitation, perhaps without thinking it through clearly. And yet the weight I felt had dropped from me the day before did not come back. I felt very calm.

I called my dad at his office—collect.

"Hello, Dennie," he said. "What's the matter?"

"Nothing, Dad. Listen. I'm going to be a priest."

A short pause was followed by, "We must have a bad connection."

"No, we don't. I've decided I'm going to be a priest."

"You mean, in the Church?"

"Yeah. Where else?"

"But you can't be a priest."

"Why not?"

"Well, if for no other reason, you're getting married. And you're starting law school in two months. And I had to practically buy the place to get you in, you know. This is no time to start playing your usual games."

"I'm not playing games, Dad. I know what I'm doing."

"Well, if you do, your timing is brilliant. Your fiance's picture was in the paper two days ago with your engagement announcement. If you're serious . . . Listen, what time is it in Rome?"

"What time . . . ?"

"Have you been drinking?"

"Dad, I know what I'm doing."

"Dennie, you haven't known what you were doing twice in your whole life. Have you talked to anyone about this?"

"No. I thought you should call Bishop Maguire and get things set up."

"I should call the bishop? I should call the bishop. You're lousing up your whole life and I'm supposed to call and set it up?"

He was yelling, and I wanted, impulsively, to hang up to stop him. But I didn't, and he finally calmed down, somewhat. He said, "Now listen to me, do you hear? Don't you dare speak to anyone until you get home here and you and I will have a good long talk and get this all straightened out. Do you understand? Now I love you, Dennie. You know I do. But for once in your damned stupid life you're headed in a normal direction and now you're going to blow everything up, just as you've always done."

"Well, I already did write Gaelin."

There was a long silence.

"You still there, Dad?" I asked.

"I'm here, Dennie. You can't do this to Gaelin. Don't you care anything about her?"

"Yes, I do, Dad. But that's not . . . it's not . . . I've just got to be a priest. That's all there is to it. Gae will understand. She's really religious."

"No girl is that religious when her engagement has been announced in the paper."

"I've got to do it, Dad."

"None of your brothers ever did things like this. Why have you always done everything backward?"

"I don't know, Dad."

"Well, promise me you won't say anything else to anybody till you get your ass right on a plane and get home here. We'll keep this quiet until we get it all straightened out.

Well, the family didn't exactly keep it quiet, at least not among themselves. They were all waiting for me at the airport like I was going to come stark raving mad out of the plane and they were all set to straitjacket me.

Gaelin was calm. All she said was, "I guess I never really knew you, Dennie."

Haltingly, afraid of opening wounds within her and within my own acting heart, I said, "Gae, it's not that I don't love you . . . or that I wouldn't want you to be my very own for the rest of my life. I can't imagine these past few years without you being a part of me . . ."

Her tears ran down her cheek, washing away my strength.

To maintain my resolve, I blurted, "But Gae, if I didn't do this I would feel that I missed what my whole life was meant to be."

She sighed from emptiness more than anger.

"Well," she said, "I suppose you've got to get this out of your system—like every other thing you do."

I winced. "Maybe. But I've got to do it."

"Okay," she said, "but when you give it up, don't expect me to be waiting for you."

Even now, I look back and wonder how I came to the decision. Was it Mike's influence or the example of Maguire and the other ordinary but strong men who as priests had shaped my childhood? Perhaps. And yet their influence was secondary. It was the priesthood itself. Because Christ had commanded it, an ordinary man took on the power to call God's presence into his hands.

9

*M*Y best preparation for what I found at St. Bernardine's came from the summer I had spent at Fort Sill in Oklahoma. This preparation would only have been complete however, if at Fort Sill we had worn armor and used crossbows instead of rifles, for the outward form of a seminary rule hadn't changed appreciably since the Council of Trent in the sixteenth century.

The institution's grounds, covering several acres of heavily wooded land, were cut off from the rest of the world by a ten-foot-high stone wall. The buildings of massive, dark gray stone were in a Victorian-Gothic style. High-ceilinged rooms with creaking wooden floors were lighted by cathedral windows that rose to a point at the top like hands joined in prayer. Every part of the main building—even if it was only a short distance from another part—seemed connected by interminably long corridors, where mandatory silence emphasized echoing footsteps.

Bells rang throughout the day at St. Bernardine's, ordering us through a minute-by-minute schedule. The first bell went off each morning at 5:45, calling us to the darkly medieval chapel to recite the prayers of the office, meditate for twenty minutes, and then attend Mass. The office prayers, which were repeated at other times during the day, were, like our textbooks in class, in Latin. I would sit totally lost, reading out meaningless syllables, thinking occasionally that for all I knew we could have been reciting a foreign-language dictionary or a dirty novel.

Other bells called us to meals, classes, periods of study, and more meditation. There were times when no talking was allowed. We were permitted to remove the black cassock, which was our constant uniform, only when we were in our rooms or playing sports during assigned recreation times. In the evenings we studied, forbidden to leave our desks. At ten o'clock the lights had to be turned off.

Father Fufferd, the vice-rector and prefect of discipline, was a middle-aged man with black hair plastered back like a silent-film actor. He made a point of speaking harshly and used a clenched fist to punctuate almost everything he said; and yet for all this dramatic flourish he added to his authoritarian role he often seemed befuddled about what he was doing.

One day at the end of lunch, shortly after I had entered the seminary, as we stood and began the long litany of Latin prayers recited from our prayer manuals, Fufferd suddenly waved his arms to silence us. "Enough!" he screamed. "Enough of this!"

The litany, already feeble in volume, ground to a stumbling halt.

"How many of you don't have your prayer manuals?" he demanded.

A good percentage of the student body acknowledged the lack by a raised hand.

"You're supposed to have them at all functions, including meals!" he thundered, stomping back and forth behind the head table as if he were controlling an unruly mob instead of the motionless herd we were. "This is outrageous—total disrespect for the Church's discipline of prayer. I want the name of every man here without a book. The bishop will have an account of this. That way he won't be surprised when you aren't recommended for Orders."

We were to pass by him at the doorway so that only students with books could leave. As the few who had them lined up, he painstakingly opened each cover to see if the manual presented belonged to the man in front of him. Not understanding how serious the situation was, I instinctively turned to Mike (now a six-year veteran of all this) at the back of the refectory, looking to him to tell me what to do.

Mike was quietly opening a window. He climbed out, dropped to the ground, and ran off in the direction of the chapel. In a few moments he ran back with an armload of books that he handed in through the window; then he headed back for a second load. In three trips he had everyone's book and had climbed back into the hall. Father Fufferd began to get confused, and as more and more books were presented he took all the longer looking at names and the man in front of him.

An atmosphere of comedy took over and the students began playing games: handing Fufferd the wrong book to see if he knew them by name, which in many cases he didn't. Several seminarians, including Mike, went around outside, climbed back in the window and waited in line a second time. Afterward a number of people insisted that when Fufferd, thoroughly rattled, looked at Mike suspiciously, Mike smiled back at him and said: "I'm my cousin"— and Fufferd, with a blank, puzzled expression nodded him through.

Television and radio were forbidden as a matter of routine, but on Saturday nights a movie was shown in the gym. Owing to the schedule, most of the men were so desperate for diversion they would have sat through a test pattern. What they got wasn't much better. The local distributor, a good Catholic, prided himself on seeing that the boys got "the right sort of entertainment," and the films he sent were generally of the caliber of *Clarence the Cross-Eyed Lion* or *Mister Limpet Becomes a Fish*.

The second week into the semester, Mike told me to skip the movie and join him for a walk. The seminary was such a bewildering world to be thrown into cold, I had all but decided I wanted to go home to pick up reality where I had left off.

"Don't be dumb," Mike said as we pushed our way through the acres of backwoods owned by the school. "You haven't been here long enough to air out your suitcase."

"I've been here long enough to see that this whole business is unreal. I keep waiting for the Wicked Witch of the West to come out of the walls."

"So, how real was Fort Sill?" he asked.

"I know, but that was different . . ."

"Wait. Shut up a minute," he cautioned, putting his hand up.

"Huh? Why?"

We had reached the gateway in the wall, where we could see the dirt road bordering the seminary lands.

"In case any of the faculty is out," he whispered. "If you see anyone walking, just separate and slip into the woods."

I was confused. We were allowed to leave seminary property on one afternoon a week. But we hadn't left the place. We weren't breaking any rules. It was pitch dark along the road, and we waited in the shadows. After a few minutes a car drove up slowly with its lights off. It stopped and when Mike walked over to the driver's window the kid inside told him, "I couldn't get pepperoni. They were out. I got sausage instead."

"Was it any more?"

"Buck more."

He fished out a bill, handed it to the kid, and took three pizza boxes from him. When the kid drove off, Mike led me back into the woods and explained, "One of my runners. I've taught him in release-time religion for the past two years. You got to be careful who you pick though."

In a clearing, four of Mike's classmates were waiting with cans of soda. They had been, along with Mike, my bosses during the summers I had worked at the diocesan camp. We had gotten along poorly back then. They had been as hard as nails in handling their jobs, no doubt because we junior counselors had been such screw-offs.

"What the hell took you so long?" asked one who had once been my cabin boss.

Long ago, this crowd of my cousin's friends had shattered any childhood preconceptions I held about the clergy. They were ordinary men who lived the life we did, who lost their tempers, who drank beer, and played poker at night. Now they proceeded to shatter my view of the seminary rule.

"The kid got messed up with the order," Mike told him.

"My God, how can you guys do this?" I asked, taken aback.

"Are you kidding?" Mike laughed. "What would you rather do? Go nuts? Like I started to say before: Think of the navy—or the army if you will. You do two things at the same time. You live with the rules, and then learn to live under the rules."

"A lifer in the military and the kind of guy who ends up running a seminary," added another, handing me a piece of pizza, "are cut from the same cloth. They're in love with a system, and most of them don't know their ass from a hole in the wall."

"Do you ever read Beetle Bailey?" Mike asked me.

"In the comics?"

"Right. It's my best spiritual reading. I have the Boss mail it to me all the time. The parallels are total. Father Fufferd, blustering away, is Sarge; Monsignor Buck, running a system he'd never have invented, is General Halftrack; Father Nolan jumping each time he bumps into his own shadow is Lieutenant Fuzz, and I'm Beetle. When things get really down, I figure that if Beetle can make it through, I can too."

I still couldn't get over what they were daring to do right under the noses of the nearby faculty. "But," I objected, "if you guys get caught . . . you'll be . . ."

"Screwed," said one.

"And it's 'us' guys," Mike added. He leaned back against a tree with his pizza and laughed.

10

SEMINARIES should have had saloon doors to facilitate the sudden entries and sometimes faster exits of candidates. This world is filled with men who lasted a month, a year, two years, right up until the day before ordination. The students with whom I shared life at St. Bernardine's fitted no more of a mold than any cross section of men I had met in college or at Fort Sill.

There was a small percentage of seminarians who did fit the quiet mold of the cleric that most Catholics imagined. At the other end of the spectrum were men who, for as many reasons as they themselves were, had wandered onto the scene. A good number of them quit because they came to realize they just weren't meant to be priests. But many of them left, or were told to leave, because they were unable to fit into the clerical system as it was set up. This was sad because many of them, though they would indeed have made the worst of clerics, had the potential for becoming the best of priests.

And then there were the rest of us: very ordinary people fighting our way through a system as abnormal to everyday life as had been the army. We accepted it because we had other reasons for wanting the priesthood. To survive it, everyone stuck together. Tight rule intensified everything. Friendships were cemented that would remain lifelong. Aggravations blew up larger than life. The dirtiest sports I've ever seen played anywhere were played at St. Bernardine's.

The local hospital must have had a special rack in the emergency room for broken limbs and concussions sent with loving care from us to them. In most games rules went by the boards. A basketball foul wasn't generally called until someone was smashed into a wall and lay unconscious. Even then the whistle wouldn't have been blown if the man didn't have to be dragged out from underfoot. It was all a way of relieving tension.

At least twice a week, after night prayers in chapel, Monsignor Buck would deliver a sort of progress report on our conduct. A heavy-set man nearly sixty years of age, the Buck had shaggy gray hair that defied combing, and a lantern jaw that gave him both the appearance and sound of trying to hold back spittle while he talked.

He would begin almost every sentence with an elongated "Eh..." while he thought of what he was going to say, and it was his custom upon hitting some point of a rule or regulation he felt wasn't taken seriously enough, to comment, "Eh... What do you think you are? Funny?"

Because the Buck was so easily imitated and because that was such a catch phrase, it was an almost emblematic sentence in the seminary—one student going so far as to translate it into Latin and hang it with a coat of arms on the wall of his room.

When the Buck was absent, Father Fufferd as vice-rector would fill in. Fufferd had one basic theme: obedience.

"The Church is like a machine," he would bellow from the pulpit, "and we are simply cogs in that machinery. The Holy Spirit makes his will known through our superiors. When we are disobedient we slow down his very own machinery. Obedience must be the hallmark of every priest."

Before he got to the particulars Flufferd would be sure that we had all made the logical conclusion that he was, as our immediate superior, the manifestation of God's will to us. The second such talk that Fufferd gave was about our laxity in observing the 10:00 P.M. lights-out rule. Because we were so negligent in observing this, he declared we were to forfeit our recreation time after lunch and take an enforced nap every afternoon for the rest of the week.

63

For a brief moment I thought that he was joking. But for the next three days we lay in bed for an hour each afternoon while he patrolled the corridors. The students did their most to make a game out of it, snoring loudly whenever he'd walk by; but for the most part I just lay staring at my ceiling, listening to the midday traffic from the road and the occasional squeaking of Fufferd's shoes, trying to connect all this with learning to be a priest, with being twenty-one years old, and having just given up my officer's commission in the United States Army.

Father Fufferd pursued the possibility of disobedience with the tenacity of a private detective. The 10:00 P.M. rule was his most active worry, and one of his favorite tricks was to endure the olfactory torture of hiding in jock closets throughout the building to see if people left their rooms after lights-out. It was such a common ploy on his part that students took to hanging doorknob signs on each closet door with inscriptions such as "OUT TO LUNCH" or "THE DOCTOR IS IN."

One night when my cousin Mike was coming back from the latrine in the dark corridor, he caught the glint of Fuffern's eyeballs peering out from behind the hooked sweat clothes. He stopped by the door, which was open just a crack, shook his head, and muttered loudly, "Jeez, this stuff is gonna get stolen if they keep this door open."

He slammed the door shut, locked it, and walked off. Only when Fufferd, choking and desperate, screamed and banged on the door did Mike go back and in amazed innocence exclaim, "Father, what happened? What did you do—take a wrong turn in the dark?"

It was the escape mechanism of practical jokery, carried on by all the students, that almost ended my career when it had barely begun. It had started off slowly and then built up to a war of one-upmanship between myself and another student on my corridor. We had reached a plateau whereupon, after he had filled my room from floor to ceiling with trunks from the storage room, I had emptied his of every piece of furniture and reset it up in perfect order on the service elevator. My adversary had a gift for mimicry and was known for an inflection-perfect imitation of the Buck. With this he took me in.

One evening there was a knock on my door during study hall and when the familiar voice commanded, "Eh . . . Mr. Hogan, open up; I want to talk to you," I opened the door without hesitation and caught a faceful of water.

I didn't know quite what I was going to do with it; but I filled a bucket myself and put it in my room, planning to work up something after lights-out. At 9:30 there was a repeat of the knock on the door.

"Eh . . . Mr. HOgan," he said again, "could I talk to you for a moment?"

"Talk through the door," I yelled.

There was the briefest moment of silence. Then he commanded again, a little more loudly, "Eh . . . I said, 'Open this door.'"

"Eh . . ." I said back, quietly picking up the bucket, "open it yourself, you big tub of shit."

The door flew open. I hurled the water. It hit Buck—the real Buck—full force in the face. For an eternity of three seconds it cascaded like Niagara off his shoulders, down over his belly, drenching his red satin monsignor's belt, and splashing to a sudden puddle around his feet. The bucket dropped from my hands with a hollow clatter to the floor.

"Oh, my God," was all I could say. He blew a spray of water—perhaps steam—from his lips and choked out: "Eh . . . What are you, Hogan, a wiseguy?"

He turned and stalked off down the corridor. About ten guys rushed out, stunned at what had occurred, and without a word mopped the place dry, as if by eliminating the evidence that Buck might presume that he had imagined what happened.

At 9:55 the place was deadly silent, everyone for some reason having decided to turn in early. I wasn't surprised at the knock on my door.

"Who is it?" I asked, my voice sounding almost normal.

"Monsignor Buck," he said. "I want to talk to you, Hogan."

I obediently opened the door, expecting the worst. But not the kind of worst I got. The Buck stood with a filled bucket. An almost maniacal look of triumph spread over his face.

"Ah-hah," he yelled, hauling back and hurling its contents full in my face. The water finally came to rest, and we stood looking at each other. Then he burst out laughing, dropped the bucket, turned and walked down the corridor.

11

WHEN I first arrived at the seminary, people took Mike and me for brothers, and I spent the tail end of almost every introduction saying, "No, we're really cousins."

I had never previously thought about our relationship. Our family was so close we just took each other for granted. But, in October of 1963, distinctions that other people made were brought home most painfully to me. Eddie and Ann got married. I had presumed that Mike and I would go home for the wedding; but when the time came, Mike was allowed to go and I was refused permission. It was simple to the Buck, who shrugged away my plea for reconsideration.

"Eh . . . The rule states plainly, Mr. Hogan, that the only weddings and funerals seminarians can leave here for are those of the immediate family. Mike's brother is being married. You are only a cousin."

"But, Monsignor," I pleaded, "you don't understand. We're not just cousins. We grew up together. We slept in the same bed more often than not. My dad is like Eddie's father. It's more like we're really brothers."

"Eh . . . But not really," he answered, looking over the rim of his glasses in a way that said that no more explanation was necessary. "If we made exceptions such as this, Hogan, the rule wouldn't stand for anything. We'd have to stretch it to make more exceptions all the time. Everybody would be going home for their next-door neighbor's birthday parties before we knew it."

I tried to object again, but he put his hand up and closed his eyes. The interview was ended.

The Saturday of the wedding I wandered around, totally down and even jealous of Mike. It was the first time I had ever been separated from my family for an important event, and I resented what I considered a needless seminary rule. I felt physically ill, but I knew my illness was homesickness.

At five in the afternoon, when we were heading into chapel for spiritual reading, I was called out of line and told to report to Father Fufferd's office. He was sitting behind his desk when I entered, and without changing his expression he pointed to the telephone receiver, which was off the hook, saying, "You have a long-distance phone call."

As I reached to take it he added sharply, "You know that you are not supposed to receive phone calls without permission."

I figured it had to be Eddie and Ann, but it wasn't. I said hello into the phone and a burst of yelling and laughter roared back through. It was a bunch of my friends at the reception and obviously at the bottom end of the punch bowl.

I pressed the earpiece as close as I could to my head to muffle the noise. Father Fufferd never moved. "Oh, hi," I said, wishing he would leave and ask about the call afterward.

It sounded like there were ten guys fighting each other for the phone.

"Uh . . . it's nice hearing from you . . . uh . . . Dad," I said, "but you're not supposed to call like this, you know."

That didn't help stop the confusion on the other end. "Hey, stupid, it's me, Jack," and then after thuds and a number of yells, "I mean, all of us. Hey, here's Eddie."

Fufferd kept staring at me. Eddie stammered and sounded almost shy: "Hey, Dennie, it's me . . . I'm married now."

My throat tightened all at once. I wanted so much to be with him. I was depressed and yet happy. And most of all, a feeling that was just a part of being family seemed about to overwhelm me. I felt tears come to my eyes and could hardly speak.

"Yeah . . ." I said finally. I didn't want to talk over a phone. Some things shouldn't be put into words.

67

"Ann is on the other side of the room. We were going to call you later. Together. These guys just grabbed me."

I looked at Father Fufferd. "You can't, Eddie. I wasn't supposed to get this call." Then realizing that he didn't understand, I added, "Talk to Mike. He'll tell you why."

The operator broke in and Eddie hurriedly asked if anyone had more change. No one did. He talked fast, "We'll get hold of you somehow before I go away. I'm going ahead and then Ann's coming after me. We'll be at Fort Benning next week. Write to us a lot. Hey, do you want me to say something to Gae? She's with Ann."

"Uh . . . no. No, don't," I said, reddening as if Father Fufferd could read my mind.

"Okay. Listen, Dennie . . ." he said, and then we were cut off.

I put the phone back on the receiver, and Fufferd went into a long roundabout warning as to how another such performance could terminate my seminary career. He went on and on talking, but I scarcely heard him. I was angry at my friends for calling because if they hadn't, Eddie and Ann's call would have come through.

But mostly I just felt totally frustrated listening to this foolish old man in front of me. It was downright wrong that I couldn't be a part of Eddie's wedding. In every way that mattered, we *were* brothers.

That incident always remained with me as a bitter memory. It was the last time I ever spoke with Eddie.

12

*I*T was a warm, almost hot afternoon for November. I had found Mike walking up and down a path in the woods behind school. He was reading, and when I asked him what he was doing he shook his head in exasperation.

"Canon law," he grunted. "Fufferd makes up the damnedest tests. What he does is print different canons on the test paper and leave out words to be filled in. Only he doesn't leave out important words, just picky crap like 'atque' or things like that. So you have to memorize what you can of all the canons he's covering."

"In Latin?" I asked.

"What else?"

"Do you understand Latin?" I was getting depressed.

"Hardly a word," he laughed.

"Hell, Mike, what are we going to do when we get out of here?"

"Since when did you become the all-time great intellectual?"

"Well, I . . ."

"I work under the great Navajo theory myself," he cut in. "I invented it. Want to hear it?"

I gave him a perplexed look.

"I figure—who gives a shit?"

Before I could digest this theory in its essence he elaborated upon it. "Jesus gets beaten to death with theology anyway," he continued.

69

"The way I see it, the only things you're going to need when you get out of here are a Bible and a jockstrap."

"Ah . . . it's more than that, though . . ." I said, and we walked along without saying anything for a minute.

He put his arm around my shoulder as we walked and finally said, "I know, Dennie. The whole thing stinks sometimes, doesn't it?"

"I don't know. It's just that the whole damned world is out there falling apart in 1963 and we're here pretending it's the thirteenth century or something."

"Sure," he said, stopping our walk abruptly. "But don't blow the whole thing just because you haven't got it figured out yet." He paused as if considering whether or not he should continue and then said, "You know, you're kind of simple. Has anyone ever told you that?"

"Yeah, you," I said. "About ten thousand times."

"I don't mean when I'm putting you down. But you really are. When you were a kid, whenever you went off, like even to go downtown, I used to wonder if you'd find your way back home. I don't think you know how to figure situations out. Like even with that phone call from Eddie. There were a dozen ways you could have called him back if you had just used your head."

I started to pull away so I could argue more effectively with him, but he held on to me.

"No, wait a minute. I'm not trying to hurt you, Dennie. Believe it or not, I wouldn't hurt you for anything. But it's what you are. You always walk into a situation, play it as you see it and then end up taking it on the chin. You've got to be a little cagey. You've got to measure things out before you play your hand."

"What does that have to do with this?" I retorted angrily.

"Everything, damn it! Look, what about being a priest? Could you see that saying something to the world of 1963?"

". . . Yeah," I admitted.

"Well, okay. So you live in a medieval monastery for a while. Big deal. But don't be an idiot and throw away the priesthood just because your bed isn't comfortable or your cornflakes are wilted. That's what I can see you doing . . ."

He finally let go of me so he could gesture. "You're not the only person who ever went through this. We all did." He laughed again. "I remember when I first got here. There was one night when about fifteen of us were in a guy's room during study period and the place was so crowded the bed was pushed out from the wall for more space. Anyway, I was lying on the floor with a pillow behind my head and I fell asleep. All of a sudden everybody was jumping to their feet, and the bed got shoved over me against the wall."

After a brief pause, he continued: "It was Fufferd doing a spot check and he was madder than hell. By the time I fully woke up and realized what was happening, the place was cleared out and just Fufferd and the guy whose room it was were left. Fufferd began ripping into him and about every offense he had ever committed against the rule at St. Bernardine's. It was embarrassing. It was like overhearing a guy's confession, but it was too late for me to come out. Fufferd had his sandals on and so I just lay there on the floor for almost half an hour with his dirty toenails in my face, trying not to breathe. There I was, a totally grown man, hiding under a bed from that featherbrain. And if that isn't eating crow, what is? Hell, I was so hacked off I would have left if the priesthood didn't mean anything. But I thought it all through."

I still wanted to see things from my perspective. "Aw, I don't know . . ." I started.

"Well, I do," he countered. "So if you walk away from this willy-nilly, I'll knock your stupid head in. Remember, just keep thinking Beetle Bailey."

We were almost to the back door of the seminary building. One of the deacons was standing on the walkway, his face strangely blank, as if he were in shock.

When he didn't seem to notice us, Mike socked him on the arm, remarking with a laugh, "Hey, Bob, what's the matter? Price of beer up?" Then when he looked at us without changing expression, Mike added, "What happened?"

"Didn't you hear yet?"

"Hear what?"

"Kennedy's dead."

"What?"

"He was shot in a motorcade in Dallas. He died about five minutes ago."

I watched the President's body taken off the plane in Washington that night and thought back to when I had seen him during the summer. He had been the most forceful personality in the country when I was in college. He was of my own kind—Catholic and Irish. Now the sight of him dead rekindled in me all the emotions I had felt in Rome about doing something for the world. So, too, the clerical realm in which I was caught seemed all that smaller in the perspective of the tragedy that had just occurred.

It was a time of great confusion for me. For weeks after that I lived through the daily schedule attempting to sort things out. If John Kennedy's death had stirred up in me what I had experienced watching him during the summer, it also brought back what I had felt that same day at Pope John's tomb and the mind-shaking realization that had hit me from nowhere that day.

I was drawn to the Church—above all to the Eucharist. What it was remained a magnetic force compelling me toward the priesthood. To have God's trust to command his own presence—a man couldn't walk away from that.

13

ENNEDY'S death was a watershed moment of history, even though his death was not the cause of what was about to occur. Had he lived he would have been held responsible the following year for the growing war in Vietnam; the cities would still have erupted in racial riots; violence would still have taken over as the most effective form of American politics; and one of the greatest cultural upheavals mankind has ever lived through would still have taken place. But for a brief while of stunned apparent inactivity, there was a sort of quiet time before the winds of change began to stir. So, too, if nothing seemed changed in American society, nothing seemed changed at St. Bernardine's; nothing seemed changed for the Roman Catholic Church.

And yet it had. The world was too preoccupied to notice at the time; but twelve days after the shooting in Dallas, and after two years of what seemed ineffectual debating, the Second Vatican Council issued its first official statement—a decree on the liturgy. I had thought of the council as being a routine Church exercise, something Rome had done as a public relations gesture. The issuance of a decree meant nothing to me. Nor was it spoken of as anything important at the seminary.

Since secular newspapers were forbidden to us at St. Bernardine's, if we were to keep up on anything it had to be through the

Catholic press or nothing. I was in the library one evening between supper and night prayers, reading the Jesuit publication *America,* which was at least a window to the outside. Because the magazine was still filled with emotional tributes to Kennedy, I looked for anything else to read, even columns relating what was going on in the ecclesiastical world. There was an article by an archbishop from Australia and it caught hold of me by a strong insistence on the part of the author, so unlike the usual harmless rhetoric expected of the clergy. He declared that the council document issued that month was an "implicit call for an evolution in the Church's existing juristic structure."

"Some may be misled," he pressed on, "into viewing the constitution as a mere catalogue of minor changes in the liturgical discipline of the Western Church. The fact is, however, that this catalogue adds up to a quiet but deep revolution, one whose impact will be measured only in generations to come."

The bell sounded for compline, and I wandered to chapel, pulling on the white surplice needed for formal prayers. Perhaps because the article had contained such an insistent force, perhaps because I was always lost at compline, the archbishop's comments remained with me after I had sat in my choir stall, fixed my biretta on my head, and we had begun to alternate the Latin psalm chants from one side of the chapel to the other. The word "revolution" was so strong a term for a representative of the hierarchy to use. I puzzled as to what he could have meant. By the time we had knelt for the final blessing, however, I dismissed the statement from my mind. Whatever he had been trying to say, a revolution was not the sort of thing that came from a meeting of the Pope and his bishops. I left chapel that night and headed for my room, unaware that I had read an understatement as powerful as any a churchman had pronounced in the twentieth century.

Years later, after the Church had been ripped apart, a good number of Catholics would complain that the Vatican Council had opened up a Pandora's box of problems—a box that should have been left untouched. But if a revolution was coming, my age group was to be passively ripe for it; and as far as the Church was concerned, if the Pandora's box hadn't been opened, it would only have rotted out from the bottom.

My parents and much of their generation, including the faculty at St. Bernardine's, had more than just accepted the external rituals, symbols, and trivial regulations of the Church. They had internalized them as real values, along with what was truly essential to Catholicism.

I had grown up in a post-World War II, media-filled world. The external trappings of the Church were a comfortable enough backdrop for me. But the authoritarian rules that, so I was now told, were supposed to reflect my relationship with God, meant nothing to me. I saw them only as rules written by human beings who wanted to exercise power over others. Nevertheless, the essentials of Catholicism were very real to me, and the quest for the priesthood was worth the garbage we had to take.

As we moved into 1964 I learned to adopt Mike's Beetle Bailey philosophy. He was right. Ignoring the situation was the only way to survive in it. Father Fufferd could keep us for a half hour after night prayers lecturing about how our window shades weren't properly half up or down as specified and I could see the humor in it. I would listen to the saints' lives, which were read to us through half of each meal, hearing for instance, the story of St. Lawrence being roasted to death while we were trying to eat Spam, and I would figure it was worth the price of admission. I even managed to laugh when during the routine mail censorship Fufferd opened one of my sister's letters and corrected her spelling with a red pencil.

From the day I had entered St. Bernardine's I had tossed and turned for a good hour and a half after 10:00 P.M. each night. Now I got into the habit of flicking my light back on twenty minutes after lights-out, knowing that once we were in bed the priests would go to their recreation room in a far end of the building. I could usually read safely enough for about an hour before the prefects would begin to head back to their floors. One night, however, I got overly absorbed in what I was doing and was startled when my door opened to reveal Father Ben Nolan, the prefect on my corridor. He was a timid, balding, scarecrow of a man in his late thirties, whose attempts at affability were hampered by his constant fear that the harshness of those about him might bring about the recurrence of his recent nervous breakdown. Now, standing with his thin gray eyebrows knitted in perplexity and embarrassment, he asked, "Mr. Hogan, isn't it well after lights-out?"

"Yes, Father, it is," I said, upset at being caught.

"How can you expect God to bless a disobedient life?" he clucked, shaking his head sadly.

"Oh . . . uh . . . well . . . you see, Father . . . I was lying in bed and I kept getting these impure thoughts, and the more I kept getting them the more I was afraid I was going to . . . uh . . . well, uh . . ."

"Oh, yes. Oh, well, fine," he said, blushing and backing out of the room.

After that I kept my lights burning half the night and he never bothered me. Near the end of that semester, however, Monsignor Buck called me in and asked if I wasn't having an extraordinary problem with impurity. So I dropped that business, figuring that if I didn't they would have to expel me for being some kind of pervert.

Instead I developed a regular excuse of night diarrhea, even asking for Kaopectate from the infirmary so I could be covered in staying up every now and then to sit in the latrine. But it was a hell of a way to read and all I got out of it were red indentations on my rear end like some people get on their nose from wearing glasses too much.

14

THE changes ordered by the Vatican Council arrived at St. Bernardine's in the person of Father Mulqueen. Still in his mid-thirties, he was crowned with silver hair that gave him the distinguished look of a scholar; and though he spoke with a slight lisp, he was the most convincing of speakers either in a pulpit or behind a lectern. He had worked at the first two sessions of the Vatican Council. Now that he was back home in the States, he was busily preparing a book based on his experiences and giving lectures to both Catholic and Protestant groups as to how Christian churches were on the verge of a new age.

From the first day of the fall semester of 1964 he began to push to make that new age a reality in the seminary, and the fourteen priests on the faculty quickly divided into two battle groups—pro-Mulqueen and anti-Mulqueen.

We had been used to such a seamless solidarity on their part that this breach in authority was, at first, difficult to accept. It took little time for Father Mulqueen to develop into a sort of hero in the students' eyes and the natural leader of the faculty members who joined the ranks of the followers of Vatican II. Almost overnight the seminary became the staging ground for a small war, though at first this fighting remained on a faculty level, because the students were afraid of expulsion.

There were bizarre dichotomies. Father Mulqueen would invite a Presbyterian minister to speak to us, while on the same day in moral theology Father Tucker would be expounding upon the paragraphs in our textbook that questioned whether it was morally permissible for a Catholic working in a hospital to call a minister for a Protestant patient. We would be getting previews in one class as to what the Church was preparing for a decree about conscience and religious freedom, while in another class we were being taught how many ounces of meat eaten on a Friday made for the difference between a mortal or venial sin.

But it was the liturgy that became the most divisive issue, for the beginning of the approaching Advent season in 1964 was to be the date to implement the first changes set forth by Rome. The faculty at St. Bernardine's had apparently presumed, like so many men at all levels of authority in the Church, that the new directives would be dead-letter orders just as so many directives had been in the past. After all, in the late 1950s Pius XII had directed that the Latin responses at Mass be recited by the entire congregation, and he had been roundly ignored. These directives would simply be a repeat of that. When the orders became specific many of the professors simply refused to discuss them.

What course the changes would have taken at the seminary without the insistent direction of Father Mulqueen I could only guess at. Certainly they would have eventually taken hold, for they did so in even the most reluctant citadels of conservatism throughout the Church. But as Mulqueen kept insisting, it was our duty as a seminary and house of theology to assume a role of experimentation and leadership.

To this end we were not only to do what was basically expected— that much of the Mass was to be said in English now rather than Latin—but we were also to do that which was allowable though not ordered. The altar was to be turned so that the priest faced the congregation, and we were to begin singing hymns during the Mass.

An atomic blast might have shaken the seminary less.

"Like a bunch of Protestants, that's what it sounds like," Father Fufferd said, pounding on his podium to answer a question put to him by my cousin. "There hasn't been any provision made for a proper study of the whole matter."

I was half asleep at the back corner of the lecture hall, but the sound of Mike's voice had brought me to attention. He had been a worry to me of late. During our first year together in the seminary he had played a quiet game very well, but now he had begun to reassert himself more and more in the natural leadership role in which I had always known him: the child manager of the cemetery, the boss of the summer camp, the master of sailboats. Now he and Fuffered were arguing about the changes in the liturgy and Fufferd's absolute opposition to any innovations.

"But, look, Father," Mike insisted, "if we don't hash this out here, what'll we do next year when we're in pulpits? I mean, you people here can fight with each other till the cows come home if you like, but don't take it out on us. Right now we're going from class to class, with all of you contradicting each other. I'd just like everybody to get together, hash it all out, and decide whether we're supposed to obey what the Church is teaching now or not."

"The Church is teaching what it has always taught . . ." Fufferd began.

"No, it's not," Mike interrupted, cutting off the beginning of Fufferd's standard statement on the issue. "The Church is saying a whole lot of new things. Every magazine is writing about what's going on, and we can't even discuss it civilly in a school of theology."

Fufferd raised a hand in the air, shaking his forefinger. "In 1570 Pope Pius V decreed, absolutely and for all time, that there was to be no further change or experimentation in the Roman rite."

"But in 1964," Mike argued, "Pope Paul says that we have to change. Is he wrong?"

There was an odd moment of silence. Then Fufferd said, "Yes, he is. For every reason you can give me, Mr. Hogan, for turning an altar around, I can give you a better one for keeping it the way it is."

Mike half laughed and said: "Wait a minute, Father. You're jumping to a kind of far-out conclusion. I don't care if the altar gets turned around. I never in my life gave a single thought as to whether Mass should or shouldn't be in English. I hate the idea of singing at Mass and I like Gregorian chant—I really do; if it goes I'll miss it. What I'm trying to say is, I didn't invent any of this. We were told to change by the Pope. You're always talking about obedience and the Church being a machine and all that, and now here you are saying we shouldn't listen to the Pope. I mean that's a little hard to digest."

79

Fufferd glared at him; his mouth snapped shut in a pout, and then his face went red. He started to say something, then stopped, threw his book down, and stalked from the room.

I grabbed Mike coming out of the classroom. "Hey, what are you trying to do?" I asked. "Get screwed in your last year here?"

"Look, Dennie," he said, "I really meant what I said then. I don't care about any changes. I'd be just as happy if things stayed the way they were. I got some Jesus reasons for wanting to be a priest. I don't give a damn about English or Latin or songs and positions of altars. Hell, I'm no great intellectual about what's going on, but I think it's a question of honesty. The Church is saying something, and these guys are running around in circles with their hands clapped over their ears."

"What about your Beetle Bailey games?" I objected. "How could you put up with five years of hundred-miles-per-hour horseshit and then get upset about this now?"

He shrugged. "I don't know. I guess because it scares me a little. At least before, no matter how unreal things were, we all—both we and they—seemed to realize that above and beyond all the nonsense, we believed in something. But since the beginning of this year all any of them are doing is fighting about trivia and poor old Jesus seems to have been tossed out a window somewhere along the way."

He kneaded his forehead, then continued: "Hell, Dennie, what if everyone in the Church started to react the way Fufferd is? We'd go right down the drain with the whole damned world looking at us, scratching their heads. It scares me. It really does."

"Yeah. Okay. But why," I insisted, "don't you worry about it after you get yourself ordained?"

15

*I*N late November and early December, the faculty tangled horns backstage. At first all we saw were a few clues. After the liturgical changes began, Father Fufferd refused to celebrate the liturgy for the students and would only say a private Mass after everyone else had left chapel. He became petulantly reclusive, refusing to speak to students in the halls. His classes turned into monologue harangues about the destruction of the Roman Catholic Church by newfangled changes.

Then, abruptly, there was a notice on the bullpen board that announced that Father Fufferd had decided upon a transfer and that Father Mulqueen would be assuming the office of vice-rector and prefect of discipline. It was a total surprise.

Fufferd was one of those people who seemed to be one of the very foundations of a place. I had never really liked him, but then I had never disliked him either. He hadn't been personally mean. If anything he had been a little foolish. It was just that he had done an overtime job of enforcing a mean system of rules. There was a general rejoicing among the students about the changing of the guard from him to Father Mulqueen. But I didn't feel like rejoicing about his being gunned down. Somehow it seemed to me to be a sad commentary on us as a Christian community—as if we had turned an old grandparent out into the cold. I felt as if I had somehow been responsible for his misfortune.

Impulsively, I decided to give him a gift, to try to make up for the hurt. I had no money to buy anything, but I did have a handsome set of liturgical commentaries that someone, probably Maguire, had steered my dad into buying for me. I had never used them and they looked new. With the volumes tucked under my arm I knocked on Fufferd's door. It was the first time I had ever gone into his room without being in trouble.

He was sitting behind his desk cleaning out drawers, stuffing papers into boxes. "What do you want?" he demanded without pause in his work.

Awkwardly I mumbled, "I ... uh ... wanted to give you these. As a sort of good-bye. I thought you might like them."

He glanced at the books and snorted: "Pius Parsch? Those won't be worth much in a little while. Not with you people having your way. Soon enough you'll be able to make up your own Mass every time you perform it."

He then looked me in the face for the first time since I had come through the door and said, "Your cousin told you to come here, didn't he?"

"What? No. I just didn't want you to go off without saying anything to you, that's all."

He almost smiled. "Blood is thicker than water, after all. Put them over there with that one."

He pointed to a trunk next to his bookcase. There was a copy of Romano Guardini's *The Lord* placed on the edge of it. I put the Parsch set down next to it and with my back to Fufferd opened the lid of the Guardini book. The old owner's inscription was scratched out and a new one written under it: "Best of luck ... and don't forget the great class of 1965—Mike Hogan."

"He really didn't say anything to me. Not at all," I apologized.

Fufferd sat looking at me with neither friendliness nor animosity. I was totally uncomfortable and wanted to get out. "I guess we can't see it now," I said lamely, "but the Church must have really needed this or it wouldn't have happened."

"Do you know what I think we really need?" he said, squinting his eyes bitterly. "I think we need missionaries to be sent to places like this to tell you people who are tearing Catholicism apart just what the Church is supposed to be."

"Yes... well..." I reached to the farthest limits of my philosophical range, going from bad to worse. "I guess, like Jesus, we've just got to keep loving in spite of everything."

I had never talked to an older man in such a situation. I didn't know what I was supposed to say. He took the words as they were meant, however. And rejected them.

"Some people aren't worthy of loving," he replied acidly, and then stared down at his open desk drawer as if I were no longer present.

I nodded and backed out of the room without saying anything else. That encounter so depressed me I never talked about it with anyone, not even to share with my cousin the coincidence of what we had both done. He must have been rebuffed as I had. And yet it was not the rebuff that was depressing: It was seeing a man like Fufferd cashing in everything, choosing to stand at a dead end. It didn't make any sense to me.

The departure of Father Fufferd did not mark the end of the difficulties of transition. In that respect we were only at the beginning of a long tunnel.

For a time many of the Fathers tried to straddle both the old and new—jumping from the recent directives to their old notes and back again.

Father Mulqueen's canon-law course housed as many transition-age contradictions as the courses taught by the older professors. Everyone learned but Mike. It wasn't that he was stupid. It was that the situation was so much smaller than he was. I began to worry. I would watch him put his pen down, fold his hands into his cassock sleeves, and knit his red eyebrows together, and I'd think to myself, "Oh, God, he's thinking again." A freckled fist would bolt out and he would insist on having a point clarified, usually a point that, with the way things were, couldn't be clarified without some double-talking on the part of the professor.

With ordination only weeks away, Mike was called into Monsignor Buck's office. I waited on tenterhooks, because summonses by the rector were seldom for good news.

"The faculty voted that I'm not ready for ordination," Mike said when he got to my room. "Mind you, the vote wasn't unanimous," he added.

"What were their grounds?" I asked, as if I couldn't guess.

"Well, Mulqueen turned in as evidence that term paper I wrote for canon law. You know, where I said that the synod of bishops being called was to forestall a real episcopal authority from emerging in the Church. Seems I wasn't showing proper respect for the Pope.

"And?"

"Oh, general complaints. Like I'm openly rebellious, and rash, and I don't take seminary discipline seriously. And of course I ask too many questions in a questionable tone of voice."

Mike was grinning, seemingly entertained by what had happened. "Well, maybe they're right," I said, getting angry. "You're sure as hell not taking this seriously, are you? They're pushing you out the door and you're acting like it's an intramural game they're playing."

"Aw, Dennie, stop worrying," he said. "They're not going to stop me. Where the hell is your faith? I'm going to be a priest and that's it. If they get me thrown out of this diocese I'll tramp around till I find a place that needs priests badly enough. South America is starving for priests."

"You'd go to South America?"

"Wouldn't you?" he asked.

That stopped me for a moment. I wanted to say yes, but it sounded so stark a reality to have to face. "I don't know," I finally said. "I think maybe I'd tell them to go shove it."

He looked at me for a second or so, the sort of impatient glare which years before would have prefaced his calling me "Chickenshit."

"Well, it won't come to that anyway. This is serious business, so Maguire will have to come down to examine the case." He smiled again as if anticipating it. "Hell, Dennie, it's a challenge."

"What's Maguire going to do? Help you pack?"

"Nope. He's going to meet with the whole lot of them, and me, together. I insisted on it, and after some balking the Buck agreed it was the only fair thing to do."

Mike stopped, walked over to his bookcase and picked up his notebooks, saying, "Dennie, I'm not going to be a sacrificial victim because of a time of confusion. If they're going to go after me because

I don't know which end is up about the Church, then each one of them is going to have to explain every blasted contradiction they've boxed themselves into since this whole business of change started last year.

He was grinning as he concluded, "Dennie, this might just be about the only halfway intellectual experience I'll have ever gotten out of this place."

Were it not for the basic justness of Monsignor Buck, or the open-mindedness of Bishop Maguire, Mike might have been rail-roaded out of his own diocese to search through the world for a bishop to ordain him. But with the faculty forced to bring their own confusions and disagreements to an open inquiry, the whole business fell apart like a house of cards. Mike kept asking questions from his class notes, asking for clarifications. By the time he was finished, before any of them got a chance to speak, he had made it clear that everyone present was in the same situation as far as confusion with Church teachings was concerned.

Monsignor Buck ended the matter after about half an hour of exposition. "Eh . . . I think we've got to admit," he said, "all of us—that we're living through something that's hit us broadside. The council's made us all students again. We've got no right to victimize someone for what we're struggling through ourselves."

Maguire asked if there were any accusations other than those mentioned, any complaints bearing more directly upon the candidate's personality. There was a brief interplay of grumbling about a "total disregard for the spirit of the rule," but as with a patched truce in a war, the losing party only needed some demonstration of face-saving. The matter was ended.

When Mike walked with him to his car, Maguire stopped before getting in and told him: "You know, Michael, I can't help but wonder—a little fearfully—how this might have turned out if I didn't know you as well as I do. This might have been the end of your vocation."

"No, it wouldn't, Bishop," Mike said. "I'd have gotten to the priesthood. I don't know quite how, but I would have."

Maguire smiled, saying: "You're too direct, Mike. Learn to have a little reserve, will you please? Let me feel a bit grandiose about this."

He put his hand on Mike's shoulder, then continued: "I threw you

85

out of high school once and you could have hated me for that. You never showed an ounce of bitterness. It wasn't in you. When I say I know you, that's what I mean, not that I'm a family friend. I want you to know that I came here prepared not to repeat a mistake I made once before. Even if that meeting had gone badly just now, St. Bernardine's final recommendation to me would have been that— simply a recommendation. I would have ordained you anyway, Mike. You're too valuable a man to lose."

Mike was the reverse of a grandstander, preferring people to think worse of him than to undergo the embarrassment of praise. He backed away uncomfortably as Maguire spoke and Maguire, knowing this, got out what he had to say quickly. Then to change the subject he lifted his hand from Mike's shoulder, clapped him on the back and asked, "Have you filled out that form I sent about what kind of job you'd want after ordination?"

"Yeah," Mike said. "I haven't sent it back yet."

"What did you put in for?" Maguire asked as he climbed in behind the wheel of his car.

"Auxiliary bishop," Mike answered, shutting the door for him.

In May of 1965, Mike was ordained. Assigned as the bishop's miter bearer during the elaborate, courtly ceremony, I stood next to Maguire as each young candidate knelt to receive holy orders. When Bishop Maguire lifted his hand from my cousin's head, Mike, now a priest, looked up. It was the first time I ever consciously thought of him as looking more like a child than a grown man. There were tears in his eyes. And then he smiled at the bishop. I couldn't see the bishop's face; but when Mike stood up and turned away, I heard Maguire take one strongly audible breath.

It was as if I had intruded upon ground where I had no right to be.

16

$\mathcal{M}$Y own pathway to the priesthood should have remained uneventful. I was no crusader for intellectual honesty or the changes in the Church or, for that matter, anything. And yet, because of what was deemed aberrational behavior, I spent the winter of 1966-1967, my last year at St. Bernardine's, talking to a psychiatrist. By decision of the faculty and approval of Bishop Maguire, the psychiatrist was to decide whether or not I was fit material for the priesthood. In a sense their decision was a kindness, for the penalty for what I had done should have been immediate expulsion.

"So, you took a swing at the vice-rector," Dr. Cohen, a thin man whose small beard and mustache formed a circle about his mouth, smiled cautiously and made the statement with noncommittal lightness.

I sat nervously in a chair opposite him. "I didn't hit him," I objected, trying to choose my words carefully. After all, it was Cohen's business to find hidden depths behind everything I uttered. "I just threw him against a wall."

"I see . . ." He casually jotted something on a small pad.

"But, it's not like it sounds," I insisted. "It was something that had built up over a long time."

"Had you ever been in a fight before?"

"Oh, yeah," I said. Then remembering the hurdles I had yet to jump with Cohen I hastened to add, "Not in years though. I mean, never since college."

He waited a moment or so, as if I should have elaborated. When I said nothing he pointed out, "Your permanent record states that you have a police record."

"Well, that wasn't for fighting," I assured him.

"What happened?"

"I exposed myself," I said, wishing immediately I had let it remain in his mind a fight.

That first session didn't go too well.

Neither did the second. If the first point we had established was that I was a pervert, the next was worse. After about twenty minutes of monosyllabic guarded answers from me, Dr. Cohen had stopped and commented, "We're not getting very far together, are we?"

"I want to be a priest," I told him, as if the declaration would explain my reserve.

"So... if I'm to help you make a decision in that regard, you're not being very open..."

"Well..." I ventured. He seemed to have moved two steps back, from professional inquiry to a normal discussion. "It's just that... well... if we're talking about a matter of God and... grace and all that, I can't see what right a psychiatrist has to be any part of the matter. Hell, most of the saints the Church tells you to imitate were as mad as hatters."

"Nonetheless, Dennis, we're dealing with concrete behavior in an everyday social setting. Right?"

"Yes... but... I can't see how you... I mean... you're not even a Christian."

"Ah," he said, smiling.

I blushed. "What I mean is, you are a Jew. You don't believe Jesus is God."

"I'm not sure I believe he existed at all."

"So... how can you be the one who decides whether or not I should be a priest? You're about as qualified to do that as I would be to decide if a man should be a rabbi."

"Would you prefer to have the vice-rector decide?"

"Well..."

"Perhaps, not being that close, I can be in all the better position to help you line things out clearly for yourself."

"Yeah . . ." I admitted, still on the defensive.

"And as I understand it," he added, "from the position you are in . . . what have you to lose?"

From this backward beginning we moved on to firmer ground. Cohen was friendly. And he was right. The only other alternative had been expulsion. So we talked about everything. Things from my childhood. My relationship with Mike and whether I might possibly have coattailed myself onto his vocation. We talked about the Mass and what I felt about it, how I felt this was what drew me to the priesthood. And then we got to the matters which had led up to my present troubles.

Since the changes had started, all that the priests ever seemed to do was fight one another. The divisions among the faculty at St. Bernardine's affected the morale of the students, and in the space of the one year after Mike's ordination, the enrollment at St. Bernardine's, which from time past remembering had been over two hundred men, shrank to almost half that number.

Regardless of how so many of my classmates felt, I couldn't walk away from the priesthood no matter how ugly it looked at the moment. I had no desire to get involved in the fighting about cultural patterns that engulfed the seminary. I only wanted to get past it all to get to the world outside, to be a priest for others, as priests had been for me when I was growing up.

But the world made cracks in the cloistered walls, already unsteadied by uncertainty and change within.

Father Ben Nolan had joined the faculty as a patrology and Greek professor the same year I had entered the seminary. When asked he was, despite his shyness, surprisingly open as to the reason for his assignment. He was an alcoholic and had suffered a severe nervous breakdown in the large parish where he had last been stationed. Because the seminary had traditionally been a secure enough place to send a man with problems, Maguire had put him at St. Bernardine's. The fighting about the changes, however, had destroyed whatever healing qualities a house of studies might have had. Father Ben, a gentle friendly man, withdrew from the conflicts swirling about him and spent most of his free time clearing out dead trees in the school's vast expanse of backwoods.

Almost every afternoon I would join him at work for a couple of hours, and gradually we became friends. He became a sort of saving grace for me. Father Nolan was, with all of his problems, a steady reminder of why I wanted to be a priest.

He was unfailingly kind; and he had a strong devotion to the Mass, not to the old or to the new Mass, but to the Mass itself. We didn't talk much. In truth, both of us being quiet people, we hardly talked at all. It was simply the work that cemented our friendship.

One day in mid-May, the two of us were removing an old dead elm, wrenching it out with chains and chopping away at its roots. We were so intent on what we were doing I didn't hear my name being called until the student yelling was almost upon us. The Buck wanted to see me right away.

Ignorant as to what I could have done and covered with dirt, I walked into his office, embarrassed that I was soiling everything I touched. Without saying anything to me he picked up the phone and told the operator to put the call through. He got up, came around the desk and put his hand on my shoulder.

"Your dad wants to talk to you," he said, and then turned away from me so that the operator might save him from saying anything more.

"What happened?" I asked. A flooding sense of dread filled me. Buck knew and was holding back. "What's wrong?" I insisted.

"Yes," he said into the phone, then handed the receiver to me.

"Dad?" I inquired, barely hearing his voice as the operator told him his party was on the line. "Dad, what is it?"

"Hello, Dennie..." he said. He sounded tired and more quiet than I had ever heard him speak.

"What's wrong, Dad?" I asked again. The blood pounding within my head became almost like a scream inside me. It was as if time had stopped and I couldn't pull the next few seconds into being.

"We just got word," he said dully. "Eddie . . . was hit."

"Bad?" I pleaded, shaking my head no as if to make that the answer.

"He was killed, Dennie."

I kept away from people. I wanted to be alone. What I had to accept

90

was beyond belief. Eddie couldn't have been killed. Young people didn't die. Other people died far away. But he had been far away. In Vietnam. It didn't make sense. Eddie didn't want to go to war. He didn't hate any Vietnamese. He had only gone into the army because it was something he had to get done with. Ann and he had a son Eddie hadn't seen yet. His whole life was still ahead of him. It was so damned senseless.

When Eddie's body arrived home, Monsignor Buck was away at a conference of seminary rectors. I checked in with Father Mulqueen to tell him I would be leaving for the funeral. Apparently he knew nothing of the situation.

"This is your cousin's funeral?" he asked me.

"Yes," I said.

He shook his head as if I had been misinformed. "I can't give you permission to go to a cousin's funeral."

"But, Father, I have to go," I said. "He was ... well, he was Mike's brother." At the sound of Mike's name Mulqueen's eyes narrowed for a moment. Then he shook his head more decisively. "No," he said.

It was a repeat of the situation with Eddie's wedding two years before, when it had been useless to explain that Eddie was more than a cousin. I looked at the top of Mulqueen's head, for he had already busied himself with something at his desk by way of dismissing me. This was the man who had come to liberate the Church into the twentieth century, who was always talking about the freedom of the children of God and the law of love.

"Father," I said, "I'm sorry, but I've got to go to my cousin's funeral. I am going home."

Mulqueen looked at me. "The door here swings both ways, Mr. Hogan."

I stood trembling for a moment. Then, outside his office I took my cassock off, hung it over a chair in the main hall, walked out the driveway to the main road and started hitchhiking home.

17

*I*N my memory the next few days kaleidoscope into a series of dreamlike scenes. I find it hard to remember what, as a family, we said or did with one another. The long hours at the wake were a fog: the endless faces of people, the friends we had grown up with all saying how sorry they were. Yet, the first instant I saw Eddie's body in the coffin is like a still frame that, to this day, unbeckoned, flashes into my mind.

He didn't look like himself. He seemed made of wax, and because he had been shipped in from out of the country, the top of his open coffin was sealed with glass. For all of her dealings with burials Aunt Gert couldn't be made to understand why this had to be so and kept pleading, "If only I could touch him. If I could just touch him once."

Each time she would say it we would all try to make her understand, but I knew what she felt. He had been like my twin for all of our lives. We had shared the same bed so often and talked each other to sleep; we had wrestled and run together until the adult world had separated us. I couldn't accept that he was lifeless. What I saw in front of me wasn't him.

We buried him in Aunt Gert's cemetery on a hill where, when we were very little, we had built a mock fortress. Mike read the prayers at the graveside and never once betrayed a loss of control except that the book he held trembled while he spoke. As we prayed and I watched Mike, I suddenly thought of him years before when, as a teenager, he had done an Indian dance, throwing stones on an old man's coffin. I pushed the image from my mind. We had all come such a long way since then. Why did it feel like yesterday?

After we left Eddie's body in that hillside I never again felt any closeness in time to my childhood. His death was a dividing point in my life. From the time I reached full height, I had always had difficulty imagining myself as being grown-up. After that I would never think of myself as anywhere near youth again. The carelessness of our younger years was laid to rest with Eddie and I never had the heart to want to re-create it again.

A week after the funeral, Mike and I spent the afternoon working on the lawns around the mountain resort church where he was stationed. Both of us had yet to talk openly with one another, so locked were we in our own private world of shock. It had been selfish to seek out Mike to lean upon; yet it had been a natural thing to do. He had always been the source of strength, always the leader with a sense of direction. Now he was as lost as I was. He had withdrawn into silence, throwing his energies into every kind of janitorial work at the church in order to avoid contact with people.

I had no place to go. My clerical career had ended abruptly three weeks before I was to have been ordained a deacon—ended without my having a chance to wonder if I cared that it had. The loss of my cousin was all that mattered to me at the time. And so I came to be with Mike, even if only to help him mow lawns.

The place was a shrine to Our Lady of Fatima; and because it was situated in a heavily Italian resort area, Mike's shrewd pastor (a man with a W. C. Fields eye toward profit) had instituted about every kind of money-making venture that traffic would allow—from gambling games to neon-glowing pieties sold in a two-hundred-percent-markup shop. Statues banked with flowers and dollar vigil candles dotted the shrine's acres, honoring about every saint I had ever heard of and a few more I would doubt were known by anyone. From dawn until dusk the grounds were covered with waddling fat ladies, praying their way up and down the paths that led inexorably to the gift shop. Their husbands, dressed in Bermuda shorts and black socks, smoked thick cigars and guarded the church parking lot, their hats pulled low over their eyes to avoid recognition.

It wasn't that Mike's pastor was a money-grabbing huckster. No Barnum or Bailey was ever so devoted to his public as was Father Tom Boyle at his shrine. If the place was a religious Coney Island, it was because it was what a majority of the people in the area wanted, for they came in hordes from the surrounding resorts. Yet, for all the religiosities shoveled out, Boyle seemed to use the externals to get to the people themselves. He spent the bulk of each day moving from one group to another, and to find his whereabouts one had only to listen for the sound of his booming voice followed by rounds of laughter.

The operation of the shrine required a great deal of caretaking, and for the time being it was a kind of salvation for Mike. It was already summer-warm, so we were stripped down to cut-off dungarees while working. When we were done for the day we ended up resting on the ground next to an altar to St. Philomena. I was lying back with my eyes shut to ward off the sun, when Mike finally broke our silence. "What are you going to do?" he asked.

"Dunno," I said, then, after a vacuum of thought, added, "I was thinking I'd get a job at the power company. I worked for them a couple of summers. That should be a pretty good in, don't you think?"

"Do you want that?"

I didn't know what to say. Then to defend it as an option I said, "Yeah . . . I like it. I enjoy just working with my hands. It lets me get lost in my thoughts."

"You mad at God?" he asked.

I still couldn't answer. I hadn't gone to church since the funeral. It was the first time in my life I had consciously missed a Sunday Mass. But I couldn't go; I guess I wanted to hurt God for the way he had hurt me.

"I guess I am," he said when I didn't say anything. "And you know what, too?" he went on. "There's something I didn't know before about being a priest. It's that you've got to be an actor. Like, if I showed what I was feeling inside me last Sunday, I'd have scared people right up a wall . . . and there I was saying, 'The Lord be with you . . .' to them. Like I really meant it. Even if I wanted to tell everyone there how bad it was . . . to say my brother is dead. My kid brother is dead. Because of a lousy, stinking, half-ass war to defend people who, if they came over here, you wouldn't ever let live on the same goddamned street as you . . ." He stopped and took a deep breath, as if to pull anger deep from within himself.

"If I had showed my true feelings," he continued, "they still wouldn't have given a crap. They don't know who I am. I was a *priest* . . . not *me*. And I thought, you really have to be an actor. They never mentioned that in the seminary."

Then he looked down at the ground between his legs, shook his head and said, "Oh, Jesus . . ." and started crying.

He put his hand up over his eyes and bent his head down, but the tears ran through his fingers, and he cried for a long time. I didn't even realize at first that I was crying too. I put my arm around his neck and we sat for a time saying nothing. A stern, commanding woman's voice intruded upon us.

"Hey," she called a second time, walking toward us from behind. "Where's the *fath*?"

I stood up, intercepting her from Mike. "What?" I asked. She was holding out a dashboard Jesus statue and leading another woman who had a fistful of plastic rosaries and medals.

"Where's the priest?" she demanded again in a heavy Italian accent. "The lady in the store, she say the priest over here . . . gonna bless these."

Mike stood up, composed, his tears lost in the sweat on his face. "Sure," he said, "I'll bless them for you."

The woman's eyes went silver-dollar-size and ran from his face to his shorts, then back again.

"You a priest? Nah, you notta priest."

"Yeah, I am," he said. "I was just working on the lawn." He took her statue and the string of beads from the other lady, blessed them and handed them back, smiling.

The first woman looked at him with suspicion just a shade short of the evil eye. "You not joking? You really priest?"

"Yes, I am. Really, I am," Mike assured her. "I'm the assistant here."

She took the objects back and the two of them walked away.

Mike, drawing a breath, laughed and said, "She'll get those blessed again, just to make sure."

When we walked in the back door to the kitchen, Mike's pastor was cooking linguine for supper. He was tossing pieces of pasta against the wall to test its doneness while he bellowed at a middle-aged woman swathed in black who kept dabbing at her eyes with a handkerchief.

"Rose, it's been over a year. You're too ravishing a beauty to coop yourself up like this. Play the Merry Widow. Live a little," he ordered as he bent over a steaming pot.

"Ah, Father," she said, and tried to laugh for him but with little conviction.

"The next time you come here, Rose," he said, ignoring her protestations and shaking a spoon at her, "I want to see you in red. Flaming red . . . with sequins. Catch another man, Rose. I'd offer you myself . . . but look at me. I'm fat and old. Take my assistant. Look at him, Rose. He's a young Adonis."

Turning to my cousin he ordered, "Michael drag this wild creature to your lair and teach her that life is worth living. It's your assignment for the evening."

The woman cast a glance at Mike's sweating body, blushed wildly, and finally gave in to laughter, for which she received an immediate but feigned reprimand from Father Boyle: "Rose, stop thinking things like that and hold this colander for me. And you boys clean up. I invited Ben Nolan for supper tonight."

Father Ben Nolan was going to Peru for the summer to work with one of his classmates.

"It's therapy for me," he said as we finished dinner. "I could have worked in a parish over the summer . . ." He toyed with his dessert for a moment, then added, "But I don't think I'm quite ready for that yet."

"The missions are better for you than a parish?" I asked. "I should think you'd want to take it easy."

"I do," he said. "Do you think what's happening in parishes is any different than at the seminary? Our good Catholics are ready to shoot on sight."

"Like that lady with the beads this afternoon," Mike said to me.

"The missions are much easier," Nolan said. "Catholics in Latin America are so eager for priests they couldn't care less about the changes in the Church or what a man looks like. They take him for what he is."

"Which, of course," said Boyle, "brings us to the point at hand."

Ben smiled. "This is a conspiracy, Dennie."

"I think every man should have a taste of the missions," Boyle expanded. "That's why I invited Ben down, Dennis. I've decided to sponsor you as a missionary for the summer."

"Me?" I said. The thought wouldn't have entered my mind. "Why?"

"Because . . . well, because it's there to be done," Boyle said. "It's not that the Church has to be listened to. It's that it has to speak out. And that's what the missions are about."

He pointed his coffee spoon at me authoritatively, adding:

"And that's why you're going with Ben this summer."

"I don't get it," I said. Boyle had me thoroughly confused.

"Let's talk strategy," Ben said calmly. "That's what we're really up to Dennis. What were you going to do about the seminary?"

I shifted uncomfortably. "What can I do?"

"Do you still want the priesthood?"

I had to stop for a long moment. Grief had so overwhelmed me that I had not focused in on what I had done to myself. Ben's words crystalized the situation. The desire to be a priest surged up inside of me again so suddenly that the desire itself surprised me.

"Yes," I answered. "*Yes.*"

"Well," he said, ". . . and this is between us here. Remember . . . I come from the enemy camp. I say, don't do anything for the moment. Things are at a stalemate. Your class gets diaconate next Saturday. If you were to try to go back now, Mulqueen would have no problem drumming you out. The faculty would have to vote. But as it is now, they can only presume you have quit. And there's no use in voting on a man who has quit."

"I don't understand."

"Let the diaconate—the semester end—go by. Then, come with me to Peru and while doing so present your case to the chancery. Tell them the truth. You were under mental stress. You didn't know what you were doing. Right?"

"Well . . . ."

"Believe me," he smiled, "I specialize in mental stress."

"But why Peru?"

Boyle couldn't believe my stupidity. "Good God, child, have you no sense of theatrics? Maguire's a good man; he'll want you back.

But give him a weapon to use. If the case comes up while you're working away with Ben in the missions, the seminary will look satanic if they reject you."

I started to shake my head.

"Besides, I have it all arranged," he went on, waving off my budding objection. "I have a dear friend who edits the diocesan paper. Just as the matter comes up he will run an article on what our seminarians are doing over the summer. And there you will be, with your sunny little Irish face, sitting atop a burro in the hinterlands of Peru for all who are voting to see. They wouldn't dare drop you. They'd be stormed by hordes of little old ladies."

"Aw, that's cheap," I said, looking to my cousin for support. Mike shrugged.

"Nothing that I do is cheap," Boyle said, arching an eyebrow. "It's simply good showmanship."

18

*H*OW did you function in Peru?" Cohen asked.

"Well," I ventured, "I don't think I'd make too awfully great a missionary. I pretty much just trailed around after Nolan for ten weeks."

"What about the language?"

"Believe it or not I could speak Spanish. Even I was surprised. I took it for two years in high school and two more in college without ever having to speak a word. But when we hit Peru it just came naturally after a couple of weeks."

"Did you get along with the people?"

"Yeah . . . well enough, I guess," I said. "But do you know what made me feel funny? While we were down there trying to show them how to live and all that, their newspapers kept reporting stories about race riots here at home—and with pictures. You'd see photographs of our cities and it would look like scenes from a war. I kept thinking to myself, 'Hell, what are we doing here? It's the United States that's mission territory. The people in Latin America live all mixed together racially. They're not dropping bombs on any other countries. And we're supposed to help them to be like us?' My God, they should be sending missionaries here."

Cohen laughed a little and nodded. "But Nolan's strategy worked," he said.

"Yeah," I admitted. "He and Boyle had that worked out like a game plan, even with the dumb picture on a burro. I'll get you the newspaper clipping."

"No other repercussions from the seminary?"

"Well," I said, "here I sit, with you deciding if I'm crazy or not."

"You're making a couple of jumps. There's an altercation somewhere between that and this. Let's take it as it happened."

When I got back in September I checked in with Father Mulqueen. It was a brief encounter. Neither one of us pretended any friendliness.

"Convenient to have a bishop in the family, isn't it?" he said without looking directly at me.

He played around with a couple of papers on his desk. I said nothing.

"You're on probation. You realize that, of course," he stated matter-of-factly. "However the faculty votes on you this semester we will have to see. I personally have grave reservations about your being mature enough to be a priest in less than a year's time. As for your leaving campus last spring after I expressly forbade you to, that remains an open account."

He paused again, then passed sentence: "You will not leave this campus for any reason—without exception—until further notice. That includes any apostolates, teaching, or parish work . . . *until further notice*," he repeated with emphasis.

"Let me get this straight," Cohen said. "You were forbidden to leave the property at all? No one mentioned that to me."

"You could check if you . . ."

"I didn't mean that," he broke in. "I simply don't see a purpose to it."

"Oh, that's Mulqueen's big thing." I said. "He once campused my cousin for two months for talking to a guy who stopped in a car out in front of the seminary."

Cohen seemed fascinated. He rested his head on his fist, leaned over his desk, and tapped his pen.

"I thought you said this Mulqueen was the man who modernized everything after the Vatican Council."

"Yeah . . . well . . . he brought in all the new things. I think I'm developing a theory about that."

"What is it?"

"Well, it's like our whole culture got picked up, shaken, and changed, and we're living in almost a whole new system now. But the way I see it, aside from changing the trappings, things have stayed pretty much the same. I mean—there were great guys and real bastards under the old system, and it's the same in the new. A lot of guys I know seem to take the stand that anything of the old was bad and everything of the new is good. But that's not true. I think it's the individual man that counts. Like Buck throwing a bucket of water in my face. He enforced all the old rules, but underneath he's a really great guy. On the other end of the spectrum, Mulqueen pushes all the things that are new, but as a person . . . well . . . I don't know . . . It's the men, not the method."

"Don't forget, though, Dennis," he said, "you're being trained to preach this new system. What if Catholics, refusing to accept you as an individual, choose to brand you for doing that?"

"I don't understand."

"How would you react if you experienced a strong and personal rejection from the very people you set out to serve?"

"Well . . . I don't really know."

"How did you end up attacking Mulqueen?"

"Well, I guess being campused got to me more than I would have thought—just knowing that there was always a leash around my neck. By November I was pretty uptight. If I hadn't been campused, maybe the fight wouldn't have happened. But then maybe it would have. One thing I've never been able to take is standing around and watching somebody getting bullied."

St. Bernardine's attitude toward academic studies had changed since I had entered. Once at the bottom rung of seminary values, academics now were emphasized. Students were urged to be scholarly, "professional." Many of the new breed of professors couldn't care less about the man who devoted his time to private pieties in-between the regular chapel exercises. They pushed for the guy who could understand—and pronounce—theologians like Küng, Teilhard de Chardin, and Schillebeeckx.

101

Father Mulqueen had the deacon class teaching seminars to the new men who came to St. Bernardine's from colleges. He'd preside while we presented the topics and where the church stood on them at the present moment. There was this one kid, Joe Walsh, who had just joined the seminary after his sophomore year in college. He was shy of his surroundings. In fact he was much like I had been when I first arrived. I sort of took the role with him that Mike had taken educating me, but Joe just couldn't get on to the whole scene. Even without this incident happening I think he was about ready to throw in the towel.

In class Mulqueen tended to be sarcastic with students who weren't up to following his train of thought. Maybe he couldn't help talking down to people. It was a constant nit-picking sort of thing and, what with all the pressure I was under from being campused and on probation, he was beginning to rub on me like acid.

During this day's seminar, Mulqueen began grilling Walsh about some readings that had been assigned—readings which I, in charge of conducting the seminar, could barely understand.

In answering, Walsh got confused and didn't know what direction he was headed in. Mulqueen suddenly lost his temper. "Stand up, Walsh," he commanded.

Joe stood.

"You didn't read the assignment, did you?"

"Yes, sir, I did," Joe answered.

"You're lying. You didn't," Mulqueen accused.

Joe reddened. I began to get angry. It was a scenario written for a grade-school teacher and student, not for two men.

"I told you I did," Joe repeated.

"Well, then," Mulqueen retorted, "if you're too stupid to learn something as basic as this, perhaps you don't belong here..." As Joe took his seat, Mulqueen added, "... you fathead."

The bell rang, ending class. There was no premeditation involved in what I did. When I got out into the hallway, Mulqueen was almost to the faculty lounge.

"Father," I yelled after him, "hold it a minute!"

He turned and waited impatiently.

"You had no call to do that," I said.

He stared at me, surprised.

"I what . . . ?" he said, incredulously.

102

"I said you have no right to do something like that." I was shaking, frightened by my own anger. "Walsh doesn't even know where he's at in this place yet. I think you . . ."

"Who do you think you are, Mr. Hogan?" he broke in, leaving no doubt that he had remembered who he was.

My words spilled out without forethought. "Just one human being telling another human being that any teacher who has to resort to name-calling, or browbeating his students, has to be something less than a man."

"With the situation you're in, Mr. Hogan," he said his voice climbing, "you're hardly the person to be dictating how a seminary should be run."

"I'm not trying to tell you how to run a seminary. I'm saying that you're in a position to destroy people. And I don't think Joe Walsh is ready to play your kind of games yet."

"You'd be an expert at judging, of course," he said, turning away from me.

I grabbed him by the collar and pulled him around to face me. His note pad and several pencils fell clattering to the marble floor. I yanked his face to mine and through gritted teeth said, "I should be. I've had to play them long enough."

I let go of him, pushing him back against a wall. For the space of three seconds we stared at each other. Then he turned and stormed into the faculty lounge, slamming the door behind him.

"I'm surprised you weren't thrown right out," Cohen reflected.

"Yeah, so was I at first," I said. "But when the Buck called me in, it turned out that nobody on the faculty knew Mulqueen had campused me. He had done it on his own and he was supposed to have consulted them. I guess it was Ben Nolan who held the line and insisted that Mulqueen had created what happened. And so, here we are. Going to you was the compromise."

"What about Bishop Maguire?" Cohen asked. "What did he have to say?"

"Well . . . when I saw him he said that going to you was probably good. He said he was worried about me."

"Why?" Cohen sat forward a little as if this created a particular interest.

"He said . . . well, he started comparing me with my cousin—with Mike."

"How?"

I hestitated as if I were breaking a confidence. "Well, of course, he's known us since we were born, you know. It makes it kind of a personal observation."

"I know. That's why I'm interested."

"He said that people always take Mike and me for being alike, but that we're really very different. He says . . . he said I'm guileless."

"Guileless?"

"This is embarrassing," I said. "He said it's a real attractive trait and all that. That it's a young trait. It means I don't know how to work angles with people and so I just take them straight on. He said that it looks like innocence, but that it isn't. A lot of young guileless people end up being bitter when they're old, because they can't handle hurts."

"And your cousin knows how to work the angles."

"Right. So people would never think of him as being innocent. But then Maguire said that Mike was one of the most innocent people he has ever known. He said that innocence means to be unaffected by evil. And even when Mike gets really kicked down—like after fighting with somebody or being expelled from high school, and very nearly St. Bernardine's—he always shrugs it off. Other people hold grudges; but with him, when something's done with, it's like it never happened."

"That's interesting."

"Anyway, Maguire said that's what I have to learn to be."

"Can it be learned?"

"He says so."

"Could you learn it?"

"I don't know . . ." I answered slowly. "I just can't brush things off like that. Things stay with me. I've got to admit I'd like to stomp Mulqueen's face in."

Cohen smiled. "What would you do if people turned on you when you're a priest?"

I felt as if I had talked myself into a trap. "Your point," I said finally.

"No, no," he protested. "Don't misunderstand me. I'm not being judgmental. Whether you become a priest or not is your decision. But to tell the truth, Dennis—and after all these talks I hope I say this as a friend—I can't see what there is in you that's attracted to the priesthood, especially with the turmoil in the Church right now."

"I already told you," I said. "It's hard to explain. It's the Mass. Anything else about the priesthood you could do by being something else. But it's the Mass. What else can I say?"

"Is it worth a whole life?"

"I can't see how I can explain it to you. Hell, you're not even sure Jesus existed. How am I to tell you what the Mass means to me?"

He reflected for a long moment. Then he conceded: "I think maybe you have."

Our sessions ended on that point of agreement. In March of 1967 I was ordained to the Roman Catholic priesthood. It is a fascination to me that, owing to a historical moment of confusion and division in the Church, I was ordained not with the confidence of my religious superiors, but by the faith in my faith of a Jew who was not even sure he believed in the historical Jesus.

19

"**Y**OUR knowledge of Spanish gives you a unique quali-
fication in relation to your classmates," Bishop Maguire
said as he opened a folder from among many on his desk. "I'm
sending you to Holy Innocents—in the south end. Do you know
where it is?"

"Yeah, it's in the gut," I said.

"Inner city, Dennis," he corrected, smiling. "You'll be envied. It's
apparently the key place to be at this moment in history. Do you
know anything about the parish itself?"

I shook my head no, saying, "Just that it's near that hospital down
there."

"Well," he said, "it used to be an Irish-German area. But when
blacks started moving into the neighborhood, everyone else moved
out. There's only a small percentage of diehards who have hung on.
Few of the Negroes were Catholic, of course, and Monsignor Adams
... well ..."

He paused and then interrupted his own train of thought. "In any
event, in the last handful of years more and more Puerto Ricans
have been settling in this city—especially in that area. They're
Catholic. And we're not ready to help them. It's an entirely new
culture for us to deal with. So you see where your experience puts
you at an advantage?"

"I liked the people in Peru," I said. "It sounds good."

"There's the hospital too. You'll be responsible for that. There was so little to do in the parish it was a good place to put the chaplain. But as for the future, we'll see how things start to move there. You'll have Father Kudirka to help. He doesn't speak English well, but he's a good old fellow, and he seems to get along at the hospital."

I thought he was finished and started to stand up.

"Do you know much about Monsignor Adams?" he asked.

"No, nothing at all," I replied.

He seemed to hesitate. Then he simply said: "Be patient, Dennis. Go slowly."

Holy Innocents' rectory stood out starkly from the brownstone fronts surrounding it. Niched securely into the courtyard of the gray stone church and encircled by a high, spiked wrought-iron fence, it had the stolid look of a small Victorian mansion. There were no lights on in any of the windows, and there was no response the first two times the bell rang. After the third ring the black front door jarred open six inches, stopping at the length of a chain lock. An older man who was notably drunk pushed a baseball bat into the opening and demanded, "State your business, man."

There was a small scuffle, a deep-voiced woman's command, and he disappeared.

"What is it you want?" the woman asked. Her fleshy cheeks and jutting chin sharply defined the angry crease lines from her nostrils to her mouth. A single hair sprouted from the mole on the end of her nose.

I had been apprehensive enough carrying my suitcase through the neighborhood from the subway; now I felt as reluctant as if I were being welcomed into Dracula's castle.

"Uh . . . I'm . . . uh . . . Father Hogan," I said. "I'm the new assistant."

"Where are your clericals?" she asked suspiciously.

"My what? Oh," I said, "I'm wearing them."

I buttoned my open collar and slipped the white tongue-depressor piece of plastic into place. She hesitated a moment, slammed the door, reopened it, and admitted me to a dark hallway.

"Was that Monsignor Adams?" I asked, looking for the man with the bat.

"No, that was Mr. Adams, the Monsignor's brother," she said, her voice betraying a touch of brogue. "He lives here."

Everything was dark. The woman's huge figure was swathed in black; the rooms leading off the hallway were all a heavy, faded brown and decorated in stiff Victorian furniture. I almost asked if she wouldn't mind turning on a light. But they were on—all small, yellow, candle-shaped bulbs that gave a muted funereal appearance to the surroundings.

"The Monsignor's busy," she said. "You can't bother him now. Father Buckley will be over from confessions. You can wait for him here. You'll have his room, of course, but you'll sleep in the guest room until he goes. There's a radio beeper for you to carry—to catch calls from the hospital. Now, when you're here, you're not to have guests outside these parlor rooms here. The Monsignor doesn't want any outsiders going above the first floor. In the morning you'll be taking the 6:30 Mass . . ." She proceeded to list my duties. She hadn't introduced herself, nor had she changed the expression on her face. She was like a female Father Mulqueen or Fufferd, laying down the law.

I had had enough of that to fill me for a lifetime. After about two minutes I cut in. "Who are you?" I asked. "Do you work here?"

At my question she stopped, and her eyes snapped with indignation that an introduction was needed. "I'm Mary Murphy," she announced. "I'm the housekeeper here."

"I think I'll go over to church and see Father Buckley," I said.

Like the rectory, the church was cavernous and dark, lighted by inadequate, dusty fixtures suspended from the ceiling. A lean, friendly looking man with wispy blond hair was sitting in the front pew. When he saw me he closed his breviary and walked down the aisle toward me.

"Just waiting for any last-minute sinners before I lock up," he said. He shook my hand, introducing himself, "Jim Buckley. I hate to be deserting you here. I would like to have seen how the hospital could have been worked with a young team, but I did ask for a few days to show you the ropes at least. Did anyone fill you in about hospital work?"

"Not really."

"God. More on-the-job training. The priesthood is great for that."

He paused, as if he had said something unpleasant. Then he proceeded, "It's a good hospital. Even though it's not Catholic they treat us well. The nurses are good about calling. They do so even if they're not sure the person is Catholic. For this first week, we'll go on calls together. I don't want you to be alone."

"What about the other two?" I asked.

"Well," he said, and began walking from door to door, locking up, "Kudirka is a nice enough guy. He's a Lithuanian refugee, and he's suffered a hell of a lot in his lifetime. But I wish they'd put him in a real soft country parish somewhere. The trouble is that he speaks horribly broken English. I get embarrassed because even I can't understand every other word he says."

Buckley shrugged, adding: "He's got to go somewhere though. And he's really not bad. He sticks to the geriatric wards, and he'll sit with old people and pray the rosary with them. But he just can't be a part of any emergency situations, so you're pretty much on your own."

"What about Adams?"

"Did you meet him?"

"She said he was busy."

He laughed. "Mary?" He laughed again. "She stands between him and the world. That means he's in the bag."

"Hey, what about the guy with the baseball bat?" I asked.

"'State your business, man!'" Buckley mimicked in a deep brogue. "That's Patty. His whole role in life is to guard the moat around the castle. 'Keep the god-damned niggers away.' His reception doesn't have too many people beating a path to our door."

"Doesn't Adams hear confessions?"

"Not in twenty years. He won't take any calls from the hospital either. He's only sixty years old, mind you. But he was angry with the bishop when the hospital was built and they assigned the place to Holy Innocents. Adams insisted it was in the boundaries of the next parish; so he just refused right from the start to take any sick calls. He's one of those guys for whom becoming a pastor meant 'on-the-job retirement.' When the neighborhood went black, he got as bitter as any of the parishioners who got left behind."

Buckley double-checked one of the doors before continuing. "And then when the changes in the Church happened . . . well, that was the end of the world for them all. Adams refused to implement any of the changes until Maguire came down here and made him. We turned the altar from the wall only a couple of months ago. Dinner-time conversations usually center on the destruction of the Catholic faith and of the neighborhood. Somehow, I'm responsible for both." He stopped and patted my back. "I bequeath that role to you now."

I must have looked pretty set back, because he added quickly, "I don't mean to make it sound that bad. The work here is good, and you can pretty much ignore the Adams family. Besides, they're here only about half the time. Monsignor owns two—count 'em—two houses: one uptown, and a summer home at the shore. That's why he's never bothered to paint the inside of the rectory. He doesn't have to live there. The assistants do. He's an absentee landlord. On Saturdays he, Mary, and Patty arrive, and we all have dinner together. It's too bad you missed that tonight. It's a real sideshow."

"What do you mean?"

"Mary presides over the whole thing. She sits at one end of the table. Old Kurdika and I sit and shovel our food in. Monsignor and his brother shout, argue, and drink each other under the table. It's very stimulating."

He stopped and mused a moment. "I read somewhere," he said, "that Irish women subconsciously push their men into being heavy drinkers. It's a way of preserving a strange sort of matriarchy in the home."

It seemed as if he were describing a marriage. I said so.

Buckley burst into a laugh that echoed through the empty church. "God knows, they deserve each other."

20

*B*UCKLEY took me to meet the sisters. After the crowded grime of the streets and the haunted-house rectory, the spotless convent—with every downstairs room a bright institutional yellow—seemed an oasis. There were five nuns, still dressed in the old habit. Their order hadn't yet been touched by Vatican II, and as we sat at their table, Sister Dolorosa, the superior, assumed the role of spokesman for all.

The setup reminded me of St. Bernardine's seminary, a system I wanted only to forget. There was little opportunity to learn what the other sisters were like, for Dolorosa intercepted every question of importance, whether it was addressed to her or not. She had been stationed with Adams for twelve years, and she went well out of the way of the conversation to let me know on whose side of the fence she stood.

"Monsignor Adams is a very priestly man," she informed me, whereupon the older nun to her right, Sister Jude, silently rolled her eyes up to the ceiling.

Of the two younger sisters, Marie Bernard, with an energetic, attractive face, was the more aggressive. When the introductory conversation ground to a polite halt, she remarked, "You look like an athlete, Father. Are you?"

"I wish you people would call me Dennis," I said. "I hate losing my first name."

"So, you are good at sports, Father?" she said, repeating both the question and, pointedly, my title. "I was thinking you might take over that end of the summer program."

"Be careful with her," Buckley interjected. "She can make you feel like an idiot playing baseball."

"That's enough from you, Father," she laughed.

"She cheats," he insisted. "If she misses she cries foul and claims her wimple got in the way. I think that's why they refuse to change the habit. It's a good excuse."

This got a frown from Dolorosa.

"What's the summer program?" I asked.

"It's great," Marie Bernard enthused as she leaned her elbows on the table and took command of the conversation. "We get a government lunch—and it's more food than a lot of these kids ever see at home. Plus transit passes for trips. All sorts of arts and crafts— games and sports—which you'll take care of. Won't you?" It wasn't a question. It was a statement.

"Well, I don't know how much I'll be around," I said, smiling at Dolorosa. "I own a house uptown, and one at the shore."

Dolorosa's frown deepened to an expression I had met earlier in the evening. I began to wonder if she and Mary Murphy might be related.

Letter-perfect seminary liturgies were not a good preparation for a man going into a parish. At Holy Innocents the church was, at best, a third filled, and no one sat more than halfway toward the front.

That first Sunday, I started to preach to the dimly seen huddle of faces in the dark, but stopped after a few sentences, feeling stupid. After hesitating a moment, I got out from behind the pulpit, opened the altar gate, and walked the length of the church to where the congregation was.

"I'm sorry," I said, in response to their shocked expressions, "but I couldn't even see you."

Father Kudirka's Mass, including the sermon, though friendly in tone might as well have been in Latin. Monsignor Adams gave a stream of consciousness talk for some twenty-five minutes at his Mass and then hurtled through the canon in another seven. There were no young people at Holy Innocents. It was not difficult to determine the reason. Were it not for the Mass at the hospital, I would have found that first day on the job most discouraging. Buckley said the Mass; but he took me along to see where everything was.

The chapel was filled to overflowing with patients and hospital personnel, and though it was the fourth Mass I had been to that day, it was the first that seemed to be a community of people consciously praying together. Even then, this brief interim of sanity was marred by a bizarre touch. A young girl sitting near the back of the chapel had a pathetically thin but pretty face. Whatever illness she was suffering from had given her an almost elfin appearance. Shortly after Buckley began his sermon, an elderly black man tiptoed in and got into the pew behind her. As he took his coat off, he somehow caught her short brown hair with his arm and yanked it off. It was a wig. She was completely bald but for a few patches of crew-cut short strands.

Flustered with embarrassment, the man picked the girl's hair off the floor and handed it to her, apologizing in a loud whisper. She reddened and hastily pulled the hairpiece into place, trying to assure the man it was all right. If I had been preaching I would have lost my train of thought completely, but Buckley smiled at both of them and continued without drawing more attention to what had happened.

Back at the rectory we all had our first midday dinner together. We sat around the massive oak table while Mary waddled into the half-darkened room with the first course, a nondescript barleylike gruel. She carried the serving bowl to Monsignor, her thumb well below the surface of the contents.

Buckley, who waged a nonstop war with her, noted, "Mary, you've got your thumb in the soup."

She threw him a baleful glare and muttered: "That's all right, Father. It's not hot."

Monsignor Adams, as evidenced by a framed portrait on the parlor piano, had once been a powerfully built, good-looking man. Now he looked dissipated and older than his sixty years. Under shaggy white hair and rheumy eyes, loose flesh hung in slack jowls, and a red, heavily porous nose shone out in a face that had not been exposed to fresh air or sunlight for a very long time. As dinner was

113

served he took his teeth out, wrapped them in a napkin, said that they were hurting and that he could do better without them.

I decided I could do better without the soup.

Mary served everything that came out, slopping food on our plates and handing it to us. She then brought Monsignor's meat out separately. She had either put it through a grinder or chewed it for him. It lay in a big pink pile next to his squash.

I took a sip of water and said that my stomach had been bothering me all day.

"What are they teaching you in the seminary now besides how to play the guitar?" Adams asked, his tone hinting that he wanted an argument.

Father Kudirka smiled as if by doing so he could make Monsignor's query a pleasantry.

"Probably the same things you had," I said, "except, of course, for the ideas from the council."

"Pah," he spat disgustedly, rolling his food from one cheek to the other. "Aren't worth the paper they're printed on."

"Read any of them?" Buckley asked.

"I did my learning in the seminary," Adams answered. "I need no one trying to put me back in school now."

Patty, a carbon copy of Monsignor except he had his own teeth, interjected with much the same tone as his brother, "Mary tells us that you jumped over the altar rail this morning."

"I what . . . ?"

Mary, sitting silently at the foot of the table, shot me an imperious glance as if she were the head of the tribunal.

"Jumped over the altar rail," he expanded, "and skipped down to where everyone was sitting."

I felt myself blush. He made it sound so stupid. Monsignor waited for my answer as if they had rehearsed the scene beforehand.

I said nothing.

"Well, did you?" he persisted.

"I walked down to where the people were," I said. "There were so few of them, and I was half a football field away."

"Well, that's the last time you'll do that. You'll preach from the pulpit," he said.

"Why?"

"Because I said you will."

114

21

*E*ARLY Sunday evening, Jim Buckley took me on a walking tour of the parish.

"There's a cold—sometimes hot—war between blacks and whites here," Jim said. "The old parishioners don't really accept the idea that their priests are to have anything to do with the blacks or Spanish. They feel we're helping the others get control of the neighborhood. I guess in a way we are. They're the majority of the population here."

We walked, it seemed, for miles of blocks, touring tenements overflowing with stoop sitters. Most people knew Buckley, and in the several blocks that were predominantly Spanish, he seemed like a local celebrity. I was in a culture shock. Streets and sidewalks were strewn with the always present broken glass; piles of broken couches, mattresses, and almost all kinds of rubbish lined the curbs. The constant human noise was deafening. About every other parked car was filled with men passing around bottles in paper bags. It was different from anything I had ever known. Even working in the poorest kind of country area in Peru had not prepared me for this noise and crowded confusion. I kept thinking: How could people live, all jammed in like this?

"I walk around at least an hour or two a day," Jim said. "It's perhaps the biggest part of the job. I know it sounds like nothing but if you get to know people the rest just happens. This place is a dumping ground. Eighty-seven percent of these people are on welfare. There are people here who don't know what it's like to work. Their parents didn't either. They're caught in a dead end and they can't get out of it."

Youngsters would come along and hang on Jim while we walked, and he would stop to talk with them. I kept noticing groups of kids in alleys or behind stoops, pulling rubbish together to start fires. As we passed one such group, a mulatto teenager separated himself from the others, ran alongside us, yelling, "Hey, what's happening, man?" and slapped Jim's outstretched hands with both of his. He was too tall for his babyish, freckled face topped with red, almost blond, frizzy hair. His features were distinctly Gaelic. If one parent had been black, the other had certainly been Irish.

"Hey, Jerome," Jim answered, returning the double slap. "Nothing much, man."

"Gotta go," the boy announced immediately, trotting back to his intended conflagration.

Jim shook his head as he said, "That was Jerome Simmons. He's a pain in the neck at times, but you can't help but love the kid. You'll get to know him real well—he craves attention. He lives with his sister who's all black. I think there's a big rejection thing there."

"Why don't you stop what they're doing?" I asked, looking apprehensively at the blaze kindled under a front stairway.

"That's like the national pastime here," Jim shrugged. "After a while you won't even hear the sirens. I never interfere. I don't try to break up fights either. You're not a cop. Always remember that. You're not a social worker either, but I'll get into that later. You got to meet my special girl."

We stopped at a stoopful of people and Jim addressed a very elderly black lady with snow-white hair.

"Mother Miller, I want you to meet Father Hogan. He's going to be with us a while."

"Well," she said, "it's nice to meet you, Father. I'm a Baptist, but sometimes I come to your church with Irene Williams."

I'd have guessed her age at seventy and was surprised when I was told she was eighty-seven. While we talked, Jerome, finished with his fire, ran up and interrupted the conversation. He immediately launched into an angry tirade about his superintendent.

"This is Jerome," said Mother Miller, "but I call him 'Mouth.' You can disregard about ninety percent of what he tells you."

Jerome went on with his complaints about how his building wasn't kept up. "Man, he leaves garbage layin' all 'round those halls. He never cleans it and that's his job."

"Well, you've got to live there," said Mother. "You clean it up."

"Yeah, well..." he said, puzzling on what she said for a moment, "I'd rather walk on dirt that high than clean it for nothin'."

A middle-class impulse stirred itself within me. I would have argued with him, but Buckley seemed to read my mind and shot me a look that said "shut up."

An attractive black woman of about forty, wearing a yellow, flower-print dress, came out on the stoop to join the sitters. She was Mrs. Williams, a Catholic, and she needed no introduction as to who I was.

"I was at your Mass this morning, Father. My God, did you scare everybody when you walked down that aisle. You woke me up—that's for sure. But I looked at you and I thought to myself, 'My, he's too pretty to be a priest—that hair is like shiny copper. He won't last long.'"

This got a laugh from the people on the stoop, and I felt myself get red.

"Now, Father Buckley," she went on, "I look at you and I think, 'There's Father Confessor. I could tell my sins to him.'" Then directing herself again to me, she said, "You, I don't know. You got a look about you; in those blue eyes ... sort of ... well ..."

"Shifty-eyed?" I volunteered.

"No ... not that ... well, maybe ... you don't seem like a priest. Not like you were sure of yourself."

"I am," I said, imagining her being interviewed by the faculty at St. Bernardine's.

She laughed. "Ah, that's what you say. But wait and see. One of these nights you're gonna be out on the town and meet a girl, and you won't even come back for your bags."

22

THERE had been nothing in any seminary course that had taught me how to be a chaplain. My first week at the hospital was a disaster. I had no idea what anybody expected me to be. The only time I had ever even been in a hospital had been after my bogus football injury in high school, and my only experience with a priest at the time had been with Maguire, sitting on the edge of my bed and laughing at me. Now it was my role to wander up and down the long hospital corridors, to poke into other people's rooms and be, I presumed, some sort of professional visitor. The slight experiential knowledge that I had from my past gave me the only resolve I carried with me into the job—that being never to laugh at any high-school kid who had fainted during a football game.

The first day I figured I would start in the private rooms and work my way up to handling the wards. I knocked on a door and walked in to find a lady about my mother's age sitting in bed. She looked startled to see me, and I thought perhaps I had checked the list incorrectly.

"Are you a Catholic?" I asked.

"Oh, yes, Father, I am."

"I guess I came in too fast," I said, reacting to her expression.

"Oh, no, that's all right."

We were both uncomfortable. I tried to make small talk. "Um . . . It's a nice day out, isn't it?"

"Very nice, I should think, Father. I haven't been out today."

"Of course."

It's probably that she was in a bad marriage or something, I thought, and that was the reason that she was so uncomfortable. I wondered what I was supposed to ask. "Well, is there anything, like any problem, I can help you out with maybe?"

She smiled graciously. "I don't think so."

"Oh, okay, I just wondered. Uh . . . you seemed a little ill at ease."

"Well, it's just that . . . well, I'm sitting on a bed-pan, Father."

"Oh," I said, embarrassed. "Well, I guess I'll come back later." I half turned, backed to go, and caught a vase of roses with my arm.

"The flowers!" she yelled, reaching out as if to stop me, almost falling off her pan. The flowers crashed to the floor. I knelt and started to pick up the broken glass.

"Leave it, Father," she said, almost impatiently. "It's all right."

"That's okay. I'll get it," I said, cutting my hand.

"I'll get a nurse to take care of it, Father."

"I'd appreciate that," I said. I had hit a vein and was bleeding all over the place.

"I meant the vase . . . well, your hand, too, if you want."

"I'll just grab this towel," I said.

"Father, that's my bathrobe." She was almost screaming.

A nurse fixed up my hand for me, and I started to hit rooms again. Somehow, I had trouble convincing people I was a priest. I had a Roman collar on, but people would seem either a little frightened or doubtful and say something like, "You don't look like a priest."

"What does a priest look like?" I began to ask. I wasn't trying to be smart—I was just trying to figure out what I was doing wrong.

I got through about an hour of visiting and opened the door to a private room where a grim old man snapped his head around to see me. He had no doubt about who I was. "Get the hell out of here!" he snarled.

"What?"

"I told that other feller, I don't want to be bothered by no priests."

"Why?"

"Waste of time. That's why. What do you want, going around here anyway?"

"Well," I said, wondering why myself, "it's just that . . . we're trying to help you . . . see what we can do . . . maybe . . . to help you get back on your feet again."

As these words were coming out, I noticed that he was an amputee. No legs. "Well," I said, "I'll see you later."

I quit for the day. The next morning it took all the courage I had even to enter the building.

I received a phone call from a priest in another downtown parish half a mile away from Holy Innocents. There was to be a meeting during the week of a group of people who called themselves the Urban Christian Council. Presently they were in the midst of plans for a march on City Hall, the purpose being to protest the inadequacies of the welfare system.

"Has Buckley been working with you?" I asked.

"No," he laughed. "Jim's a great guy, but he's kind of a stick-in-the-mud when it comes to getting involved."

When I asked Jim later, he shrugged, "I guess I am. Sometimes I end up working with that crowd when I agree with what they're doing. But, as I said to you the other night, we're not cops, and we're not social workers."

"Yeah, but we can't just ignore the world," I objected.

"Maybe I overreact to some of the people in it," he said. "The college ministry crowd, running from one protest to another. They get their ankles wet down here and rush back to their own sophisticated worlds to discuss what they've done. The way I see it, our biggest job is just simply living with these people, helping them realize what they should be toward each other. There's damned few of that crowd who would want to leave their campuses to come down and do that."

Perhaps it was that I was so disorganized and confused by my surroundings, but I was attracted by the meeting. I knew I would be at a loss for what to do in the neighborhood after Buckley left. At least following their lead would be something concrete and a direction to head in.

"I don't think I agree with you," I said.

"Well, go ahead then," he said. "I'm a great believer in every man working out his own scene. I just think that between the hospital and the summer program with the sisters, and the stoop-visiting at night, there's more than enough for you to do."

"I don't want to get you pissed off at me."

He laughed. "Good God, Dennis, I'm leaving in two more days. Do what you want. Who knows, maybe for you it's right."

The sacrament of the anointing of the sick frightened me. Most Catholics still insisted on calling it "the last rites," and I was always afraid people would see me as the Angel of Death when I came in to administer it.

At first I operated under the shadow of Buckley or Kudirka, going with one or the other of them when there was a call from the hospital. I was surprised at how comforting a person Father Kudirka was. Perhaps because he was so obviously a man of prayer, he inspired confidence. Even with his pronunciation barrier, he would smile, pat people's hands, or stroke their brow, and somehow he would manage to make each patient feel as secure as if they were in the presence of an Old World grandfather. Rather than stick to the ritual, he would recite an Our Father, Hail Mary, and Glory Be along with each person. It would seem almost as if they were performing the sacrament together instead of his doing it by himself.

I had no such calm to share. The day Buckley left for his new assignment, I went on my first call alone. It was in the coronary care unit. When I entered the curtained partition around the bed, a sturdy, middle-aged man looked up at me. He looked healthier than I felt, but he had been admitted after a mild heart attack. He saw the Roman collar, and groaned almost in exasperation, "Oh, my God, is it that bad?"

"Oh, no," I said, attempting to make light of the situation. "No, it isn't, really. We anoint everybody who comes in here, sometimes even the janitor. You're fine. I mean you're not fine, but I mean . . . it's just . . . well, it's a . . . would you like to be anointed?"

"Sure, Father, I guess I would. Coming in here was fright enough to cover anything else."

I took out my ritual and the small thumb-sized container of oil, trembling so badly that I could hardly turn the pages.

"Are you nervous, Father?" He laughed at me.

"Oh, no. Well, I guess a little," I said. "You're my first anointing. I just got ordained."

"Is that so?" He mused on this for a moment. "Well, isn't that something? I guess this is kind of an honor. Well, don't be nervous, son. Just take your time. You don't have to be letter perfect for me."

"Thanks," I said, and began the prayer.

"Lord," I read, "as I enter here with a sense of my own unworthiness, bless what I do . . ."

The sacrament explained itself. There was a gospel about Jesus curing a sick boy. Forgiveness was asked for any sins committed, and oil was applied to the man's forehead as a sign of strength in God. Then the prayers asked the restoration of the sick person to good health. There wasn't a mention of death.

I finished, and the man said, "I never knew how beautiful that was."

"Neither did I," I thought.

23

THE Urban Christian Council met in a vacant neighborhood storefront. When I walked in late, some thirty-five people were sitting, crammed onto benches and rickety chairs, perspiring in the humid heat and fanning themselves with the mimeographed fliers that explained the purpose of the meeting.

A wiry, gray-haired woman had everyone's attention. "Well, you just can't deal with a hierarchy," she was saying, "which gives five-hundred-year-old answers to modern-day problems."

Mrs. Heidrich taught sociology at a local Catholic college. I recognized her because she was prominent in the antiwar movement and frequently in the news. Only recently a Sunday paper had interviewed her as a leader in what was labeled the "underground Church," a group of Catholics who operated apart from what they called "the structure."

Three priests, dressed in sports clothes, their black pants a dead giveaway, sat at the head of the room. The rest of the crowd was a mixture of college students and neighborhood leaders. For a long time the meeting was more gossip than business, and mostly gossip about the Church, which was sometimes referred to as a home base, sometimes as an obstacle, sometimes as an enemy. The day had been endless and humid. I sat on the edge of the display window, wishing I hadn't come, wishing I had the nerve to get up and sneak out.

Then I saw the nurse from the hospital squeezed in a far corner of the room.

She was looking at me, and she grinned and gave a little wave. She wasn't a pretty girl. She was just heavy enough not to have a good build, and her light brown fuzzy hair was pulled back and tied in a bun. Her large dark eyes crinkled with a constant liveliness, and her face dimpled attractively when she smiled. At the hospital I feared the emergency room a little less when she was on duty, for she did much to make it seem a less clinical and inhuman place. She was good at soothing children's fears, sometimes kneeling on the floor to talk to them, holding a child's face in between her hands. Though obviously not Spanish, she spoke the language perfectly, and sometimes she was the only one in the emergency room who could understand the Puerto Ricans who were brought in.

Harold Tremblay, whose chubby face and body seemed to belie the militancy of his words, was the priest who had called me. Apparently in charge of the meeting, he finally steered the interminable conversation toward business. In another month, he explained, a number of coordinated groups planned to stage a city-wide protest march in front of the mayor's office to point out the inadequacy of the welfare system. Neighborhood people would be mobilized and bused to the protest area. It was hoped, if the volunteers canvassed their blocks well enough, that several thousand people would be produced for the march. When he finished his pitch, he began dividing our district among the student volunteers present. I didn't know Tremblay except for the one phone call, and was thus surprised that he knew and addressed me.

"Dennis," he said, "you game to canvas a neighborhood?"

"Sure," I shrugged. "Why not?" Immediately I wished that I had held back the "why not." It didn't fit the zealous mood almost everyone else seemed to share.

"Great," he went on. "Now, all you people have to do is to pass out fliers, explain the protest, and get as many names on the petition as you can. Don't forget that there'll be a free lunch at the rally. That's a big draw. We'll hit all the neighborhoods in the next few weeks, and then on the day of the rally, sound trucks will go around as a reminder. Come up front when we're finished, and I'll show you which blocks you'll hit."

When, finally, I escaped from the stuffy storefront, the night air, though hot, felt blessedly cool. As I started toward my car, I noticed the nurse walking alone down the block. I knew that she was called both "Lips" and sometimes "Lippsy" by the hospital personnel, but her name tag said "Smith." I hesitated.

"Hey, Miss Smith," I yelled.

The breaking bottles and cars racing up and down the street could not have covered my loud call. When she didn't respond, I tried again. "Hey, Miss Smith . . . Hey Lips."

She stopped and turned. "Oh, me? Sorry."

"You need a ride?"

"I can get a bus right at this corner."

"I'll drop you off," I insisted.

"It's far."

"Nonsense," I said, opening my car door and gesturing for her to get inside.

"Oh, it's been a long, long day," she laughed as the car started. "I like it when I'm on the night shift. Then I can sleep all day. I'm a night person."

"Aren't you afraid walking around here at night?"

"Nah," she answered. "If anyone starts coming toward me, I clutch my bag and scream, 'I got syphilis viruses with me.' Haven't been touched yet."

I laughed. We were stopped at a light, and I looked at her. She seemed a little more attractive than I had thought at first. When she was laughing, she reminded me a little of Gaelin.

"How come everyone calls you 'Lippsy'?" I asked.

"It's my name," she said, "Oh, that's why I didn't catch you calling me. I just wear the 'Smith' name tag to stifle some of the idiots who come into emergency. My name is Lipschitz. When I had that on my chest, too many wise guys coming in with broken arms almost got fat lips to match. Lucille Lipschitz. How's that grab you?"

I smiled, sympathetically I hoped.

"Can't you just see my folks standing over my crib saying, 'Hey . . . Let's call her Lucy Lipschitz. That'll fix her in school'? 'Course you have to take my father from where he was at. His name was Emil."

"Did you ever think of changing it?"

"I've thought of that, believe me. I was even thinking of going into the convent just to get a different name."

125

We came to a corner where a group of kids had broken off a hydrant cap. With a tin can opened at both ends they were directing the force of the spray to blast passing cars. We slowed down to roll up the windows.

"How come you're into this thing with the Urban Christian Council?" I asked.

"Who knows?" she shrugged. "I don't know what I think about welfare, or that whole crowd back there. But I saw one of their fliers, and I decided to see what it was all about. You know, you see so much during the day at work. Sometimes I just don't like to pack up and go home to my nice little apartment. I wish I could help some of these people in some way. I really do."

My Volkswagen got hit with a deafening explosion of water so forceful I feared we would be turned over.

"Want to get out and help them now?" I shouted over the roar.

She laughed. As soon as we were out of range, she rolled down the window and shouted, "Bulls-eye, kid!"

"Were you really thinking of going into the convent?"

"No, I was just kidding," she said. "I'm not even Catholic."

"What are you?"

She shrugged. "My father was Jewish and my mother was Episcopalian. The whole business confused me. To tell you the truth I don't think I'd label myself anything."

"Did your parents practice religion?"

"They celebrated Christmas and Chanukah. They liked holidays."

"Do you believe in God?"

"Good grief! Twenty questions! I don't know. Sometimes I think I do, and sometimes I think I don't."

"I didn't mean to pry."

"Oh, go ahead. Pry away," she laughed. "You need the practice."

But she did most of the talking, telling me about the hospital, splicing in directions to her place. It was an awkward situation for me. I kept thinking of things to say, but what came naturally to my mind wouldn't have fitted who I had to be to her.

When we got to where she lived, she shut the car door, started to walk away, then turned and stuck her head inside the window, saying with a smile, "By the way, stop walking around with your thumbs stuck in your belt. You always come into a room like a cowboy looking for a saloon fight. A couple of nurses have started calling you 'Red Ryder.'"

"I didn't know that."

"It's nerves. You'll get over it."

"Red Ryder?" I repeated dejectedly. It was a stupid image.

"Hey," she called, "it beats 'Lipschitz' any day of the week. I'm just glad they hung 'Lips' on me instead of the last half."

I waited until she climbed the front stairs of her brownstone apartment house and unlocked the front door. She turned and waved with her keys before going in. As I drove away I realized I was still smiling. In the previous few weeks it had been so difficult to adapt, at the age of twenty-five, to people addressing me and treating me as "Father." Lippsy had treated me as if I were still really me. She had a take-charge sort of warmth that reminded me of Gaelin. Being with her felt *good*.

24

WHATEVER else the welfare march might have been, it provided an opportunity throughout those first weeks to get into homes in the neighborhood. In touch with the hospital by a pocket beeper, and armed with explanatory fliers, I started through my assigned area, moving from door to door in each crowded apartment building. In the first I tried, I stopped at a fourth-floor door that wasn't even tightly shut. A radio blared loudly. Where a peephole should have been, an opening gave any person at the door a view of the living room and kitchen. Rubbish and clothing lay scattered on the floor. I knocked. A young girl's lethargic voice called, "In."

Cautiously, I pushed the door back and entered. No one was in the living room. In the second room a heavy-set black girl of about twenty, wearing a red T-shirt and dungaree shorts, lay sprawled on a bed. Two young babies slept soundly alongside her. She stared at me blankly, not saying a word. For all she knew, I could have come in to beat on her.

"Uh . . . I'm Father Hogan," I said. "I'm going around for the Urban Christian Council. They're trying to get people out for a welfare march at City Hall . . ."

"Yeah," she said, not moving a muscle. "M' girl frien' tol' me. Someone been to her place."

"Do you think you'd be interested in coming to it?"

She shrugged.

I pulled the clipboard out from under the mimeographed forms.

"Maybe you could sign the petition they want to present to the mayor."

I put the board on the bed. She rolled over, looked at the petition, took the pen, and signed without reading it.

I thanked her and backed out of the bedroom. At the apartment door I called back: "Do you want this shut?"

She didn't answer. I closed the door and then opened it again part way, feeling stupid.

That was my best sale of the day. For the next few hours I went about pushing the virtues of protest, following a pattern that varied little from door to door. The buildings in the area, which had once been attractive residences with marble entranceways and tile hallways, were now broken-down and covered with grime. Each time I entered the dark hallways, I would hold my breath against the strong garbage and urine smell for as long as possible and then inhale it all in one bad gulp. At almost every sticky metal door a voice would suspiciously answer my knock with, "Who?"

"It's Father Hogan from the Urban Christian Council."

A slight pause would be followed by another "Who?" Then they would open the door, hear out the spiel, and often invite me in—sometimes to an apartment worse than the hall, other times to a tidy refuge from the rundown surroundings. They would be sympathetic, nod while they read the sheet, and say things like, "Yes, that's right. That's a fine thing. Oh, I'll be there. Don't worry."

Still, I couldn't help but feel as I left each place that I was being politely written off. I didn't care that much about the march; however, I was still in a sort of culture shock. I kept thinking, "Why don't they get shovels and mops to clean the place up, or at least escape and move out?"

I stopped pushing the rally on the Spanish blocks, and went from apartment to apartment saying simply that I was the new priest at Holy Innocents and wanted to say hello.

Worn down from the heat that had baked the concrete streets to oven force, I stopped early in the afternoon at a hole-in-the-wall Spanish eatery where plastic religious statues and pictures lined the shelf behind the counter. The small dark curlyhaired proprietor recognized me right away. "Hey, Father," he asked, "what is it you like?"

It was as if I were God's vice president, dropping in. Nothing was too good. Mr. Cruz was a regular churchgoer and had five children. As I downed four glasses of water, he insisted that I come to his house within the week, for dinner. His daughter, Clemencia, about nineteen years of age, with lively black eyes, gave me a plate of rice and beans. While I ate, the two of them leaned on the counter, talking. Clemencia, angrily bitter about the neighborhood, tried to explain how, to them, it was a trap.

"Do you know what it is like to be here and not to be white?" she asked. "When I was growing up in San Juan I would hear of this country and see it in the movies. And the picture I had of it was . . . was . . ."—she stopped and with her hand gestured as if to pull a picture out of the air—". . . well, all friendly and blue-eyed, freckled people, and little rivers and beautiful hills. And then we came here. Agh. All dirty brown buildings and cold unfriendly people who don't want you.

"When I got a job downtown, once some friends and I, we tried to eat in a nice restaurant. They did not say, 'We don't want you,' but they treated us so bad. Impolite? They served our food one at a time, some fifteen minutes apart. And the food was purposely burned. And you know? We were neat, and well dressed. So they didn't say, 'Get out,' but that is how you are treated."

"The Church is the same," Mr. Cruz said, absent-mindedly mopping the counter and switching back to the Spanish tongue in which he was obviously more at ease: "We are Catholic and our children are in the Catholic school. But we are not wanted. The school meetings are an insult. When they talk about problems, it is not what children do that is a problem—it is *our* children who are the problem. Women will stand right up and say so. I will not let my wife go anymore."

As he talked I suddenly thought of something I might be able to do. Maguire had explicitly sent me to break ground with the Spanish-speaking people.

"Do you think more people would come to Mass if there was a Spanish Mass?" I asked.

Clemencia answered: "Most of the people know English well

130

enough to understand. Even if they do not, it is no less understood than when it was in Latin."

Then her eyes brightened, and she added. "But it would be a way to say, 'This Church is for you as much as it is for anyone else.' And it would tell the others that it is ours too. Yes, it would be good. Are you going to do it?"

"I guess so. Yes, I am," I said, still trying to work the idea out.

"Hah!" she snorted and laughed knowingly. "That old priest. He will not let you. He does not like us and he is the boss. Right?"

The radio beeper in my pocket would sound off and I would telephone the hospital. Whatever section had phoned for a priest would fill me in on what was wanted. On one occasion the hospital called because a middle-aged woman whom Father Kudirka had anointed a week before was having another attack. When I entered the coronary care unit, nurses and doctors were crowded around her bed. They worked at a quiet, frantic pace. The woman was in pain and frightened. Oxygen tubes were stuck into her nose and wires connected to machines in the corner of the room recorded the pace of her heart. When she saw me her eyes widened in recognition. She tried to smile. A nurse made room for me at the head of the bed. I eased in, took the woman's hand and as gently as I could placed my other hand on her forehead. She closed her eyes, trying to steady her rate of breath. For some fifteen minutes the attack and the work continued without any change.

I gradually became conscious of what one doctor was doing. He was cutting into her leg to get to a vein, snipping away with a small scissors. Each small methodical snip sounded like the work of a nail clipper. It began to affect me—a dizziness swam into my head, along with a feeling of nausea. I had been afraid of getting sick right from my first day at the hospital.

"Don't let it happen," I told myself. "Don't think of it. Think of something else."

The woman kept looking up to me for reassurance, squeezing my hand tightly. I smiled at her. To battle my nausea, I flashed movies into my head and thought out popular songs. The snips continued persistently. The nausea got worse.

Then the sound stopped. Foolishly I looked down. The doctor had an incision made and was working a small wooden depressor under a vein. The room began to swim. When I pulled my hand away from the woman she looked up at me, her eyes begging desperately.

"I'll be right back," I assured her.

I went out the door, holding onto the wall to steady myself; I opened the window and hung out of it, breathing in gulps of air. A nurse who had been in the room followed me out, pulled a chair behind me, and, touching my back lightly, ordered, "Sit down. Put your head between your knees."

After a few minutes my head and stomach stopped reeling, though a draining sense of weakness remained. The nurse returned and handed me a glass of water.

"I'd better get back in there," I said, and started to get up.

She shook her head. "She expired, Father."

I sat for a long time, my elbows on my knees, sick now from a sense of failure. The woman's pleading eyes, the way she had clung to my hand as I pulled away—remained frozen in my mind. If only I had held on for five minutes longer, I would have been with her when she died.

Father Kudirka came in the door of the coronary care unit. Apparently, when I got sick someone had called him. After a whispered conversation with the nurses at the desk he came over to me and put his hand on my head. "Don't worry, boy," he said, pronouncing the word "vorry."

I could only shake my head. If I had tried to speak I probably would have cried from frustration.

"It was just a minute you missed," he said, bending over to enclose us in the privacy of a whisper. "Just a minute before the angels were with her. They are better company than you."

25

I had been setting up the summer program with the sisters and had come into the house late for supper. As I washed my hands in the kitchen sink, the noise of animated discussion, even above the running water, rang through the dining-room door. It was so unlike the usual morose mealtime atmosphere that I turned off the water and listened. An outsider's voice became distinct, then recognizable. I pushed open the door and Father Fufferd looked up at me.

He hadn't changed. He still had his Francis X. Bushwacker hair-cut and flabby jowls. Now he smiled and lurched at me as if I were an old friend. "Well, Dennis, we didn't think you were coming. Haven't seen you in a long time."

"Four years," I said and shook his hand guardedly.

Kudirka had a disapproving scowl on his face and the Adams family had such a look of resurrected triumph about them I knew something was wrong.

"I heard about the trouble you had with Mulqueen at the seminary," Fufferd said as I took a chair. "That would never have happened under the old system . . . sending a man to a psychiatrist." He clucked and shook his head.

"I was pretty messed up," I offered. "My cousin died in Vietnam. Everything kind of fell apart. It was nobody's fault." I was tempted to add, "You'd probably have thrown me right out," but held my tongue.

"The story I heard was that Mulqueen had you campused for a year and nobody on the faculty knew."

I didn't want to rehash something I wanted only to forget, so I said nothing and busily slopped food onto my plate.

After an uncomfortable silence, Adams plunged back into their previous discussion. "But this has doubled your attendance in the last six months, Bill?" He was excited, the first time I had seen him so intent since I had arrived at Holy Innocents.

"At least doubled," Fufferd said.

"What's this?" I asked, looking instinctively to Kudirka.

Kudirka tightened his lips and waved off the question with a disgusted movement of his hand.

"The Counter-Reformation," Patty smiled.

"The what . . . ?"

"The Tridentine Mass," Fufferd corrected. "The Mass as Pius V declared it had to be for all future ages."

Fufferd took a paper which lay on the table next to him and handed it to me. "Una Via" said the bold red masthead, above a letter announcing an organization bent on the return of the Latin Mass. The several paragraphs sounded like Fufferd's last bitter classes at St. Bernardine's after the changes. As the author and spiritual leader of the new movement, his signature was at the bottom of the letter.

I put the paper down and looked up at him. "But you can't do that," I said.

His friendly facade dropped. The investigator of prayer manuals and jock closets returned. "And why not?" he growled. "If all you hippie priests can do as you please, playing guitars and bringing nightclub acts up on the altar—why can't we innovate as well, but with something that is right?"

"Bill has been attracting people who drive as far as fifty miles to hear a Latin Mass at his church," Monsignor pronounced. Then pointing a fork at me he demanded: "What does that say to you?"

I stared at the fork until he lowered it.

"Not that Mass should be in Latin," I said. "I think if people could vote to bring back twenty years ago, they'd do that too."

Mary Murphy took a deep breath, heaving her breast almost to

134

chin level, and entered the fray. "And here's this one, objecting to that, but wanting to put in a Spanish Mass."

I didn't see any connection. "Well . . ." I objected, "that's the venacular for Puerto Ricans—just like English is for us."

"Don't you understand?" Adams said, slamming his hand on the table. "If you people hadn't thrown out Latin, the Mass *would* be the same for everyone."

"If you put in a Spanish Mass," Mary concluded for him, "you'll have to put in a German Mass, an Italian Mass, one for every nationality."

Patty grunted a laugh into his glass. "And blacken your face for niggers."

"Bill is filling a church at a far end of the diocese," Adams said. "If people begin to respond right here at the diocesan seat—and if this catches on in other places as well—it just might begin a movement to turn the tide."

I didn't know what to say. It was Father Kudirka who spoke up. "Then you will say that Mass yourself. You will be alone in your disobedience."

"I am the pastor here," Adams bellowed.

"And who is the bishop?" Kudirka asked angrily. "And the Pope, and the Holy Spirit?"

"I won't say a Latin Mass either," I said, echoing Kudirka. Then, drawing further strength from the older man's objection, I added, "Bishop Maguire sent me here to help the Spanish people. If you don't let me use the church, I'll just get a vacant storefront and say Mass there."

Monsignor looked at me and sneered. "How typical of the New Breed. Two months ordained and you would set up your own schismatic Church."

I looked forward more each day to the welfare protest, if only to end my commitment to it. I might have been a failure at the hospital and a fifth wheel getting the sisters' program started, but at least I could see how they were connected with being a priest. I was less sure about what I thought of the whole business with the Urban Christian Council.

After the first week I took to canvassing blocks, wearing a T-shirt and cutoffs. I had felt sort of phony, pushing my way into people's apartments with a Roman collar. If I were dressed like one of the student volunteers, the response to my political ideas could be more direct.

After a long day—first, playing ball with the kids in the summer program, then touring the hospital—I spent a couple of hours unenthusiastically passing out fliers: being waved off; agreed off; flaked off by the tenement dwellers.

The sun had baked the streets to a dry wafting heat. I stopped, bought a can of soda and leaned against a building to rest. A young guy, bigger than I was, with his shirt off and a rag tied around his head, sauntered by me and stopped.

"Hey, man," he said, and snapped his fingers once in disdainful aggression. "How 'bout you let me have a quarter?"

"Why?" I answered guardedly.

"Well, you got money to buy yourself a soda pop. You can give me a quarter."

His cool demand enraged me. My arms shook with wanting to react. But I held myself in check. I had to. I was on his turf, not mine.

I shook my head slowly. We stared at each other. He shrugged, laughed a little as if the encounter wouldn't be worth the trouble and moved on. I started to walk in the direction of Holy Innocents, replaying the scene, wishing I could have said, "Kiss my ass, buddy," and hit him before he could have hit me. I kept playing it over and over in my mind that way—each time bloodier and more victorious for me.

As I ran through something like the twentieth replay I passed a guy sitting on a stoop. He wore an oil-covered mechanic's uniform and was holding a bottle of beer.

"Hey, you," he demanded.

I only half looked at him. He was my own age, and bigger than the guy who asked for the quarter.

"What are you passing around? I've been watching you."

"Fliers on the welfare march," I said curtly, and kept moving. I was done being a politician for the day.

"Let me see," he insisted.

I walked back to the stoop and handed him one.

"I'm not on welfare," he muttered as he began reading the sheet. "I just want to see what you're doing."

I looked at his face for the first time. My mind spun back to high school, to a city track meet in my freshman year. It was in the novice eight-eighty. A black kid had tripped me, fighting for a lane. After the race I had picked a fight. Before we started swinging he had called me "whitey"; I had called him "nigger." When they pulled us apart the coaches and officials made us shake hands. Only afterward did I realize that the officials had made me say I was sorry for using the word "nigger," but that he didn't have to apologize for saying "whitey." Every meet we would both be in after that, he was the only person I would be running against. It did great things for both my time and his. When we were in a race together it was just him and me. No one else would touch us. I hated him so much I got to like him. By the end of our senior year we had gotten to look for each other at meets.

We had talked, grudgingly at first, and then a slow steady sense of camaraderie had grown. Now, I watched him read for a moment or so, and then interrupted him. "Brooks," I said.

He looked up at me from the paper. The hostility melted and his face broke into a smile.

"Holy shit!" he drawled. "Holy shit! Hey, man, I didn't even look at you. What are you doing?" He reached out and grabbed my hand, then yelled back into the open first-floor window, "Hey, Rachel! Come here a minute! Bring two more beers!"

A slim girl with a ready smile stuck her head through the white curtains and handed out two bottles.

"Honey, this is . . . Hogan, right?"

"Dennis, Dennis Hogan," I nodded.

"We used to run against each other in high school," Brooks said. "Actually he used to watch my ass for four years while he ran after it."

"I can still blow your drawers off," I retorted.

"You put your legs where your mouth is," he laughed. "I'll leave you in my dust."

"When?" I said.

"Right now," he challenged.

"George, you can't," his wife ordered. "We're gonna eat in two minutes." Then, smiling at me, she said, "Want to join us? Cold chicken and potato salad. Too hot to cook. I got plenty."

We ate in their kitchen while two toddlers played around the

137

table. Only about halfway through the meal did it come out that I was a priest. Somehow I had presumed it was self-evident, as if the fact radiated from me.

"Not from the way you're dressed," Rachel said. "You don't see too many reverends walking around in T-shirts."

"I started wearing this when I got into the welfare protest . . ." I began.

"Yeah, that's a bone I wanted to pick with you," George said, angrily. "What the hell are you mixed up with that for?"

"I really don't know," I said. "I just fell into it."

"Man, that is the sickest thing I know. Welfare keeps this place a hell, that's what it does. It's degrading. It goes to the woman, so she's more boss than her man. They should give coupons if they give anything. Food stores here charge more than stores in rich places. I won't buy here. Just a lot of people making easy money on a system, that's all it is."

"George doesn't make as much money working as some of these people on welfare get," Rachel put in. "And wait till you see the night the eagle flies—when the checks come out. They might as well send the money right to the liquor stores." She sounded angry.

"I'm saving up," George said, pointing to the two babies. "I want them growing up in something better. I'm going to buy a home in Clinton Heights."

"But up there's not much better than here," I wondered out loud. "If you're buying a house, why don't you get out into the suburbs or the country?"

Even as I said that, I remembered how when I was in high school, a black doctor had almost moved into our upper-middle-class white neighborhood. A near panic ran up and down our entire block. It was our ghetto, and blacks weren't wanted. Even my parents joined in worried discussions about property values. One man wanted to form a buyers' group to get the house off the market. But to the great relief of all, the doctor decided not to buck everybody. We had been saved from becoming a slum.

That thought filled me with guilt after I made my suggestion to George, and I reddened with embarrassment. George seemed to know already. "Yeah, well maybe," he said, and we dropped the topic.

Later that evening George and I drove to the same track where our city meets had been held, and raced a four-forty. It is a shock to the human system to wrench muscles that aren't being used regularly, and neither one of us had raced in years. We kept neck and neck almost all the way around half of the track, but when we got to the straightaway George pulled ahead of me. I poured out every ounce of strength I could muster, but it wasn't in me. He beat me by five feet.

We collapsed, got up, and made ourselves walk to keep from cramping, then collapsed again. My chest felt as if a sledgehammer had pounded it.

When I could breathe enough to talk, I pulled myself to a sitting position and challenged him again. "I can still kill you in any distance you name over a mile," I gasped between deep breaths.

"What makes you think that, little man?" he puffed as he massaged his legs.

I laughed and rolled over to face him. "Because I always figured niggers couldn't run anything over an eight-eighty."

"You just name any distance you want," he said. "I'll give you more of what you just got." Then, with a slow gleaming grin, he added, "Honky."

26

THE welfare protest had some big money behind it. Scores of buses unloaded thousands of people near the park right in front of City Hall. Free baloney sandwiches, along with soft drinks, had been supplied for the protesters. It was a grand sort of picnic.

As I stood at the edge of the park, a vendor accosted me, hawking bright green T-shirts emblazoned with the message "Make Love not War!" His price was an exorbitant eight dollars.

"Naw," I laughed, waving him off, "that's too much."

"Don't you want to help the cause?" he insisted.

I didn't know what cause he meant, but it was obviously a day to support causes. Reluctantly, I purchased a shirt and shoved what I could of it into my back pocket so that it hung out like a trailing handkerchief.

I sat against a police barricade, uneager to wade into the crowd. As I watched, a mammoth white woman of about forty, wearing thongs instead of shoes, moved up to me, laughing softly to herself. Having imbibed heavily on something more than the soft drink she was carrying, she leaned up against me and wrapped her arm around my neck, drooling on me as she did so. I unwrapped her arm, tested to make sure she wouldn't fall as I moved my body away, and tried to disengage myself. She kept laughing, softly, almost threateningly, and held onto my arm. It was like being caught in a ton of fleshy, sweating quicksand.

A voice broke in from behind us. "Hey, lady, get your cotton-pickin' hands off my husband."

It was Lippsy, dressed in dungarees and a tank top that barely concealed her large breasts. She bore down on us and the lady in thongs moved back, releasing me.

"Hi, love," said Lips, kissing me on the lips. Then, turning back to the woman, she added, "Eat your heart out."

My heart was pounding. Nobody had kissed me like that ever in public. It took me seconds to find my voice.

"What are you doing here?" I finally asked, anxiously looking around to see who might have seen what had happened.

She acted as if nothing had happened, as if she had kissed priests every day.

"God," she said. "I wouldn't miss a show like this for the world. You had your free baloney sandwich yet?"

People had brought lawn chairs and blankets; a loudspeaker system had been set up to blare music, and people sat in groups, singing and laughing. It was almost like being at the beach. Harry Tremblay came up to me in a fair state of agitation. It was the first time I had seen him in a priest's black suit.

"Where is your collar?" he asked, his sharp tone insinuating mental retardation on my part. I was wearing the cutoffs I had worn canvassing the neighborhood.

"What difference does it make?" I asked.

"Well, damn it," he exploded, "the press is here! How the hell are people going to know you represent the Church without your collar?"

I was puzzled. "You were the one saying at the meeting that you never wear the collar because it stood for all the wrong things in the Church."

"This is different, Hogan. Can't you see that? We're *supposed* to be representing the Church here."

"I don't think I'm representing the Church here at all, I'm just . . ."

He cut in angrily. "Christ, you really are out of it, aren't you?"

He started off, papers in his hand, toward a group of organizers surrounding Mrs. Heidrich.

"My, my," said Lippsy, "seems you have a reputation to live up to."

The protest got underway. Newspaper and television photo-
141

graphers arrived and the delegation that was supposed to get in to see the mayor stood on the steps of City Hall to talk to the crowds. Picket signs dotted the gathering, along with chalk scrawls on the walls of the government building. "MORE WELFARE," "POWER TO THE PEOPLE," the signs proclaimed.

A hefty woman community leader stood on the steps yelling, "We want more food for our children, and clothes for their backs, and insurance so's we don't hafta be buried in potter's fields!"

Everyone responded in unison: "Amen!"

"What's that? Yell louder! I want to hear you!"

"Amen!" everyone repeated and a cheer followed.

Harry Tremblay introduced Mrs. Heidrich who was to tell the crowd what she intended to say to the mayor. As she opened her mouth to speak, a woman from somewhere in front drowned her out and filled in for her voice, so that it sounded as if Mrs. Heidrich had announced, "I gets hit with anythin' else an' somebody gets this chair over the head."

Lippsy shrieked and doubled over, laughing. If Mrs. Heidrich had something to say other than that, I never heard it, for Lippsy's laughter was so infectious I ended up laughing as hard as she was.

Everyone began singing "We Shall Overcome," and moved about carrying their pickets. "I want a picket sign, too," Lippsy said, and moved off toward a bearded young man distributing hand-painted signs. A little kid about a year and a half old, obviously lost, sat on the grass, crying his eyes out. I picked him up and tried to stop his crying, looking around for whoever might own him. I noticed a photographer focusing in on me. I pulled the kid up in front of my face as a shield.

A cop behind a barricade was directing a puzzled glance at me, and beckoned me over.

When I got there, he asked, "What are you doing here?"

"What do you mean?" I wondered if, perhaps, he knew me from somewhere.

"You're not on welfare, are you?"

"Oh, hell, no."

"I didn't think so," he said. "You look too uncomfortable. Why are you here?"

The baby was screaming all the louder. "I don't know," I shrugged. "I really don't know."

142

The mayor came out on the steps to speak to the crowds. My brother Jerry, who was a lawyer and worked at City Hall, stood next to him. It was too much. I looked around for someone to deposit the kid with before he had a chance to see me. Then I crawled under a barricade and disappeared to where the buses were parked.

After the protest, the community organizers from our area returned to the storefront to celebrate. It had all been a great success. The number of people who had shown up at City Hall far exceeded anyone's expectations. The priests who were there decided that a liturgy would be in order, so Harry Tremblay stood at the small desk at the front of the room and presided over a Mass.

I lay on the floor in a back corner and propped my head against a radiator, becoming progressively more disturbed. Not because Tremblay made up the Eucharistic prayer as he went along (sounding not so much unorthodox as just banal), or because he went out of his way to use a Dixie cup for a chalice when real glasses were in the room, but because he kept referring to the Eucharist as "the breaking of the bread of fellowship" even after he had consecrated it and changed it into the body and blood of Christ.

I began to get angry at him, the way I had at the hero in college who called out to the priest to "make it fly."

The loaf of Italian bread was passed around the room. I watched large crumbs flake off and fall to the floor. What I felt must have been reflected on my face, for Lips, from across the room, mocked me with a scowling imitation. She didn't take communion when she was handed the loaf. That made two of us.

After Mass they discussed the news coverage.

"Watch channel seven tonight," Tremblay said. "They had cameras all over the place down there."

"Speaking of television," Mrs. Heidrich put in, "did any of you see the film clip of the Mass at the bishop's conference? Did you see Maguire kneeling at the side of the altar saying his rosary while everyone else was concelebrating?"

The room echoed in appreciative groans and laughter.

Mrs. Heidrich kept going, making a joke of Maguire. It was too much for me. I wanted to interrupt her and say, "Mrs. Heidrich, you're so full of shit it's spilling out of your ears."

Instead I got up and walked out.

27

$\mathcal{I}$T was frightening when the hospital called during the night. As soon as the phone would ring, I'd sit bolt upright and grab for the receiver, still half asleep. The tone of the nurse's voice would be an indication of what to expect.

Sometimes the voice would be calm. "Father, this is Four North. We have a patient whom we think you should see."

At other times the nurse would speak hurriedly, suggesting that the faster I got there the better. "Father, this is the coronary care unit. Would you come up? We've just admitted a man and he's in bad shape."

Sometimes the voice would be tense, with no time allowed for details. "Father, this is the emergency room. We could use your services right away!"

At times like those, I'd start praying as I pulled on my clothes that I wouldn't get sick when I got to the hospital.

I had been tired after the welfare march and depressed by that Mass. I had gone to bed early. When the call came it was Lippsy on the other end. "Better get up here," she said. "Car accident. They're both dead."

"I'll be right there," I replied, automatically looking at the clock. It was still before midnight.

144

In another ten minutes she was leading me to a back cubicle, carefully curtained off from the rest of the emergency room.

"They were just kids," she whispered by way of warning. "Cops said they were doing about one hundred and ten when they went off the expressway. They hit an embankment. Brace yourself. There's not too much left to them."

She pulled back the curtain and there they were. All that could be made out of the two bloody forms on the carts were the clothes and the rough shape of human bodies. They had been mashed beyond recognition. When I made the sign of the cross, Lippsy did so along with me and then stood next to me while I said the prayers for the dead. The two boys were lying face down. When I anointed each of them I closed my eyes and reached under the top of the skull, signing the cross in oil where there was no longer a face.

According to the identification in their wallets they were brothers, eighteen and twenty years old. It was Lips who called their home. "Is this Mrs. Russell?" she asked, her voice carefully noncommittal. "This is the emergency room at Memorial Hospital. There has been an accident. Could you come down?"

After a pause, she said, "Yes, it is serious."

Another pause, then: "Yes, both. Both serious."

After she hung up she looked at me and half smiled in apology: "It would be worse to tell them any more than that. We don't know what situation we're calling into and they have to drive here."

We sat in silence for a moment. I looked at my hand. There were specks of dry, caked blood on my palm from lifting the boys' skulls. I needed to wash my hands.

"Would you like some coffee?" she offered, taking off her cap and placing it in front of her on the desk. "It could be awhile before they get here."

I shook my head no. Then I realized that she had been on the go since the welfare march. "You must be pretty tired," I said.

"No . . . I like this shift."

For a moment the incongruity of that statement worked on both of us. The hospital was eerily quiet at that hour. Where we sat, it was just she and I along with the two corpses.

"I don't mean that," she said, pointing to the pulled curtains. "But you can't think of that after awhile. You force yourself to think of other things. God, if you didn't you'd go crazy. We end up talking about movies and politics even after the worst sorts of things in here. If an outsider walked in, they'd be scandalized."

We sat for about a quarter of an hour without saying anything. Then recalling how she had blessed herself at the anointing I asked, "By the way, how come you made the sign of the cross?"

"I don't know," she said. "The nurses who are Catholic do. It seems like the right thing, a way of supporting the priests. The people too, maybe. Who knows?"

"You didn't go to communion at that Mass today," I pointed out.

She almost laughed as she remarked, "With the look on your face I was afraid you'd come over and hit me. You have a big hang-up about that, don't you?"

"Well . . . it's sacred to me. I really believe it's Jesus," I said. "Tremblay was making it a toy. He didn't have to use that dixie cup."

"I thought you were going to take a shot at that Heidrich bitch," she laughed.

"I came close," I said.

"The way she was knocking that old bishop for saying his prayers at Mass? What's it her goddamned business how he says his prayers?"

I had never thought of Maguire as old before.

"I mean," she went on, "isn't it kind of funny—all those raving liberals? And yet they're the most intolerant people who ever came along. There they are, bleating away about how straight the Church is. But, boy, if you're gonna march out of step with old Mrs. Heidrich . . . hey, you better get outta the way. She'll . . ."

The outside door opened. Lips stopped and quietly put on her cap. We went to the emergency room door. A state trooper had been sitting in the waiting room. Now when a man and woman, along with a teenage boy, came into the hall, he stood up to meet them.

The mother looked frantically from the trooper to me. Addressing me, she asked, "Oh my God, is it that bad?"

"Yes," I answered, wishing I could look away from her eyes. "I'm sorry, it is."

"Are they dead?"

There was no way to slow down what was happening. The situation explained itself too immediately.

"Yes," the officer said.

"Both of them?"

"Yes," he said, then added, "I'm sorry."

The mother dropped her pocketbook and clapped both hands to her face. She started to crumple. Both the state trooper and I grabbed her. We helped them all to the waiting room and sat them down. The man and boy stared dumbly, as if they refused to believe what they had been told. Lippsy came in with paper cups filled with water. While the woman drank, Lippsy rubbed her back as if she were a small child.

A positive identification still had to be made. The father, the trooper, and I went in to where the bodies were. As soon as we separated the curtains the father gasped, burst into tears and moaned, "Oh, God. Yes. Those are their clothes."

For a long time we sat together in the waiting room, I attempting to give comfort where none could be given. After a while, I realized that the boy, unnoticed, had slipped into the emergency room. I went in and found him standing next to what was left of his brothers, staring down at them. I touched his arm and suggested, "Why don't you come back in with your mom and dad?"

He wouldn't look at me, but muttered through gritted teeth, "Get away, priest."

"Please," I insisted, gently tugging on his sleeve, "your folks need you now."

He yanked away, hissing, "I said get away, priest."

After a moment he turned and pushed past me back to where his parents were.

When, at last, they were settled enough to go back home I walked them all to the door. The boy started to go out, then stopped and without looking up from the floor, said, "I'm sorry . . ." Unable to finish he choked on tears. I put my arms around him. He hugged back and sobbed. When they were gone I felt myself shudder from the release of tension.

Lippsy was standing behind me. "I'm off now," she said softly. "Want to give me a ride home?"

28

"*I* seem to recall you describing this as a 'neat' little apartment," I remarked, knocking an empty box out of the way to get into her living room. Salvation Army furniture crowded the place. Tidy housekeeping didn't seem to rank high on Lippsy's list of values.

"Ah, it's lived in," she said, then added with a wink, "real lived in. How about a glass of wine?"

"No, thanks. I'd go right to sleep."

"Do you smoke?"

She had plopped on the couch, opened a canister, and was rolling a joint.

"Pot?" I asked, shocked. "What the hell are you doing with that?"

"You tried it?"

"No."

"Well, don't knock it." She lit up, took a drag, and handed me the smoldering joint. "Here. Get it into your lungs," she ordered. "Let it out slow."

I held it as if it were alive. "Uh . . . no . . . I don't think so, Lips." I handed it back.

"I figured you needed something after that last scene. That takes a while to get used to, you know."

"Yeah," I conceded. The broken bodies of the two boys flashed into my mind. I sat staring into this thought until I felt one of Lip's hands on the back of my neck and the other on my arm.

"Don't think about it," she whispered. "Put it out of your head."

Her touch was as startling as an electric shock. I pulled away, blushing.

"God," she said loudly, "do you have hang-ups, or do you have hang-ups?"

"I am a priest, Lippsy," I countered.

"You're a friggin' human being too," she said, throwing her hands up. "I was just trying to calm you down. You're halfway up the wall from that accident, for Pete's sake."

"I'm sorry," I apologized. I edged away from her on the couch.

To change the subject, I took note of the wood carvings she had on her bookcase. "Where did you get these?" I asked.

"Philippines," she said testily. "When I was traveling around in the Peace Corps."

"No kidding. How come the Peace Corps?" The more I learned of her the less I could figure her out.

"Jesus, Red," she protested. "Does there have to be a reason for everything? I just like people. You don't have to be a religious fanatic to help people, do you?" Then, her tone returning to normal, she added, "Sorry. I didn't mean to bellow. You're hard to figure out, that's all."

I laughed a little. "That's what I was just thinking about you. That's where you got your Spanish, right? You speak it really well."

"Yeah," she smiled pensively and gestured to a couple of boxes in the corner. "He was a Spanish teacher, too. He got my pronunciations right."

"Who?"

"My . . . well him." When I looked at her stupidly, she explained. "He lived with me the last couple of years. We just broke up."

"Oh . . ." I said. "That's . . . too bad."

"Well, it was good while it lasted," she smiled pensively.

"What happened? Did you have a fight?"

"No . . . not really."

When I started to ask another question she broke in: "Actually, I'd just as soon not talk about him. I mean, I'm not brokenhearted or

149

anything. We broke up nice and easy. But I don't like it when I get talked about. So I don't like to rat-fink on anybody else. Not when I've had a relationship with them."

Then she laughed impishly and, winking, said, "*Now,* can you relax just a little?"

29

SISTER Marie Bernard and I ended up arguing a good deal. Though she was only two years younger than I she still refused to call me by my first name, addressing me as "Father" both before others and when alone with me. A tomboy, she was better at baseball than I was. She was also better at ending fights. I always made the mistake of taking one side or the other, pouring more oil on the flames. She simply pulled everyone apart and made them stop.

About halfway through the summer she walked into the main office in school as I hung up the phone. "Who was that?" she asked casually.

"The head of the youth office," I said. "They're setting up a display from the different summer programs around the city. They wanted to know if we had any artwork we could contribute." I stopped and laughed, adding, "I told them the only thing our kids could draw was blood."

She didn't laugh with me.

Father," she said, drying her hands on the apron she wore over her habit, "have you stopped in, even once, to look at what these children have been doing in arts and crafts?"

"No," I said, realizing as soon as I made the admission that I was in for it and quickly added, "I mean, I've seen the kids working. I just didn't get a chance to check the stuff out."

"Well, then, how can you say something like that? Come here and see."

She led me into the large classroom where Sister Jeanne supervised artwork. A number of youngsters sat at tables, so deeply intent on painting ceramics they didn't notice us when we walked in.

Marie Bernard dropped her voice to a whisper, "When these kids get onto something creative," she hissed, "there's no end to what they can do. Look at them. They're the same ones who create riots in the playground."

She led me around the room, picking finished pieces off shelves, pointing out paintings on the bulletin boards.

"There is a lot of real talent here," she lectured. "We've just got to teach these kids how to use it."

She picked a sketch pad off the main desk. "You know Jerome Simmons?" she asked.

"Our friendly neighborhood arsonist?" I smiled. Jerome, my Irish mulatto sidekick, spent most of his non-incendiary hours talking my ear off whenever I walked around the streets.

"He always carries a pad around," she said, ignoring my sarcasm. "He sketches all the time. He left this on the ground last week when he was playing basketball. Jeanne can't believe it."

She turned pages, unabashedly indicating lurid, melon-breasted nudes, stretched out and beckoning to Jerome's imagination.

"Look at the form here, the shading. This is without an ounce of training. And do you know, at fifteen he already has a record as long as your arm? What's going to become of him? What could he be even now if someone had taken him in hand when he was little?"

I felt chastened. "I'll call the office back," I agreed.

"That's a minor point," she said, her sharp blue eyes still flashing with indignation. "It's your whole attitude."

"What do you mean?" I objected testily. "It's not like I'm over there with Adams, holding the fort. Hell, I don't sit down from the time I say the 6:30 Mass in the morning till about eleven at night."

She backed down, a little, putting her hands up to shush me. Then on a lower key she resumed the attack. "That's not what I meant, Father. I know how hard you work, but ... you're not ..."

"What?"

"Well ... like this matter with the art. These children aren't

152

individuals to you; they're just there, and they're your job—as if they were things. I don't think you like people."

"What people?"

"Just people."

I digested this for a second or two. Unable to think of a way to answer such an accusation, I decided out loud, "That isn't true."

That evening, she sent a cake over to the rectory, along with a note asking me to forgive her for flying off the handle.

Shortly after that incident, George Brooks and I took a group of about forty-five kids to the city zoo. It was a bad-news trip from the start. Our first mistake had been in packing oranges in the kids' lunches. Subway rides were bad enough anyway. People sitting in cars would cringe in horror when the doors opened and our charges flooded in, whooping and leaping for the hand bars. But the day we had packed them oranges, which could be used as weapons, a trip-long battle ensued. Within five minutes the train was like the inside of a mixer at Nedick's.

I hugged a pole, closed my eyes, and pretended I was somewhere else.

"Young man," a woman demanded, angrily yelling above the train's roar and the screaming of kids, "are you in charge of these children? An orange skin just landed on my head." She held up the sloppy peel as proof and awaited my judgment.

I looked at her as innocently as I could and asked, "What children?"

Our second mistake was taking them into the monkey house at the zoo. The place was crowded. Our group went yelping and pushing their way around and into people until they stood before a cage filled with fat sleepy orangutans. The animals sat on perches, staring back at us. One male lazily reached above his head and began to toy with a lady friend directly above him. I figured it was time to move on, but suddenly this became a super circus for the kids.

"Hey!" bellowed an eight-year-old. "Look at that! He fingerin' her!"

George was always quick to point out my white mentality in dealing with black people. Thus as the crowd about us howled in laughter, I disowned them a second time, clapped an arm around George and said, "They are all yours, baby, all yours. This honky's gonna take himself out on the grass and wait for you there."

It was a good half hour before they emerged.

The third mistake, the one that counted, happened on the way home. My only concern was to shovel everyone onto the subway; but as we were leaving the park one small youngster, no more than seven, balked. "My brother ain't here yet," he fretted.

"Look," I yelled, and started to wave everyone on, "I told all of you to meet here a good twenty minutes ago. He can get home alone."

The boy hung onto the park's fence as if he feared I might pull him with me. "I ain't goin' without my brother," he insisted. As he said this, tears welled up in his eyes.

Suddenly, Marie Bernard's angry accusation echoed in my mind. She was right. This kid was a thing to me, not a person. I would never have deserted someone in my own family, but I expected him to leave his brother.

Immediately I was filled with remorse. I got down on my knees to the kid's face level and took him by the shoulders. "I'm sorry," I pleaded with him.

The little guy was crying very hard without making a sound.

"Come on," I said, brushing his tears away with my hand. "You and me will wait together, okay?"

George left for home with the group. I bought the kid a comic book and we waited on a bench a good half hour before his older brother came running along. When he did it was the kid, not I, who yelled at him for being late.

When I got home I returned Sister Marie Bernard's plate to the convent with a note saying, "Thanks for the cake. I got to eat my words, too."

30

ONE evening toward the beginning of September, Kudirka stalked angrily into my bedroom, shaking a newspaper in his fist. "Did you see, Dennis? Did you see this? Look what this fool has done."

He slapped the paper on the desk in front of me. In a three-column, six-inch-high ad, Fufferd and Adams had signed an announcement that Holy Innocents would be the diocesan seat's Una Via headquarters. A Latin Tridentine Mass would be celebrated each Sunday at eleven; along with this there was to be an active crusade for the return of the Roman Catholic Church to sanity. In small print, with a number of references to centuries-old papal pronouncements, Fufferd and Adams pointed out that it was they who were truly orthodox, that it was the greater part of Catholicism including Pope Paul who were marching out of step by adapting the Mass to modern culture.

And so Una Via went into business.

The response was immediate and strong. Within three weeks Monsignor added a second Mass to handle the crowds. Our parking lot, usually empty on Sundays, was filled to overflowing.

Monsignor Adams announced from the pulpit that he had to give out all of the communions because neither of his self-willed assistants would help him. He was easily portrayed to his sympathetic audience as an overworked man carrying a parish on his shoulders alone. I listened to him, thinking of battered old Father Kudirka who got up in the middle of the night to attend the sick and dying, while Adams had refused to answer a sick call in over a generation. My stomach churned in frustration. It was a frustration as well to refuse to help with communion. It seemed so terrible a thing to do—to cause a turmoil over the Eucharist. But Kudirka insisted that since Adams was using the Mass as a weapon against the Church itself, our only role should be to keep away from the whole scene.

At the same time they were reviving the Latin Mass, we were starting our Spanish one. The Spanish Mass wasn't said in the church. That was Adams' appointed domain, and he flatly refused permission. It was no great problem. I got hold of an empty storefront down the block. Advertised only by walks around the Spanish neighborhoods, we began. The storefront was small, and we soon had to add a second and then a third Mass. Kudirka insisted on learning the canon in Spanish, so that he could take one of the Masses. It was important to him that all the people in the parish knew he was their priest, he said.

But while we were successful, I felt constantly weighed down by the sense of guilt and frustration that came from being part of a parish-sized schism. I kept thinking back to what Mike had said at St. Bernardine's when the seminary professors had begun to divide and fight over the changes.

"Hell, Dennie," he had told me, "what if the whole Church started to react the way they are? We'd go right down the drain with the entire goddamned world looking at us, scratching their heads . . ."

In the unreal, nightmare world of Holy Innocents, I felt as if I were standing at the edge of the drain.

A very old lady was dying in the hospital. Kudirka had already anointed her several weeks before, but one day when I checked into her room she was failing noticeably. I stayed with her, along with her doctor and a nurse.

She was comfortable enough, but as she looked at me she became agitated. Her brow furrowed, and she lifted a hand to get my attention. "Father, I almost forgot," she whispered. "I wanted to have a Mass said for my husband. It bothered me all day yesterday. I have one said every year. But I've been so sick."

"That's all right," I assured her. "I'll say the Mass for you. Don't you worry about it at all."

"Oh, you're a dear, Father," she said, relieved. "Here. Get me my pocketbook. It's in the drawer."

She struggled to sit up. The doctor gave me a cold, hard look. I wanted to crawl under the bed. "No, please," I objected, "that's okay. I don't want the money."

This upset her. "I insist, Father. I want it said right and proper."

I tried to protest, but the nurse, a stolid white-haired woman, interrupted, tapping me several times on the back as she did. "I'll get the money, Mrs. Meyer," she said.

She took five dollars from the old woman's purse and stuck it in my shirt pocket. Mrs. Meyer lay back and smiled. In another hour she died, all accounts squared with God and with us.

At the main desk in the hallway I spoke to the nurse. "I feel awful about this," I said, pulling the money out of my pocket. "That doctor isn't even Catholic. He must think I'm some kind of a vampire."

"Father, you weren't there for him," she said. "You were there for her. And that made her happy."

"I know, but it was wrong, I—"

"Look," she cut in. "Don't try to reeducate people on their deathbeds. If Christ were in there, *He'd* have taken the money.

31

*M*IKE called. It was a rarity to hear from him during this time. He was chaplain at the county jail, which was a good distance from the city, and his schedule was as tight as my own.

"Had the damnedest thing happen the other day," he announced. "This kid thought I was you. I was walking along the ground floor of the cellblock and from the second tier he started yelling, 'Hey, Father Hogan . . . Father Hogan.' When I went up to where he was, he just looked at me. Then he said, 'You ain't Father Hogan.' I told him I was. Then it hit me what was wrong. He's yours. His name is Simmons."

"Jerome?"

"He's in for arson. He tried to burn down his school."

"Yeah," I said, "Jerome is big on urban renewal. Tell him I'll come up to see him."

"Don't bother. He's underage. They can't keep him here. I'm bringing him home. Don't go anywhere tonight."

Mary Murphy had admitted Mike and Jerome before I could get downstairs.

"Hey, this place is beautiful," he said to her, running his hand over the faded brown wallpaper. "What do you do—rent rooms out to Wolfman?"

The founding fathers of Una Via were meeting in the dining room. Seeing them, Mike walked into the room, Jerome trailing in his wake. The boy had never been in the rectory before. He looked about, hung-jawed. Patty's eyes ran from Jerome to his baseball bat, propped and ready in the corner.

"Father Fufferd," Mike said, "how are you doing? Hey, I saw you on the news about your Latin Mass."

"Did you?" Fufferd acknowledged without smiling. My own negative reaction to his endeavors was enough to prepare him for my cousin's. But if he expected an attack none came. After casting a cruious glance at the handbills piled on the table Mike turned to me and said, "You ready to go?"

We went out to his car. "You're losing your punch," I said. "I was waiting for you to chop Fufferd into six-inch pieces."

"Peanuts," he laughed, waving his hand as if brushing away an insect. "That Una Via crowd is pissing against Niagara Falls. They're only important if people let them think they are."

"Well, they're sure packing them in here on Sundays."

"So is Busty Russell down at the Showboat, but she ain't gonna change history and neither are they."

Jerome's half sister, a beautiful twenty-year-old black girl with a child of her own, was less than enthusiastic about having him back home. She took an unaffectionate swipe at him as we walked into her cluttered apartment.

"Family court," she spat at him. "I ain't goin' to no family court for him. I got a family of my own to take care of."

Jerome's demeanor had changed as soon as he entered the door. Normally a dervish of loud activity, his shoulders slumped and he hung moodily to the far end of the room. He answered questions with monosyllables.

"I'm tellin' you, Jerome," she said, "this is the last time I'm puttin' up with any of your bullshit. I wish you was sixteen. You could stay where you was and I'd be rid of you for good."

After a few more such pleasantries we left Jerome to whatever the fates and his sister had in store for him.

32

I can still feel the pain of the day Gaelin got married to a man she worked with.

From a kneeler at the side of the altar I watched her walk down the aisle with her father. It was a vision that, long before, when I had felt young, I had imagined a hundred times, with me waiting for her as her groom. Ann was her matron of honor, as she would have been had Gaelin and I married four years earlier. But now a three-year-old redheaded ring bearer stumbled before them with shy uncertain steps. He was my godson—the son my cousin had never lived to see. Little Eddie looked like his dead father. He looked like me. He looked like a child of mine might have looked if I had started a family when we left college.

I went running with George Brooks that afternoon, a hard driving run in which I pushed the pace far beyond our usual limits.

"Hey," George demanded when we collapsed to an aching halt, "what are you trying to do? Kill us? That wedding really got to you, didn't it?"

We started walking around the track, sweating and laboring for breath.

"Hey, man," he persisted, "you had no claim on her. Now's a late time to get worked up about it all."

"That's not it," I pleaded. "What got me was that I was like a ghost to everyone. I mean . . . she wasn't embarrassed I was there, or sad or glad or anything. I didn't exist. I belonged to God. I was as dead and as part of the past as my cousin Eddie."

"So?" he shrugged. "For her you are."

"Yeah, I know," I said, "but it made me feel that way, too. It was like I was a ghost. A dead man."

33

ONE of the nurses told me that Lippsy wasn't in because she had been mugged earlier in the afternoon. I went immediately to a pay phone.

"Aw it's nothing," Lippsy said, slurring as if she had difficulty pronouncing the words. She tried to laugh. "It happened so fast, I didn't have time to pull my act about the syphilis germs."

"What happened?" I insisted, ignoring her attempt at humor.

"I made the mistake of cutting through a side street. I was late. I was heading for the bus stop and I passed a car filled with men drinking. One of them yelled out, 'Hey, if she's a case worker, I'd like her to be mine.' Well it was the best compliment I'd gotten all day so I turned my head to see who said it. All of a sudden a kid about fifteen ran past and grabbed my pocketbook. He pulled me so hard we both whirled into the street. I hung on to it, screaming, 'no . . . no.' I think we were both just as scared. There were hundreds of people around sitting on stoops and the men in the car. All of them just sat and watched. The kid finally swung out and started punching my face. I let go and he disappeared with my bag into the cellarway of one of the buildings. I stood there and broke into tears."

I almost knocked Lippsy's door in.

"Jeez, hold it, willya?" she yelled when she opened the door. I

162

could see that just talking hurt. Her face was bruised, her lip cut, and her hair was straggly. Her thin robe was tied carelessly, revealing her breasts. Below the line where she was tanned, they looked white and soft. The instant my consciousness got the flash, I tore my glance from them and studied her swollen face.

"Goddamned animals," I exploded. "Somebody should drop a goddamned bomb on the whole goddamned area."

"Yeah, that sounds good," she mused, making her way to the sofa and flopping down. "You're a real Santa Claus. Anyone ever tell you that?"

I went over and sat with her.

"Watch it, love," she warned, "the last time we were this close you acted like I was going to jump you."

"Don't you take anything seriously?" I asked. I was frustrated, and angry enough to kill.

She touched her lip gingerly, saying, "Yeah, I take things seriously."

A wave of shame swept over me. I was adding to her hard time. She was so damned kindhearted. I was the one who was all nerved up with everything that had happened. She just took things the way they were. As if by apology I put my arms around her. Almost afraid she would take it as a joke, I reached over and kissed her.

"To make it better?" she asked. After a moment of reflection she said, "Do you know what was nice? After it happened I stood there not knowing what to do. This tough-looking bunch of teenagers passed me and one of them stopped and said, 'Hey, lady, why are you crying?' He sat me down on a stoop, and then made one of his gang go somewhere and call a cop. They all even helped look in the cellar-ways to see if the kid had thrown the pocketbook away. It was worth getting beat up, just to have that happen." She laughed and then winced again in pain.

It was almost dark. The only light in the room was a short candle stub on a corner bookcase, glowing in a small, motionless flame. I stared into the flame until it became the only thing I could see. I could feel Lippsy breathing, her body against mine. My heart was pumping fast and a nervous warmth began to flood and fill me. For a moment I fought off becoming aroused. I grappled with a slipping sense of conscience only long enough to feel anger that there was any kind of morality that dared to exist with the world and the

163

Church as screwed up as it was. Then, shaking, my chest pounding to the bursting point, I reached under Lippsy's wrapper and put my hand on her breast. I knew she wouldn't stop me. The way I could hear her breathing, so close, it was almost as if she were already part of me. I moved my hand from her breast to her waist, and undid her loosely tied belt.

Afterward I lay in her bed staring at the blank ceiling with almost as blank a mind. Lips breathed deeply and contentedly next to me. I could not believe what had happened. I had kept my virginity all the way through school—kept in check by all the adolescent fears of hellfire, clap, crabs, and the unshakable certainty that even if I had worn ten rubbers simultaneously, they would all have been defective, and I would have gotten someone pregnant.

Even with Gaelin, for all that we had gone steady for seven years, I had remained remarkably chaste. The few times, either drunk or just getting carried away, I had tried to move on her, she had shot me down with the admonition: "We should wait." Gaelin was so pure I had even begun to dread what our wedding night would be—wondering if, after all that buildup, there would be something difficult about making it with her, that I would botch my performance first time out.

I was wrong. The first time out had been so very easy.

The night was warm. Lippsy was only half covered, with a sheet pulled up as far as her navel. I watched her body move up and down with her breathing. She was deeply asleep. I propped myself up on my elbow and lifted the sheet all the way from her naked body. I had made love to her without looking at her. Now I studied her large, beautiful breasts and her soft, smooth stomach.

I started to promise God that I would never let anything like this happen again. But, even as I did so I reached over and placed my hand gently on her stomach as it rose and fell. She opened her eyes, and for a moment caught her breath, startled out of sleep. Then she looked at me. Even happily. More conscious of what was happening than when I had been pushed by unstoppable heat, I kissed her. Conscious of her body and the enjoyment of what was happening, I made love with her again.

Mary Murphy looked up from the morning paper with distaste
164

but no surprise when I opened the kitchen door at 6:15. For all she knew I might have been at the hospital all night. Still, I felt defensive as she watched me pour a cup of her tar coffee. I was sure that the marks of lovemaking were all over me, sure she would break the silence at any moment to announce with her grunting brogue: "You've got a hickey on your neck."

But her eye was more on the clock than on my skin, and her judgment instead rested darkly upon the out-dated sin of my breaking the fast before going over to say Mass.

In the dark cavern of the church, only the nuns could be counted as a congregation, grouped together in the first two pews, neatly answering the responses. The only other regulars were a powdery-faced old lady who hid behind a pillar to say her rosary, and a man who left every morning on schedule, immediately before communion.

I looked at everything but the host in my hands. "This is my body," I pronounced, commanding the presence of Christ. Instead of his body—broken, ripped apart—the use of the word flooded my mind with the image of the night before. I kept seeing Lippsy's naked body, kept thinking of my own and what I had done with it.

It would have been easier if I could have reduced Jesus to remote or theological terms, to the "breaking of the bread of fellowship." But I held Christ in front of me, and felt as much a betrayer as Judas.

During the previous day I had realized, writing the day's date, that it was the six-month anniversary of my ordination. I had ruefully calculated that it had seemed more like a hundred years. This day marked the same for my first Mass. I prayed the prayers of the canon by rote. But my conscious prayer was more direct.

"Poor Jesus," I addressed my thought to him, "we're ripping you apart. You got Fufferd and Adams using Una Via to beat you to death. There's Tremblay and the urban Christian Council bravely showing the world that they're not afraid to reduce you to a handshake. And I really do believe. God, I really do believe. Guys like me are all you've got . . . And I can't even keep out of the first bed I'm invited into."

When it came time to consume the host I held it up for adoration while the sisters prayed: "Lord, I am not worthy . . . but you say the word . . . I will be healed." In a whisper I added, "Happy anniversary, Jesus."

34

I avoided Lippsy's floor when she was on duty and managed to go almost a week without seeing her. Then, at ten o'clock one evening, I was called to the hospital to anoint a man in intensive care. Afterward I went into the deserted cafeteria. She was sitting alone at a table sipping coffee. Our eyes met and I felt myself blush. I had had intercourse with her; had studied her naked body while she slept; had spent an entire night in her bed. But since then we hadn't spoken. Now we were both in our work clothes: she in starched white, I in black clericals. Awkwardly I walked to her and sat down.

"Hi," I managed.

"Hi," she returned and smiled. She was not embarrassed, "Sick call?"

"Yeah."

There was a moment of silence. She looked around; we were alone. She reached over and traced her finger along my forearm.

"I get off at eleven."

I felt the hairs on my arm bristle from the excitement that suddenly filled every part of me. My heart was pounding. For a split second I thought of my resolve, then pushed it away. I just wanted to be with her again. I took her hand.

"My car is in the front parking lot," I said, "I'll wait for you."

Mike was stationed in the small town where I had gone to college and was chaplain at a county jail situated there. We hadn't seen much of each other in months. Our jobs had kept us chained seven days a week to where we were. Even when I went to visit him at St. Mary's, I didn't get to be alone with him until several hours after my arrival. We first had to eat dinner with his elderly pastor, Monsignor O'Donnell.

A frail man in his early eighties, Monsignor was genteel to the point of being ladylike. I decided he must have developed this trait late in life or been born an old man, for such delicacy was unimaginable in a man younger than he. We sat in a finely decorated colonial room, eating off bone china and drinking from crystal.

I wanted to talk to Mike alone. I was now staying with Lippsy several nights a week. I loved every minute spent with her, but I could not bear the sense of guilt and depression that filled me as soon as we were apart. I wanted to unburden myself to Mike. In order to get the meal done with I was all but rude to my courtly host.

Before an hour had passed, however, O'Donnell had shamed my first impressions. He was genuinely friendly. He listened to both Mike and me and he was open-minded about what was happening in the Church. Soon after our meal started, I drew attention to the one discordant note in the exquisite room: a harsh "NO SMOKING" sign placarded under an oil painting of a pastoral scene.

Monsignor laughed. "Oh, that was Alice Fortune. The priests who were stationed here called her Miss Fortune. She was my predecessor's housekeeper for years and years. I keep that up there as a conversation piece in her memory."

"What do you mean?"

"Oh, Lord," he clucked, shaking his head, "she was a tyrant. The 'no smoking' signs were for the priests. No one was going to dirty up her house. She wouldn't even let them have a cigarette on the front porch. They had to go out on the sidewalk."

"They took that?" I asked.

"That and a good deal more."

Mike broke in, "No one in this parish saw a priest without seeing her first to state their reasons. She decided who would and wouldn't get in. She was the pastor. It was her regime."

"I would have thrown her through a window," I started. But even as I spoke, I thought of Mary Murphy who just by force of weight could have made mincemeat of me.

"You would have been transferred the very next day," Monsignor

167

insisted. "That was the whole system. Ironclad paternalism. I remember my first assignment. I was ordained in 1913. Old Jim Carroll was my pastor. He imposed a curfew. The curates had no keys to the rectory. At nine o'clock the doors were bolted. If we were still out, we were in trouble. I got locked out one night, so I went home and stayed at my parents' house. Well, I was not only rebuked, I was called down to the chancery and laid out in lavender."

He pursed his mouth in an expression of distaste and concluded, "I haven't much sympathy with these fellows who want the good old days back. The good old days are now. Oh, I think we are throwing the baby out with the bathwater and we're going to suffer for it. But we needed the Vatican Council badly . . ."

Then, with a twinkle in his eye, he handed Mike a salad and laughingly added, "Even if it has unleashed all sorts of hippies on the Church."

"I'm the 'hippie priest' to a lot of folks around here," Mike explained, adding with a shrug, "I give it the old Navajo theory."

"Well, they just have to get used to a priest who likes to wear old work clothes," Monsignor O'Donnell said. "If they woke up to their own history, they'd realize that was how men who took vows of poverty started wearing habits."

Having announced that paternalism was dead, Monsignor proceeded to serve me my salad, first pouring oil and vinegar over it. I can't stomach vinegar, but this seemed to be a ritual to him. I didn't dare object. Instead I commented on what he had told us. "I don't think I could have been a priest back when you got ordained. I probably would have blown up and walked away from it."

"Oh, no, you would not have," Monsignor said, and with that he became so intensely serious he stopped serving the salad. "You would have done exactly as we did. You would have loved the priesthood and you would have taken that to have been a part of it."

"No," I objected, "I don't think so."

Monsignor had busied himself with his salad. Without looking up he shook his head. "You would have done it," he said again, quietly.

It was Friday night so there would be a long wait before we could talk privately. Mike had a wedding rehearsal and then had to baby-sit the high-school hangout he ran.

"This is my baby," he announced, his face lighting with pride as I looked around the church's basement. The ceiling was hung with fishnets. A jukebox stood in the corner. Pool tables and old couches filled the large center area.

"I was going to give the place a fancy name, but I waited so long the kids began to call it 'the room under the church' and now it's just 'the Room.' When I arrived here at St. Mary's there was no place in this whole hick town for the kids to hang out except down at the railroad tracks. So I started this. Wait till you see the crowd we get."

Throughout the evening, teenagers drifted in and out of the basement while Mike sat in a chair by the doorway. At times he stopped a few, checked for the telltale odors of beer or pot and threw them back out. One boy, wearing a faded green army jacket and an aggressively pug Irish face with naturally puffy eyes, interrupted Mike as he walked by. "A little cards, Padre?" he invited, shuffling an invisible deck in his hands.

"Not tonight, Kevin. I got company."

"Who's he? Your brother?"

"Cousin."

"Jeez, you could be twins. I don't know, Padre. I think you fixed this. I got to get back at you for last week."

He walked off and I turned to Mike, saying: "You're not still hustling, are you?"

He stretched back lazily into his chair, put his hands behind his neck and grinned. "Hell, Dennie, it's an art. You wouldn't want me to lose my touch, would you?"

"No wonder their parents don't like you."

"Naw, don't be stupid. I'm careful about whom I hustle and why. Like Kevin Baldwin there. It's good for him to be knocked down a peg or two. And he's got his hands on more ready cash than a kid who doesn't have a job should have."

His eyes narrowed a little as he watched the boy break into a pool game, grabbing the cue from a smaller kid who immediately relinquished his place rather than oppose Baldwin's pleasure.

"Interesting study," mused Mike. "Old man Baldwin owns a bar where all the local hardhats gather. He runs C.Y.O. basketball . . . Little League . . . Pop Warner. He's into anything that has to do with sports. Boys' sports. Girls' sports don't exist. Except that he's got no hair, he'd remind you of Fufferd. Everything is discipline—'Got to make men out of these boys.' You can imagine how he likes me. I invented the changes and destroyed the discipline of the Church.

169

And that somehow was the cause of every political upheaval that's happened in the last several years."

He dropped his voice almost to a whisper. "Ironic. Two years ago the old man's crew was caught falsifying kids' birth dates for Pop Warner football. Doing that somehow didn't break his code of discipline. Sadder still, I know for a fact that Kevin is one of the biggest drug pushers in town. But I can't prove it, and with his old man being who he is I ain't saying a word unless I've got the goods."

The crowd in the Room fluctuated between one hundred and one hundred fifty kids until almost midnight. Mike was the only chaperon. He seemed to be all that was needed. Being Mike's look-alike, I was the big attraction for the evening. At around eleven, while a group of girls gathered around us, asking about who I was, a fight broke out in the far corner. Mike groaned and got up, saying to me, "Here's what makes this job a pain in the ass."

He walked over almost indifferently. When he got to where the two kids were still squared off, he suddenly lashed out, grabbed the one nearest him and hurled him against the wall. Before the other youngster—it was the Baldwin kid—could back off, Mike had him by the nape of the neck, dragged him off balance, lifted him by the seat of the pants and shoved him toward the door.

"That's twice now, Kevin," Mike yelled.

"I didn't start it," the boy screamed back, his voice cracking with anger. "He . . ."

"Shut up and get out of here," Mike cut in. "You too, Joe," he said, turning to the kid plastered against the wall. "And neither one of you comes in this place for a month. Got that?"

His business completed, he came back to where we sat, resumed the smile that gave him a child's face, and picked up the conversation as if nothing had happened.

"Good Lord!" I said to him. "Don't these kids hate you?"

He shook his head, explaining, "Dennie, they know my limits. It's hard enough fighting the rumors about this place without giving people real problems. Last winter one nitwit girl got drunk out of her mind somewhere. She collapsed on Main Street, and before she passed out the only thing she managed to say was that she was headed for the Room. Well, damn it, that incident alone almost got this place closed. No, the kids cross the limits I've set and I'll break their heads open. Other than that we get along great."

"Except for the two you just wiped out."

"Nope. You're wrong. Grudges are against the rules. They'll be back in a month. If they're not, I'll look for them. Do you remember the way Maguire used to be in school?"

"Do I remember? I got scars all over my body that won't let me forget."

"But I'll bet he was your favorite priest when you were growing up."

I thought for a second. "Yeah," I agreed, "he was."

"He was everybody's. Kids don't want a big buddy."

Finally, after midnight, we were alone together for the first time. In the rectory kitchen Mike took two bottles of beer out of the refrigerator and plunked them on the table.

"Isn't O'Donnell a great old guy?" he asked as he looked for an opener. "He reads. He's on top of everything that comes out."

"Yeah... well..." I started picking away at the label of the bottle in front of me.

"Well, what?"

"It's just... well... isn't it sort of like visiting Grandpa and never getting to go home? I mean, why do they have to put guys in their twenties with these ancient people?"

"It's not that bad. It's just that the changes ..."

"Holy Innocents is a goddamned zoo," I blurted out, cutting him off in mid-sentence.

"Well, you're caught in that Una Via trap. I think Maguire is just letting Fufferd and those birds hang themselves. They look like idiots on the news."

Now that I was with him, I couldn't even tell him what I had wanted so desperately to see him about. I had peeled off the whole front of my beer bottle. I sat staring at it.

"Want another label?" he offered, pushing his bottle toward me.

"Mike..." I didn't know how to begin. Then, because the form of the sacrament seemed to make it easier, I asked, "Can I go to confession?"

He looked surprised. I had once jokingly told him that I would rather go to hell than go to confession to him. "Sure," he said.

"Well . . . okay . . . I, uh . . . well, bless me, Father, for I have sinned . . ."

I paused for a second, then began speaking rapidly, "I've been . . .

171

having intercourse ... a lot ... with a nurse from the hospital. I don't know how it happened, Mike. It started about a month ago. It happened just the once ... and then all of a sudden, it's become a part of my life. And I can't stop it. It's like ... when I'm with her is the only time I feel like a human being ... and everything else is so messed up." I started to cry.

"What about her?" Mike asked.

I got hold of myself. "She doesn't give a healthy crap," I said. "She doesn't think anything of it."

"Don't be stupid ..."

"No, really. She's a beautiful person. She really is. She's one of the most naturally Christian people I know. But her idea of emotional involvement is to say: 'Hey, you know, you're a great lay.' Each time we climb out of bed she scores me on performance, like I was taking a road test or something."

I couldn't tell if Mike was angry, or puzzled, or what. His red eyebrows were knotted; he sat studying me. Then he asked, "You using anything?"

"What?"

He sounded angry. "Like a rubber. I can see you being dumb enough to be screwing somebody and being afraid to disobey the Pope about birth control."

Somehow it felt secure to have him putting me down. When we were kids that always meant he had the situation in control.

"She uses something," I assured him.

"Yeah, I'll bet she does," he said. "She probably had her tubes tied when she was ten."

"She's not like that, Mike."

"Okay, okay, she's not the problem. What are you going to do?"

"I don't know. I was thinking, maybe if I got away from there ..."

He looked at me almost pleadingly. "Dennie, can't you just hold your water? You're only out a year. That's not enough time to adjust. Holy Innocents isn't the problem. You can't run away from yourself."

He leaned over the table and pulled my hand away from shredding the label, as if that suddenly annoyed him. "Can you do that?" he asked. "Just hold your water for another year until you've got your feet on the ground? Hell, you haven't been a priest as long as you'd have to put up with a tour of duty in the service. Be grown-up about it, will you?"

I said nothing.

After a moment he muttered: "Well, anyway, let me give you absolution . . ."

35

NINETEEN sixty-eight was a sick year for just about everybody. Lay people kept ripping their priests apart about the changes. Pope Paul issued an encyclical telling the world what it should do about birth control, and about eighty percent of the Church told him what he could do with the encyclical.

In the spring of that year, the assassinations of Martin Luther King and Robert Kennedy caused areas such as ours to become caldrons of hatred. Riots broke out almost nonstop throughout that summer. After a rooftop sniper shot and killed a ten-year-old not far from our neighborhood, we had to discontinue the children's program at Holy Innocents. Simply having white and black youngsters together was enough to spark trouble among extremist elements. Our neighborhood would be quiet for a couple of weeks at a time and then unpredictably, and often over a trivial incident—an insult passed, a window broken, or just the effect of a humid evening—all hell would break loose.

The night after that boy had been shot, a shopping district— owned mostly by whites—was destroyed in a devastation as powerful as a bombing in World War II. I had always felt as if I were well known and thus safe walking around the area, but the increased racial tension had changed this.

One hot afternoon as I walked past a group of black teenagers at a street corner, one of them yelled out, "Hey, whitey," and hurled a metal pipe. It cleared my head by an inch, bouncing with a sharp clatter off a "NO PARKING" sign.

I turned, neither frightened nor angry, almost calmly wondering what would happen. We faced each other. Futility burned in the boy's eyes rather than any antagonism aimed at me. When he said nothing and made no move, I turned and continued walking.

Even my friendship with George Brooks was burdened with a new strain. I told him about the metal pipe incident, saying, "It's frustrating. I've been getting along well here with everybody for a year. What the hell did I do to earn getting rejected?"

He was unsympathetic. "Now you know how we felt when we went up to meets in your end of town. Just us spooks and a thousand whites."

"I'm still me, though, George," I pleaded. "I mean, isn't friendship enough?"

"It's like Stokely Carmichael says," he spat, his voice acid with bitterness. "King getting killed was the whites in this country declaring war on the black race."

Even when things were at their worst that year, however, we kept running together. For all that we were living through, George was not a hate-filled person.

Nor were most people in the neighborhood. If anything, most people were gripped in an almost constant lethargy. When things were quiet, everyone sat on their stoops at night as convivially as ever. The atmosphere itself, however, was like dynamite. It needed only a spark for an evening to blow sky-high.

One night during dinner, Mrs. Cruz called the rectory so shaken with panic she couldn't explain what was wrong.

"Hurry, Father," she wailed. "Please, please, please come."

While still two blocks away I could see hundreds of blacks pressing toward the front of Cruz's place. From all directions people were leaving their stoops, running to join them. The air was filled with the noise of violent anger. Jerome Simmons stood at the edge of the crowd, hopping up and down with excitement. I grabbed him and asked what was happening.

"Man went after a kid with a machete," he said, barely paying attention to me. "The cops got him and put him in the spick's store."

This was a mistake. Cruz was white. What had been a simple assault was now, with the mad tension existing that summer, a racial matter. The fuse to the dynamite keg had been lit.

The police took the man, in handcuffs, from the restaurant and put him in the back of their van. For the space of a minute, after the whirling lights of the squad cars disappeared around the corner, everyone milled around in ominous silence. Mr. Cruz, frightened, stood inside his eatery, peering out. No law-enforcement personnel of any sort had remained. I wondered if perhaps I should move into the restaurant with Cruz. But it seemed as if inactivity would be best. Maybe the crowd would begin to melt and return to their stoops.

Then a beefy woman ran forward from the front ring of onlookers. She lifted a metal kitchen chair high above her head, then hurled it at the plate-glass restaurant front. It broke with a hollow thundering crash. The mob, as if possessed by one will, let out a roar of approval and surged forward. They pushed into the eatery, wrecking everything in sight, tossing things out the window. There was no time to think things out. I plowed, wrestled, and punched my way through to the door. Inside, I got to Mr. Cruz who was cringing in a corner. I threw my arms around him to protect him. Even as I tried to keep him from becoming a target, I was scared out of my mind that a knife or broken bottle would end up in my back, but the worst we got were sporadic punches.

In the space of a few moments, as suddenly as the violence had begun, the restaurant emptied. A number of police cars arrived and everyone dispersed, running away from the corner. Mr. Cruz was so shaken he couldn't speak. I helped him into his apartment where his wife and children waited in a worse state of agitation than he. It took me a good hour to calm everyone down to a level where we could even talk. I promised to come back the next morning to help them clean up, then slipped out a back door into an alley. The police were still watching the area out front. Without meaning the officers any offense, I didn't want to be aligned with them in the eyes of the neighborhood.

The newspapers would make it seem as if such scenes reflected a steady mood of the inner-city area; but once each riot was ended,

176

anger melted away like a wave receding from the shore. Everyday living resumed.

The very evening after the riot at Cruz's restaurant, I was helping a Baptist minister drum up support to get a block park built into two adjacent vacant lots. I was working my way toward his church some fifteen minutes before he was to start a meeting with city officials. Though it was 6:30, the sun was still piercingly warm. None of the stoop sitters whom I had approached were psyched up to listen to talk about community projects, but I was especially struck by the apathy of a group at one apartment doorway. They had been front-runners of the night before.

Sitting on the very kitchen chair she had used as a missile was the woman who had broken Mr. Cruz's window. Wanting to tell them I was still black and blue from the pummeling they had given me the night before, I smiled instead and explained about Reverend Small's meeting, getting from them a friendly round of, "Oh, yes, that's fine. I'll be right there," which really meant, "Get lost."

I was determined to channel some of their rioting energy into a positive cause. "Well, the meeting's going to begin just about now," I explained, pointing down the avenue to the Abyssinian Church.

"Right. I'll be there. Right."

I was as bewildered by their torpor as I had been frightened by their violence. "You're just saying that to get rid of me," I told them. "You're not going to the meeting."

One young man answered, "Too hot to move."

"Yeah, I know," I pleaded in anger born of frustration. "But how are you going to change things around here? You're always complaining about how bad the place is and how the sanitation department doesn't clean up. But it's you who've got to start. Reverend Small set this meeting up and he has people from the city government coming. Hell, if nobody is there the mayor will think we don't give a crap about the park and he won't do a thing about it. It's our kids who will suffer because they'll have to keep playing in garbage and broken glass all the time.

The woman who had thrown the chair was fanning herself with a comic book. "Well, I'm plannin' to be movin' out, soon's I can," she murmured, almost to herself. "To someplace a whole lot different."

36

I thought about Lippsy a lot, and about how what we were having wasn't a love affair. I *didn't* love her. At least not in a way that tempted me to quit the priesthood to make her my wife. Still, we had a great thing going. We were friends and we really liked going to bed together. It was second nature to Lippsy, about as serious a moral problem as eating after-dinner mints. To me, it was a torment. I felt like the worst phony in the world. Each time I spent a night with her I would leave vowing that it would never happen again.

But it would. Pressures would build up in the neighborhood, the hospital, or with the Adams family and their Una Via club, and I would be right back in the rack with Lips. Sometimes when I was in bed with her it seemed as if she were the only sane and normal experience in my life. But as soon as we were finished, the physical tensions released, Lippsy would drift off to sleep while I lay back amazed at what a shallow person I was.

Kudirka knew that something was wrong, for I would be gone whole nights, with the hospital beeper. He was too much of a gentleman to say anything. George, of course, didn't know. Every now and then, to be funny, he would suggest that Sister Marie Bernard and I could make it together and that nobody would be the wiser. I was tempted to tell him, "Will you shut up about it? I'm already balling with somebody three nights a week."

I found myself comparing Marie Bernard with Lippsy. The one had vowed her life to God's service: the other didn't seem to care if there was a God or not. I shrank from involvement with people. Only my sense of duty made me mingle with people. Yet both women were by nature compassionate; both reached out naturally to do good things for others. Lippsy would care for a neighborhood baby brought in with a concussion and, finding out that the child had fallen off a bed, she would get on my back until a crib could be found for the mother to use.

Marie Bernard was the same. She sought out situations for involvement. She noticed a six-year-old boy who continually clasped a balled-up handkerchief to his mouth to catch saliva. He had a severe cleft palate that could have been at least partially corrected but had never been attended to. She went to his home and all but dragged his lazy mother to the hospital. She refused to let up until the child was in the hands of someone who was committed to healing the youngster.

The occasion brought her and Lippsy together. I introduced them, fearing that my relationship with Lips would be transparent to Marie Bernard. Lippsy, however, was circumspect, as she always was at the hospital, and Marie Bernard gave no sign she suspected our secret.

My life would have been immersed in the world of Holy Innocents, the hospital, and Lips but for the force of Mike. He insisted that I take a day off each week, and that I spend it with him. Most often, during the summer, we went to the family place at the shore and took a sailboat out. It was good, and yet, each time we did, I couldn't fight the feeling that I was shirking my duty. One sunny day, drifting about with the calm air and sea, I mentioned this to Mike.

"Nope," he said, without reopening his eyes. He was stretched out on the bottom of the boat, his legs dangling over the side, "You're wrong. So was I four years ago."

"How?"

"When I first got out, I had this big thing about fixing the world up. I guess any guy who's worth his salt does when he's ordained.

But the thing is, Dennie, a guy can't be that way and survive. Especially the way things are right now. For about a year and a half I went at it twenty-seven hours a day. And then I started to dry up. I began to resent people hanging all over me. I overreacted to the fighting about the changes—the whole bit."

He opened his eyes for an instant, as if to make sure I was still listening, then he went on: "Some of my classmates began to leave the priesthood. I thought about it. Then, one day, Tom Boyle opened my eyes. He said to me, 'It's interesting to watch young priests. The most zealous ones get out and for five years they have time for everybody and everything. Then, when the glow wears off and the whole game begins to fall flat, they take up golf . . . or drinking . . . or a woman.' It's like distance running, Dennie. That's what *you're* good at. You're too smart to burn yourself out in a sprint. Go easy for the distance."

For a long while we drifted along in silence. Then he opened his eyes and looked at me. "What's with your nurse friend?"

After dinner, Gaelin's husband Harry poured Cointreau for the three of us. That I was Gaelin's long time boyfriend and, briefly, her fiancé had caused no tension during the meal we shared in their new home. I was part of her schooldays' scrapbook. Had she been tossed over for another girl, she would have excised me from her memory. But, owing to my priesthood, I was harmlessly relegated to the vaguely pleasant past.

Harry, a banker, was a decent sort of fellow, despite a proclivity to talk endlessly about the state of the economy. The evening had been mellow, made all the more so by plenty of wine. When I finally said that I had to get going, Gaelin remembered that I hadn't inscribed the gift edition Bible I had given them for their wedding. She got it from a bookshelf. When I opened it, the binding cracked. I was giving it its maiden use.

"Really into reading the Bible, huh?" I asked, impishly.

Harry laughed with me.

"Studying theology can't have clouded your memory that badly," he said. "If you wanted to give Gae something she really wanted, you should have gotten her jewelry. She's heavily into silver bracelets at the moment."

Gaelin, loosened with wine, declared:

"Dennie was never a gift-giver. I used to remind him of my birthdays a week afterward just to have an excuse to fight."

Lippsy had mentioned her birthday several days ahead of time. It never occurred to me that she might have been hinting for a gift. Had she been? No, I decided. Lippsy wasn't like that.

Gaelin had always been strong on doing the correct thing, and to her one of the correct things was not just remembering birthdays but giving gifts, like most people. Even now, her house looked like everything in it had its particular, correct place. What a contrast with Lippsy's apartment, always a mess, everything helter-skelter. It reflected a basic difference between the two women, I thought.

I had loved Gaelin. Even now I felt a strong affection for her. But she had always made sure we did what was correct. Even with lovemaking—if it could be called that. She had rigidly kept us within the boundaries of what was considered correct morality. In that respect, it had been a relationship of constant frustrations.

With Lippsy I was totally comfortable. Being with her was the only time and place in the whole world now where there were no rules, no expectations. It was the only time I didn't feel like a rusted tin man. Lippsy was giving, and a comfort to me.

She mentioned her birthday, only to bemoan the marking of another year, not to hint for a present. I would get her one, I decided, just because she wouldn't expect it.

On the way home, I stopped and rummaged through my car's back seat, which served as a spare closet and garbage bin. Running shoes, jock clothes, books, and church missalettes lay all about. I still had the as yet unworn T-shirt I bought at the rally. I held it up. "Make love, not war!" it screamed. There was a box containing a new black clerical shirt I had just bought. I put the T-shirt in the box and then decided I was cheap just to give her something I already had.

At a late night drug store I looked for something that seemed like a gift. Harry's remark about jewelry was still in my mind, and the store had a small jewelry display. I got a paste pearl necklace.

I honked as Lippsy came out of the hospital at eleven and handed her the box as she got in the car.

"Happy Birthday," I said.

"God, just what I always needed," she said, reading the box. "A clergy shirt."

"Open it up," I told her.

She pulled the top off, looked at the two gifts for a moment, then burst into laughter.

"'Make love, not war!' And pearls? Together? Oh God, Red, it's really me. It's the real me."

Her laugh subsided a bit. She reached over and placed her hand on my cheek.

"Even more, it's really you," she added.

The thing I dreaded most was getting an emergency call while I was at Lippsy's apartment. I had developed a mental fog; inside of it I could forget my priesthood while I was with her. The sound of the beeper meant not merely snapping out of that fog but having to move immediately into that realm between life and death where the priesthood meant so much to people.

One night I had to get out of Lippsy's bed to answer the beeper. The head nurse who had called informed me, "Father, you wanted to know if there was any change in Judy's condition."

"That's right."

"I hate to get you out of bed, Father, because she could linger on. But just in this last hour she's gotten much weaker."

Judy, the elfin child who had lost her wig my first day at Holy Innocents, had been in and out of the hospital four times during the year. This time we knew would be the last. She had wasted away to almost nothing.

We had become close friends, and each day I would stop at her room with a chocolate milk shake as a supplement to the bland hospital diet she loathed. Recently, she couldn't even drink the shake. She lived for what seemed an impossibly long time on sips of water or grape juice—becoming so fragile I was afraid, whenever she asked me to move her, that she might break in my arms.

Now, as I arrived at the hospital, her older sister was keeping watch, as someone from her family always had for the previous several weeks. When I came to the side of Judy's bed she smiled and breathed a small, "Hi . . ."

She had no strength to say anything else. I put another chair next to the bed and for an hour sat holding her hand. There was no

182

reason to talk. Listening would have been as heavy an effort for her as talking. But she was awake and her luminous brown eyes conveyed to us that she needed our strength. I felt shamed—the kind of strength she needed I no longer had to give. I wondered if she could read this lack in my eyes.

Once during the night she asked for a sip of water. Then, shortly before dawn, without so much as a noisy breath, her body released its hold on her spirit. After a few moments I thought of her in heaven, having regained liveliness and youth, looking down on me with eyes that could see my soul. "Well, Judy," I thought, "now you know what I really am."

If 1968 was a sick year for everyone else, it was a great year for Monsignor Adams. He had found a new purpose in life. Una Via grew by leaps and bounds. Newspapers and even magazines noted its progress, and during the year Fufferd was interviewed on a network television news show. It seemed as if their movement would eventually have to result in one of two things: a return to the Latin Mass by the American bishops, or a schism. Fufferd, in his television interview, insisted that if the latter happened, the bishops and not Una Via would be in heresy and departing from the "true faith."

Each Sunday the parking lot at Holy Innocents, guarded against the neighborhood by a contingent of hired off-duty policemen, was jammed to overflowing, with cars and even busses carrying people from considerable distances. As the movement became more organized, our rectory turned into one of its centers of operation—and a very lonely place to be.

37

GEORGE Brooks was my only close friend in the city at that
time, except for Father Kudirka, who was more like an
elderly uncle than a friend. Over the almost insurmountable barrier
of my middle-class white mentality, however, a number of people in
the area began to take me in. Mrs. Williams insisted that with the
size of her brood an extra plate was always kept for whoever might
be dragged in for dinner. Mr. Cruz was indignant if I didn't stop to
eat with his family at least once a week, especially after I had helped
him in the riot. In any case, the neighborhood stoops were a far more
comfortable place to spend evenings than Holy Innocents.

The evening was Indian summer warm as Rachel, George, and I
sat on the stoop with people from their building. There was an Una
Via meeting going on at the rectory, and Kudirka was away on a
retreat; so I was in no hurry to go back there, even though the
welfare checks had just come out and a lot of people were drinking
and drunk. As we talked, a fight between a husband and wife broke
out three stoops down from us. Both were drunk, both were yelling
obscenities, squaring off in front of each other as if they were
prizefighters in a ring.

George, sitting behind me, whispered in my ear, "There's the
woman for you, Dennis. If she gets rid of him, she'd be perfect for
you. I'll fix it up."

Knives suddenly materialized in each of the opponents' hands. They moved into the street where a small crowd gathered around them. Everyone on the stoop, including Rachel and George, got up. I went with them, but being the only white man present, I hung back at the edge of the crowd, uncertain as to what role I should play.

As the wife turned to meet her adversary, he shifted his knife to his left hand and with his right he swung out and punched her face. She grabbed him and locked him in a stumbling embrace. Then, reaching up between his arms, she cut into the side of his neck with her knife.

I held my breath. I wanted to pull them apart. But no one else had moved; I didn't dare. Finally, two men stepped in, dragged the man off and everything quieted down. We sat on the stoop again.

Jerome Simmons, magnetized as always by such scenes, came over and plopped down with us. "Man," he said, his voice filled with admiration, "did you see that knife? That was a K-55. I'm gonna get me one. When it's closed it's that long, but when it's opened . . ."

He stopped momentarily when he noticed that I wasn't paying attention. "Hey, Father, you looking? When it's opened it sticks out that long."

Then he pointed a finger at me. "Hey, if you supposed to be a preacher, how come you didn't stop them?" he asked accusingly.

I didn't know what to say. I was working up something stupid about folks working out their own problems, when George answered me. "What's the matter with you?" he interjected. "That wasn't his scene and you know it."

A police car had rounded the corner. "Maybe somebody called?" Rachel wondered. They stopped in front of our stoop.

Jerome jumped up, waving his arms and pointing to where the fight had been. "Hey, you don't want here, you want there!" he shouted.

The cop ignored him and called to me. "Father Hogan?"

"Yes?"

"The hospital's been trying to get you. You don't have your radio."

I clapped a hand to my pocket. I had changed shirts and forgotten it.

"We'll get you over there," he said. As I climbed into the car he added, "The hospital called the priest's house. The old priest there said to call us. He said you were out on the streets." The old priest? Father Kudirka was away.

"Adams?" I asked.

"I don't know," he said. "He said he was too old to go."

An hour later I walked into the rectory. In the dining room, the Una Via officers were working on campaign material with the Adams brothers. I stood in the doorway for a moment, watching them. They were in the midst of mailing out some sort of newsletter.

When she saw me, Mary Murphy interrupted the business at hand. "Did the police find you?" she asked.

I looked at Monsignor Adams who sat at the table's head. He had a cigar stuck in his mouth. He looked hale and hearty except for the effects of the evening's drinking, this "old priest" who couldn't answer the call.

"The man died before I got there," I said to Adams, ignoring Mary. I could feel blood pounding against the inside of my skull.

"Why didn't you go?" I demanded. "You let him die without a priest."

A fat, youngish man with a brush cut and thin bow tie stopped stuffing envelopes to stare at me.

"This is the one that won't help his pastor distribute communion," Adams explained to him through his cigar. "He's going to lecture me on duty." Then, not even looking at me, he added, "The hospital is your job."

"You let a man die . . ." I repeated, more incredulous than angry (the table was filled with the Una Via brochures) ". . . to do this?"

"You're to blame," Mary interjected, "for not having your radio. Now get on with you." They ignored me and resumed work. Pent-up fury had me so frustrated I didn't know what to do. I wanted to fling the table over and beat the daylights out of all of them. I could scarcely breathe. I turned and left the house. It had only been a few weeks since Judy's death and my resolve to live my vows, but I was overwhelmed with frustration. It was too much for me. I drove straight to Lippsy's apartment.

38

*H*ALF a foot of snow blanketed the ground when the call came from the hospital shortly after midnight. My car turned over poorly in cold weather. For just such emergencies I kept an electric warmer (connected by an extension cord running from the back kitchen window) plugged into the dipstick shaft. A howling wind swirled snow about my face as I poked about under the hood to remove the stick, and my hands were black before I finished. I cursed Adams while I worked. These were minutes between life and death. His own new Chrysler, that never needed to be used at night, sat in the heated garage.

When at last the car started, it took a frustrating amount of time to move through the unplowed streets. It would have been easier to walk. When I finally reached the hospital and rushed into the emergency room, brushing off snow, an orderly grabbed my arm, saying, "Over here, Father."

I always needed to brace myself for what I would encounter. As he pulled, I hung back, asking, "What was it—an accident? Are they alive?"

He was all business, failing to pay any real attention to me. I caught the odor of burned flesh. "Was it a fire?" I asked.

"Yes. Right here, Father." We entered a back cubicle as he spoke.

Without any further comment he pulled the sheet from a mound on a cart.

It was a woman burned to death. Her skin was charred black. Yet her eyes, a bright blue, were popped open, staring unnaturally at us. I looked down at the floor and prayed, "Jesus, don't let me get sick."

I was shaking and could barely take the top off the container of holy oil. I glanced at her quickly to position myself, then anointed her forehead without looking again. She had been alone at home, smoking in bed, had fallen asleep and set herself afire.

Within minutes after my arrival her two married sons, along with their wives, arrived. We took them into the waiting room and comforted them as best we could. Then the police brought in the husband. He had been in a bar and was drunk. The shock hadn't sobered him. He reeled and yelled his anguish. When he went in to identify his wife's corpse he threw himself on her, kissing her horribly disfigured face over and over again.

Then, his mind working in a bizarre pattern, he said, "We won't have an open coffin with this, will we, Father?"

We got him back to the waiting room, and he slumped into a chair, weeping in a half stupor. I went to the hospital kitchen to get coffee for the sons and their wives. When I returned, the two young men were whispering heatedly.

They stopped arguing when I entered the room. The cause of their dispute boiled to the surface when I gestured to the father and asked, "Will one of you be taking your dad with you?"

"That bastard isn't coming into my house," one of them snapped.

"You take him," the other cut in. "I don't want him near the kids."

I was dumbfounded. "What?" I exclaimed.

The older son gestured to the room where his mother's body lay, and said, "This was his fault, that damned lush. He's left her alone every night for years. And now look . . . ."

I didn't know what to say. "Somebody has to take him," I ventured. "You just can't leave him here."

As we argued, the outside door opened. A stretcher was lifted from an ambulance. Dr. Stewart, who was a Catholic, climbed out of the ambulance and walked beside the cart, holding an oxygen mask over the face of a young man. The doctor looked at me as they went by, but made no indication that I was needed. I got back to the business of trying to reconcile the sons and father. Ten minutes later they came to some kind of a compromise and grudgingly dragged the old man out of there between them.

I thought again to check on the boy just brought in; but I presumed that if I had been wanted I would have been called over the public-address system. I went out, got into my car and had skidded and pushed several blocks when my pocket beeper went off. I turned around, angry at myself for not having checked the matter out.

This family was gathered near the fourth-floor intensive care unit. Again brothers, four of them; and one young woman. They stood around a thin woman with silver-blonde hair who sat clutching rosary beads in her trembling hands.

She stood when I approached. I took her hand. "Father," she said, "we saw you downstairs. I was hoping you'd come up. It's my son Bill. He's very sick; it's his kidneys."

I left them and went into the room. The intensive care unit staff and Dr. Stewart were working on him. Machines surrounded his bed. Dr. Stewart looked up at me and shook his head. "It doesn't look too good, Father," he whispered. "Start praying."

I looked at the young man on the bed—tubes and electronic devices attached to his body. He looked to be my own age. Carefully keeping out of the staff's way, I read the full form of the anointing, whispering into his ear as if he were conscious. "Return this man to your Church, Lord," I prayed. ". . . Grant him health in soul and body."

I went out and joined the family. The mother sat, her head down, intent on her prayers. The girl, who hadn't spoken before, stood up and smiled wearily. "I'm Bill's wife, Father," she said. Then she added, "We were married three weeks ago."

"It's pneumonia," one of the brothers offered. "He's always had bad kidneys. Ever since he was a baby."

I thought of how repulsive the display of the brothers downstairs had been. In contrast this family seemed so much like my own. Their mother even looked like my own mom. I sat with them, knowing from what I had seen in the intensive care unit that this would almost certainly be a deathwatch. I tried to pray, but the burned woman's face kept flashing into my mind. I felt sick to my stomach with tension.

We waited for an hour and a half, attempting every now and then to talk. But for the most part, we remained silent. At last Dr. Stewart came out of the room and told us that Bill was gone. As expected as the announcement had been, it crushed the family. The mother put her hands to her mouth to stifle a sob; the brothers turned away. Dr. Stewart, a family friend, put his arms around the mother. I felt terribly awkward. I should have had something to say, something that could comfort. I was struck dumb. The mother reached up and took both my hands. Tears ran down her face. She kept saying, "Oh, Father, St. Ann failed me. She failed me."

I tried but couldn't say anything. A nurse insisted on giving each member of the family a tranquilizer. Then we sat for a long time. They walked to where Bill lay to look at him one last time. Then there was nothing else to do. We put on our coats, and I walked with them to their car. The wind had died down; the snow fell now in heavy silent flakes. Bill's bride helped her mother-in-law into the car, then turned to me and said, "Thank you, Father. You were so good to us."

As they drove away, I thought to myself, "Why 'good'? What did I do but stand and gawk helplessly?"

I drove back to Holy Innocents, pushing slowly through the half-plowed drifts. In the church parking lot, the car crunched to a stop in front of a street light. Exhausted, enveloped in warmth from the car's heater, I sat staring ahead. A song written after the assassinations of Kennedy and King played on the car radio:

> *. . . Has anybody here seen my old friend*
> *Bobby . . .*
> *Can you tell me where he's gone . . .*

It had been such a sick year. I turned the car off and kept staring ahead. The quiet of the storm seemed to move me out of reality. Snowflakes floated and danced about the light. But they had turned black. I watched them, only half conscious that I did so through tears. Then I leaned my head against the wheel and fell asleep. At dawn Sister Marie Bernard, a snow shovel in her hand, awakened me, worriedly tapping on the car window.

190

39

$\mathcal{M}$ONSIGNOR Adams kept his forays into the neighborhood limited to a thirty-yard walk down the block to our convent. I sat in the parlor one Saturday evening as he left to see Sister Dolorosa, watched him close the iron front gate, and resumed reading the paper. His bellow of surprise and anger, sounding so much like the end of one of his sermons, launched me from my chair and brought Mary Murphy crashing through the dining room door from the kitchen.

Whatever preceded the scene that now occurred I could only guess at. A skinny middle-aged black man fleeing past the rectory had smashed into Monsignor. As they both got up, the man's pursuer rounded the corner—a huge bleached-blonde white woman fortified against the November cold only by her body fat, a brassiere and a pair of panties. The man held on to Adams, placing him as a shield between the woman and himself.

She, then, grabbed hold of Monsignor's collar front. As if Adams were the hub of a wheel, the three of them spun about in a circle, the woman screaming repeatedly, "You black bastard . . . you black bastard," while reaching over Monsignor's head to swing punches. It was a truly remarkable sight.

Mary Murphy rushed to the window next to mine, screeched in

horror, and then began pummeling me. "Call for help!" she shrieked. "Call for help, you idiot!"

"Help," I murmured, trying to keep her from blocking my view. "Help."

She spat in disgust and ran, her broom still in her hands, out the front door. Like the gong figurine on a life-sized Swiss clock, Mary stood at the edge of the spinning trio and flailed the broom up and down, hitting Adams at least as often as she connected with either of the other two. At length, perhaps realizing that the custom of sanctuary was no longer honored in the Church, the man pushed Adams into his adversary and fled, the woman following in heavy pursuit.

Moaning and gasping for breath, Monsignor was helped into the house, where he had three drinks to recover from his ordeal, snarled at me, got into his car, and drove through the closed garage door. He was admitted to the hospital with a concussion.

The next morning Adams, for the first time in Una Via's history, was not present to say the Tridentine Mass. At eleven o'clock I went out to face the church packed with his followers. They knew simply by my presence that something was amiss. At the altar gate I confronted a crowd whose expressions would have made the rioting mob outside Cruz's eatery seem friendly by comparison.

"Monsignor Adams is in the hospital," I told them. "Father Kudirka and I are the only priests here. Either one of us will be happy to say Mass for you . . . but . . . we would have to say the Mass in English."

As the congregation stirred I added. "I'm sorry, but that is what we're supposed to do in this diocese."

This was too much for Mary Murphy who, though she had all the authority of being co-pastor, lacked the power of holy orders. She stood up in her front pew. "This is Monsignor's Mass. It's to be said in Latin," she ordered. A hesitant smattering of applause followed— hesitant I was sure, only because of the surroundings.

"I beg to differ with the lady in front here," I said, as if I had never laid eyes on Mary Murphy before, "but the Mass is not Monsignor's. It is simply the Mass.

Again, as tentatively as the applause, a few boos echoed through the Gothic structure.

I didn't see the object thrown and had no chance to flinch. It caught me in the eye. Blinded by it, I instinctively turned, shielding myself from anything else that might follow. Nothing did. When I could focus my eyes, I saw the book that had hit me, lying on the floor. It was a St. Andrew's Missal.

The petty violence had stunned them to silence—and me to some kind of courage.

"I will say this Mass," I announced, "in English—after those who wish to remain have composed themselves."

A low murmuring broke out; people turned to one another. The aisles began to fill with an angry exodus from the church. Barely a tenth of the congregation had remained.

After Mass, I changed and hurried out to my car, determined to get to Lippsy's as fast as I could. Someone had let the air out of my tires. As I ran down the subway steps, I damned a whole litany of people.

40

LIPPSY whistled, touching the edge of my blackened eye. "You know, Red, you ought to get out of being a priest and into something safe, like rattlesnake wrestling."

"You wouldn't have believed it," I told her, "If the press ever gets hold . . ."

"You haven't been listening to the radio?" she interrupted.

"It was on?"

"'Near riot at Una Via Church when young priest refuses members a Latin Mass,'" she quoted. "You're a celebrity."

"Riot my ass," I said. "Three people booed and one threw a prayer book."

"I don't know, Red. I mean it. I can't see you putting up with all this. If you're so hopped up on helping people, why don't you skip all the crap and join Vista or something?'

"It's just this Una Via thing, Lips. They're an aberration."

"Are they?"

"Sure. Look at the hospital. That's the priesthood that means something."

She lit up a cigarette and started rummaging through the refrigerator, finding a wine bottle. "Do you know Mrs. Hanrahan on Three North?" she asked.

"Which one is she?"

"The fat one at the desk. She's got blue hair."

"Oh, yeah. She's nice."

"The hell she is. She's going around bragging how she wrote a complaint about you to the bishop."

"For what?"

"For giving communion to Protestants. She can't take seeing Jesus get chewed by unbelievers—especially if they're black."

I felt myself redden, not from anger but confusion. Mrs. Hanrahan always went out of her way to give a showy, loud hello. If she had such a complaint, why hadn't she talked to me about it?

"But they're not unbelievers," I shouted. "They wouldn't ask if they didn't believe."

Lips came over, put her arms around my neck and said, "She didn't complain to me, Red. I don't care. Come on," she whispered, pulling my head down, turning my swollen eye to her, "let me kiss it and make it better."

The beeper went off about 11:30 P.M. We'd been asleep. When I called the hospital, the operator told me that Bishop Maguire wanted me to reach him at a number she read to me. I dialed it and Maguire answered the phone after half a ring. From the background noise it sounded as if he were at a party.

"Where are you?" he asked. "I tried to get you at the rectory and nobody was home."

"I must have been up at the hospital then," I lied.

"Then we crossed paths. Where are you now?"

"Oh, now . . . ? Well . . . I'm in bed now . . . I came right home and turned in."

"I see. Well, why don't you turn your light on?"

"My light on . . . ?"

"Yes, your light. I'm sitting in the bar down the block, looking at your window. Turn your light on."

There was a long, long pause. Excuses never had come quickly to me. I looked at Lips, modestly holding a sheet over herself out of respect for the bishop's verbal presence.

"I'll be right there," I told him. I hung up and sat at the edge of the bed, wondering what the hell I would say.

Lippsy, who had no sense of time or situation, reached over and tickled the back of my neck. "So what can he do?" she asked. "Dock you three weeks' pay?"

I shook my head, murmuring, ". . . Probably just throw me out of high school again."

She climbed over and sat next to me, "Huh?"

I shrugged. "Nothing."

"You couldn't just cash in your chips," she suggested, "and do something normal with your life?"

I didn't answer. I got up and started pulling on my pants.

In my entire life I had never been able to get past Maguire with a lie. Instead, presuming that the best defense was an offense, as soon as I let us into the rectory I stormed at him for not stifling Una Via.

"What? Force them into a heroic position? Don't be stupid, Dennis. Let them show themselves as the childish individuals they are."

"I can't see you not going after someone like Adams," I insisted.

"If I go after him, I should go after you as well—for giving the Eucharist to non-Catholics."

Had it not been for Lips, this would have caught me broadside.

"That's not fair," I said. "At least that's a good. It's not something done out of hate like Una Via."

"Is that where you got the black eye?"

"Yeah."

All at once the absurdity of the earlier bedlam struck me. I laughed, "I was hit with a St. Andrew's Missal."

He stopped, looked at me, then laughed himself. "Oh, my God," he said, "what a terrible time to be a bishop! Right now I'm dealing with your old friend Mulqueen and his entourage. They're encouraging me to come out with a strong stand against birth control—so that they can be quoted attacking me. On the other hand I've got most of the chancery men at my throat for giving a hundred thousand dollars toward inner-city projects. Is there any such thing as a middle course nowadays?"

As he talked he went ahead of me into the kitchen, turned on the light, and put water on the stove.

"But let's you and me get down to brass tacks," he said, picking up a jar of instant coffee. "Why did you lie to me on the phone?"

196

41

BISHOP Maguire should have worked for the F.B.I. He didn't stop until he had everything right in his lap.

"You don't understand," I said as he leaned against the sink, his indignation growing with every word I uttered. "It's like that time I got arrested. You just don't realize how things are in today's world."

"Damn it!" he bellowed, and I nearly fell back. I'd almost forgotten about the time he swore at me when I was an altar boy. "There's one thing that never changes, Dennis. A man is a man and a woman is a woman. And if you're stupid enough to start playing games with chemistry, things are going to happen."

"I think we have a beautiful relationship."

"You have an escape, that's all. An escape from yourself. Tell me your priesthood means that little to you."

"To me? What about Adams? And Fufferd? Who's selling the priesthood short? Go after them, not me. I work like hell in the hospital and on the streets. The priesthood is fine out there. It's this place that's a hellhole. It's them . . ."

"I don't want to talk about them now," he cut in. "I want . . ."

"Well, screw you," I interrupted right back.

He swung out and hit my face so abruptly I had no chance to back off. His fist caught my swollen eye. It felt like a knife. I turned away, pressing my hand to my eye. The moment of violence had quieted us both.

Just as my dad had always been deflatedly contrite after yelling at us, so too Maguire pulled at me from behind, apologizing. "That wasn't a bishop hitting a priest, Dennis," he almost begged. "That was just me hitting you. Do you understand that?"

"Yeah." I nodded.

"I'm sorry." He tried to laugh. "I guess I forgot the time and place ... by about ten years. You sounded like a snotty brat I used to have to deal with." He let go of me and walked to the other end of the room.

"I should never have thrown you into a special ministry," he continued. "I should have put you—*you* of all people—in just a simple, ordinary parish."

"I know. I'm guileless. I'm the family retard. You told me."

He sat down and ignored me. For a long time he doodled with his finger on the table as if measuring something out.

"What if I put you with Michael for a while?" he said, half to himself. "O'Donnell is getting so old. No one would think anything amiss ..."

"You mean so he could baby-sit me?" I interjected.

"So you could get your feet on the ground in an ordinary parish ... That will be good ... yes." He had stopped listening, having made a decision. Thus, branded as a problem by a man whose love I had always taken for granted, I was sent into exile to learn how to be a priest. I tried not to think of Lippsy. I was almost successful.

Jensen's Falls was a small community little more than half an hour's drive from the metropolitan area. Yet, nestled in snowy hills and surrounded by dairy farms, it seemed remote from all the concerns that had so swamped me in the city. It was a town of colonial buildings and picket fences; in the center of its business district was a park where bronzed sentries guarded a memorial for those who had died in the Civil War. When I arrived in Jensen's Falls that January of 1969, Christmas decorations were still on the lamp-posts, and a large fir tree in the park was hung with lighted bulbs. A soft flurry of evening snow gave the place the appearance of a greeting card.

I took the greeting to heart. Besides the large county jail that gave employment to a good number of people in Jensen's Falls, the area housed a Catholic college that added a youthful campus atmosphere to the town. Simply to drive along Main Street was to awaken memories of a happy time when weekend forays with Eddie and a carefree gang of friends were the concerns of my life. The people of this town were of the same background as the people who had raised me. If I had been a failure with people who suffered in slums because of a sick society, at least now I would be able to be a priest for my own kind. I felt I was going home.

As small as Jensen's Falls was, its Main Street boasted two large, high-spired Catholic churches, along with two rectories, two convents, and two Catholic schools. This was the result of the influx of nineteenth-century immigrants that had swelled the small town to serve the needs of a textile mill now long gone. The newcomers had been Irish and Italian, and each had set up a separate religious ghetto. Though the ethnic divisions had blurred considerably over the years, the two churches remained—each half filled on Sundays, each fiercely supported by its loyal parishioners as if the other parish were of a different religion. The relationship between St. Mary's and St. Francis of Assisi had always depended upon the relationship between the priests assigned. In that respect, Catholic ecumenism in Jensen's Falls was at an all-time high at the end of the 1960s.

I had already met Fathers Bianco and Savage on previous trips to see Mike. They were perfect playmates for my wily cousin. Bianco had the face and mind of a Prohibition era rumrunner and Savage, borrowed from priest-glutted Ireland, seemed born to fit his name. The only misfit in the group was the genteel Monsignor O'Donnell, who appeared to be getting an education from the others, which a high school seminary teaching career and the carefully ordered pre-Vatican II world had denied him.

The four of them had formed a habit of sharing dinner with one another at least twice a week. On the night of my arrival, they gathered to welcome me. Though all concerned knew that Maguire had sent me to be straightened out for some reason, nothing was said. Instead they initiated me into the work that was carried on in a simple, ordinary parish, dwelling for a moment upon the duplication of parish services for so small an area.

"We tried to merge the schools last spring," Bianco said, leaning his elbows on the table and upsetting his salad bowl. "It would have been beautiful. Primary grades in one building, a middle school in the other."

"They wouldn't go for it?" I asked.

"Agh," he snorted, pushing a fist in the air, then bringing his elbow back into his salad a second time. "I laid it right on the line for them. Seventy-eight cents on every dollar at St. Francis goes into our school. It serves only thirty percent of the families we've got. We have two nuns—that's all. There used to be ten before the changes hit. Now I hire who I can. I'd have to take Jack the Ripper if he were the only science teacher around. So I said to them, 'Merge. Join St. Mary's.' Would they? Ninety-three percent voted no. And why? St. Francis has *always* had a school, damn it. And St. Francis always will have a school. They're so damn ignorant." He went back to eating.

"The meeting was a corker," Savage said. "I was waiting for them to yell for a rope to lynch the old man here. I even had a rope in case they did."

"You dumb mick," Bianco said.

Even with squabbles about schools and parish boundaries, these were still my own kind of people. I looked forward to moving, once again, into the world I knew.

I went to bed that night feeling as if I were almost being given a chance to start all over again in my priesthood. Before I drifted off to sleep, I thought back to the priests who had been a part of parish life when I had grown up, even to the old priest who had given me money when I was hitchhiking in France. What those men had been for me was what I wanted to be for other people. I slept easily and soundly that night for the first time in months.

42

ON my third morning at St. Mary's, wrapped in a fog of half sleep, I made my way to the church in predawn darkness, unlocked the doors for the handful of regular worshippers, and vested for the 6:30 Mass.

No real wakefulness had enlivened my system even after I began the opening prayers. It was when I looked up at the sparse congregation to begin the "Glory to God" that I noticed a woman performing what appeared to be a slow waltz in the back vestibule. She was so large and her hair so short, she might have passed for a man but for her long, blue, greasy coat and the graceful dance she was carrying on. I rubbed my eyes and looked again. She was humming to herself, stopping her movements occasionally to straighten a wall poster or look into a confessional. I was by this time fully awake.

With one eye on her, I nervously began the epistle. As I did, she stood momentarily at the back end of the center aisle, hands clasped piously, almost as if she were a bride awaiting a wedding march. Then, with slow measured steps, she started toward the altar. When she reached the rail I stopped reading. "Uh ... lady ... you're not supposed to come up on the altar," I said.

She shook her head as if in a trance, and with her hands still clasped piously she mounted the steps to where I stood. Four feet away from me, she lunged into action, grabbing my throat.

The handful of people sitting in their pews looked up, startled but unmoving. It was almost as if this were an everyday occurrence. Maybe it is, I thought. I had fallen so far behind the times battling Una Via, for all I knew this could be some outgrowth of the handshake of peace.

"No more rockets!" she screamed at me. "Got to send a telegram! No more rockets to the moon!"

"Okay . . ." I whispered hoarsely, trying to unclasp her fingers from my throat. "Okay. We'll talk about it later. Why don't you just sit down for now?"

"No. Got to send a telegram now."

She was bigger than I was. I struggled to get hold of her hands, wrenched them from my neck, and announced an intermission to the motionless audience, several of whom had continued saying their rosaries. "We'll be right back, folks," I promised.

The woman was easily enough propelled into the sacristy where I pressed her firmly into a chair. Then, assuming a tone which I hoped was parentally strong, I commanded, "Now don't you move from here until I come back. Is that understood?"

She put on a petulant expression but didn't move. I backed out of the sacristy as if she were some wild animal, went back to the altar, and said the fastest Mass of my career, waiting all the while for her to sneak up from behind and strangle me. At communion time, the sacristy door slammed loudly. She was gone.

O'Donnell and Mike were in the kitchen.

"Did you send it?" Mike asked, laughing.

"What?" I asked.

"The telegram."

"Who the hell was . . ."

"Virginia," he cut in. "She just left here." He held up a scrap of paper and read, "'Dear Mr. President, don't send any more rockets to the moon. Love and kisses, Virginia LaPoint.' You should have taken it during Mass. It would have saved you all sorts of grief."

"Is she a regular?"

"She's our resident weirdo. She's usually content to sit in her pew and imitate whatever the priest does. I don't know where she gets them, but at the consecration she whips out her own host and holds it up above her head. At communion time, she gives it to herself and leaves."

"What do you do about it?"

"Well, you see," he said, leaning over the center counter as if taking me in his confidence, "I've been practicing with a rifle. One of these days I'm going to pull it up from behind the altar and blow it out of her hands."

"Poor Virginia," Monsignor lamented as he shuffled about, getting his breakfast. "I'm afraid she's about ready for shock treatment again."

"Wait till you meet Willie, our jerk-off artist."

"Mike," O'Donnell admonished, wrinkling his nose in distaste.

"Willie likes to go to confession to the high school girls who work here at night," Mike went on. "About three times a week he rings the doorbell, tells the girl that he's played with himself three thousand times, and then runs off. When he leaves here he goes down to St. Francis. Whichever place he hits first, the girls call the other rectory and warn that he's coming."

"It's not that bad, Dennis," O'Donnell said.

"Right," Mike offered. "They're used to it. If you ask them who was at the door, they say, 'Just Willie,' like he was the paperboy or something."

"He always comes at the same time," O'Donnell went on. "So if you hear the doorbell around 7:30, try to get it before the girl does. That's all you have to do. Sometimes he leaves notes on the altar. Just wad them up and throw them away."

"I thought this was supposed to be such a simple, ordinary parish," I said.

"Oh, hell. It is, Dennie. They're our sane ones. Wait till you see a few of the folks at the home/school meeting tonight."

The meeting was held in the church basement that doubled for Mike's drop-in center. The somber middle-aged crowd looked wholly out of place in a room garishly decorated with peace symbols, fluorescent paint, and psychedelic posters. Mr. Baldwin, a squat fleshy-faced man with puffy eyes and a wide shining dome, was the president.

While waiting for the meeting to start he sat next to me, pointing disgustedly at the decorations. "This is no way to build up respect," he snarled. "You feed the kids on this kind of stuff . . . the next thing you know they'll all be down at the college joining in all that yippie, hippie business. I don't know what's wrong with our government, sitting back while all this protesting is going on. We could win this war like that,"—he snapped his fingers—"if they had the guts. We could move in and mop up Hanoi in a month. The problem is a lot of pinko fellow travelers in government, that's what's the matter."

"Yeah . . . well . . ." I began.

"We're being destroyed from the inside," he went on, uninterested in any response I might have. "McCarthy tried to say that and look what they did to him."

At last he had hit a point on which I could politely agree. I said, "Yeah, I think if the Democrats had nominated him last summer they would have won."

"I mean Joe McCarthy."

His inaugural to me finished, he pounded on a gavel, and the hundred or so adults settled down on the metal folding chairs to begin the meeting. The minutes were read, then we got down to the serious business at hand—sports. The C.Y.O. basketball games were almost over. Thus, a series of playoffs and tournaments were scheduled to last almost till summer. Plans for the parish Little League team, which Mr. Baldwin coached, were discussed, then plans for a sports night banquet.

When new business, presumably sports business, was asked for, Mike raised his hand and said, "I wonder if we could discuss a few of the rules about dropping youngsters from teams."

When this was given approval by Mr. Baldwin, Mike continued, "It seems to me that we tend to treat these little guys as if they were professional ballplayers. Now, the rule about throwing a kid off the team if he misses two practices—do we have to be that strict? From what I can see we could be creating hurts that might grow as the boys grow. I'm thinking of the Church. I don't want to see anyone bitter against religion because of a basketball rule."

Mr. Baldwin stood, drew a deep breath and turned to accuse Mike. "Listen, Father," he began. "I happen to believe in discipline. I know that isn't very fashionable with you people nowadays, but discipline is going to be a strong principle in any sports program I'm running. If some of these campus radicals had been held to discipline while they were growing, perhaps they'd have the guts now to stand up for their country instead of starting peace rallies and running off to Canada to beat the draft."

This led into an active one-sided debate, Mr. Baldwin triumphing easily over Mike's suggestion. I kept out of it. My own feelings about middle-aged high school heroes went back to when I was about nine years old. I was in Little League playing first base. A grounder was caught and thrown to me, an easy catch. I missed it. A kid on third scored, my mistake costing the game. I was so ashamed and frustrated I started crying as I came in.

As I neared my team's bench—my misery increasing with the rising noise of grown men and women shrieking cheers for the team I had let win—I saw one man leaning against the fence, pointing at me. He was fat, so fat his belly button was like a valley in his yellow stretch shirt.

He was jubilant over his team's victory. "Aw," he taunted, "look at the little crybaby. Boo-hoo, baby. Cry away, baby. You blew it."

It burned inside me. More hot tears came and I pulled my hat down, looking at the ground so no one could see my face. That man remained in my memory for years. I had seen his face in every screaming pseudo-hero at the sideline of any game that I or any member of my family ever played.

Looking at Mr. Baldwin, jabbing his pudgy finger at Mike, I saw that man again. We were not destined to be friends.

Every Monday night, come hell or high water and about two hundred fifty ladies, bingo was played at St. Mary's. On Wednesday nights the identical crowd of ladies would scramble to St. Francis' hall to play the same game. The V.F.W. post hosted their patronage on Thursday nights, and the Italian Community Center, along with the K. of C., rounded out their week. About the only institution in town without a bingo sign over its front door was the jail. There were women in Jensen's Falls who might not have seen nighttime television, or their husbands, in years.

Lined up and down the tables in the smoke-filled gym, they placed their bingo cards (sometimes as many as a dozen simultaneously) before the good luck charms that sat on the tables like tiny shrines. Using the same intensity and thought concentration that scientists might channel into sending men into outer space, they hunched protectively over their cards, placing the plastic markers on the numbers.

Responding with computerlike movements after each call, they

205

would fill their cards, looking left and right to check the progress of their fellow players. The intent silence was broken only by occasional yells of, "Shake 'em up!" When a number was called out erroneously, thus necessitating a recall, they would sit up straight, turn, and of single heart and voice boo the luckless caller. Each time a win was claimed, everybody sat tight until it was verified by the hand of the officials and the eyes of every woman in the vicinity.

I was put on a work detail selling extra playing cards between games. I walked about the aisles along with the other men, a money belt tied around my waist, hawking my cards. I did this my first Monday night in the parish, drawing silent pride from my ability to sell greater quantities than any of the other men on the floor. Then I found out why. I bumped into another seller as he approached an old woman beckoning for more cards. Seeing me, she pushed the man off and pulled me toward her, saying, "No, I get from Father . . . blessed hands."

After that I gave up sales and took to calling numbers with Mike. One of us would yell out the number picked from the bin, while the other would light the illuminated corresponding number on the large electric bingo board behind us. I wasn't too bright and frequently called or lit the wrong number, causing the sweat-prone crowd in front of us to boil over.

On my second Monday in St. Mary's, I sat at the head table, surveying the women as they waddled to their seats and set up their shrines. I turned to Mike, commenting, "Christ, what a zoo." My voice echoed from the rafters. I swear I didn't know the mike was on.

43

THE jail stood like a fortress about 200 yards back from the main highway. Mike took me to show me the ropes. We stood in the dirty slush of a week-old snow, staring together at the blackened stone of the outer walls. It looked like an old castle.

Mike clapped me on the back, saying, "Remind you of anything, Dennis?"

"Yeah," I replied, laughing to cover up my nervousness. "We're supposed to bring back her broomstick, aren't we?"

"Close. Every time I walk up this driveway I think of St. Bernardine's. I'll bet that's why Catholic priests make the best chaplains. All those fighting Father Duffys—they weren't so much bucking their wardens as their rectors."

"It is intimidating," I said. "Look at the place. No wonder the college is always protesting about it."

"Oh, hell, they're assholes, Dennie. They're protesting about stuff that bleeding hearts have harped on for the last hundred years. They want them to have soft toilet paper in the crapper, and make the guards take the Dale Carnegie course."

"Well?"

"I mean, they're angry because the jail is a jail. They think everybody in there is Adam before the fall. Some of the inmates here would just as soon kick the shit out of you as look at you."

We had walked to the front gate. Through a heavy glass window a guard recognized Mike, waved and threw a switch. We entered a vestibule. As the door shut behind us, a second door like the first opened. In the bare green hallway to which we were admitted, a thin, older guard greeted us.

"Hey, Sergeant," Mike said, "how's your wife doing?"

"Much better, Father. She ought to be up and around in another week or so . . . hoping, anyway. You going up in the tiers?"

"Yeah."

"Wait till I get the keys."

He led us up a long, wide stairway to the second floor. Turning, he looked at my shirt pocket and remarked: "I'll bet you don't smoke either, do you?"

"No, I don't," I said.

"Like I told Father, here, when he started: Keep a pack with you anyway. Won't hurt your popularity if you can offer a man a smoke when you're talking."

I was surprised at his thinking to mention a thing like that. I had expected that the guards would all be angry men.

The three of us went through two more sets of bolted metal doors. After the last, the guard left us. We stood in a wide expanse the size of a basketball court. Behind a wall of fencing were three separate wings of five-story tiers.

Next to where Mike and I stood, several prisoners waited at a desk. A guard dealt with them one at a time, taking down messages. A fat prisoner with black greasy hair and pock-marks on his face walked by us. He half waved and grunted a hello to Mike.

When he was out of hearing range, Mike, gesturing in his direction, said: "That guy committed sodomy on an eleven year old girl. Being sky pilot for someone like that is when I find this job hard to take. I'd rather hug a snake."

"How does he act toward you?"

"Oh, he loves to talk. He'll talk to you all day long if you let him. But you see, we've got to be as cozy with him as with the curly-haired kid who was busted for smoking pot. What I'd like to do is bring that guy to speak at the next college protest about this place. It would blow their minds."

When we reached the fencing separating the tiers, another guard unlocked the gate. A man with a large pot stomach, he barely acknowledged our presence, walking away as soon as the gate slammed after us.

"The guards here are as much a cross section as the prisoners," Mike whispered. "Trainor, there, doesn't like young priests. He drives ten miles to Monsignor Flanagan's parish, because the youngest assistant there is forty-nine. Of course, if this place burned to the ground some night with everybody in it, Flanagan wouldn't move from his TV to come here. But he's old-fashioned, so for Trainor he's a good priest."

"Did you ever have a run-in with him?" I asked.

"Who? Flanagan?"

"That guard," I said. "Any of the ones who act like that."

"Nah," he waved the question off. "I give it the old Navajo theory. It's like the parish. Half of them love you, half of them hate you. Who gives a crap? Hey, look. See that guy down there?"

He pointed to a handful of men playing cards at a table in the cell block.

"Which one?" I asked.

"The one with the cigarette in his mouth. He's picking up his cards right now."

"Yeah, I see him."

"He's been waiting twenty-three months for a court date," Mike said, shaking his head in disgust.

"What's he here for?"

"Murder. His wife. But that's not the point. He's supposedly innocent till proven guilty, right? Two years is a long time to wait for a 'speedy trial.' Do you remember that time you got arrested?"

I shot him a look. This was a helluva place to bring up that old business. "Slightly," I said.

"You weren't in jail for twelve hours. The whole crew of you who got picked up were well-off white kids. All your daddies and even your high-school principal came running to bail you out. Wait till you see the youngsters rotting in jail month after month for minor charges before any fat-ass judge gets around to clearing his docket. It's not the physical jail that's sick—it's our whole ass-backward system of justice. That's what the students should be yelling about. The physical jail here is a sideshow."

I asked, "What about bail? Couldn't he get out on that?"

"Well, that guy down there couldn't bail himself out if he owned

209

the mint. Bail caters to our class of society—yours and mine, Dennie, not theirs. The only way out of here for most people is to throw money down a well, paying a goddamned bondsman. They're the real criminals."

I had come to a stop on the tier. The emotions I felt starting this job were like what I had felt the first night I had been called to the emergency room at the hospital. The whole business scared me.

Mike seemed to sense this. "Come on," he said. "Let's take a walk."

He led me along a tier. At each cell Mike would greet the prisoner. Almost every place we stopped at, the man would get up, come over, and talk. Sometimes the man would ask Mike to make a phone call. When this was requested, he would pull out a pencil stub to take down information. The requests were simple. A man would want his family to bring a pair of shoes or a radio on visiting day. Sometimes a public defender had to be contacted about something.

At each cell the conversation between Mike and the prisoner was low key and simple. We did this for an hour, moving from tier to tier.

Finally, turning to me on a stairwell, Mike said, "That's all there is to it, Dennie. In the afternoons you can even play basketball with the teenagers here if you want."

I felt relieved by the ordinariness of it. "Not bad," I said.

"All it takes," he said, "is an ounce of understanding. Most of the people here are just everyday folks . . . just like you were in jail."

44

TOWARD the end of February I was doing my round of the tiers. I walked past a cell where a youngster slept, his face buried in his pillow. His brown, lightly freckled arms were folded under his reddish-blond, Brillo-like hair. It had to be him, I told myself. No two people in the world could have that coloring. I reached in, touched his arm and whispered, "Jerome."

The head popped up, angry to be pulled from the escape world of sleep. Then his face broke into a child's smile.

He clambered up over the cot, and impulsively reached through the bars to hug me.

"Hey, man...I knew you'd come here. My sister called you, didn't she?"

"I thought you were underage," I said.

"That was the last time," he corrected. "A whole year ago. I'm sixteen. My birthday was last month."

"Many happy returns. What did you burn down?"

"Nothin', man. I quit that stuff. That's for kids."

"What'd you do?"

"Aw, nothin'. I just kicked in a guy's windshield. He say my mother was a whore."

His face told how angry that still made him. I patted his shoulder, asking gently, "How long ago did your mother die, Jerome?"

"Four years. That's why I live with my sister. 'Cept she don't want me around." As if to justify himself, he added, "I ain't sorry I kicked in that window though. Next time I'll kick in his head."

"How long you been here?"

"Yesterday."

"What's your bail?"

"Thousand dollars."

"For a windshield?"

"That's what they say. If I can get a bondsman, I pay a hundred. Only I ain't got a hundred."

"How long would you have to be here?"

He shook his head. "I dunno." Then, his face brightening, he added, "Hey, could you get me a pad? I ain't got nothin' in here to draw on. Just scraps."

I looked at the corner of his bed where he had piled pieces of notepaper, already covered with the sketches. "Sure," I said, keeping my promise small.

I called a bondsman, dialing the first one listed in the Yellow Pages. In my stupidity, I had always thought that bond was some form of reduced bail allowed people of limited means.

"Wait a minute," I said dumbfoundedly after the terms were listed for me. "What this amounts to is that you're putting out a loan and getting ten percent interest in advance."

The bondsman presumed I was calling for myself or a member of my family. "Find something better elsewhere," he said coldly.

"I'll go to a bank and pay lower interest," I said.

He grunted a laugh that contained no sense of real amusement. "Sure you will," he said and hung up.

I did get a bank loan, for the full amount of bail; but the banker with whom I dealt in Jensen's Falls was apprehensive.

"That's no way to start off in that job, Father. What do you intend to do, bail out every other kid you meet?"

"I told you," I assured him, "I know this boy well."

"Grew up with him, did you?"

"That's not what I meant."

"That's precisely what I meant. He's a case you met as a priest, not a friend. If you don't keep your work separate from your personal life, you'll never survive."

212

I looked at him, attempting to unravel what he meant. After a few seconds, he stood up and took me to a teller.

"Fair warning, Father," he sighed, "and I mean this in a friendly way. If you come back for another loan like this, the answer will be no."

Jerome's sister had had it. So until his court date he was eleven hundred dollars' worth of my responsibility.

I hadn't planned beyond getting Jerome out. Only as he left the jail with me did I begin to wonder what I was going to do with him. We sat in a booth at DiVecchio's Italian Restaurant, where Angie DiVecchio outdid herself filling Jerome's face. Accustomed to mothering not only her own large family, but the hordes of area college students who frequented her place, Angie was avidly sympathetic to Jerome but not to my problem.

"Hey, hon," she said to him, putting her arm around his shoulder as he wolfed down spaghetti, "any time you want to move in with my brood you're welcome."

Jerome nodded, his attention remaining primarily on the mountain of food in front of him. Sliding into our booth, as if she had just realized the need for a quick decision, Angie demanded, "Why can't he just move in with you?"

"Well . . . the thing is . . . I mean I couldn't . . ."

"Why not?" she asked. "I read an article just the other day about single parents adopting. What's to keep you from adopting Jerome?"

"Well . . . I don't know. I live in a rectory."

"Aw, for crying out loud," she interrupted. "Priests aren't supposed to be made out of crystal anymore. You'd tell others to take kids in, and not having a job, your schedule's more flexible. You'd be home more."

"What do you mean not having a job?"

"Oh, shut up and take him home," she said.

"Could he stay here?" I asked O'Donnell. "We've certainly got the room."

The old man was at a loss. He kept looking through the hallway to the kitchen where Jerome was talking to the high school secretary.

"It's not the room . . ." he said in an apologetic tone, "but . . . we just can't be bringing . . . people in to stay here."

"Why?"

213

"It . . . well, Dennis, it just isn't done."

He was visibly upset. Beyond the front office, rectories had always been forbidden territory to all but aged housekeepers and relatives of the pastor. Customarily, it was the pastor's house; the assistants merely had a room there. Mike had already changed that quite a bit. Now, small parish meetings at St. Mary's were held in the priest's living room, men were invited in for beer after coaching the basketball teams, and at least once a month the college students who worked in the Room with Savage and Mike stayed for an all-night poker game. With a less good-natured man than O'Donnell, this presumption by an assistant that his rectory was his home would have started a small war. But now I was forcing matters a step beyond that.

O'Donnell stood in the hallway, his thin face pursed in confusion.

"We can't just put him on the street," I pleaded.

At last, unable to confront the decision head on, he asked, "Where's Michael? Do whatever Michael says to do."

Mike assuaged the old man's fears, and assigned Jerome to a spare room. When the boy settled next to a nervous O'Donnell in the TV room that evening, Mike poked me and whispered, "Tell Angie DiVecchio it's going to be a fair trade-off. We're sending her Willie the Masturbator."

45

ℱOR several weeks after our parishioners learned that Jerome was a part of the rectory household, we heard sporadic complaints about parish funds being used to support delinquents from the city. The parents of one of the girls who worked in the rectory, working on the presumption that racial intermarriage was being pushed, insisted that their daughter quit her job. The only person who pushed just a bit too far was Mr. O'Brien, the Henry-the-Eighth-sized Grand Knight of the local Knights of Columbus and no admirer of my cousin.

Alluding to Jerome's reddish hair, O'Brien passed a remark to a group of men outside the church one Sunday in March, wondering if the boy wasn't a long-lost brother of Mike or mine. In doing so he entered the one area in my cousin's life upon which no one was allowed to tread without danger. As far back as I can remember, Mike was almost always overly protective of Aunt Gert. As a teenager he had almost gotten into a fistfight with a young priest who questioned his mother's honesty.

Now hearing O'Brien, Mike walked over and yanked the huge man around, demanding, "Are you saying something about my mother?" Mike had turned red. He talked through gritted teeth.

"I was just joking, Father," Mr. O'Brien said, surprised at Mike's sudden hostility, and backing away from him.

"Try it again," Mike said in a low but menacing tone, "and I'll pound your face through the back of your head."

That lost us one parishioner.

A week later we lost Jerome. He disappeared, taking the living-room stereo with him.

"That little bastard," I said, studying the empty table upon which the stereo had stood.

"Yep. Poor little half-breed bastard," Mike agreed. "Afraid to fit into anybody's world."

"Eleven hundred dollars I sank into him," I said in exasperation, "and he goes and steals the record player. Little bastard. If I could get my hands on him . . ."

"Let's go then," Mike said and walked out of the room.

"Where?" I shouted after him.

"Where the hell do you think?" he yelled back. "Hawaii? There's only one place in the world that he knows."

Jerome's sister wouldn't let us into her apartment. With her door opened as far as the chain lock would allow, she brushed us off. "He ain't been here," she said. "As far as I'm concerned, he ain't gonna be neither."

"If he does come here, will you tell him to call me?" Mike asked and then added, "Tell him I'm not mad at him."

"Yeah," she agreed, as if ridding herself of a salesman. She shut the door.

"She's lying to you," I said.

"Why should she? She'd just as soon he was back in jail." He started walking down the stairwell. "Okay, where else could he go?" he pressed.

"Any place," I said.

We drove up and down streets hoping to catch sight of him, asked around without getting results, and finally stopped to see George and Rachel.

"I think he's taken off," I decided.

"Let me try," George volunteered. "You don't know the right people."

"The hell I don't," I said.

"You know them, but you don't know them. Right now, you're

guessing. I'll be back here in forty minutes and know for sure whether he's around or not."

An hour later he walked into the apartment, his hand in a friendly yet vise-like grip around Jerome's arm.

Jerome glared resentfully from one of us to the other. Finally he volunteered, "I already sold it."

I was so glad the search brought him to light, I forgot, for the moment, to be angry about the stereo.

Before anyone could say a word, Mike took command of the scene. "I thought we agreed," he said sternly, "that you weren't to go anywhere without permission."

Jerome looked back at him with a guarded expression.

"Did Monsignor O'Donnell say you could come here?"

Jerome shook his head.

"Well, I didn't and Dennis didn't. That means you left the house overnight without permission. For that, you don't go out this weekend—not even over to the Room. Got that?"

Jerome hesitated, then nodded sullenly.

"Okay. Let's get going."

"Not till everybody eats," said Rachel. "You're not getting out of here after I went and watered everything down."

About ten minutes into the meal Jerome managed to say, "Pass the bread."

In a few more minutes Mike told George that when Jerome had a basketball in his hands he could blow the drawers off any kid in Jensen's Falls.

Jerome smiled almost shyly and without looking up from his plate muttered. "None of them are good anyway . . . they're like playin' with the little kids down here."

"Hey," Mike said, turning to Jerome and tapping the boy's forearm for emphasis, "don't back down from what you are. You work up halfway decent grades in school, and you'll be able to write yourself a ticket for a college scholarship. Believe me, you're that good."

Before Rachel had cleared the dishes, Jerome had laughed twice.

$\mathcal{A}$S the early spring of 1969 melted the ice of a heavy winter, Jerome went from being St. Mary's token black to being the greatest asset Mike and I had. It wasn't because Mike managed to have the charges against him dropped, paying Jerome's accuser the price of his windshield. It wasn't because of the praise the high school art department lavished upon his natural talents. It was because Jerome could play basketball. He could play circles around the best hoop star in the area. And he was all ours. St. Mary's had finished a poor fourth in the diocesan league season, but with Jerome we became unconquerable in the post-season tournaments.

We Hogans were canonized for the moment, not so much for being parents as for being managers. Jerome became a center of admiring attention, surrounded by men such as Baldwin who dreamed of being the kingmaker of Jerome's potentially meteoric career.

The boy had no idea how to accept being a hero; he had lived most of his life in the role of delinquent. But if he was awkward in his new part, it was still a beautiful transformation to watch. He began to walk with a sense of assured pride, and if he was being used, Mike saw to it that he was being used to his own advantage.

Jerome wasn't the only person who remained in my life from Holy Innocents. Late one night in April, after I had gone to bed, Lipsy called. She had never done that before. In the city, I had always taken the initiative.

"What's up?" I asked, a little embarrassed.

"Oh ... nothing ... I was wondering how you were." She sounded nervous.

"Good," I said. "How are you doing?"

"A little lonely," she answered, her voice uncharacteristically small.

Something tightened inside me. I felt wedged between fear and desire. Throughout our relationship, she had always acted as if what we did was a matter of easy come, easy go. If it wasn't me, it would be someone else. Or maybe she had been trying to give me that impression.

When I didn't respond she asked, "How are the people out there? Anything like here?"

"Hey," I said, happy to get onto a neutral topic, "you know those people that used to drive in from the boondocks for the Latin Mass?"

"You're living in their hometown."

"Right."

We both laughed a little. Then there was nothing else to say—except what shouldn't be said.

Lippsy said it. "Am I going to see you?"

I didn't want to. I had been feeling for three months that I had conquered something in myself that was self-destructive. Now I realized that my "victory" was based mainly on geography.

"Well, Lips ... I ..."

"I miss you," she said rapidly. Then her words slowed almost to a halt. "I mean I need you ... a little."

I stammered a guilty protest. "I thought you didn't ... I mean, I thought you didn't get involved."

"I know. It's your magic charm, Red. You grow on people ... Anyhow, I feel kind of empty."

"Lips," I said, "I can't."

"Yeah," she laughed, "I know. Well, anyway, I like hearing your voice ... Record an announcement and I'll call every now and then—like dial-a-prayer."

I went back to bed. For twenty minutes I lay there, trying not to think about Lippsy, getting more and more aroused. I thought remorsefully of how wrong it had been to involve her in my life. The whole affair had been easy to write off as long as it was my personal flaw, not a two-way relationship involving the need of another person for me. She was still near enough to have. She wanted me. The tension of thinking about her was too much to bear.

I called her back. "You still up?"

"I'm a night person, I've told you that," she said.

"I'll come down."

I let my car roll down the slight incline of half a block before I started it. I was afraid Mike would come after me, as if I were Jerome going out without permission.

Forty-five minutes later I was in bed with Lippsy, back in the rut I had been in at Holy Innocents. When I was living in the city I had pleaded an excuse for making it with Lips. My relationship with her was the release I had needed from the frustrations of life with the Adams family, Una Via, the streets, and the hospital. Now, desolate and happy, I had no excuse.

47

THE mystery of what others believed, what my own beliefs were about the priesthood, was still beyond my grasp. One day in May I passed the cell of a boy who had been brought into the jail over the weekend. He sat on the floor next to his cot, thumbing through a paperback book. He was young, with long, clean, curly brown hair. In his green prison coveralls he didn't look too different from many of the other teenage inmates.

"Hello," I said. I had learned to take a slow approach, leaving room for a rebuff or sarcastic remark.

He nodded, saying nothing. Then he looked from my face to the collar. "Are you a reverend or a priest?"

"Priest."

His face stretched slowly into a reluctant smile. "Hey, Father."

"How're you doin'?" I ventured.

He shrugged.

"What'd you get picked up for?" I asked.

"Me and my friend took some medicines from his father's drugstore," he said. "We got caught. We got hit for possession of dangerous drugs."

"Is he here, too?"

"He got probation. First offense."

"How many times have you been arrested?"

"Two," he said, holding up two fingers as if it were a peace gesture.

"What was the other charge?"

"Stealing tires."

"Did your folks come down?"

"I'm with a foster family. They came."

"What did you get sentenced to?"

"A year." As if to defend the judge's injustice he added, "We had a lot of stuff . . ."

I must have looked unconvinced.

"Well . . ." he reasoned, "it was his father's store. If it's your own father you can't really steal from him, can you? So he got off."

He scrambled to his feet, dusted the seat of his pants, walked over to me, and held on to the bars between us. As if to change the subject, he said, "You know that Little Flower Home in the city? I was there. I know a lot of sisters . . . priests, too."

"That place is for small kids."

"Yeah. I was there."

"Your folks dead?"

"My mother is. My father's around someplace. I haven't seen him in about ten years."

"How old are you now?"

"Seventeen. Those sisters at Little Flower . . . boy, I couldn't take them. They must have been about the meanest bunch of people in the world."

"All of them?"

"There was this one, Sister Redempta. She used to beat the hell out of me all the time. One time I slammed her hand in a doorway."

"Weren't there any nice ones?"

"Yeah . . . There was this fat one . . . in the kitchen. She used to laugh a lot and give cookies. She wasn't bad."

"Why don't you remember her instead?"

"Yeah . . . I suppose. But they were still pretty bad."

He leaned back, holding onto the cell as though it were a jungle gym, and looked at me as if wondering what category I would fit in.

I searched in my mind for something to say. Just as when I had to talk to hospital patients with terminal illnesses, I didn't want to deal with the reality in front of me. It was as if everything had been stacked against him before he was born.

222

Then he asked, "There's Mass here, right?"

"Sunday morning—at nine."

"Do you do it?"

"Sometimes. Sometimes my cousin says it. You'll see him; he looks like me. There's an Irish priest, too."

He said nothing. So I added, "Okay?" then made to move on.

"Do you have to go to confession to go to communion?" he asked.

"Only if you want to."

"Could I go then?"

"You could go now if you want."

"Right here?"

"Sure . . . Do you want to?"

He thought it over a moment, then said, "Okay."

He let go of the bars, looked down at the floor for a moment, then, slowly, with a somewhat hesitant sign of the cross, he mumbled, "Bless me, Father, for I have sinned. It's been . . ." He stopped, his brow knitted, trying to recall.

"You don't have to have it exact," I said.

". . . Two years," he finally said. "I went with my girl friend. It was Christmastime."

"Okay."

"Let's see . . ." he threw his head back, closing his eyes for a moment. It was not unlike listening to one of the grade school children before first Fridays. "I swore some . . ." he said. ". . . I don't know how many times . . ."

"That's all right . . . forget the times. God probably knows."

". . . I fought . . . I had impure thoughts, some . . . I did impure things . . . I lied to Mrs. Johnson once."

"Who's Mrs. Johnson?"

"They're the family I was with. They're nice people . . ." He paused.

"What about the store?"

"Was that a sin?"

"Stealing."

"Oh, yeah." Then he looked at me and shrugged. If there were to be any more sins I would have to give them to him.

"That's all?"

"Yeah."

"What's your name?" I asked.

"Billy Morton."

"Billy," I said, tracing the sign of the cross over his head, "May our Lord Jesus Christ forgive you your sins; and by his authority I forgive you your sins, in the name of the Father, and of the Son, and of the Holy Spirit. Amen."

I felt ashamed somehow. I took my hand from the top of his head where I had ended the blessing and patted the side of his face. "Be good, Billy," I said. I started to move on.

"Hey," he said, "don't I get a penance?"

I turned and looked at him—looked at the bars, the small cell, thought of how long this setting might be his home. I came back to him. "Say an Our Father and a Hail Mary. Okay, Billy?"

That incident was not strikingly unusual. What caused it to stand out was the contrasting experience that occurred that same evening. Mike and Savage had opened the Room. I had remained at the rectory with two young people, to arrange their wedding. As the couple was leaving, a well-dressed man in his late thirties walked onto the rectory porch.

"Father Hogan?" he inquired.

"Yes . . ."

He extended his hand a trifle self-consciously as he introduced himself, "John Reagan. I . . . uh . . . I'm sorry to come without an appointment. This is sort of on an impulse . . . I was at the jail anyway, and . . . uh . . ."

"You're an attorney," I broke in. "I thought I recognized you from somewhere."

We walked inside.

"You look a little different close up, Father. You look taller from a distance."

"There are two of us," I said. "I think you want my cousin. We're both priests here. I'll get him."

"No, no, that's all right," he said. As if to draw attention from his lack of ease, he said, "That's a little unusual, isn't it—cousins as priests?"

"There are about five sets of brothers in this diocese."

"In the same parish though?"

"Well," I said, offering the excuse I always answered such questions with, "I guess so many people confuse us anyway, they figured

224

they'd put us in one place and get all the confusion done within one shot. Want to sit in the parlor?"

"That would be good."

He sat on the couch and lit the first of a chain of cigarettes.

"Well . . . I asked one of the guards at the jail your name—or your cousin's name. I wanted to talk to a priest. It's been so long . . ."

He hesitated, almost as if he were going to insist we forget the whole thing. Then, drawing a deep breath, he began: "I'm in trouble, Father, a lot of trouble. It's . . . I don't know how to make it short. You see, I've been into investments for the past few years and somehow, a long time back—not to steal, but just to keep things moving—I began shifting funds around, illegally. And not alone. There were several of us in on this. Well, Father, one thing led to another and the whole affair has become like a Gordian knot. They've caught up with us. They've got investigators in on a few of these deals. It's all bound to come out. There's no way of escaping an indictment."

He was talking about a world of which I was not a part. "I lost you somewhere there," I finally managed. "Did you steal money?"

He tried to laugh, choking on smoke as he exhaled. "It's not exactly stolen. It was used for the wrong purposes. It involves a little less than a million dollars. I've glossed it over for you. It would take hours to explain fully. It's so complicated, my own lawyers say it will take a court a couple of years to unravel it all. They say if a jury convicts me, they'll give me a standing ovation afterward for having managed to work out the whole scheme."

He stopped and then sat back, as if I were supposed to pass judgment on the matter. "Why see me?" I asked.

"I don't really know, Father," he said. "I guess, being knocked on my tail like this has made me think . . ." He paused, then went on. "I'm a Catholic. Nominally Catholic. I went to Catholic college— even Catholic law school. But I haven't thought of God, or about any teachings of the Church in so long I can't think when. This mess I've gotten myself into has affected my marriage . . . my children . . . we live in an attitude of mistrust now. I guess I'm searching for some basic values to hold onto again."

I looked at him for a minute, thinking of Billy, thinking of his backward, childlike confession, his stolen tires and paltry break-in. "I've got to say this," I blurted out. "It's bursting inside me. You see what the jail is like. I mean, I was talking today to a kid who's going to rot there for a year for doing practically nothing. He's got no one to help him. And here, even if you go to prison—and you're saying you may not—you'll never be inside the county jail."

He pulled out another cigarette, coughing another hollow laugh. "Well, it's like they say, Father: Never steal anything small. That way you always have your bail ready."

"But that's so unfair."

He reddened. "Father, you don't have to tell me that. If I hadn't already said that to myself, I wouldn't be here. I'll get to talk to a judge in court. I came here to talk to a priest."

His sharp reproof burst my hypocrisy. Deflated, I apologized. "I'm sorry. I had no right to make comparisons."

"Oh, don't think anything of it," he said, waving his hand as if I had knocked over an ashtray. "I'd better be going. Sorry to have bothered you, Father."

I tried to keep him from going, but he would have none of it. He was polite, but he had had enough of me.

I stood in the empty hallway after he left. I had blown it. The man had reached out to me for healing, and I had shoved him away. What a hypocrite I was, telling him Mike and I were in the same place to get all the confusion done with with one shot. Why didn't I tell him my cousin was supposed to baby sit me because I couldn't keep my pants zipped? What right did I have to sit in judgment of him? What kind of a priest was I?

48

AT Eastertime a petition to have me removed from the parish was sent by a sizable number of parishioners. The Sunday gospel reading spoke the Easter message, with Jesus saying, "Peace I leave with you, my peace I give to you." With Eddie in mind, I couldn't preach about peace. I spoke about Vietnam. I wondered if the attitude of the United States in waging war against civilians was very different from the tactics of Nazi Germany in World War II.

It was an impolitic sermon. It enraged the commander of the local Veterans of Foreign Wars post, who sent a letter to Bishop Maguire calling for my ouster. I was a traitor to God and, inseparably, country. For a week or so the matter caused a local furor. Even Mike was angry at me. "You dumb chickenshit moron," he said. "When the hell will you ever learn to look before you leap?"

I was stung by his attitude. "Oh, come on," I insisted. "Stand up for what you really think."

"Look, what you really think is one thing. How you deal with people is another."

"So I back down and agree with the goons at the V.F.W., right?"

"No, damn it! You learn how to handle them. Like that Una Via crowd. You only give them stature by railing at them. Make a joke of them."

"Of the war . . . ?"

"Yes. That's where students are wrong. What they should do is show up at pro-war rallies and cheer like crazy. Make it satire. Carry signs saying, 'To Hell with Civilians,' or 'America Rules the World'—crap like that."

The petition seeking my removal went to Maguire with my cousin among its signers. Mike had gone to the commander's house, reminded the man that he had served two years in the navy, and then praised the V.F.W.'s stand.

"You guys are right. This war is the best thing that happened to this country. Look what it's doing for industry."

The man had half smiled, unable to deal with Mike's encouragement. As he signed the petition, Mike added, "I was reading about those plastic bombs we drop. The ones that only go off when a human comes near. Great. Shape them like pineapples? Fabulous. You got to get these little goddamned Commies. The next thing you know, we'll have a bunch of eight-year-old gooks storming the Golden Gate Bridge. I say, Kill 'em all!"

The man looked blankly at Mike, his smile still draped across his face. If he thought anything was wrong with Mike's statement, he didn't know how to say so.

If Maguire thought anything about the petition he never said so. I wasn't removed.

Mike was a fighter, but after any clash, he insisted that peace be made. He even sought out the dislikable Mr. O'Brien after that man had jokingly insinuated that Aunt Gert was an easy woman. I could never have done that. Yet neither Mike nor I was antagonistic by nature—we didn't seek unfriendliness. The time of the changes somehow seemed to breed it.

The big hurdles still centered on the "new" Mass. At the monthly home/school meeting in early May we ran a gauntlet after initiating a folk Mass for the teenagers. Mrs. Sheehan, who disliked the Church's new wake service, used her authority as president of the ladies sodality to show up at wakes, after the priests left, to lead people in a second service: the rosary. She now led the charge at the meeting.

"The next thing you know we'll be having go-go dancers on the altar," she declared, her plastic bracelets rattling as she shook her finger at us.

Somehow Lippsy snapped into my mind. I thought of her laughing during the speeches at the welfare rally. She would be in hysterics at this meeting, I decided.

There was immediate support for Mrs. Sheehan from a man in the back row who half rose to add, "These guitars belong in a minstrel show, not church."

Monsignor O'Donnell, presiding at the front table, attempted reasoning. "I'll be the first to admit," he said, "that I don't . . . care for that type of music. If I were a parishioner, I would choose not to go to a folk Mass. That's precisely the freedom you have, my good friends. You don't have to go. Go to a different Mass. Go to eleven. The choir sings very simple music then. But if we're getting our teenagers to go back to church by having a folk Mass, isn't it a good thing?"

It was Mr. Baldwin, seated at the head table as the association's president, who objected. "Why aren't they just told to go to Mass?"

Then he turned to face Mike and me, saying, "I know for a fact that you teach the children they don't have to go on Sundays. My kids refuse to go. They say they don't have to."

"They're misquoting us," Mike said. "We tell them that it's important to go. We try to tell them why it's important."

"Do you tell them that it's a mortal sin not to?"

"No."

Baldwin began pointing at Mike as if he were a prosecuting attorney in court. "That's what we were always taught," he blustered. "Why don't you say that?"

"Because I don't believe it," Mike answered. "Do you?"

A ripple of comment ran through the crowd.

Mike turned from Baldwin to ask the crowd: "Do you really believe, in your hearts—did you ever really believe—that God would damn somebody to hell for all eternity for missing a Mass on Sunday?"

He waited for an answer. It came from Baldwin. "Well, how else are you going to get them to go?"

"Is that the reason you go?" Mike asked.

A woman with several children in the parish grade school stood. She said, "I don't think our children are learning anything about being Catholic. They don't even know what mortal and venial sins are. My children haven't learned anything about the rosary or first

229

Fridays. I mentioned Fatima to one of my daughters, and she didn't know what it was. The sisters don't even bother to look like sisters anymore. I'm telling you, I'm disgusted. It's no wonder the children don't go to Mass."

As she sat down her statement was lauded with a round of applause.

Mike got up and addressed the woman who had just spoken. "The reason young people don't go to Mass, Mrs. Hurley, is that for the last several years the only thing Catholic parents have been saying about religion is to continually tell their children what they hate about the Church. Most Catholics have never told their own children that they believe in Christ."

A small elderly lady raised her hand hesitantly. When she was acknowledged, she stood, turning to face the people behind her. "I think perhaps we are only looking at one aspect of these changes," she ventured. "We forget that things were so strict—religion was always such a fearful thing. I lived my childhood terrified of priests and nuns, and I imagine most of you did as well. I'm glad the changes happened."

Her eyes narrowed, and she looked away from her audience as if she were seeing a memory. Then she continued. "Almost fifty years ago I married my husband in St. Mary's. All my girlhood I had dreamed of my wedding day. My husband was a Protestant. We couldn't be married in the church. I stood in my wedding dress in that little front office at the rectory and Monsignor Flaherty married us over the desk. He didn't like my marrying a non-Catholic, and he was as cold and harsh as the surroundings. I cried all through the ceremony, not for the happiness of being a bride, but because what was happening was so ugly. I never walked down an aisle in my wedding dress. And my husband—God rest him—was the most beautifully Christian man I have ever known.

She stopped for a brief moment as if to compose herself, then turned to the front and said, almost fiercely, "I'm all for the changes. They were long overdue. I'm behind everything you boys are doing."

She sat down. No one uttered a word. Then Mike said, "The only thing is . . . it's not something we boys are doing. We are teaching what the Church is telling us to teach. Don't you all see that?"

Angie DiVecchio shook her head as if in dismay. "Right or not, Father, I just can't pray with the Mass in English. I miss the Latin."

"Angie," Mike said, smiling, "back in the seminary, there was a whole slew of Latin mottoes painted on shields all over the walls. And right over the dining-room entrance there was one that said, 'Fidem Scit.'" He pronounced the Latin correctly, giving the *sc* an *sh* sound.

"Michael, please," O'Donnell whispered.

"Feed 'em *what?*" Angie asked.

"Shit," Mike repeated, "Fidem Scit." He spelled it for her, then said, "It means something like, 'Know the Faith.' But that's the way it's pronounced. For six years I had to read that every time I went in that door to eat. The English is new to the Mass but we'll get used to it—and at least we'll know what we're saying."

Angie had broken into a laugh that tentatively spread through the room.

Mr. Baldwin, in defense of public morality, was not amused. "I can't see turning this into a vulgar joke," he declared, standing to look down on Michael, who was seated. "Our young people need discipline and the Mass used to be a symbol of order and discipline. Now what have you got . . . ?" He opened his arms in imitation of the priest greeting a congregation and, with a saccharine smile and effeminate intonation, lisped, "The peace of the Lord be with you . . ."

It was Monsignor O'Donnell who interrupted him. "Mr. Baldwin," he said sharply, "are you making fun of the Mass?"

"I am not," he threw back angrily. "I'm pointing out . . ."

Monsignor stood, cutting him off as he said: "You are mocking the holy sacrifice of the Mass, and I must say . . . I have never in my life seen an adult Catholic do that. I think this discussion has gone far enough." He turned and walked from the room, ending the meeting.

There were two minor repercussions. Mr. Baldwin, angry at having been rebuffed by Monsignor because of the new liturgy, began calling Mike and me "Butch Cassidy and the Sundance Kid" in his bar—and the nicknames stuck. Bob DiVecchio, who had broken into an open belly laugh with Mike's explanation of "Fidem Scit," had the motto carved with script lettering in wood and hung in his Italian restaurant where it quickly became a byword among the area college students.

Catholics like Mrs. Sheehan and the Una Via people had the

231

luxury of walking away from the changes. Those of us who stuck with the Church had to implement them. For instance, a liturgist somewhere (who certainly had never held a screaming baby) decided that the Church should try baptizing infants at Sunday Mass.

The O'Neills were good-natured people whose seventh child had just been born. They were active, interested parishioners; but they balked when Mike suggested that they be the first to utilize this latest innovation.

"I'm not worried about the baby, Father," Mrs. O'Neill pleaded. "It's the other kids. They'll tear the church apart during the ceremonies."

But they gave in. The next Sunday at the noon Mass, the hangover crowd woke up to see the O'Neill family ringed around the altar with O'Donnell, Mike, and me.

Mrs. O'Neill had worked herself into a lather worrying that the baby would cry. She had brought a bottle of milk, a bottle of water, and a teether. Even her hulking teenage sons, serving as altar boys, had been infected by her apprehension. The whole family tiptoed into the marble sanctuary as if they were a bomb detonation squad, holding the baby as if she were the bomb.

It would almost be better, I thought to myself, if the baby cried; anything to break the tension would have been a relief. Relief came from another direction. Jimmy, the oldest O'Neill boy and godfather, was handed the peacefully sleeping infant, and Mike began the ceremony.

"What is it," he read from the ritual, "that you ask of the Church for your child?"

In response came a loud muffled report of somebody breaking wind. It was so blatant I figured it had to be the baby.

Mike, caught by surprise and not using his head, looked up and whispered, "Was that the baby?"

"Well, it certainly wasn't me," hissed Mrs. O'Neill.

"I didn't think anyone so small . . ." he wondered aloud, then, catching himself, he looked down to the book and read on, asking the name they gave to their daughter. Their daughter answered for them with another report, sleeping contentedly all the while.

An air of irreverence began to infiltrate the solemn ritual. Jimmy looked up from his sister and piously commented. "And that's only her first name. Do you want to hear the rest?"

Monsignor O'Donnell, standing next to my cousin, shot the boy a menacing glare, reached over, and snapped off the microphone. A few titters of laughter rippled uncontrollably throughout the church.

Mike launched into the gospel reading, the story of Jesus talking to Nicodemus about baptism: "That which is born of the flesh is flesh, and that which is born of the Spirit is spirit . . . The wind blows where it will. You hear its sound but do not know where it comes or where it goes."

A third blast punctuated his words. That was enough. The entire church broke into a roar of laughter, the sort that only such solemn occasions can generate. The baby, startled, woke up, and started screaming.

When everything had quieted down enough to continue the ceremony, Jimmy lifted the baby over the baptismal font, whispering to Mike, "Why don't I back her into it and let her blow bubbles?"

"Jimmy," he warned, "this is a religious ceremony."

"You'd almost know it," he answered.

Afterward, Mike tried to calm the socially destroyed Mrs. O'Neill. "Don't worry," he assured her. "The next time you go through this, we'll have things all smoothed out."

"Like heck you will," she said. "But I don't care. I'm going on the pill."

49

*I*N the spring of 1960, my freshman year in college and an election year, the weightiest matter then sweeping the campuses nationwide had been seeing how many people could be gotten into one telephone booth. In the spring of 1969 campuses were starkly serious places. In mid-May a protest had been staged at the college by a visiting company of antiwar leaders. These were led by two religious order priests and a nun who had taken leave of her order to join them. They burned the American flag in front of the building that housed Jensen's Falls draft board. In the ensuing fracas they, with a number of the protesters, were arrested. They refused to post bail, preferring the publicity to be won by remaining behind bars.

The two priests wanted little to do with us jail chaplains. Our very job told them that we had to be part of the Establishment they were fighting against. An attempt to say hello at their cells brought only a cold rebuff. I was accustomed to this, however, for a number of new inmates would start off by ignoring us.

The matrons were unstrung by the presence of the sister. They were caught somewhere between respect for her vocation and a reaction to her person.

Gruff Mrs. Quinlivan greeted us, as the guard opened the door separating the men's and women's sections. "I try to help her," she said, her usually tough face a study in bewilderment. "She cuts me off. She won't even come out with the other girls. She stays in her cell. Believe me, Father, I don't know why."

"I do," the guard grunted, pulling the heavy metal door shut. "That would be bad press. She might have to say someone was nice to her here."

The women were out of their cells, sitting in the open area next to the tiers. A soap opera on television was building up to some kind of dramatic moment. Savage, Mike, and I received only mechanical waves as we walked past them. We made our way along the second floor tier to the sister's cell. She sat primly on the edge of her cot wearing a light blue business suit, reading a book. Even if we had no idea of her identity, we couldn't have put her in the same category as the rest of the women in the jail.

It was not that she would be picked for a nun. She looked, simply, as if she were used to the finer things in life. Moreover, with the other women, their almost slovenly body postures seemed to speak of a pitifully low self-esteem. The woman in front of us appeared sure of herself. She looked up only after Mike addressed her. "Hey, Sister," he said, "aren't you into soap operas?"

She stared at us for a moment, her frowning glance going from Mike to Savage to me and back to Mike. "What are you, the Three Musketeers?" she asked.

"Sort of," he said. "We find it's comfortable for everybody if we drop in kind of casually."

She stood and came over to us. The door was open, but she remained in the cell. We remained on the tier.

She was not unattractive, yet her face seemed devoid of humor. She reminded me immediately of a teacher I had had in first grade who had insisted on making me right-handed. "What are you doing for this place?" she demanded. The question was directed at me.

"Doing? I don't know," I said. "We just sort of visit."

"Do you know that this place has been listed 'condemned' by no less than three federal commissions?"

Mike, who had begun the conversation with an easy-going smile, moved on to her wavelength. In a tone as cold as hers he said, "What of it?"

"Well, don't you think it's your responsibility to do something about this . . . dungeon?"

"Hey, look, Sister," he retorted, "commission statements get publicized. It's everybody's responsibility. But I've got to work in here every day. I work with guards who are just ordinary folks. They're my parishioners. They didn't build this place—and they don't make its policies. If I were stupid enough to make enemies out of them they could destroy what I'm trying to do. I deal with the little guy—not systems. I'm not going to cut my nose off to spite my face."

"That's what's wrong with the whole Church," she snapped. "It's so easy to sell out and steal down into a comfortable little middle-class world. If more parish priests had the guts to stand up in pulpits and speak about things like this place and the war, maybe we could do something about them."

"Wait a minute, lady," Savage interrupted. I stepped back. This was going to be their battle. I was no match for any one of them. "If we're talking about comfortable little worlds," his brogue slipping, with anger to near unintelligibility, "the free-lancers from religious orders got it made. Those guys on the other side make it a career to come into a community, dump their crap, and run. They don't have to rub shoulders with the people they're yelling at, or baptize their kids and go to their wakes. All they've got to do is head back to their campus friaries, and pull up the drawbridge."

"They're in jail for what they believe . . ." the nun began.

"Oh, don't shovel that crock at me," Mike said, cutting off Savage who had opened his mouth to continue his argument. "You love the hell out of being where you are. If you go to prison, it will just give you time to write a book about your martyrdom, so the three of you can move to the Bahamas and live on your royalties. Don't kid yourself. You're on the biggest ego trip of your life."

"I'm interested in people, which is more than . . ."

"No, you're not," he interrupted, gesturing into her face with a finger. "You're interested in crowds, not people. In three days here you haven't made a move to share life with any of the inmates. And the reason you don't is because they're dumb. They're so dumb you can't stand it."

"At least I don't stand in line with the fascists who are killing the youth in this country." By this time she was practically yelling.

Mike pulled the tones back to conversational level and tried to reason. "I'm not trying to argue with your views," he pleaded. "All

I'm saying is you have no idea of who you're talking to. You go out and burn the flag and they're not going to listen to a word you say. Think of your own parents. Like my mom. She's the biggest hard-hat in the world. She's got to make this war mean something. It's got to match World War II. My dad died in the invasion of Normandy. His death meant something. And now that . . ."

"How can you talk about the past?" she broke in. "It's irrelevant to the boys who have to be cannon fodder in this mockery of a war. Tell them they have to be heroes because your father was. That really justifies Vietnam, doesn't it?"

Mike held on to the bars, looking at her. His face drained so white his skin seemed almost ghostly against his red hair.

I waited for him to finish the sentence he had started about Eddie. Instead, quietly, he said, "That's what I meant. You people don't, won't, listen." Then as if a storm had blown over, he added, "Well, let's put philosophies aside. Can we get you anything?"

"No," she said, "I don't need anything . . ." It seemed as if she were going to say "from you." She stopped in mid-sentence, went back to her cot and reopened her book.

50

O N the Friday evening after the protesters had been arrested, the college marched on the jail. The students were well organized. Around 9:00 P.M., about six hundred of them moved down Main Street in relative quiet. The police had been alerted for trouble; thus, squad cars were seen cruising alongside the students. None came. Everyone was quiet. They gathered in the park at the base of a large Civil War memorial whose cannons and bronze military figures formed an incongruous backdrop to the demonstration.

It was a warm night, so humid the air was misty. We stood— Mike, Savage, and I—at the edge of the crowd, along with the high school youngsters who had deserted the Room in hopes of excitement. A coffin was taken out of a station wagon and carried through the crowd. Up front, a guitarist had begun playing "Where Have All the Flowers Gone." The crowd sang, almost in a whisper.

> ... Where have all the young men gone,
>   gone for soldiers everyone ...
> Oh, when will they ever learn ...
> Oh, when will they ever learn ...

As if on signal, the students produced candles. As the small yellow flames began to glow in the mist hanging over the park, an eerie effect grew from the silence.

A girl with waist length blonde hair stood on the top step of the memorial. From a scroll she began to recite the names of boys from the area who had died. The list was long. With the earnest intensity of a drama student, she injected emotion into each name she read. Her pouty mouth and green eyes were too pretty. Front line protesters had militant faces and harsh ringing voices. She wore the right uniform—T-shirt, cut-off dungarees, and sandals—but her body was softly feminine, meant to be displayed at beaches rather than barricades. The roll of names seemed endless; alphabetic and monotonous. My imagination began to work as I stared at her. I fantasized her into a bikini that would reveal a soft, oiled stomach and smooth tanned thighs. Then I imagined her with nothing on. I saw her in Lippsy's bed and saw myself moving in on top of her to do some of the things I had become so adept at with Lippsy.

The girl was intoning her way through the Hs.

". . . Joseph A. Hoenig.

"Robert Hoffman.

"George J. Hoffnung.

"Edward A. Hogan."

Eddie! The name snapped me out of my reverie. Eddie. She was reading his name while I was fantasizing having sex with her. I burned with sudden guilt.

We had grown up, Eddie and I, in a puritan world where we had been taught to push such thoughts immediately from our minds. They were "occasions of sin." Until I became a priest, I had fought to control unruly passions that crept into my consciousness. I had disciplined myself to take custody of my mind, custody of my eyes. If a woman's body was sexually attractive to me, I looked away; I prayed and thought of something else in order to rid myself of temptation. Now, after having had sex so regularly and over so long a time with Lippsy, I had awakened something inside of myself that I couldn't control. A nagging sense of shame filled me constantly, along with an equally nagging desire for sexual release.

When Eddie had been killed we still lived in the innocence of childhood. Hearing his name interrupt my fantasy made me feel I had driven a wedge between myself and the innocence we had shared together. It separated me from him more than death had.

When the last name was read, the coffin was picked up and carried into the street. Wordlessly, carrying the candles, the students followed. I went with them. It wasn't a matter of joining a

239

protest. They had spoken Eddie's name. It was almost as if I was following his coffin a second time. The students moved down Main Street. At Baldwin's bar, a crowd of the sportsmen who made his place a club had gathered reserves to make a small mob.

As the students passed the corner at which they waited, the silence was shattered by something which sounded like a rebel yell. They had armed themselves with eggs. An avalanche of white missiles was hurled wildly into the line of students. Several people around us were hit. An egg splattered into Mike's ear. He winced, turning away from the hurler and toward me. Then he turned back to search out his assailant, fury coloring his face. He picked out Mr. Baldwin, still clutching one egg in his left hand. None of the students had reacted. They kept quiet; kept marching according to plan.

Mike, glaring, took a step toward Baldwin, whose mouth opened and shut once in a reaction of fear. I fully expected Mike to charge into the group and grab him. However, as if the silence of the students reminded him of proper comportment, he suddenly twisted his anger into a grin, held up his thumb and said, "Good shot, Baldwin." Then, wiping muck and shell from his face, he added, "You've wasted your wife's eggs. I'll bring her some in the morning."

The entrance to the jail was as forbidding as that of any defended fortress. A guardhouse stood by the machine-operated iron gate. Only one guard was on duty. Several police cars, however, had kept pace with the demonstrators, and now they pulled alongside the gate in anticipation of any trouble. With candles still lighted, the students milled about. Nothing had been planned beyond the march itself. The students looked confused. There was no one to protest to. Only the one man behind the window.

It was Mr. Donahue, the man who had once advised me to carry cigarettes for the prisoners. He could have moved away from the window or called for help. Instead he opened the guardhouse door, and walked out to where the students carrying the coffin stood.

There was an awkward silence. Then, apologetically, Mr. Donahue said, "I'm the only one you'll be able to see tonight . . ."

No one said anything. He continued, "I fought in Korea. I was wounded . . . I was there near the end of the war, when we were

trying to pull out gracefully. Those of us who were very young ...
well ... we just didn't know what it was all about. And then there
was no victory ... or loss ..."

He looked so alone, facing the students, I wanted to go up to help
him. Yet he seemed an impressive figure. There was dignity in his
quiet manner.

"Perhaps with all the confusion ..." he went on, "perhaps ... the
most fitting thing we can do now—if it's just between you and
me—is pray. Maybe we could pray the Our Father ... ?"

There was a slow, unsteady, murmured response of agreement.

Then Mr. Donahue began in a low clear voice, "Our Father, who
art in heaven ..."

The students joined him, almost hesitantly.

"... may your will be done on earth ...
... forgive us our trespasses as we forgive ..."

We concluded the prayer. Mr. Donahue looked up, his eyes filled
with tears. He turned, and went back into the guardhouse. The
students snuffed out their candles. The demonstration was over.

51

*M*RS. Baldwin was in charge of social affairs at the K. of C. hall. After learning that Mike and I had been present at the war protest, she declared that as far as she was concerned neither of us was to set foot in her hall, ever again. However, shortly after that, there was a benefit spaghetti supper at the hall, and it was expected that all the priests in town would be present.

"Hey, screw that," I said to Mike. "Mrs. Baldwin said we're not to set foot in that place, and I don't think we should."

"Aw, don't be a sourmouth," he insisted. "It will be a pisser. The Baldwins and that whole crowd will be there, and they'll all smile us in because they're too phony to do otherwise. Besides, even if they throw us out . . . who gives a crap? Come on. Part of the job."

I wouldn't do it. I was as petulant as an angry child about the situation. Bianco, Savage, Mike, and O'Donnell went, taking Jerome with them. After sitting alone in the rectory for an hour I decided to drive into the city to be with Lippsy. All the way in I felt depressed. I had divided myself into two people, both of them cheats. One was an adolescent lover, taking from a relationship with a giving woman while giving nothing in return. The other was half a priest who functioned well externally but who had become, while still new in the priesthood, brittle and unforgiving toward people who hurt him. I wondered if I could ever become a whole person in either role.

Pulling over to the side of the road, I told myself that I should swallow my pride, and go back to join the others at dinner. But I couldn't. I jerked the car to a start again and continued into the city.

Mike further nettled the local machine. Babysitting a weekly drop-in center gave him a vantage point from which to watch an ever deepening problem.

"Drugs are sold down at the railroad tracks and in the high school," he said from the pulpit one Sunday. "We have had to throw youngsters out of downstairs—your own youngsters—because they were high. Should this be a problem we just gossip about, or should we get together and do something?"

Outside the church, after the noon Mass, he was accosted by Judge McCauliffe who was an important figure in the local political machine. McCauliffe was angry. If Jensen's Falls looked bad, his party, which had been in power over two generations, looked bad. "Father," he called loudly as if to attract an audience, "you've got one heck of a nerve turning a pulpit into a political soapbox. You had no right to say anything like that in church."

"Political?" Mike responded. "I'm talking about a parental problem we've got to face up to."

"Look," the judge said, moving to within six inches of Mike's face, "there are no drugs in this town. I represent the law. If there were drugs around here I would know it."

"But I've had to deal with it myself," Mike persisted. "I've had to throw kids out of the Room who were high on something other than liquor. What was it, and where do they get it?"

The judge looked from Mike to Jerome, who sat whittling on the rectory stoop.

"You'd certainly know better than I, Father," he said, nodding toward Jerome. "And that's an outside problem. There is no drug traffic in this town."

"No drug traffic at all?" Mike asked. Their voices had risen. People milling about on their way out of Mass seemed embarrassed.

"That's right," Judge McCauliffe said. "This is a clean town."

Mary Ellen, a quiet, blonde sixteen-year-old who worked in the rectory, listened to the story with a smile of knowledgeable amusement on her face.

When she finally spoke, she said, "It's not like there's drug traffic in school. It's like there are kids who have stuff and they'll share it with others who'll pay."

Mike was sitting at the kitchen table, angrily stirring a cup of instant coffee. "I don't know what you'd call traffic, Mary Ellen, but that would fit my definition," he replied.

"You know what I would do?" she offered. "I'd get kids to call him up and agree with what you said. They don't have to say who they are. I'll even do it if you want."

Mike's face brightened. "Now, why didn't I think of that? Okay. get me a couple of kids."

"Man, I could do it," Jerome said, delighted by the drama that was developing.

"Forget it," Mike said. "He thinks you're the main supply for whatever he says doesn't exist here."

Mary Ellen got to work. For ten minutes, two of her friends, using two of the rectory's phone extensions, described for Judge McCauliffe the process of informal buying and selling of drugs that went on in Jensen's Falls. It was to no avail.

"Father Hogan put you up to this," he said when they had finished. "You sound like rehearsed recordings."

"Good enough," Mike said. "If he wants to play fun and games, we'll play fun and games. Mary Ellen, if I gave you money, how long would it take you to get me some drugs?"

"What do you want?"

"Anything. How long would it take?"

"Ten minutes."

"Here's twenty-five dollars," he said, pulling bills out of his wallet. "I won't even ask where it came from. It will be anonymous. Just get it for me fast."

"Sure," she said. She walked out of the kitchen to the front office telephone.

We waited upstairs. Over half an hour passed. Mike yelled downstairs, "Where is he? You said ten minutes."

"I'll call him again."

"Call someone else."

"No. I want him," she insisted.

"Mary Ellen, the time element is important."

"I'll call again."

244

In a few moments she called up the stairwell, "He says he can't get out of the house until he finishes his dinner."

"Oh, Christ," Mike yelled back, "what a world! My pusher's mommy won't let him out till he finishes his potatoes."

At last, it arrived. Mike came into my room holding a small cellophane bag filled with pot. "Let's go," he said, "delivery boy time."

At the judge's house, Mike banged on the door, ignoring the bell. When Mr. McCauliffe answered, Mike held out the bag to him, saying, "Judge, there's twenty-five dollars' worth of marijuana. I bought it from a teenager here in Jensen's Falls. You should have me arrested."

The judge took the bag and examined its contents suspiciously. "You probably had this in the rectory," he said. "That kid of yours . . ."

"Your honor," Mike said, "I have a feeling that you and I are going to end up accusing each other of being a liar before this episode is done with."

The whole thing backfired. In an overwhelmingly Catholic community where there was virtually one political party, an attack upon the local machine was considered tantamount to an attack upon the person of the Pope. When the story became known, propagated primarily by the high-school students involved, Mike's popularity with the students' parents sank to an all-time low.

"The funny thing is," Mike mused, "I'm in a position to blow this whole thing sky-high. If I were really the vindictive person they're painting me to be . . ."

"What do you mean?" I asked.

"Well, you saw the kid who sold me the pot, didn't you?"

"No. We told Mary Ellen we wouldn't look," I said.

"Oh, God, Dennis. You are simple. We said we wouldn't tell. We didn't say we wouldn't look. I watched through the blinds."

I wrestled with my conscience for a moment. "Who was it?" I asked.

He laughed: "Our own cute little Kevin Baldwin."

52

OR almost two thousand years it had been understood in the Catholic Church that a man who put his hand to the plow was not to look aside from his task until he himself was plowed under the ground. In the wake of the Second Vatican Council, however, old men who stubbornly refused to respond to the changes became a liability to the Church. A retirement ruling, effective at seventy-five years of age, was attempted in order to move the Church back toward uniformity.

Issued with lightning swiftness, the plan had its flaws. Age was not the only criterion to measure how renewed or not a man was. Pope John, in his late seventies, had been the initiator of the changes. O'Donnell, an octogenarian, was more educated and reasoned in his thinking than I. Yet, men like Fufferd and Adams, both around sixty years of age, would still have a decade and a half of destructive maneuvering before the ruling would squelch them.

O'Donnell was in the first wave of men hit. It was heartrending to experience. He was great with Mike and me. He had allowed Mike to become, for all practical purposes, the acting pastor. The idea of retirement hit him broadside.

We had a sort of ritual at St. Mary's. Each night after eleven o'clock news, we went down to the kitchen to have hot chocolate and a few laughs before going to bed. It was a comfortable way to end the day. The night that O'Donnell received word of his enforced retirement we sat despondently around the table.

At about twenty minutes to twelve, Mike, sensing the old man's need to talk, kicked Jerome lightly under the table. "It's getting late," he told him. "I'm only going to call you once in the morning."

When the boy had gone upstairs, O'Donnell sat quietly for a moment. Then shaking his head he sighed, "I just don't know what I'm going to do."

He started to cry. It was awkward. He wasn't the sort of man who showed emotion easily. Neither Mike nor I knew what to do. The old man trembled when he wept. He kept shaking his head as if saying no. When he had regained his composure somewhat, Mike reached over and put his hand on his shoulder, saying, "Why don't you stay here? You could be a kind of grandfather to the parish."

"No. The personnel board made it quite clear. They want the retirees to live at the seminary." He attempted to laugh, "God knows there's plenty of room there now."

He stopped for a moment, sighed and continued, "I suppose they're right to insist on that. There would always be the situation where the old boss would undermine the new man's position with the people."

"That could never happen with you, though," Mike said.

"Ah, but how can the diocese say to one pastor, 'You can remain,' and to another, 'You have to go.' They'll have to make us all go and that's that."

He said the words calmly. Then after a moment of silence, he insisted on changing the subject.

After that, he always spoke cheerfully about having some time to do things without being burdened by responsibilities, and told all who cared to listen that he looked forward to retirement. But I had never seen a man cry the way he had that night, and the picture stayed with me.

53

*J*EROME blew the whistle on me. We were sitting around the television, watching the Monday night ball game when, during a commercial, he asked, "Hey, where were you last night?"

"When?"

"When you went out in your car. I saw you. You do it lots of nights."

O'Donnell said nothing. Mike kept his eyes glued to the screen.

"Oh . . . nowhere," I said, glancing cautiously to see my cousin's reaction. "When I can't sleep I just drive around . . . that's all."

"Man," the boy pressed, "you must drive to the Pacific Ocean or somethin' . . ."

"All right, Jerome. Knock it off, will you?" I blurted angrily. Then, as if to normalize my outburst, I added, "Watch the game."

Only later, when we went to our rooms, did Mike stop at my door. For a minute he just looked at me. "Out of the mouths of babes . . ." he commented dryly.

"I do drive around," I insisted.

"Don't give me that crap. You go into the city to get laid. I've heard what's-her-face call you. I've known what you've been doing all along."

I counterattacked. "What are you doing, listening in on the phone? That's typically you."

"What is it, now," he taunted, "twice a week? It's like she owns you, isn't it? Stud service on demand?"

He knew nothing about Lippsy; nothing about how beautiful she was to people. He thought of her as cheap only because he saw the way I treated her.

"Well, all right, it's none of your goddamned business," I yelled. "Now get out of my room, will you?"

He turned and walked out. I sat on the edge of my bed for about ten minutes. It was the first time in my life I had ever dared take a shot at my older cousin. His quiet acceptance of my anger confused me. I didn't know what to think. Finally, I went to his room and knocked on the door.

I didn't apologize. I just sat down next to him on his bed. "I can't help it, Mike," I said finally. "I keep wanting to stop. I end up promising God I will—after each time. Sometimes I wish I could turn the clock back and begin all over again, never let this happen. And then, when I go down there, it's like I tell God . . . I figure after this is all over, I'll be a priest till I'm eighty. And I'll be a great priest later to make up for now."

"Seventy-five," he corrected. "You'll have to retire."

"Mike . . . don't you ever . . . ? I mean, what the hell. Is it just me?"

"No . . ." he said. "It's not just you. It's a lot of guys."

"Haven't you?"

"No . . ." I must have looked at him as if I were disappointed. He shrugged as if to apologize and slapped his hands on his knees. "I go out and howl at the moon sometimes, Dennie, but I haven't thrown that in, yet. Celibacy isn't impossible. Hell, we're denying grace if we say it is."

"I just can't stop. I really do try."

"Are you in love with her?"

I didn't know what to say, even to myself. After a moment, I said, "I love being with her."

"Hell, so would I," he laughed. "The only time you see her is when you're getting your rocks off. But are you ready to cash in being a priest for her?"

When I sat studying the rug without answering, he continued, "I think you've got to decide soon. You can't do both too much longer. She's going to destroy your priesthood . . . or you're going to destroy her . . . or both of you are going to end up destroying each other."

"I can't just pull away. She needs me now as much as I need her."

"Would you hurt her any less by pulling away a year from now?"

"I suppose not."

"And I don't know about you, but if I decided it had to be her, I couldn't stay a priest and compromise myself for a *day*. I would have to be one or the other."

"Mike," I pleaded, "I just don't know how to handle it."

"Dennie," he said, "You're not ten years old. You've got to figure that out for yourself. No one can do it for you."

54

THE first week of June, the month O'Donnell was to retire, Bishop Maguire conferred the sacrament of confirmation upon the older children in our parish school. A half hour before the ceremony was to begin, I left O'Donnell in the rectory where he was playing host to his priest friends and walked over to the church where Maguire had gone with Mike.

The two of them were standing next to the vestry case in the sacristy. When I opened the door they were arguing. "Of course it wasn't thought out," Maguire said angrily, as if he had just then gotten a word in edgewise. "Can you tell me what has been, in the last decade?"

Maguire turned to see who had entered the room. Satisfied that it was merely me, he turned back to Mike and resumed his defense. "I look forward to retiring, myself. Believe me I do. Ten years ago I was a simple pastor in a parish. I lived an easy, ordinary life. Do you have any idea how lonely it is to being in a position of authority? I want to retire if only to regain some of my friends."

"Okay, so you're in the hot seat," Mike said. "That's a different issue. I'm talking about the guys like O'Donnell who have gotten steamrollered by a moment of history. Who's supposed to scrape them off the pavement when everything has passed by?"

Mike had started gesturing with his arms. Maguire held up a

hand to shut him up. "Do you know you have a Messiah complex?" Maguire demanded. "It isn't all on your shoulders, Michael. Let somebody else carry the world for a while."

"I'm not trying to carry any world on my shoulders," Mike insisted. "I'm only . . ."

"Yes, you are," Maguire cut him short, then laughed in exasperation. "The cool, baby-faced card shark whom nothing bothers. Wouldn't you say that was the image, Dennis?"

"It's the Navajo theory . . ." I offered. Mike shot me a quick glare.

"It doesn't hold water, Mike," the bishop went on. "You're still the boy who got thrown out of school hustling to earn your sister's tuition. You're a worry-wart Michael."

My cousin reddened, turned, opened the closet and began yanking out the vestments for confirmation. "You're avoiding the subject," he said angrily.

"I am not," Maguire answered. "I'm working out something for the retired men. Just give me a chance, will you? You've stated your case, Mike. Now let it be on my conscience, not yours."

Mike shook his head and kept on sorting the vestments. The door flew open, and three altar boys came in talking loudly.

Maguire said hello to the youngsters, then lowered his voice to a private conversational level. "If you really want to worry about redeeming a small portion of the world, why don't you help me with something?"

"What's that?" Mike asked.

"Well," Maguire said, addressing himself to me, "when I began to rearrange assignments after this retirement business came out, I presumed I'd have to break up this happy twin act. It is going well, isn't it . . . even with the petitions?"

I blushed at the reference. "Yeah," I said. "It's almost like living at home again. It's so comfortable, after Holy Innocents I feel guilty."

"That other matter is all cleaned up?"

Luckily, I was already red. "What . . . ?" I began.

Mike broke in with an easy-going lie, "Everything's fine, Bishop."

"I knew it would be," Maguire smiled. "Anyway, I had planned to move you out, perhaps into high school teaching in the fall, but then two things happened. The parish realignment committee pointed out that the iron would never be hotter for merging these two

252

parishes here. God knows we haven't got enough priests to go around as it is. Then, while I was mulling that over, a man asked me if he could be assigned here with you. He'd teach an easy load at the college and just be in residence. It would be perfect. He's older. People could think of him in terms of a pastor, though he won't be. Then, gradually, with no one being the wiser, the priests of both parishes could ask to move into a sort of community together. We could let the merger happen naturally."

"Why don't you just make him pastor?"

"He couldn't take it. He's been in bad shape. But he's spent time away. He's dry and he wants to make it this time. When I suggested the college he was wary. Then he realized you were here, Dennis. He's very fond of you and . . ."

"Who?" I broke in.

"Ben Nolan."

"Ben?" I said. "I didn't know he was having problems again."

The church was beginning to fill with people. The sisters were busy lining up the children in the courtyard outside the sacristy window. It was no longer the place to hold a private conversation.

Maguire finished in a whisper. "The only enemy that Ben has ever earned in life is himself," he said. "He's one of the gentlest men I've ever known. All I want for or out of him is to see him happy and for him to realize what a fine priest he is. What do you think?"

The door opened again. O'Donnell, laughing, led a number of old priests into the sacristy. There was no chance for us to agree with Maguire. But that didn't really matter. Maguire had not asked a question. He had issued a directive. If I had disagreed with him, I wasn't at a point at my life where I would have dared tell him.

55

ON the day Ben Nolan arrived, the teenagers were running a car wash to raise money for the Room. I had come into the kitchen to get more rags. Ben was sitting at the table with Mike. At my entrance he stood. He broke into a nervous grin, then extended his hand to shake mine. I said a lame hello. It was a stiff and awkward greeting for two men who had known each other for so long.

I didn't know what to say without referring to his absence from priestly work. "I think it's going to rain," I announced at last, turning my attention to Mike. "You sure picked a great day for a car wash."

"I was listening to the radio," Ben said. "We're supposed to have thundershowers."

It was a stupid conversation. "I only came in to get rags," I apologized, happy for a quick escape.

"I'm on my way out," Mike said, holding up a laundry bag.

"Do you want help?" Ben asked.

"Sure," Mike said, "if you don't mind getting rained on. If the skies don't get you, the kids will."

Mike introduced Ben to the crew of youngsters. "Father Nolan is going to be staying here," he told them. "He's taking Monsignor O'Donnell's place."

"Are you the new pastor?" an older girl asked.

"No," Ben said. He blushed slightly. "I'm going to teach at the college. I'm only a resident here."

"Who's going to be the pastor then?" the girl pressed.

"Well," Mike said, jumping into the conversation, "that's kind of an old idea—having a pastor. We're going to have what they call a 'team ministry.' Nobody is boss."

Jerome, using his thumb as a nozzle, released the water pressure on the hose he held and shot a remark at Mike: "Nobody is boss? Man, I got to see that. What are you gonna do? Tape up your mouth?"

Ben was an easygoing scarecrow sort of a man. The hours we had spent clearing out woods together had been an oasis of contentment for me during the fight about the changes at St. Bernardine's. In 1966 Ben had saved my seminary career by taking me with him to Peru. We had traveled and worked, subsisted on beans, and roomed together.

Within an hour, he was as comfortably a part of the work crew as if he were back chopping down trees at the seminary. And I was at ease with him.

Jerome knew nothing of Ben's condition. But the boy was so outspoken, we knew it would only be a matter of time before he would notice that something was awry and demand a full explanation. We were watching the Monday night game of the week. Ben went to the kitchen, and asked if anyone wanted another can of beer while he was up. When he came back without one for himself, Jerome seemed to study him for a moment, piecing together a pattern. Finally he asked, "Hey, Ben, how come you never take any beer?" Ben smiled as if it were a question he had been waiting for Jerome to ask.

He replied: "I can't, Jerome. I'm an alcoholic."

Jerome's face, always brightly inquisitive, lit up with a special interest. "What does that mean—you can't take a drink at all?"

"Yep . . . nothing."

"How come?"

"It's poison to me, Jerome. If I started I wouldn't be able to stop."

"Just one beer?"

"Right."

255

"Huh..." Jerome sat studying him, fascinated. "How did you get to be an alcoholic?" he asked. "By drinkin' a lot?"

I was embarrassed. Jerome was blithely charging in where I would never have dared to tread.

"No. It's not just drinking," Ben admitted to the boy. "I let drinking become a crutch for me to get through problems I had before I ever took a drink."

Jerome pressed on, innocently intrigued. "What are your problems?"

Ben laughed. "You're about as subtle as a grenade, Jerome."

He paused, as if weighing how much or what to say—then shook his head, "My own problems really. Nothing that would make much sense to you—or that would take me less than three hours to explain."

I looked guiltily at the can of beer in my hand. "Does it bother you when others drink?" I asked.

"No," Ben said. "No more than to pass a bar knowing I can walk in and put money on the counter. What I mind is somebody forcing a drink on me. You know—those people at weddings who are so aggressive about buying Father a drink."

"What do you do then?" Jerome asked.

"Well, some people simply won't take no for an answer." He stopped and smiled philosophically. "I hold a ginger ale in my hand. People can't offer you a drink if you have a full glass in front of you."

Within a month after Ben's arrival, a real friendship developed between Jerome and him. Perhaps it was because they had both met a great deal of rejection in their own lives, but they seemed to go out of the way to try to build each other up. I actually began to feel a sort of jealousy about both of them.

"Jealous?" Mike asked, when I mentioned it. "Jealous of what?"

"I don't know," I said, "I guess it's like . . . I guess I had a role in both their lives . . . and both of them are moving into the role that I always had . . . with each other. Does that make sense?"

He looked at me a moment, puzzled. "Nope," he decided.

Then his face brightened into a sarcastic smile. He patted me on the back and said, "Don't worry though, Dennie. If nobody around here loves you, you've always got your hot little number burning the home fires for you back in the city."

I wished I had never told Mike about Lips. If I hadn't, he wouldn't be able to sit on me like an unwanted, second conscience. He didn't understand that when I needed to be with Lippsy it was almost beyond my control. I hated him because he didn't understand that. I hated myself because I didn't either.

56

*I*T was quarter to midnight, almost time to close the Room. A girl hurried in from outside and communicated something electric to the group gathered around the blaring jukebox. There was a flurry of activity, then a mass exodus toward the door. I shot a look at Mike. No doubt a fight outside. We got up and trudged wearily up the stairs after the excited herd.

It wasn't a fight. A state trooper's car, its red and white lights still flashing, was nosed in behind a beatup Chevrolet that I recognized immediately. Three boys were lined up, their hands on the roof of the car, while two troopers examined the license of the driver—Kevin Baldwin.

We stood, mere spectators, along with the gathered kids. Kevin looked over his shoulder, and caught sight of Mike. "Padre," he demanded, his voice thick with inebriation, "tell them to lay off, willya?"

Mike shook his head apologetically without answering. To the youngsters around him he quietly said, "Can't cross lines of authority, folks."

At the word "Padre" one of the troopers looked up. He gestured to us to join him, out of earshot of the crowd.

"We chased him all the way in from near the college," he said.

"Got him clocked at better than ninety. Get close enough and you'll smell the pot."

The second trooper was rummaging through the car. When he backed out of the front seat and stood up he was holding a plastic bag about one-third the size of a pillow. He opened it as he joined the three of us. Inside was a good quantity of loose marijuana, as well as several plastic bags of carefully measured pot. "Looks like a good business," the trooper said.

In a cell next to that of my young penitent Billy Morton (now halfway through his year's sentence for drug possession), Kevin sat naked, hugging his knees. His face, puffy in any event, was more so from a hangover. When my footsteps had sounded on the metal tier, he thought I was the guard.

"Hey, where's my friggin' clothes?" he yelled. Then, in a somewhat abashed tone after he saw me, he asked, "Padre... How come I ain't got no clothes on?"

He pulled his feet in closer to his body as if to make himself less visible.

"I don't know, Kevin," I said. "All I know is they do it when someone comes in stoned or acting crazy. I think they're afraid of suicide and so they leave a guy with absolutely nothing."

To make sure Billy didn't feel I was ignoring him, I backed up and asked him, "How you doin', buddy?"

"Okay," he said, standing up and coming over to the bars.

"I wasn't that stoned," Kevin broke in.

"Downstairs they told me you took a swing at the captain when you got here."

He frowned, leaned his chin on his knees, and ventured in an unsure voice, "I . . . don't remember."

"You were pretty much out of it when they brought you up here," offered Billy, separated from view by the metal cell wall. "You were kicking like hell. You told them you'd get them all fired."

A guard rounded the corner of the tier with a pile of clothes under his arm. Kevin jumped up and with a muttered "Christ," pulled each article through the bars with a resentful grab.

By the time we were alone again, I was getting angry. "There's no call to act like that," I said.

259

"Goddamned pigs," he snapped, stumbling as he pulled on his underpants.

"Wait a minute," I objected. "He didn't put you in here—you did that to yourself. He's just doing a job."

I caught myself. As he finished dressing, I asked, "What are you doing selling drugs? You don't need to do that."

"My old man does it," he shot back.

"What?" I asked, startled before I caught his meaning. Then I realized, "The bar? Oh, come on."

"What's the difference?" he insisted. "He makes money selling drugs. And pot doesn't rot your guts out like liquor."

"Did you get to call him?" I interrupted.

"Yeah," he shrugged.

"Is he coming down?"

"All he did was scream. He said they should throw away the key."

"He'll be down," I said. "You know the way he blows off steam."

Sure enough, Baldwin was in the front office when I came in off the tiers.

"What are you doing here?" he demanded, his small eyes angrily lost in a red face, thirty years puffier than his son's.

The desk sergeant looked up, surprised at the sudden outburst.

"I work here," I said.

"I don't want you anywhere near my boy, do you understand?" he continued. For the benefit of the confused sergeant, he waved a hand in my direction.

"This wouldn't have happened if him and the other one didn't have all that hippie, yippie stuff going on. I know where the kids get hold of any drugs there are in Jensen's Falls. It's in that place they got down there under the church. And there wasn't any of this stuff until they got that nigger from the city up here."

He turned his back to me. "The other one shows Judge McCauliffe there's a drug problem by bringing some to his house. Took him all of fifteen minutes to get it. Now you tell me, how far did he have to go to find it?"

His voice sounded fainter as he reached the end of his diatribe— not because he had lowered it but because I was walking out the door.

Kevin was released from jail immediately, and according to our dual system of criminal justice, his case was taken care of through political channels. Some technical fault was found in the manner of his arrest and the matter, but for a stern parental warning from Judge McCauliffe, was tossed out of court. Billy Morton continued serving his year for possession of drugs.

57

$\mathcal{B}$Y the middle of the summer, word had begun to spread about the proposed merger of parishes. At dinner Mike decided, "This will kill Baldwin. Here he's gone and switched parishes to get away from us, and we're going to move right with him."

"He knows already," Savage said. "According to the gospel preached over his bar, the whole business is a power grab by you. He hears you've got the bishop wrapped around your little finger."

"He wants to fight you with a petition," Bianco added. "But none of his friends know how to write."

"Ah, empire," Mike mused almost to himself. "It makes me feel like Alexander the Great."

His remark seemed weighted with depression. As if embarrassed by how heavy he had sounded, Mike quickly switched to a joking vein. "Jerome," he offered, "why don't you reawaken some of your childhood talents and just burn the place down for us? Think of all the problems that would solve."

"Make sure we've mailed in the insurance premiums first," Savage aded.

"And we'll all sit back in the rectory and pray for a total loss," Mike said.

"Amen," finished Bianco.

Jerome was frowning. I realized we had touched a sore spot that had not yet healed. We moved on to a different topic. Meals were no place to discuss problems.

Neither Mike nor I were especially talented dealing with very small children. After Ben's arrival we had to get used to the rectory being filled with preschoolers from the neighborhood. The kitchen seemed perpetually crowded with knee-high people getting drinks of water or milk, and draining our supply of cookies. Feeding the fish in Ben's aquarium became a sought-after privilege, and the elevator, which a luxury-prone pastor had once installed between the first and second floors, became a neighborhood amusement park.

Ben also seemed to have compassion for those at the bottom of the pile—perhaps the reason he befriended me at St. Bernardine's. Bums, and people who were disturbed, seemed to be his special apostolate.

Willie the masturbator, like Zorro, struck almost every day—either leaving notes on the altar, or spilling his confession to the high-school girls who answered the door. Everyone was used to him. Ben wouldn't let it go at that. If he saw Willie come up the walk, he would talk to him for awhile. Once, when Ben saw Willie off, patting him affectionately on the back, I was surprised to hear Willie laugh. I didn't think Willie had it in him.

Bums were something else. I didn't know how to deal with them. On the one hand, there was Jesus, breathing over one's shoulder to say we had to be Good Samaritans. On the other, it was evident that a man could make a fortune out of panhandling, simply by going from rectory to rectory. So we tried to make a habit of giving food, but not money. Ben sat with the bums while they ate, oftentimes for as long as an hour, listening to the interminable stories each man told about which priests he had known back in the 1940s and how he had been an altar boy—the story-teller stopping at that point to recite the Confiteor or Suscipiat as proof. Ben always gave them money. I told him he was being taken.

"Oh, hell, Dennie," he retorted. "Take a look at the stinking old suit coats they wear piled one on top of the other, and the head rags they use for hats. Feel their hands. They're like cracked leather from being exposed both winter and summer. Sure, they're trying to take us. But do you think there isn't a single one of them who wouldn't break out and become something else if it were humanly possible for him to do so?"

I started to object. "Well . . . I don't know . . ."

"Well I do, Dennis," he insisted. "I've been there."

While I admired Ben's capacity for taking care of people who were hurting, I began to see his inability to cope with aggressive people who used pressure tactics. Teenage pregnancy marriages were always sad, often ugly affairs that we had to deal with all too often. They were sad because of the youngsters, and ugly because of the irrationality of the parents involved. The family name was the only sacred value in these situations. A father who had been forbidding his daughter to date a particular boy he didn't like would, within a month's time, insist because of pregnancy that she be bound to the same boy for life in a sacramental marriage.

Ben became involved in such a case near the end of July. Both parties involved were nonchurchgoers, an important fact in light of the insistence placed on having a Catholic ceremony. The girl was seventeen, the boy sixteen. Both were immature, and their own solution to the problem had been an attempted elopement.

"I thought we could just go to a justice of the peace," the boy said, adding, "I thought that would fix things up."

"Why not?" Ben said to the parents. "That way they can be legally married, and wagging tongues will be stilled. If everything works out in three or four years, then get the marriage blessed."

"How can you suggest such a thing?" the girl's mother balked. "I won't have them living in sin. I want my daughter to have a church wedding."

"I don't mean to be abusive," Ben said quietly, "but let's keep matters straight. You've already missed the boat about them living in sin, correct?"

He got no response. "Gail," Ben said, turning to the girl, "when was the last time you went to church?"

She smiled timidly. "I don't know. Pretty long time, I suppose."

Having made his point, Ben turned back to the girl's mother, saying, "Again, if you were worried about sin—and if you are going to stick to your own interpretation of morality and the need for sacraments—keep in mind that you've been allowing her to live in sin for missing Mass. So why complicate her life at this juncture by forcing her into an indissoluble church contract? For all practical purposes, everything can be solved by a civil ceremony."

"I won't hear of it," the mother said.

"Gail, I'm sorry," Ben said at length. "Believe me, it would be so much easier for me to marry you and not care. It would be no skin off my nose at all. But I couldn't have you on my conscience. You aren't ready for marriage."

When both Mike and I refused as well, the parents complained to the chancery. Whoever was making decisions there decided that we had to perform the ceremony. The case was sent back to Ben who had been the object of the complaint. The parents were as triumphant as if they had defeated us in battle. The youngsters were married.

After the ceremony Ben said to us, "I hope that the chancery idiot who approved that marriage has to handle their annulment plea when they come back in two years. If I had any guts, I would still have refused."

I had never seen Ben so upset by anything. He was depressed for days about it—so depressed he worried both Mike and me.

58

OR the first time in weeks I slipped into the city to see Lips. I had been fighting it—had willed a hundred times over that I would turn the lie I had told Maguire at the confirmation into the truth. Then she called me. We talked for a long time on the phone. I tried to back off from her, suddenly terrified that she was beginning to have a claim on me. But I was just as scared that she might never call again. I gave in to both of us.

It was five in the morning when I drove back from the city. As I passed the college at the outskirts of Jensen's Falls, I could see the smoke rising lazily into the predawn sky above the center of town. When I got closer, I saw that it was coming from our property. I floored the accelerator, jolting the car into speed. My mind was filled with an inexpressible fear of what I might find.

As the highway curved into Main Street, relief flooded through me. It wasn't the rectory that was on fire but the church. The massive gray stone outer walls still stood, but the front rose window was smashed, and the roof had fallen through at the front end of the building. Thick smoke and steam poured out of every opening. The loud hiss of water and flame fighting one another penetrated the morning air. Fire engines ringed the property.

I deserted my car and cut through the throng of townspeople. I searched frantically for Mike, wanting only to see that he, and then Ben and Jerome, were safe. Finally I saw him standing in the middle of the front lawn with the fire chief. The latter bellowed commands at the men who played fire hoses into the building. Mike looked dazed. I ran up to him and tugged at his sleeve. "Is anybody hurt?" I asked.

He turned, glared at me angrily, then pulled his arm away. "Heavy sick call?" he asked.

He walked over to where Jerome and Ben stood with a crowd of onlookers. I followed, pleading with Mike for information. "What happened?"

"Who knows?" he said. "Too bad you weren't here when it was really going. You could have gotten your picture in the papers."

He wasn't about to give me any information. I asked Jerome, "What time did it start?"

"I don't know," he replied, continuing to look past me to the blaze. "It woke me up around two o'clock. I thought it was a dream I was havin'. It sounded like a wind. Then you could see the colored windows with lights behind them.

"What started it?"

"Wiring probably," Ben put in. "I don't know what starts fires. Where were you anyway?"

I made as if I hadn't heard his question and continued pressing for facts. "Maybe a cigarette left in the Room," I said, "like in a couch or something?"

"The Room ain't touched," Jerome assured me. "They could open that right up again."

Ben smiled, staring at what was left of the church. "Won't that make the parishioners happy?" he commented dryly. "Mike can go right back to pushing drugs."

"I'll bet it was one of those statue candles," Jerome said. "They got them leanin' all over the place—right against the walls practically."

I turned to look at him. He was happily intent, watching the firemen douse wherever the fire showed signs of renewed life. The accusation flashed into my head: Jerome did it. He had probably figured it was a way of thanking us by solving our problems. All he had had to do was push a tray of vigil lights into something flammable like the papal flag.

267

I searched for the answer in his lively brown eyes, electric with the spectacle filling them. But Jerome was too open a person to hide anything. If he had done it he would have run, just as he ran when he stole the stereo. Besides, there was no reason for him to have done it—no reason, except that we had told him to do it. I quickly mashed the suspicion into the back of my mind. It continued to lie there, uncomfortably suppressed.

The church building hadn't been totally destroyed. The outer walls still stood and the basement, though it had been flooded, was intact. The one totally unscathed part of the building was the section Mike used for the Room, situated under the main altar area and elevated by a half flight of stairs from the rest of the basement. To the near outrage of many a parishioner, he reopened this for the teenagers as soon as we were assured of the basic safety of the whole structure. At first glance, it seemed as if the merger problem had been solved. It would have been against common sense to do anything other than merge.

When the metropolitan press asked Maguire to comment on the fire in the light of the rumors of a merger, he said, "The present shortage of priests had forced questions to be raised about the existence of the two parishes even before the fire."

The bishop's statement broke open a hornet's nest of resentment. The parishioners of St. Mary's swarmed into action, intending, at first, only to steer the bishop toward their point of view by way of petition and protest. When an insurance payment of $410,000 was announced, however, they were handed a real weapon to use against him.

Mr. Baldwin, chairman of the committee formed to save the parish, called a meeting at the Knights of Columbus hall, a meeting to which the press had been invited.

"I mean no malice or bad feeling to the bishop," he announced. "We hold full respect for his office as spiritual leader. But as an administrator of our property, he has allowed himself to be led by these younger priests who have no respect for the true Catholic faith. What the bishop is doing, he is doing with our money. It's our right to rebuild our church with our own money if we choose to do so."

When Baldwin's declaration of independence appeared in the newspapers, Maguire issued to the press the carefully worded statement that he had already had us read to the members of both parishes the previous Sunday.

"Fortunately, because of the diocesan insurance program," it read, "St. Mary's Church building was adequately protected. The $410,000 insurance payment is deposited in your name and is drawing interest, while you collaborate with one another and with your bishop in planning for the best use of your resources and facilities. May I encourage you to consider opportunities in your own town to help care for the poor and the elderly, to improve your schools and programs of religious education, your ministry to young people, and other possible community projects."

Still, the talk in Jensen's Falls was: "The bishop wants to take our money and spend it on himself."

59

AS Mr. Baldwin had declared himself the protector of St. Mary's, it was logical that he return to the parish. As he had declared himself the parish spokesman, it was logical that he be able to say he had spoken with the parish priests. On the second Sunday in August, Mr. Baldwin followed Mike out of the school gym where Mass had just been celebrated, and into the room off the stage where the sacristy furniture had been placed. I had hung up my surplice after giving out communion and, turning to leave, I bumped into him as he barged through the door. I was a cipher as far as he was concerned, a shadow carbon of my cousin. He brushed past me.

"Father Hogan," he demanded of Mike, "I think it's time you and I cleared the air."

"Oh?"

"You know, a lot of people realize that it's been you all along who's been pushing for a merger."

"So I understand," Mike said as he removed his vestments.

"And Mrs. Sheehan tells me that your family has undue influence over the bishop."

"My mother runs a cemetery. How influential is that?"

"You know what I'm getting at, Father. From the day you came to this town, you've turned the church we knew—even the society we knew—upside down. You've . . ."

"Wait a minute," Mike cut in, piling his liturgical clothing on a bench and turning his full attention to the argument. "When I came here the church, and the society you knew, happened to be changing. Look outside your little world, Mr. Baldwin. The changes happened. I didn't invent them."

"Admit you've got a stake in this merger," Baldwin charged.

"What stake?" A smile of amusement played around the corners of Mike's mouth.

"Well, it's common knowledge that the bishop has agreed to make you pastor of the combined parishes."

"Well, if you don't mind my saying so," Mike said, "all the common knowledge in this town put together isn't worth the powder to blow it to hell."

"Let's clear the air, Father," Baldwin repeated, his voice lowered to a theatrical snarl. "When you manipulate something, you're pretty ruthless about getting what you're after. I can certainly attest to that after the way you had my son set up."

Mike stood with his arms folded, saying nothing.

Baldwin plunged onward. "I'm telling you frankly, Father, I'm not satisfied as to the origins of that fire."

"You think I started it?" Mike asked.

"I think you'd use any means to gain your own ends. That nigger you have with you . . . is a convicted arsonist."

Mike's lips went tight. Up to that point, he had been brushing the barrages aside. He moved a step closer, and pointed his forefinger at his opponent. "Baldwin," he said slowly, "if you accuse that boy of having anything to do with the fire, I will sue you for slander."

"That kid is a criminal . . ." began Baldwin, stepping back from the jabbing finger.

"So is your son," Mike interrupted. "The only difference between the two of them is that Jerome never had anyone to pull political strings for him with a local judge. If your son were poor, he'd be doing time in jail right now."

"You bastard," Baldwin snapped.

"Very good," Mike congratulated. "You've cleared the air beautifully. But now you go tell this—and tell it straight—to all your cronies who know more about running the Church than the Pope. They can play any game they want about this whole damned business. They can go into schism if they like. But Jerome Simmons is as much my child as your boy is yours. The first one of you who makes an accusation like you just tried to make, and does it publicly, will answer to me. Got that, buddy?"

Baldwin stormed out, slamming the door. Mike walked up and down the small room twice, looking caged. He stopped and held his hand pensively over his mouth, apparently trying to think something through.

"You know what?" he said finally. "I think I should send Jerome to basketball camp. I've been thinking about it all summer. I want him to be able to buy and sell these hicks on a basketball court this year. I want him to know this game backward and forward."

"Mike," I asked, "you don't suppose . . ."

"Dennie," he interrupted, grabbing hold of my shirt and pulling me toward him, "thinking isn't one of your strong points. So don't, okay?"

"But, Mike . . ."

As always, in those moments when he lost control of a situation, his face looked almost childlike. "Please, Dennie . . ." he pleaded. "Look. There is no way of knowing how that damned fire started. So don't ask Jerome . . . don't ask me. Let me worry about it, will you?"

"Sure," I agreed, backing away.

The committee to save St. Mary's fought on, utilizing the natural interest of the press as best they could. At the height of the campaign, the committee issued a statement that they intended to petition the Pope to have Bishop Maguire's decision revoked. Maguire, hoping to stop the publicly embarrassing foolishness, announced a meeting with the parishioners. It was meant to be a forum for reasonable discussion.

"Don't you see?" Maguire said, standing on the school stage to address the packed auditorium. "Right now the Church is going through a crisis as disastrous as anything she has ever experienced in the past. We have no more priests."

"It was the changes that did it," someone offered.

"Whatever did it," the bishop said, "there are no more priests. Look at the announcement I had to make in June about closing St. Bernardine's. We only had thirty-five seminarians. A decade ago we had two hundred. Even merging as we did with the next diocese, we barely have enough students to conduct a seminary. The situation in Jensen's Falls is not an isolated problem."

272

"But why pick on us?" a voice yelled.

Mr. Baldwin stood to take command. "Bishop, there's a skunk in the woodpile here somewhere. If there really is such a priest shortage, then how come we've got three priests in this parish now when there used to be only two?"

He received a round of applause; but before Maguire could answer, Ben stood up. "The reason why I am here at St. Mary's," he explained, "is that I have had two nervous breakdowns. I am an alcoholic. When I came back to the priesthood after having been away, Bishop Maguire put me with these two men because . . . because he wanted them to take care of me."

He sat down. There was an awkward silence. I almost expected someone to stand and ask me why I had been allowed to do something so human as to live with my own cousin. They wanted no human consideration to be allowed to the priesthood. I turned Baldwin off. I was filled with disgust. No wonder there aren't more priests, I thought. Why would any sane young man want to walk into this cage of animals? I stared down at the floor, attempting to block out from my mind the scene of which I was part. Sometime later, I heard Maguire say, "I am sorry. Believe me. If I could change this situation, I would. But I am responsible for the needs of the whole diocese, not just Jensen's Falls. I simply don't have the priests to rebuild a parish where a parish is not actually needed."

Baldwin stood again, declaring, "We have made contact with a priest who says that he would be willing to come here."

"Who?" Maguire asked. Baldwin's claim appeared to confuse him. It was as if Baldwin had taken over his role.

"Father Fufferd."

Maguire's face went red, and his expression moved quickly from confusion to anger. "I suspended Father Fufferd three months ago. He will remain suspended until he ceases his activities with the Una Via movement, which is in marked disobedience to the Church."

"He's still a priest, isn't he?" Baldwin pressed. "You can't take that away from him."

"He is not an acting priest in this diocese right now," Maguire said. "He's only using you because he needs a place from which to operate."

"He's still a priest," Baldwin insisted.

Anger had drained from Maguire's face, replaced by an almost despairing sadness. "Would you really opt to separate yourself from

273

the Church," the bishop asked, "when the Church is in such desperate need of finding her sense of unity again?"

There was silence, then a general but hesitant murmuring. What the parishioners of St. Mary's were on the verge of doing was beyond their own ability to appreciate.

Before any further debate could start, Maguire spoke again. "I had hoped to avoid this because now we will have to appear ugly before the world. I will make one final statement and after that nothing more will be said this evening."

He stopped for a moment. Then, in an authoritative tone, quite different from the conciliatory manner that he had held himself to throughout the evening, he commanded: "If you decide to do something so disobedient as to leave the universal Church and set up a schismatic Latin parish under Father Fufferd, you will do so without this property. Contrary to the well-publicized claims of this committee, you have no legal claim over the money gotten from the insurance. As I have already stated, that money will be used for charitable work in Jensen's Falls and in no other place. But legally that money belongs to the diocese. It is not yours. St. Mary's Church will not be rebuilt."

An angry protest welled up from the audience. Maguire nodded a curt good night and stalked from the stage. It was only after we had returned to the rectory that his shell of purposefulness crumbled. He looked ill. "Well, I don't know who won," he said and shook his head, "but it certainly wasn't the Church."

60

TRUCE negotiations followed. Within a week a compromise was reached. All were agreed that St. Mary's would not be rebuilt. Calling a press conference to supplement the statement issued by the bishop, Mr. Baldwin tried to make it clear to the news media that it was Bishop Maguire and not his committee that had backed down.

"We will still have two parishes," he announced. "St. Mary's will continue to exist. We will only be using St. Francis' Church for Sunday Masses. Both parishes will maintain their own schools, rectories and convents, along with separate records. We will not lose our identity."

During the last week of August, eight days after the confrontation between the parishioners and Maguire, I was visiting men along the top tier of cells at the jail. It was lunchtime. The two bottom tiers of men were out, eating at barrack tables, four stories directly below me. I barely noticed the first couple of yells. Then, for a moment, I presumed that a fight had broken out. I turned around and looked over the railing. As if a volcano had erupted, the one hundred men eating had turned into a mob.

Food was being hurled, tables overturned. The few guards watching over the eating prisoners retreated quickly to places of safety behind the fencing that fronted the tier area. Alarms blasted. More guards swarmed into the cell area from all directions. In a frenzied rampage, the prisoners ran amok through cells, ripping and throwing mattresses into the cellblock's open space. Stools were hurled through the windows high above the men's heads.

I stood frozen, to my knowledge the only nonprisoner in the tier area. Within minutes, fire hoses were force-spraying the men against the back walls. Dogs were brought in.

Order was restored quickly. Under the threat of guns, but more so the dogs, the men were told to strip naked. Dehumanized, defenseless, they were brought in small groups back to their cells. The single case of resistance that I saw was met with quick and effective brutality. My presence had been forgotten by the guards.

When I reached the ground floor area and approached where the prisoners stood naked, their hands on top of their heads, a tall young black man noticed me and yelled out as if I were some kind of arbiter, "There was goddam maggots in the soup!"

Yells from several guards shut him up. I looked down at the debris on the floor. Water covered everything—the overturned tables, the broken glass, the soaked mattresses. Nothing remained of the potatolike soup that had been in the bowls. Then I saw one—then another, and another. Maggots. Like living rice kernels, they squirmed in the mess underfoot.

One of the guards, a friendly man who was generally good both to the prisoners and to me, came to my side. "Father, get out of here," he said in a tone that, though nervous from fright, was still amiable. "Come back later when this is under control."

Immediately the incident was on the radio and TV. The commissioner who had rushed to the scene came out with a categorical denial that there were maggots in the soup.

"There were a couple of fruit flies, that's all," he insisted, adding, "My own wife's soup gets fruit flies in it."

He then assessed that the damage done by the inmates came to $200,000.

"Oh, my God," Mike said. He snapped off the radio and laughed. "They must have slashed the Raphaels. You couldn't do $200,000 worth of damage to that place if you used it for nuclear testing."

"Mike," I said, "I saw it. There really were maggots in that soup."

"Oh, well," he shrugged, "maybe that's what his wife serves and he doesn't know the difference. Anyway, that's what they get for saving money by having winos do the cooking."

"I can't believe the way they put the thing right down," I exclaimed.

"Yeah, but look at their side of it. For all the guards could know, that might have been some sort of planned break."

"I guess," I conceded. "But why did the commissioner have to lie about it on the news?"

"My God, you're dumb, Dennie. After what we've just lived through in this town? Politics, pal, politics. You think they're going to let the local machine look bad? Come on."

Several hours after the riot I went to the Knights of Columbus installation banquet, only because a priest was needed for the blessing before the meal.

I sat at the head table, frustrated and anguished for the inmates in the jail, while ministering to the local politicians who made their plight worse than it had to be. I kept wondering why I was there—wondering if my whole life was going to be like this. The more I looked at the smug crowd in front of me, the more futile it all seemed. Impulsively, I finally leaped to the irresistible temptation, just to be free of all this pain. I deserted the K. of C. Hall, leaving the Knights to say grace for themselves.

Jerome was at basketball camp. Only Ben and Mike were at St. Mary's rectory. Knowing that we could never discuss the matter rationally, I avoided bumping into them, got a few things together that I would need immediately, and left a two-sentence note. Feeling as if I had climbed out of a frying pan, I walked away from the priesthood.

61

SOME unwritten code demanded that former priests leave their hometowns to live a fugitive sort of life hiding from what they had been. I had no intentions of doing that. I was finished living my life according to what was expected of me.

I fantasized encountering Mr. O'Brien, Mrs. Sheehan, or Mr. Baldwin, imagining that I could tell them where to go; that my life and my religion were no one's business now but my own. And yet, my parents' homes, either at the city or the shore were out. In my parents' middle-class Catholic world, having an ex-priest in the house would be like having a leper in the family.

George and Rachel let me sleep on their couch while I looked for an apartment. I got a job with the power company, where I had worked summers as a college student. There the only person who found my former priesthood a difficulty was Mr. Poplovski, my crew boss, who had relatives in Jensen's Falls. Nothing had been said to the rest of the crew about what I had been; and for almost a week no one knew. A heavy, tanned and crewcut man of fifty, Poplovski called me Dennis in front of everyone else; but if we were riding alone in the cab of the truck, he would make a point of going back to "Father," which to him was my indelible title.

He insisted repeatedly upon bringing the subject up, and once almost drove off the road because his emotion required his hands to italicize his words. "What am I supposed to tell my kids, Father?" he demanded. "What do I say if they ask me what they should call you now?"

"Tell them anything you want, Stan. I don't care."

"What does your poor mother think?" he pressed. "You must be breaking your parents' hearts." I didn't like being reminded that my parents *were* hurt by my leaving.

"I don't live my parents' lives," I muttered defensively. "They don't have to live mine."

One hot day as we ate lunch in the shade under a bridge, the men on the crew were trying to outdo one another with reports on their love lives over the weekend. The only two noncontributors were Stan and me. My priesthood was a blight to Stan. Without me around, he probably would have joined in the conversation. As it was, he sat on the ground gnawing angrily at his sandwich. With every off-color remark, he shot a look at me to see what effect it might have had. The only thing that was having an effect on me was his rigid observation. I would rather have had Maguire testing my reactions.

Finally, a young crew member drew a verbal picture of a girl who, if she did exist outside his imagination, should have been immortalized in "Believe It or Not."

Stan got up and disgustedly cut the kid off in mid-description of a trapeze act. "Ah, why don't you guys clean up your goddam language?" he growled. He got up, scooped up his lunch pail, and walked off to eat in the truck.

"What's eating him?" someone asked. The situation was unfair to Poplovski.

"He's upset because I used to be a priest," I told them. "I quit a couple of weeks ago."

"No shit?" the kid exclaimed in pop-eyed disbelief. "Can you quit just like that?"

"That's what I did," I said.

"No shit," he repeated.

"A lot of priests are leaving," said an older man. "Don't you read the papers? What's that one guy ... Kavanaugh? He wrote a book."

For several days there was an intense interest in finding out the "inside dope" about the Church. But after a week of monosyllabic responses from me on the topic, this waned.

The younger members of the crew did dub me with the name "priester," but this was to get Stan riled up. If he was standing by the truck when we punched in in the morning, one of the guys would yell some comment like, "Hey, Priester! Who was that piece of ass you had down on the strip last night?"

Stan would get all upset, not sure what to believe, and he would resort to screaming orders. "Get this truck loaded up!" he would yell, walking away from us. "What are we gonna do? Sit here till lunchtime?"

Lippsy sat waiting for me in a popular downtown hangout. It was the first time we had ever been together in public. I wore a sportcoat and tie. Wearing the outfit somehow made me more nervous about meeting her than I had been all day. She was accustomed to seeing me wear a roman collar—or nothing. My tie symbolized the fact that we had to redefine our relationship.

She saw me in the mirror over the bar before I got to her. "Great tan you're getting there, Red," she commented, talking to my reflected image.

"Yeah, well, I'm outside all the time now," I said, slipping onto the barstool next to her. I ordered a bottle of beer and got another drink for her. We sat in an uncomfortable silence, each of us searching for something to say. It was a whole new scene. I was a free man—free to make a commitment.

And that was the problem. My relationship with Lippsy had been such an escape from my problems in the priesthood that it had become intricately woven into those problems. If I stayed with her now, I felt I'd have to answer emergency calls from the hospital! I had barely known her when I leaped into a relationship that should have demanded some sort of commitment. But I hadn't made it, and I wasn't ready to now. I had to feel free—totally free so that I could start again and do things in the right order. Maybe it would be with her after all. But we would have to get to know each other first. And I had to begin by getting to know myself better.

"You're staying with those friends of yours," she remarked, ending an awkward pause.

"Just till I get my own place.

"Oh."

"There's an apartment complex near the power plant," I added quickly as if apologizing. "I think I'm going to try there."

She toyed with the cherry in her drink. I knew what she had to be thinking. There was that great wrestling-mat-sized bed in her place. What did I have to go and waste money for? Nothing was said. I drank my beer down, ordered another, and then quietly drank half of that as well.

At last what I needed clicked. I had a relaxed, heady feeling, enough to give me courage.

"I need to pull back, Lips," I apologized, "I mean . . . I really . . . would want to be with you . . ."

"But it wouldn't work," she finished for me.

I breathed a nervous sigh of relief. "Yeah . . . I mean, right . . . no. It wouldn't. Not the way we've been."

"But . . . you're thinking of marriage," she objected.

"I suppose."

"I don't know, Red," she said lightly, almost philosophically. "You got upside-down ideas about morals. Why an ironclad marriage? Why don't you just enjoy life . . . enjoy this year . . . enjoy . . . us?"

She put her hand on my arm. Her words were spoken lightly, but the tug of her hand belied her tone, felt like pleading.

"I'm sorry," I said. "It . . . can't be. I mean . . . it's got to be 'either-or.' I know that sounds stupid after what we have been doing all along. But . . . hell, Lips . . . it wasn't . . . I mean the way you were about everything . . . it was just . . . it wasn't a commitment."

When she didn't respond, I admitted, "But it was, I guess, wasn't it?"

"Oh, Jesus, Red. I didn't do it purposely. You make it sound like a trap. It just happened."

I suddenly felt the same tenderness I had felt for her when she had been beaten up. Fighting the entrapment of my own emotions, I asked.

"What about that Spanish guy?"

She took her hand off my arm and picked up her drink. "Don't bring that up. That was nothing like this."

"I thought it was."

281

"Why? Was that reassuring to you?"

"Yes . . . I guess."

"Oh, I get it," she said, her voice suddenly sarcastic and loud. "The old 'Once the loaf is sliced, nobody will miss a piece' routine, right?"

"No," I objected.

"Yes," she insisted, then laughed. "Except you grabbed about half the loaf."

"Okay. Lower your voice, will you?" I pleaded. "Half the god-damned place is listening to you."

"Sorry," she said. Her voice caught. She was going to start crying.

"Lips, please," I said. "I don't want to hurt you."

"When did you start thinking about that?" she sniffed. A tear spilled down her cheeks. She wiped it away angrily.

"Let's get out of here," I said.

"What for?" she said. "A nice ride around the city? No thanks."

There was nothing else to say without hurting her more. "Let me take you home," I offered.

She shook her head no, looking at me in the mirror. I got up and took my wallet out to pay for the drinks. I started to pull out a five. Then, knowing that Lips would stay to drink more, I took a ten-dollar bill and put it on the bar. Still looking at me in the mirror, she asked, "Is that to pay him or me?"

I walked outside and stood for a long time, staring at the heavy nighttime traffic as it honked and jostled through the busy intersection in front of me. I could feel sweat on my forehead that had broken out while I was talking with Lips. I hated myself and felt depressed for what I had done. Lippsy had been the innocent party in our relationship. I had used her. When I left her, I had almost said, "I'll call you." Even now—perhaps wanting to soften my callousness—I wanted to go back in and tell her I would. I decided no. Lippsy was right in pushing me away. It was over and done with. I gulped a deep breath of air, guiltily wiped my forehead with my jacket sleeve, and got into my car.

62

$\mathscr{A}$T first, my daily routine was almost like a return to the carefree existence I had known in college. We would start at eight each morning, straighten out materials on the trucks, and then head out to wherever we were to work, wasting half the morning for a coffee break on the way. I could spend each day digging the holes for power-line poles, enjoying the smell of air and earth—and not have to think about much at all while I did.

At four in the afternoon, a new experience in my adult life happened. We punched out. After that time, whatever I was or did was nobody's business. I had two full days off out of each week. It seemed a great luxury. I traveled around, visited people, and did things I had never found time to do as a priest. I spent weekends at the shore, sharing my life with no one but sea gulls. When it rained, I sacked out and logged the weekend in front of a television set.

Each Friday afternoon, after quitting time, most of the men I worked with would stop to spend an hour or so shooting darts at a bar close to the company plant. One Friday, almost a month after I had started working, Savage walked in and joined several of the crew at the bar. Angrily I jumped to the conclusion that he had come to butt into my personal life. I was wrong. He ignored me.

Three of the guys I was working with were from Ireland. There were a number of young men in our city who had come to the States to get work. Savage went out of his way to be someone they could turn to for help. He played soccer with them each week, and became a kind of big brother to the younger ones. If he was free on Friday afternoons, he joined them after work for awhile.

Having first been angered that he would intrude into my life, I now grew nettled that he ignored me. I shot darts, ignoring him in return. Finally I offered to get my group another pitcher of beer and pushed in next to where he sat at the bar.

"Well," he asked, seemingly surprised to notice me, "have you started writing your book yet?"

I refused to pick up on the sarcasm in his voice and asked, "What book?"

"You know, *A Modern Man Looks at His Ugly Church,* or *How I Got Hot Rocks,* by the former Father Hogan. Make a few bucks on this, why don't you. All the rest of them do."

I told him to lay off. I didn't want to talk about the priesthood. I didn't want to think about it. I just wanted to start off fresh. He backed down, and for the remainder of an hour we talked about neutral topics. But later, when I left, he followed me to my car.

He returned to the subject I wanted to forget. "Are you content with yourself?" he asked.

"Are you kidding?" I said. "I've punched out for the day. No meetings, no goldfish-bowl rectory life, no neurotics . . ."

". . . No bums," he finished for me, "and no barflies calling at two in the morning to ask if burning the flag is a mortal sin."

"Did you get that?"

"Two nights ago. I hope he didn't mind a foreigner saying it, but I told him what he could do with his flag."

"Well, it's all yours and you can have it," I replied, "all one and a half parishes on the same block in Hometown, U.S.A."

"Oh, you have to play it as it lays," he said. "You know that."

I had sat on my car fender to work at a sliver in the palm of my hand.

"You don't miss it at all?" he finally ventured.

"No," I assured him, my defenses up.

"Nothing at all?"

I couldn't lie about that. "I miss saying Mass. But that's the only thing."

"You still believe in it?"

"Hell, yes. I didn't stop believing. It's goddamned Catholics I can't take."

"Do you go to Mass?"

"Yep." I forced a laugh. "Maybe that's why I miss saying it. I get bored listening to other guys preach."

"And you put in poles all week?"

"I like it."

"Grand," he said. "Tell me, how is it for relevancy?"

63

ONE night Rachel invited Mike over to dinner without telling me. Of course, she could say he was their friend as well as my cousin. She certainly didn't have to tell me who she was having to her home. Yet, I couldn't help feeling that it was some kind of plot. If I had run off and married Lips, it would have been the end of it. But the way everyone was on my back, I felt as little freedom as Jerome must have felt when we were pursuing him. It was unsettling.

"Ben is really worried about you," Mike said almost as soon as we had sat down to eat.

"Well, tell him not to be," I said. "I'm fine."

"You know him. He feels as though he's responsible in some way."

"Well, hell. What am I supposed to do? Be a priest to make him happy?"

A family fight wasn't going to make for an enjoyable meal, so we kept off the topic and talked about everyday things like the war and crime in the city. But when we finished eating and went to the living room to watch the ball game, Mike returned to the subject like a magnet.

"Angie DiVecchio says hello," he said. "It's funny. With all the crap going on, it's easy to forget that there are people who really do like us."

"Hey, that's good," I said, meaning to brush him off. "When did they discover we didn't belong to the Hell's Angels?"

He watched the game for a minute or so and then said, "Ah, poor Dennie. Poor little Dennie. Everybody's against him."

I ignored him for an equal length of time, then said, "What's that supposed to mean?"

"Nothing," he shrugged. "Just that you are a spoiled brat."

Rachel sat forward in her chair, hugged her knees, and tried to be intent upon the television picture. She was embarrassed.

I took a make-believe mike and pushed it in front of George. "All right, and now let's have a few words from another spectator. Tell the audience what you think about this, George."

"I'm watching the ball game," he said, shoving my hand away.

"He's watching the ball game, ladies and gentlemen. Beautifully said, sir. I think I will watch the ball game, too."

This left a vacuum of silence broken only by the sound of the television. But soon Mike started again, speaking faster as if to prevent my interruptions. "It's kind of interesting," he said. "Ever since you could talk, you always ended up crying and walking away from any game that wasn't going your way. Everyone always fought your battles for you—your mommy and daddy, your big brothers and sisters, your cousins. Everybody always gave in to Dennie. You weren't just the youngest, you were the runt of the litter."

I started to respond. He cut me off, stabbing his forefinger into my face. "Dennie, I've never once seen you get into trouble in your whole dumb life but that someone didn't buy your way out of it for you. Not once. You're like Baldwin's kid. I remember it used to make me worry about what would happen to you when you grew up and had to stand on your own."

"Look," I said angrily. "Don't blame me because the Church is all screwed up."

"I'm blaming you because *you* are screwed up. *You,* buddy, not the Church. And do you know why you haven't gone the whole route and married your pigpen pal? It's because you don't have the guts to make that kind of a commitment. Even if you did marry her, it would fall apart in a year. Then you would blame her, and say it was because you should have been a priest after all."

"That's none of your damned business anyway," I said. My voice caught. As much as I fought it, his words hurt. As if to prove his accusation of childishness true, tears of frustration sprang to my eyes. I wanted to punch him.

"Did you ever read a biography of Lenin?" he demanded.

"Lenin?" Rachel asked, eager to jump at any change in topic.

But Mike, as I knew both from experience and the tone of his voice, had no intention of letting up. "Yeah," he said, "Lenin . . . or Martin Luther King . . . or even Hitler. Any man, no matter how good or evil, who really changed history. They were dedicated, goddamn it! They lived for years—starved and struggled to make what they believed in a reality. And that's what the Church has lost, for Christ's sake. Men who would live so that their lives can say: 'This is how much I believe.' What's the matter with us, Dennie? Why can't our age produce somebody who will believe in Jesus as much as Lenin believed in Marx?" He was sitting next to me—and as if to emphasize what he said, he had grabbed hold of the back of my neck. Unconsciously, his hand tightened like a vise.

I yanked away from him and said, "All right, damn it. Stop, will you? Look, I just want people to leave me alone for a while. Okay?"

He got up. "I can't stay," he apologized to Rachel. "I've got to get back. It was a great meal." He stopped at the door.

Then half looking at me, he asked: "Do you want me to say hello to the kids in the Room?"

64

THE bar that the power crew frequented after work was part of an Italian restaurant—a family sort of place, much like the DiVecchios'. One afternoon as we killed the end of a day, I was walking back from pulling darts out of the bar's dart board when a young woman walked in from the restaurant. She smiled a hello to me, then looked a little confused and asked, "Father?"

"Yes?" I responded to the title without thinking. Instantly, not wanting to and feeling very awkward, I assumed the role of "Father" for the young woman, whose face relaxed with relief.

"I wondered if it was you the way you were dressed," she said. "Where were you, out digging?"

"Yes," I searched my memory to place her. Finally I apologized. "I'm sorry . . . I don't recognize you."

"It's been a long time," she said. "I'm Elizabeth Chura."

Nothing connected. "You were with my husband when he died in the hospital," she explained. "We had just been married."

The scene flashed into my mind. The night a lady burned to death; then the boy who died of the kidney infection—his mother saying, "Oh, Father, St. Ann failed me."

"Oh, my God, yes," I said. "I felt so bad for all of you that night."

"I'm with my mother-in-law now. We're having dinner. Why don't you come in and say hello?"

"I'm all caked with dirt," I said, hoping to beg off.

"She would love to talk to you. We saw you when you came in the door."

I nodded and gave the darts to a member of the crew, who took them respectfully, as if I were handing him an altar vessel. I followed her into the dining room.

Mrs. Chura (a younger-looking woman than I had remembered, attractively dressed) stood up, extending her hand. She said, "Father, how are you?"

"Fine, thanks," I answered, thoroughly embarrassed. "How are you doing?"

"Very well, Father. You know, I always meant to write you a thank-you note and never did. You'll never know how great a comfort you were to us when my son died."

I felt like a fool.

"Where are you stationed now, Father?" she asked.

"I'm not," I said, mustering the courage to drop the facade. "I've left the priesthood. I'm working at the power company."

They both looked surprised, then flustered. When neither of them said anything, I added, "I had to think things out."

"Yes," began Mrs. Chura, "but, Father . . ."

"Dennis," I corrected. "You see? Priests do have first names."

It was a bad attempt at a pleasantry. She shook her head. "Well, uh, Father—you did help us at a very terrible time."

I studied her for a moment. She looked a little like Mrs. Sheehan . . . a little like my own mom . . . like that whole category of Catholic middle-class leaders of society. I wondered what she would have felt toward me if we had simply met in Jensen's Falls. If I had not met her at her son's deathbed, would she, like Mrs. Sheehan, have hated me for being part of the changes? Would she have joined in the fight against the bishop?

"What is going to happen," Mrs. Chura asked, "if everyone leaves?"

"I don't know," I said, half impatiently, half apologetically. "I'm not part of that world anymore."

When I left them and returned to the bar, somebody had gotten me another beer. For a few uncomfortable minutes, I remained half priest, half real person, to the men I was with. When handed the darts, I tossed them one at a time, aimlessly, at the board. None of them were anyplace near the bullseye.

65

AUTUMN was rainy and cold. My truck crew had planned to play ball at the end of the day; but at four o'clock heavy clouds promised rain, and the game was cancelled. I was glad of the cancellation. Without knowing why, I had been depressed all day. The thought of steaming off the day's dirt in a shower and settling down with a beer was all that preoccupied me as I left the plant and headed for the parking lot.

As I walked up to my car, I saw Jerome sitting on the hood. He didn't smile when he said hello. His manner was almost hostile.

"What are you doing in the city?" I asked.

"Came to see my sister."

"Didn't you have school today?"

"Family's more important, sometimes."

"I thought you don't get along with your sister."

"Still family. That counts for somethin', don't it?"

He was playing some kind of game. I unlocked the car. We got in. "Where are you headed now?" I asked.

"Back."

"I suppose if I translate all this into polite conversation," I said, "you're asking me to take you out to Jensen's Falls."

He slumped in his seat, his lanky legs doubled up in front of him, unanswering.

"How is school going?" I asked. "I mean, when you bother to go."

"I go," he said. After another sullen silence, he added, "Why don't you ask how church is goin'?"

Reluctantly, I gave in to the topic. "How is church going?"

It was an odd conversation. I was used to having the parental edge in dealing with Jerome. He made it clear that we were talking now as peers.

"Bad," he said, almost muttering. "Ben's been drinkin'."

A pang of guilt clutched at my stomach. Jerome's tired hostility toward me suddenly made sense. As soon as the rush-hour traffic came to a momentary halt, I looked at him. "When?" I asked.

"'Bout a week now," he said. "Mike—he figures it was at a weddin' last Saturday. Sunday, Ben came in the kitchen after he did Mass—he just stopped for a second. Mike asked him somethin', and Ben talked fast, all mixed up, like he just woke up or somethin'. Then he went upstairs and he locked his room."

"Did Mike do anything?"

"He's just been chasin' him around. Ben keeps on disappearin'. He got in a fight in a bar somewhere two nights ago. His eye is all cut up. I say his nose is broke too."

He thinks this is my fault, I thought.

"Did you really see your sister?" I asked.

"Nope."

"What was that business about family?"

He didn't answer. I realized that he meant family business that I was ignoring.

Mike was in the kitchen opening a can of something for supper. When we entered the back door, he looked up. "I thought maybe you were Ben," he said. "He's been gone all day. Did Jerome tell you?"

"Yep," Jerome answered, sitting at the table.

Mike dumped the can into a saucepan, then rummaged through the refrigerator to get more food. "If we can only get him signed into a hospital, we can start from there," he said. "He wasn't really bad until today. He's a sober sort of drunk. I don't think people could tell unless they know him real well. What changes is his basic personality. He looks like he's got a real hatred for everything and everybody. He's been staying in his room. He's simply locked himself away from us. Today he came down to say the noon Mass. He was so

292

drunk, I wouldn't let him go over. When I got back from saying it, he was gone."

"Where?" I asked.

"No trace. I called the police. They've got the troopers on a quiet lookout for him. I don't know. I'm sick with the thought of it."

The atmosphere was weighted with depression. "What are you cooking?" I asked, feebly trying to dispel some of the heavy mood.

"I don't know," he said. He picked up the can and read the label. "Turkey hash. How's that grab you?" It was not a meal to lighten anyone's spirits.

During the evening, while we anxiously awaited word of Ben, Mike kept an appointment with an engaged couple, went to a wake, then ran a parish school board meeting. This last was an uncomfortable session for everyone present. Ben had been drinking in area bars, and, in a town like Jensen's Falls, people didn't go out of their way to keep that sort of thing quiet. Nothing was said about Ben at the meeting. As if by tacit agreement, business was gotten over with quickly, and everyone left as soon as possible.

Savage and Bianco joined us as we waited. At ten o'clock, the phone rang. It was the police. A state trooper had spotted Ben's car about twenty miles to the south. It was parked at a bar on the main highway. They were bringing him home. In another thirty minutes, two troopers half propelled, half carried Ben through the back door. He seemed oblivious to what was going on until he saw me. He half straightened up and blurted, "What are you doing here?"

Then his head slumped and he mumbled incoherently. We carried him upstairs, undressed him and put him to bed.

When the troopers left, we went to the parlor. Mike stopped Jerome at the door. "Bed," he ordered. "You're overtired."

Jerome nodded obediently, almost with relief, and turned back. Mike took his arm as he passed him and took hold of the boy's face. "Hey," he said gently, "I'll worry. All right?"

Jerome nodded.

"Good boy," Mike said. "Go to sleep."

As soon as we were alone, Bianco lit a cigar. "Well, I haven't been cured yet either," he announced. "How about a drink?"

Mike went to the liquor cabinet in the hallway. In a moment he returned, looking sheepish. "I can't remember where I put the key," he apologized. "I hid it when Ben started drinking."

We should have dropped the matter. But with all the built-up tension of the evening, finding the key became a project. For twenty minutes, we searched through Mike's room, his clothes, his car, finally finding the key on the kitchen counter. When we finally had our bottle, we broke down and laughed at ourselves.

"My God, man," Savage exclaimed, "we've got no right to complain about the poor guy upstairs."

The sanity of laughter lasted only a moment. Mike was sitting next to me. I gradually began to notice, then become frightened by his appearance. I had been out in the sun so long my skin had become even darker than Jerome's mulatto brown. Mike's arm, next to mine, was a pasty white. But it was more than that. His face looked tired and gaunt. Even with direct eye contact, even when he laughed, he appeared hollow-eyed, as if his mind were elsewhere.

When Bianco and Savage left, Mike insisted that we safeguard Ben's car. He pulled open the hood and yanked loose a couple of wires so that the car wouldn't start. Then we called it a night. Too tired to drive to the city, I ended up in my old bedroom.

On the way upstairs, I realized that, with the funeral, there would be three Masses in the morning. "Are you going to get Savage to take one of the Masses?" I asked.

"I'll say the three of them," he said without turning to face me. "You wouldn't believe how touchy people are about that right now. They would rather have me get the Lutheran minister than a 'non-St. Mary's priest.' We can't lose our identity, you know."

"Well, I can take the 6:45 before I go to work," I offered.

He stopped, reflected on this a moment, and then said, "No, I'll take it."

"No," I insisted. "I'll take it. You sleep."

"Dennie," he said, "you're not a priest in this parish. In fact, you're not a priest anymore."

"I am still a priest. That can't be undone. Hell, you heard what Baldwin told the bishop. You're being pigheaded now. Let me take the morning Mass."

"Listen," he said, turning on the stairs and poking a finger at me, "saying a Mass isn't like helping with the goddamned dishes. I'm glad you're here. I need you here. But you're not a priest right now.

Somebody like Ben is willing to face self-destruction to be a part of the priesthood. I'm not going to let you mock what he's doing by saying a Mass. I'm going to say the three Masses, so shut up about it. Okay?"

66

I went to work the next morning. It was the slowest day I ever lived. I kept looking to see what time it was, thinking that hours had passed when only minutes had. I kept thinking of Ben and Mike—what both of them were going through; and how, while they were, I was planting power-line poles.

Throughout the day I made several stupid mistakes. Poplovski, pointing out one of these, asked, "Something bothering you today?"

"No, nothing," I told him. "I'm just not thinking."

I got back to the rectory at five. Mike wasn't inside. I found him in back walking up and down the parking lot.

"How is Ben?" I asked.

He shook his head, replying, "He's in his room now, but he was out all day. This morning he came down and went out the back door. He came back in and confronted me and asked, 'What did you do to my car?' I felt awful, but before I could say anything he turned and went out again. What could I do? Tackle him? He looked all right. You can't just grab a grown man and lock him up."

"When did he come back?"

"Less than an hour ago. He had a small suitcase with him. I'm sure it was filled with bottles. He could hardly walk, and he wouldn't speak to me. I'm sick about it."

"What are you going to do?"

"I don't know."

We walked around the lot suddenly Mike said, "Let me lie down on the grass a minute. I got these damned stomach cramps. I'm eating too fast."

He lay back and put his arms above his head. Finally he said, "That feels better."

"How long has your stomach been doing that?" I asked.

"Ah, I don't know; off and on."

"Sharp cramps?"

"Yes."

"Do you throw up at all?"

"The other day, after I ate, I did."

"I suppose you haven't seen a doctor."

He grunted something unintelligible.

"Why don't you see a doctor?" I persisted.

"No," he said and stood up. "Let's get through this."

During the evening, Mike called the hospital. There was no way they could take Ben until the next morning. Then he got hold of a friend of Ben's who went to Alcoholics Anonymous meetings with him. He came over and went in to talk with Ben, but got nowhere. He suggested that we not try to prevent Ben from drinking. He felt that in the condition he was in, he could get very sick if we suddenly cut him off.

Shortly after nine, Ben almost managed to slip out of the rectory by going down the back stairway, but he made so much commotion undoing the door chain we heard him.

"Ben," Mike asked him, putting a hand on his back, "where are you going?"

"I'm going out for a walk," he said. He stood steadily, but his face was a mask devoid of any expression.

"Look, please," Mike begged, "don't go out. If you want liquor I've got some in the house. Just drink it here—please."

Ben leveled a hostile stare at us, certain this was a trick. He looked as if he were going to swing at Mike.

"Wait here," Mike said. He turned and ran out of the room. In a minute he came back with a bottle of gin and a bottle of whiskey.

"Here," he said, "take it. But please, drink it here."

There was a long silence. We stood at one end of the kitchen counter, Ben at the other, the liquor bottles between us. Without a word Ben took a bottle in each hand and stalked to the stairwell.

Mike was afraid that Ben, a heavy smoker, might start a fire in bed. The locks having already been removed from Ben's door, we decided to spell each other through the night. Each of us would take three hours outside his room—to prevent a fire, and to keep him from leaving the house. In the morning, we could get him to the hospital.

I began the watch, slumped in a sofa we had pushed into the hallway. Throughout the night Ben paced about. Whenever he was quiet I would get worried and look through the keyhole until I could see him. Once, when there was no sound for almost fifteen minutes and I couldn't catch sight of him, I quietly opened his door. He bolted out of his bathroom so quickly I jumped, as frightened as if I were at a horror show.

"I didn't hear you," I said. "I got scared."

The expression of hatred on his face was so unlike him I felt I was with a stranger. Yet, if I hadn't known him, I wouldn't have known he was drunk.

"I don't need anybody spying on me," he said. "Get out of here."

"I'm sorry, Ben, really . . ."

"Get out!" he screamed, hurling a package of cigarettes at me. I backed out of the room, pulling the door shut after me.

At three, Mike took over, saying: "I'll wake you up for work when I come back from the 6:45."

"Let me say it, Mike," I pleaded.

"Why?" he demanded.

"Because I want . . . because I need to say it."

I had taken a shower, and so I was clean. but the only clothes I had were those I had been digging in for two days. Putting a clean alb over them felt as strange as it looked. I tied the neck ribbon slowly, somehow wanting to prolong the strangeness of the moment. I wrapped the cincture about my waist, then opened the closet for the chasuble. The mirror on the inside of the door caught my reflection and I stepped back to look at myself.

I felt something of what I remembered feeling when I was a new altar boy trying on a cassock for the first time. The alb was highly starched, so stiff it almost had to be broken into. Sometimes altar boys showed up to serve Mass wearing ripped sneakers: my construction boots destroyed the effect the same way. I put a host on the paten. A memory flashed into my mind—the day in Rome when that priest had raced through Mass just so he could say it on St. Peter's tomb.

"Lord," I asked, "forgive me for forgetting that."

I felt a sense of exhilaration as I went out to begin Mass. When I bent to kiss the altar, there was a note from Willie.

67

I got back to the kitchen and called Poplovski, telling him I had
something important to take care of. I wouldn't be able to work
until the afternoon.

"Oh, that's all right, Father," he said. "Take the whole day off."

I thanked him and then apologized, "Stan, I don't know what to do
about giving notice or what, but I'm going to quit."

"Why?" he demanded. "You going back to the priesthood?" It
sounded as if he had jumped into the phone.

I wondered if Stan had known my mind before I did. "Yeah, I
guess I am, Stan."

"Well, why do you want to give notice? You're afraid the Church
is gonna fold and you'll want your job back? You're finished today.
I'll say you broke a leg."

He started talking rapid-fire. I couldn't get a word in. "This is
wonderful, Father," he announced, laughing. "This is wonderful.
Wait till I tell Helen. She's been praying novenas for you."

"Stan," I said, unable to resist one last jab, "novenas are out."

"Sure, they're out," he practically yelled in his excitement. "Only
don't tell my wife that, and don't tell God neither, because she's still
using them and they still work."

It wasn't a matter of waiting until Ben was awake. He hadn't so much slept as slipped in and out of consciousness. At ten in the morning we dressed him and drove him to the hospital. When we had him signed in, in safe hands at last, we went back to the rectory. Feeling a mixture of relief and depression we sacked out for some much-needed rest.

The bubble shattered almost immediately. At five in the afternoon Mike drove to the hospital to deliver some things he felt Ben might need. Ben wasn't there. He had checked himself out at 3:00 P.M. There was no way the hospital could have kept him.

He left no trace. His family, themselves distraught, had heard nothing. The state police quietly combed the area for his car and turned up nothing. We spent the evening calling every person Ben knew whom we could think of, either in our area, or as far away as he could have driven. Every direction we tried was a blind alley.

"The only thing we can do is wait," said Mike.

At three in the morning the waiting ended. The phone's jangle worked itself into a nightmare I was having. I almost knocked the receiver off the table grabbing for it. Mike had answered on the extension phone at the same time. I let him talk.

It was a priest from a diocese in the next state. Ben was in his rectory. He had been arrested by the local police after a disturbance in a bar and had been put in jail. When they found out he was a priest, they called the nearest rectory and moved Ben there. Ben was in pretty bad shape, he told us, but a judge had agreed to take care of the matter early in the morning. Would it be possible for one of us to be there?

"We'll be there," Mike said. He called Savage to cover the 6:45 Mass. We drove for almost four hours, hardly ever talking, tired beyond being tired. We stopped once, as the sun rose, to get coffee. At 7:30 A.M. we arrived at the town, found the church, and knocked quietly on the back door of the rectory.

The priest who had called us answered the door. "You guys look beat," he said. "Come on in and get something to eat. We're supposed to see the judge at eight."

"How's Ben?" Mike asked.

"I don't know," he said. "I tried to get him to have breakfast this morning. He wouldn't. He's really at sea, poor guy. He went upstairs right before you came."

I followed Mike up the stairs. He knocked gently on the door of the room where Ben was. There was no answer. "Ben," Mike said, "it's Dennie and me. We're going to bring you home."

There was still no answer. Mike opened the door. I started to follow him in. He stiffened; I stumbled into his back.

He turned, pushing me into the hall. "Don't look. Get out of the way." He pushed past me and ran to the stairs, calling down: "Where do you keep your oils?"

I turned into the room. Ben couldn't have been dead more than a minute, and when I knelt down and touched him he was still warm. His eyes were open, staring into mine, a little look of questioning hurt in them.

There was a bottle of wood alcohol in his hand. I was barely aware of Mike kneeling next to me, reaching out, his hand shaking, to anoint the sign of the cross on Ben's forehead. "Lord Jesus," he whispered, "bring this child home to you."

68

$\mathcal{B}$EN'S wake was held in St. Francis Church. At ten in the evening, after the undertaker had closed the coffin and Bianco locked the church, Mike and I walked the few blocks to St. Mary's. We were the sort of people who, when things were at their worst, kept worries bottled up within ourselves. We had been like zombies with one another since we discovered Ben's body. I didn't know what Mike was thinking, but I kept hearing in my memory the accusation he had made while I was working at the power company: "Ben is really worried about you."

I couldn't help wondering how much he blamed me for what had happened.

It was a Friday night. A crowd of teenagers stood under a street light in front of the corner drugstore. As we approached, they fell silent, as if out of respect for our loss.

Mike stopped. "Nothing to do?" he asked.

"Naw, nothin'," a girl answered.

"Come on. I'll open the Room up."

"Really?" The girl was shocked. So was I.

"It used to be," Mike told them all, "that whenever a priest in a monastery died, the monks would throw a party right that night. You've got to understand. Priests see other priests as being a special kind of brother. And if we really believe what we say we believe in—well—it's a sort of celebration. We rejoice because our brother is with God. So let's go celebrate."

They trailed after us, looking to one another for assurance that this wasn't some sort of bizarre prank.

When we reached the shell of St. Mary's Church, Mike took a key and handed it to one of the boys. "We'll be right down," he said, waving them off toward the side entrance.

After they left, Mike walked up the front steps and pushed open the heavy wooden door. I followed him. The place looked like a medieval church fallen into ruin from centuries of neglect. The Gothic windows, pointed at the top, were almost all broken, and the interior was filled with bright moonlight. I looked up through the half-destroyed roof. The sky was crystal clear. The stars shone brightly within the frame of the stone walls. It reminded me of a night long before when I had slept under a turret outside the walls of Carcassonne, had stared at the stars, and tried to sort out why the Church so mystified and attracted me.

Mike broke into my reverie, saying, "We should have had Ben's wake here." He spoke in a whisper, as if louder sound would have broken the mood. "It would have fit."

"What do you mean?" I asked.

"I don't know," he shrugged. "I guess Christians have always worked on the assumption that the Jews were God's people, but that they missed their big moment in history. Who is to say we Christians haven't as well?"

He walked farther into the church, stopping at the smoke-scarred altar rail. He spoke again, but it was as if he were addressing the sanctuary instead of me. "Strangest thing Jesus ever said . . . 'But will the Son of Man find any faith on earth when he returns?' Interesting."

He turned to me, his hands stuffed into his coat pockets, and raised his eyebrows pensively, saying, "I could see it . . . God letting us do it. It would be the finalization of the fall. We could destroy the Church from within."

"Didn't Jesus say he'd be with us till the end of the world?" I asked.

"That was an offer. We can refuse."

A sudden blare of rock music burst through the floor under the main altar, shattering the quiet.

As if that brought him back from the realm of the speculative, Mike shook his head, observing, "Catholics blame the changes. Well, that's a lot of crap," he said quietly as he tapped his chest. "It wasn't in here. Catholics didn't have it. When the externals were stripped away, we were hollow inside."

The sounds of laughter and running echoed through the burned-out building. Mike leaned his head back and forced a laugh. But when he did, his eyes filled with tears. "Gaudeamus, Dennie," he said. "Let's go downstairs and celebrate for our brother."

69

SOMETHING was wrong with Mike. His color was pale and, for a person who was so faithful an athlete, his stomach had developed a bloated appearance since the summer. One night after dinner he got sick and threw up; then he began to vomit blood. I insisted that he call a doctor. He refused. He made it clear that I was no person to be giving him orders, that *that* wasn't the pecking order in our family. But the truth was that Mike had an inordinate fear of doctors. He hadn't so much as had a physical since he had been in the navy.

When I continued to badger him, he shut me up by challenging me to a one-on-one basketball game. He was determined, almost child-ish, in his insistence that he was in better condition than I. We went over to the school gym and played until, red-faced and sweat-ing puddles on the floor, I exhaustedly gave in.

"It's only because you're bigger," I puffed. "It takes me twice as much energy to get past you. Come on. I'll race you, from here"—I stopped and measured a distance in my mind that would be at least two miles—"to the water tower out Fisher's road."

"Oh, no, you don't," he laughed softly. "We proved that once. You're a distance man, Dennie. That's your big talent. I ain't never gonna forget that. And don't you either . . ."

The use of St. Francis Church for the prayerful purposes of the two parishes was an uglier experience than had been the dramatics about the proposed merger. Both communities were determined to retain their separate identities. It was not enough to list a schedule of Masses. The Masses had to be designated as belonging to the one parish or the other, and parishioners were vehement about attending their own Mass.

When we four priests showed signs of being indiscriminate about who said which Mass or who helped out with communions, a heavy barrage of complaints was filed to remind us that we were not living up to the "deal" that had been made. One angry man wrote a letter of complaint about the four priests sharing meals at one another's rectories.

Christmas was approaching. The birth of the Prince of Peace posed a host of problems. There was no way to have two Midnight Masses. What was to be done at the one Mass was haggled about by some two dozen members of both parishes, under a flag of truce, at the Knights of Columbus hall, a building considered to be neutral Catholic territory. Mr. Baldwin was present, having recently discovered in himself a hitherto unrealized interest in liturgy. So too was the ubiquitous Mrs. Sheehan, present to play devil's advocate on every point raised.

At the head of several banquet tables shaped into a U, Mike sat alongside Bianco—the one distractedly snapping a rubber band in his hand, the other happily fouling the air with his tar-odored cigar. Neither man looked very interested as their respective flocks worked out as intricate a liturgical minuet as had ever been choreographed. If a St. Mary's priest was the principal concelebrant, a St. Francis of Assisi priest was to give the sermon. If a St. Mary's altar boy was the incense bearer, a St. Francis of Assisi altar boy was to hold the thurible.

All negotiations broke down, however, at the crucial question as to which parish's youngest altar boy was to carry the plaster-of-Paris Jesus in procession to the plaster-of-Paris manger. At this juncture, Mike dropped his rubber band and politely raised his hand, asking, "Why don't we have both boys carry up a Jesus? We'll simply announce that Mary had twins this year."

Mrs. Sheehan gasped and spat out the word "blasphemy" under her breath.

"It's no worse than what we're doing now," Mike insisted. "So we

307

pretend that God goofed and there was a biological slipup right back at the incarnation."

Mr. Baldwin looked triumphant as he gloated, "It seems to me I recall Monsignor O'Donnell objecting to people making a joke out of the Mass."

Mike smiled his old gambler's smile but without the usual light effect. I knew his stomach was bothering him badly. "Mr. Baldwin," he said, "if only you could perceive how serious I am . . ." Suddenly turning to Bianco, he asked: "What do you say, Father? This year Mary has twins. Let's nail our flag to the mast and proclaim to the world the present state of Catholicism."

Bianco pulled the smoking stub from his mouth, looked from Mike to the sullen ring of faces, and then back to Mike again.

"You're absolutely right, my boy," he finally stated. "Why destroy the faith around the edges? Get right to the heart of the matter. Twins. Two parishes. Two sets of altar boys. Two Jesuses. Next point of discussion . . . ?"

On the second Sunday of Advent, at the last Mass, Mike came out to help distribute communion. When we were only half done, he turned and walked back to the tabernacle. Beads of sweat covered his face and the ciborium shook in his hand. He was almost doubled over with pain. As he left the altar, a doctor in the pews followed him into the sacristy. Hurriedly I finished the final prayers, tore my vestments off, and went over to the rectory. Mike was staving off the doctor.

"All right, all right, all right," he said, countering the doctor's seriousness with laughter. "I'll come after Christmas."

"I'll make an appointment for you this week—tomorrow."

Mike balked. "Wait until things settle down. It's only a bellyache."

The doctor turned to Bianco, who stood worriedly next to Mike. "Don't you have some kind of seniority?"

"We tried for that," Bianco retorted, pulling the cigar from his mouth. "You people voted us down."

Then, responding to the doctor's plea, he put his hand on my cousin's shoulder, saying, "Mike, don't be an idiot . . ."

"Tomorrow," the doctor insisted.

Mike shook his head, then jabbed a thumb in my direction: "We got plans, don't we?"

He was worried about Jerome. Jerome was playing varsity basketball, and colleges were scouting him. But he had taken Ben's death hard and had been morosely quiet in the weeks following the funeral.

School or no school, Mike had decided that we should spend a little more time with Jerome. An overnight stay at the shore seemed the best solution.

"Well," I mumbled hesitatingly. "I don't know . . ."

"Doctor," Mike promised, "I'll come Tuesday."

70

IT was four o'clock that afternoon before we got to the shore. We unlocked the house, cooked for ourselves, and walked the beach, feeling the unseasonably warm ocean mist against our faces. There was no Jensen's Falls, no burned-out St. Mary's, no St. Francis. There was no world outside where we were. We relaxed, played cards for the evening; we told Jerome stories about our childhood as if he were a grandchild to be told the family heritage; then we went to bed early.

I slept with Mike. Perhaps it was because of where we were, perhaps because my mind sought an escape to an earlier, simpler life, but I dreamed long involved dreams of being a child again. It was sunny. Eddie and I were running together at the beach. There was no plot to what we were doing. But we were happy. Everything was so secure.

Somehow, I woke up in the middle of dreaming. My mind wasn't awake. Eddie lay next to me, where he always slept. I started to drift back into sleep, then snapped awake again. I forced my eyes open to stare at the soft orange hair in front of me. Mike's face could almost have been Eddie's. With an aching desire for what was lost, I allowed myself for a moment to pretend I was back there. I reached over, touched his head and whispered: "Eddie . . ."

Mike stirred, and consternation crossed his face. He whimpered almost inaudibly. I felt myself shiver from the cold of the December night. It was not summer. It was not the past. I lay awake for a long time remembering, instead of dreaming about being a child.

It was mild and calm enough on Monday to take the sailboat out. It had always been Mike's, Laurie's, and Eddie's boat, smaller than the one my brothers and I had, but faster and easier to handle. It was the boat that had once nearly caused our deaths due to Mike's disobedience on a long-ago stormy day.

Jerome had learned to sail during the previous summer. Now, for the first time since Ben's death, he looked happy. "I got to get me one of these," he decided, talking above the sound of flapping canvas, "soon's I get out of school."

"Forget it," Mike said. "You've got one."

"Huh?" Jerome was bewildered.

"This is yours."

"This boat?"

"You own it. I want you to have it."

Jerome's eyes tightened as if he were squinting into the sun. He looked questioningly at Mike. Mike said, "Unless you don't want it."

Jerome looked down at the boat.

"The only thing is," Mike added, "I don't want you to change the name. It's got to stay *Bonaventure*. My brother and I named it."

The boy remained mute, captivated by this new, perhaps first possession.

We left him at the dock and ambled slowly along the beach, passing the closed-up houses of summertime neighbors.

"God, smell that air," Mike said, stopping, eyes closed, his face held against the wind that rushed to shore with the surf. "If I could stand here for five minutes every day, I could feel there was something sane in this world."

Throughout the morning he had been abnormally quiet.

"Mike," I said, "Remember back at George and Rachel's?"

He opened his eyes and looked at me, as if he had been expecting, hoping for the question. "Which time?" He half smiled.

"You know. About me being the runt of the litter . . ."

He said nothing. Bluntly, for the remark had festered within me like a wasp's stinger that had never been removed, I blurted, "Did you mean that?"

311

Again, as if the moment had been rehearsed in his mind he nodded deliberately, saying, "Yep. That's you in a nutshell."

The sting, injected a second time—this time without anger on Mike's part to lessen it—hurt all the more. I held back.

Mike turned toward me. "Dennie, why are you a priest?"

"What do you mean?"

"Did you come back because I needed you?"

"No . . ." I began, then stammered to a stop.

"Because if that's the reason, I don't need you, Dennie. We can't go through life with me holding your hand all the time."

"That's not it," I objected. "Maybe a little, but not finally."

"Why then?"

"Because I believe, Mike."

"In what?"

"In the Mass. In Jesus . . ."

"Hey, great . . ." He clapped his hands in mock applause which sounded hollow against the crashing of waves. "It's nice to see a priest who's got the basics down."

"It's more than that," I insisted. "Maybe . . . maybe it was only that before. I mean, I always felt . . . that this power . . . in the priesthood . . ."

"You make the Mass sound like conjuring."

"Let me finish, will you?" I said testily. "What I mean is . . . that now I see the job to do, too."

"Job? How idealistic."

"You know what I mean."

"I do. And that's why I'm so afraid for you all the time. Job . . ." He said that last word with disgust. "What about love? Good God, you always talk about the Eucharist as if Jesus were on a personal appearance tour. Why don't you connect him with the 'job'? Don't you think *that* Bread is supposed to say anything about the people you share it with?"

"Like the Baldwins . . . ?" I began.

". . . The Judases, the Pilates, the Baldwins, the Good Thief . . . Why should it be different for us than it was for him? It can't be a job, Dennie. It's love or it's nothing."

The image of Baldwin's heavy-faced, fist-shaking attack on Maguire flooded my memory. "I know it, Mike . . ."

We stood in silence while he waited. "I accept that," I finally said.

312

"I'm trying. I may not make it all the way, but I see it. I am trying."

"There's something else too . . ."

"I know," I said. "Don't say it, because I know it. Like you said, I can't hold your hand. I'm my own man . . . my own priest. I really have been thinking about it. I'm going to ask for a new assignment."

Mike looked incredulous. "God, am I really hearing this?" he laughed. "Are you really grown-up?"

"About time, huh?"

He took a couple of deep breaths. "Hey, Dennie . . . that's like removing a thousand-pound weight off my shoulder."

I started to say something, but he continued excitedly, "You know what? The day you got ordained, I was going to say to you that I had lost my only brother and that you had become my brother. But I choke on that New Breed emotionalism. Sometimes, afterward, I was a little sorry I hadn't said it. Then, when you started screwing everything up, I was glad I hadn't. But hell, Dennie," he stopped and his smile broadened into a grin, "I think you've got a chance. I really think you've got a chance."

I felt abashed, and yet felt along with this a clean sense of starting anew a priesthood I was only beginning to understand. Before I could respond in any way, Mike had reached out with both hands and clasped the sides of my head in a motion that seemed somewhere in the middle of being a blessing, an ordination, and a hug. Very quietly, he whispered, ". . . Brother."

71

*W*E headed back toward Jensen's Falls. It was a long drive. The sun had gone down and I was leaning back on the seat, dozing off.

I woke up when Mike pulled over to the side of the highway and stopped. "Would you drive for awhile?" he asked.

I walked around the car, got behind the wheel, and started driving. Mike stretched out across the back seat. He shifted several times, attempting to find a comfortable position. I could see that he was in pain.

"Why don't we stop in the next town, Mike?" I suggested. "We can get something for that."

"Yeah, all right," he said. "Maybe we'd better."

It was the first time he had admitted needing medical help. He rested his head back on the seat. After a couple of minutes Jerome asked him if he felt any better. He didn't answer. I turned and looked at him. For a moment I thought he was asleep, but he was unconscious. His whole body was limp. Frightened, I pulled over and shook him gently. "Mike, Mike, you okay?"

He didn't respond. A trooper had cruised past us only a minute before. I speeded ahead, caught up with him, and signaled him to pull over. As he got out of his car I ran toward him. "My cousin just passed out. I think he's really sick. Is there a hospital near here?"

"Follow me," he said.

We got to the emergency room. Mike came to. In a few minutes he seemed to be all right and he sat up. The doctor insisted, however, that he should be admitted. Mike was strong enough again to be pigheaded and refused.

"Look, Mike," I said, for once giving him orders. "You're staying here, and that's all there is to it."

He stood up, then quickly doubled over with pain. We lifted him back onto the emergency room cart. His face was paper white. In another moment he passed out. The doctors put him in the intensive care unit. Jerome and I stood outside the unit near the desk. I heard the nurse talking into the phone, "Father, we have a new patient in I.C.U. I think you'd better come up."

I walked over to the desk. "Excuse me," I said, "was that for my cousin?"

Embarrassed that I had overheard her but more concerned that I'd be upset, she tried to reassure me by saying, "Don't be alarmed. We call for every patient brought in."

"I know. I'm a priest. So is my cousin."

"Oh," she said. This upset her all the more. "Well, . . . Father . . . he should be anointed."

The priest arrived. Upon learning the circumstances, he gave me his oils and ritual. I went in to where Mike was. He was still unconscious. I felt grateful that he was. Moving next to the doctors and nurses who worked on him, I signed the cross on his forehead and prayed the short form of the sacrament. My hand shook, half from fear, half from disbelief at what I was doing.

They wanted to operate. Immediately. I gave permission, then called home. Within an hour and a half, Aunt Gert arrived with my mom and dad, all of them shocked and apprehensive.

"I don't know what happened," I told them. "He just doubled over."

We waited. Hours later, when Mike was returned to the intensive care unit, the doctor who had operated approached us. He was cautious in his report. "It's ulcers," he said, addressing Aunt Gert. "Bleeding ulcers. The problem is that it was neglected for so long. Infection has set in throughout his whole system."

"Is he all right?" Aunt Gert asked.

"He's . . . very sick," the doctor advised. "A lot depends on his own strength."

Mike drifted in and out of a delirious semi-consciousness, but he never really knew where he was. The nurses continued to pack him with ice to keep his temperature down. At eleven o'clock they assured us he was doing better. They insisted it would be good if everyone went home for the night. Mike was sleeping, and his temperature was below the danger level.

When we reached Jensen's Falls I pulled into the driveway at St. Francis and said to Jerome, "I want you to stay here tonight. I'm going to go back."

"Why?" he asked.

I couldn't bring myself to say what I feared. When I had been a hospital chaplain, I had quickly become accustomed to the way nurses acted. I had learned to sense when they felt a case was hopeless. "Well," I told him, "I . . . think one of us should be there . . . don't you?"

When I arrived back at the intensive care unit, several nurses were at Mike's bedside. His temperature had risen to 105 degrees. They kept packing him with ice and rubbing his body with alcohol.

In his delirium he had no idea why he was strapped down. When I moved to the side of the bed he looked at me, angrily frustrated. "What are you doing?" he demanded, his voice stumbling on his words as if he were drunk. "Untie me, damn it! What's the matter with you?"

"Mike," I whispered, "calm down. You're sick. You need to rest."

"You dumb chickenshit!" he yelled. "I'll nail your ass to the wall for you . . . that's what."

A nurse pulled me gently away from him. "He doesn't understand, Father. Why don't you sit over here? You're only making him more excited."

As foggy as Mike's mind was, he knew that I was nearby. He was angry at me, and kept calling my name. "Damn it, Dennie, let me have some water."

His lips were so dry they had cracked. "Please, Dennie," he begged. "Let me have some of that water. Just a little cold water."

A nurse came over to me to explain: "We can't give him any liquids—not right after the operation."

I nodded, but it was torture to deny him that sip of water. I felt as if I were being deliberately cruel.

For hours his mind wandered, rushing through disconnected

316

memories. "Use two statues," he mumbled. "...They can both have one...I won't give it back...I won it, Mom...I didn't take it from him...I didn't make the changes...tell your cronies...they know more than the Pope..."

After a while he became quieter. I walked back to the bed. His eyes were closed, but he kept mumbling. He startled me by reciting almost verbatim the story of the Pharisee and the sinner. When he finished, he paused a moment. Then, with his eyes still closed, he said, "It's a trap. You think you're the sinner, and that makes you the Pharisee."

He spoke so clearly I thought perhaps he had come out of his delirium.

"Mike," I whispered, "it's Dennie."

A look of consternation crossed his face as he said, "You see?... You're a distance runner...You beat me...I'm a sprinter...Go for the distance...That's your talent..."

My memory was a blur of scenes until it took me to where Mike was. Senior year in high school. The mile race after I had been destroyed in football. He had goaded me into running to teach me that I had endurance rather than strength.

From the scene of that lesson he slipped into quiet. I walked back to the nurses' station, fifteen feet from his bed, and dropped into a chair. Outside, the sky was turning from black to a leaden gray. Death seemed to belong to nighttime at a hospital. I thought to myself, "If he can make it till daylight, he'll be all right. He'll get strength during the day. Then he'll be all right."

Without realizing it, I fell into a kind of sleep sitting in the chair. I was jolted by the sound of the public address system: "I.C.U. code ninety-nine. I.C.U. code ninety-nine."

I knew it was Mike even before I was awake. Machines were being rushed to his bed. I walked over and stood helplessly behind the team of doctors and nurses. For the next hour they pounded and jolted his heart to keep it going. Each time they stopped, I looked to the small screen that recorded his heartbeat. The electronic blip died down after each of their efforts. My legs began to wobble so badly I had to hold onto a nearby window sill for support. Even while they pounded on his chest I knew that he was gone. Their work became so terrible to watch I wanted to scream out, "Leave him alone, will you? Can't you see he's dead?"

317

Finally the electrocardiograph machine registered only a straight line. Mike's heart had been stopped for over five minutes. The doctors backed away from him; the nurses began to remove the breathing apparatus and wires from his body. After the desperate intensity of work, the room seemed almost peacefully quiet. I was in shock—a shock so total I looked at my cousin and calmly accepted his being dead without feeling any emotion.

An older nurse, turning from the bed, looked at me, then took my arm. "You shouldn't have been in here, Father," she said, pulling me toward the door.

"No, please," I said, slowly pulling free of her. "I'm okay."

I went over to the side of the bed and took Mike's hand. Then, concentrating as much as possible, I tried to recite from memory the ancient prayer for the dead: "Mike . . . may the angels come to greet you . . . may the saints and martyrs help you along the way . . . may they bring you home to paradise."

I stood looking at his face for a long time. I could not accept yet that he was gone. It occurred to me that it was strange to be holding his hand. It was not because his hand no longer had life. I had never before held his hand. We were not a demonstrative family. I couldn't recall ever having told Mike that I liked him, let alone that I loved him. I bent down and kissed him. It was the only sign of affection I had ever shown my cousin in my entire life.

72

THE resident chaplain had been called. He brought me to his room. I sat, unable to speak. After awhile, when I began to be conscious of time and space, I said, "I'd better call home."

"Will your folks be awake?" the chaplain asked. It was 7:15 A.M.

"Probably. They get up about now."

"Why don't you wait a few minutes?" he suggested. "It won't make any difference here. Don't hit them as they're getting out of bed."

I nodded agreement. But I had to tell somebody—somebody who would know. It was too much for me to hold onto by myself. There was a diocesan directory on the chaplain's desk. I opened it and looked for Maguire's number.

The next three days had an almost dreamlike quality to them. The notes that Mike had written to plan Ben's funeral were still sitting with a pile of unfiled papers on his desk. But I was at a loss to apply them. As soon as O'Donnell heard, he came back and moved into the rectory. He took over completely.

Jensen's Falls was stunned by what happened. Mike's youth, his sense of freedom, and his unclerical bearing—precisely the qualities that had been a target for people's criticisms—now became the reasons the same people saw his death as a special tragedy. The wake brought out virtually every Catholic in town: people whose names had filled petitions; people who had fought the changes, the merger, the bishop. They stood in line to tell Aunt Gert that her son had been a good priest.

She received them with a quiet stoicism born of shock and conditioned by a lifetime of losses. She had lost a husband and a son in two wars. Now she had lost her last son. I shook hands with them all as they passed—the Baldwins, the Sheehans, the O'Briens. I listened to their expressions of sorrow without any reaction. I was beyond feeling anything.

If there was an irony to their offering sympathy, it was no more ironic than my standing to receive them, as if I had been a dedicated priest. I knew, with a heart as heavy as stone, that if it hadn't been for me, Mike would still be alive.

I had brought Ben to St. Mary's as I had brought Jerome. Then when the going got too rough, I had walked away. There was nothing I might have accused the disobedient people of Jensen's Falls of having done to Christ, or to the Church, or to my cousin, that I had not done in greater degree myself.

I responded mechanically, without hearing, to each person who shook my hand or embraced me. I was lost in my own sense of guilt.

I saw Angie DiVecchio stop in front of Jerome. She pulled his head down, and kissed him. "Listen, honey," she told him, "if things get shuffled around and St. Mary's becomes a regular rectory again—I want you to know you'll be in my home. Understand?"

Tears were streaming down her face as she came up to me. She kissed me as well. "Fidem Scit, Father," she whispered, choking with a sob.

"What?" I asked dully, hearing only the phonetics, missing her meaning.

She tried to smile. "'Know the Faith.'"

Everyone had been sent home; the church was closed. I sat alone with Mike's body—trying to pray, trying to clear my mind. I heard footsteps in the side foyer. I remained where I was, my head bowed down, hoping that whoever had come in would leave me alone and go back out. The footsteps came closer and then stopped. I looked up. It was Maguire.

320

He sat next to me, and for a long moment he looked at Mike's face. Then, shaking his head slightly, he whispered softly, more to himself than to me, "He was the most innocent grown-up man I ever knew."

I was too weak—emotionally, even physically—to say anything. He put his arm around my shoulder. "Are you going to be all right?" he asked.

I opened my mouth to say yes, but when I tried to form the word I began to cry. I started sobbing uncontrollably, and put my head into my hands, wanting only to be alone.

"I did it," I finally said. "Damn it, I did it. It wasn't the people, or the fighting about changes, or anything else. It was me. It was like a chain reaction I set up. If I hadn't gone off, Ben wouldn't have started drinking, and he wouldn't have died, and that's what killed Mike—and there's just no way out of that."

Maguire didn't exactly answer me. He just held on to me and kept saying, "Sure. Let it out. Let it out."

"I walked away. It wasn't any great crisis of faith or anything. I just walked away because I didn't like the way things were. Oh, God. What the hell did I do? What did I do?"

"Sure," he said, "sure." He kept patting me, almost rocking me. It was a long time before what he was doing seemed absurd. I started to laugh, then started sobbing again.

When I finally got control of myself, I shook my head and gestured to Mike's body, saying, "Why him? You'd think Jesus would have better sense. Mike made things work, damn it. Why leave me and take him? I should have gotten run over by a truck or something. He's gone and I'm here for . . . for . . ."—the word surfaced in my consciousness—". . . the distance."

"Dennie," Maguire broke in, gently, "Mike didn't make things work. He had no magic personality. You above all people, know that. He . . . willed to make things work. That's why . . . I loved him so much. That's also why he was so . . . innocent."

I nodded, only half listening.

"Innocent," he repeated, whispering huskily. "You know, he could be in the worst donnybrook in the world on one day—and the next day he'd be back with a laugh, expecting all his opponents to laugh with him. That's why . . . his death is such a loss to this diocese now. I knew, because of what I've always known about him, that when the fighting was all over with, he would have worked at laughing people out of bitterness. I was . . . counting on it."

His voice trailed off. We sat for a moment. I felt his arm on my shoulder, and realized that I was letting him do all the comforting when he was hurting too. I pulled my own arm up and returned his hug. It was too open a love for two Celts to express. He stood abruptly and said, "I told Monsignor O'Donnell I would get you right back to the rectory."

I started to follow him. Then I asked, "Would you mind if I walked? I need to get some air."

It had turned bitterly cold during the course of the evening. A penetrating wind moaned through the trees and tugged at the silver tinsel wreaths strung across Jensen's Falls' Main Street. I stopped for a long time, barely aware of the cold, and stared at the Christmas decorations, thinking about Mike.

Innocence. I had been told once that I was guileless. I didn't know how to deal with people. And guileless people tended to grow into bitter people. Mike knew all the angles. He had lived a life gambling on long odds. He had been a manipulator, a scrapper, never more alive than when in a fight in which the chances of winning were all against him. And yet . . . he was innocent. Understanding evil didn't affect him.

I thought of his Navajo theory . . . and his words came back: "Hey, Dennie . . . who gives a crap?" And for the first time I glimpsed what it meant—the very opposite of what I had always thought.

"For Christ's sake," he had yelled at me once, "why can't this age produce men who will believe in Jesus as much as Lenin believed in Marx?"

That was the theory. It did not mean that he didn't give a crap. It meant that he cared so much he wouldn't let anything petty stand in the way of his caring. I thought of the eggs he had bought Mrs. Baldwin to replace those her husband had thrown at him. I thought of the book he had given to Father Fufferd during the first fights over the changes. I thought of the smile he had given Maguire at ordination—Maguire who had expelled him from high school.

There was a small department store with the Nativity scene displayed in the window. I stopped and looked at the Christ Child in the manger, then at the Blessed Mother. A laugh that was half a sob rose up inside of me. "Hey, Mary," I prayed, "if he had lived you would have had twins this year."

I kept staring at the manger. "The distance . . ." I thought to myself. "My one talent. No real strength. None of Mike's color. Only endurance. I will last . . ."

"Mary," I whispered out loud, "you are still going to have twins this year. I'll make them do what Mike was going to do . . . make them see how stupid we are becoming as a Church . . . make them nail their flag to the mast . . ."

Then, with the tears freezing on my face, I prayed: "Please, Jesus, help me to become innocent. I have to stop hating so much."

A small horde of wandering teenagers stood huddled together in the drugstore doorway, seeking escape from the wind. They had all been at the wake earlier, but now I didn't want to encounter anyone. I crossed the street while I was half a block away, hoping they would let me be. They didn't. One of the younger boys, his hands stuffed into the pockets of his parka, broke away from the group and called to me, "Father, are you going to open the Room?"

I just looked at him.

"There's nothing to do," he said, approaching me.

A surge of anger welled up in me. I wanted to punch his face in. This is the human animal, I thought. This is the goddamned human animal.

"My cousin is dead," I said, taking a step toward him. I must have looked threatening, because the boy moved backward.

"You opened it the last time," he said, his tone a plea not to be attacked. "You said priests celebrated when priests died."

I froze in my tracks. I almost yelled, "That wasn't me who opened the Room. That was my cousin. That was his crazy way of doing things." But something caught me.

"He willed it . . ." Maguire had said. "That was why he was innocent."

His innocence was his strength. It wasn't an accident, or necessarily how he felt. It was a matter of will.

I stood in the middle of the street, almost in a trance. I did believe. I believed in Jesus at least as much as Lenin believed in Marx. But belief wasn't enough. I had to will to do something about it. I had to turn a neutral guilelessness into innocence . . . and I had to go the distance.

323

The boy and I stood facing each other. He didn't know what to expect. I willed myself to smile.

"Sure," I said. I reached into my pocket for the keys. "You kids go ahead and open up. I'll be right there. We'll celebrate."